"*Seduced by Shadows* blew me away! Sera and Archer won my heart at first glance. Slade creates a beyond-life-or-death struggle for love and redemption in a chilling, complex, and utterly believable world—one I can't wait to return to again and again."

—Jeri Smith-Ready, award-winning author
of *Bad to the Bone*

POSSESSED

"Go away."

"You called. You've called forever," he said.

"I don't even know you . . . ," she said, trailing off when he raised a hand to brush back her hair. The touch sent ripples of shivery sensation through her body.

From behind, his hands slid over her shoulders, down her arms, then skipped to her bare hips.

That made her shy away like nothing else had. "Don't touch me." *Not there.* The unspoken words echoed in her head.

He framed the scars with his hands. The long shadows of his fingers hid the red and white puckers of stitched flesh. "I will make you whole again, as if you'd never been broken, nothing left behind."

He eased her back against him. The leather of his coat was cool on her backside and shoulders. Her thoughts scattered.

"I will take away your loneliness, your fear," he whispered into her hair.

"I'm not afraid."

"You will be."

SEDUCED
BY
SHADOWS

A NOVEL OF THE MARKED SOULS

JESSA SLADE

A SIGNET ECLIPSE BOOK

SIGNET ECLIPSE
Published by New American Library, a division of
Penguin Group (USA) Inc., 375 Hudson Street,
New York, New York 10014, USA
Penguin Group (Canada), 90 Eglinton Avenue East, Suite 700, Toronto,
Ontario M4P 2Y3, Canada (a division of Pearson Penguin Canada Inc.)
Penguin Books Ltd., 80 Strand, London WC2R 0RL, England
Penguin Ireland, 25 St. Stephen's Green, Dublin 2,
Ireland (a division of Penguin Books Ltd.)
Penguin Group (Australia), 250 Camberwell Road, Camberwell, Victoria 3124,
Australia (a division of Pearson Australia Group Pty. Ltd.)
Penguin Books India Pvt. Ltd., 11 Community Centre, Panchsheel Park,
New Delhi - 110 017, India
Penguin Group (NZ), 67 Apollo Drive, Rosedale, North Shore 0632,
New Zealand (a division of Pearson New Zealand Ltd.)
Penguin Books (South Africa) (Pty.) Ltd., 24 Sturdee Avenue,
Rosebank, Johannesburg 2196, South Africa

Penguin Books Ltd., Registered Offices:
80 Strand, London WC2R 0RL, England

First published by Signet Eclipse, an imprint of New American Library,
a division of Penguin Group (USA) Inc.

First Printing, October 2009
10 9 8 7 6 5 4 3 2 1

For my family—Mom and Dad and sister—who cheered over every success and commiserated through every rejection. You are my emotional bucket o' cookie dough. For MomMom, who published my "early works" and saw potential in that grade-school poetry chapbook.

And for my very own moody, broody bad-boy werewolf rock-star superhero lover.
You do inspire me.

Acknowledgments

I've read in other authors' acknowledgments how many people it takes to turn a story into a book. They weren't just kidding. My sincere and enthusiastic thanks to Kerry Donovan at NAL, whose brilliant editorial shine brought out the highlights and deepened the shadows; also to the whole team at NAL including Scott Biel, who created this great cover (with my name on it!) and copy editor Jane Steele, who pointed out where I don't know English as goodly as I thought I did; to Becca Stumpf at Prospect Agency, who was willing to take a chance with me on this wild ride; and to Romance Writers of America, especially my marvelous local chapter, Rose City Romance Writers, which ran the writing contest where I came to Kerry's attention. See how it's all one big circle?

Last, to my amazing critique partners, Joey Berube, Betty Booher and Shirley Karr, who agonized with me (and it was agony, wasn't it, guys? Yeah, sorry about that.) over every one of the nearly million final draft words it took to get me here—thank you, thank you, thank you.

CHAPTER I

"The end is nigh."

Ferris Archer braced his shoulders against the Chicago wind that whipped straight up to whistle around the balcony railing with savage glee. "Never nigh enough."

"Nigher, then. For some poor soul."

"Don't pity the bastard, Zane," Archer said. "Whoever he is, he could resist temptation."

Zane squatted in the shelter of the wall, arms wrapped around his knees. "Like we could have?"

Archer faced the dark lake. Despite all his years at these latitudes, he'd still not gotten used to how night came so early in November and stayed so long.

At least the numbing chill anesthetized the memory of anything else.

The balcony door opened. The breath of warmth was snatched away in an instant.

Zane rose to meet the newcomer. "Nothing yet, boss."

Archer lifted his chin by way of greeting. "Niall."

"Archer. Haven't seen you around lately."

"Any reason you've been looking?"

"Just wondering." In the glitter of city lights, Liam

Niall's Black Irish eyes were as enigmatic as the inky mark that rayed out from his temple and down his cheek.

"Still alive." At the mocking whisper in the back of his mind, Archer shoved his hands in his pockets. He edged past the two men to the opposite corner of the balcony. "Still kicking."

If the news brought Niall any joy, it didn't show on his face, which echoed Archer's own sentiments on the matter.

Zane cleared his throat. "What's that? Due north, this side of Division."

Archer had already seen the flicker near the raised train tracks, nothing like the strange fireworks that flamed in his dreams lately. "Reflections from the L. Keep looking."

The burning dreams had hollowed him out, left him wanting, when he thought he'd long ago lost touch with the feeling—with any feeling.

He didn't appreciate the reminder.

Zane gripped the rail. "Have either of you actually *seen* one before?"

Niall shook his head. "They're usually drawn straight to their victims, who can't see them until it's too late. And they're rare. Thank God."

Archer coughed.

He felt Niall staring holes in the back of his head. "By the way, nice trick, catching this crossing," Niall said. "Bookie's been tracking activity since you warned us. With no telltale genocides or pandemics or famine in the city, we're lucky you detected it so early." He lifted one eyebrow.

Archer didn't miss the implied invitation to share how he'd known. Since he couldn't answer, he said nothing.

As if mocking his reticence, an unearthly shimmer drew his gaze to the shadowed depths of the urban valleys. He stiffened. "There. Toward the river."

"My God," Zane whispered.

This time, Archer didn't scoff at invoking the Almighty.

Above the streets and buildings, an arch of vaporous luminescence unfolded in a slow ballet. Vortices of ghostly light pinwheeled out into the dark, highlighted in sprays of radiant sparks that caught, flared, and died.

Only the ceaseless hum of traffic and wind whining over concrete and steel accompanied the eerie sparkler. No screams. No sirens. The phantom lights played over the city, pulsing to an unknown heartbeat, unseen by human eyes.

Or merely human eyes.

Zane whistled. "Well, now we know what an unbound demon escaped from hell looks like."

Like dragonfly wings glinting iridescent as the tiny predators hunted under a bright sun, fierce and lovely at once. The spectacle echoed through him as if someone were using his breastbone as a gong.

His whole body vibrated with the unheard note. He stiffened against it. "It's going to draw every fucking djinni from Detroit to St. Louis."

"Easy to follow, at least," Niall said. "Get down there. Find whom it's pursuing. I'll send a team to run interference in case things go badly."

"A demon has breached the Veil, the only barrier between us and hell, to possess some poor bastard's soul," Zane muttered. "How exactly could it go 'goodly'?"

Archer didn't bother responding. "Arm your people well." He headed for the balcony door. "Every malice and feralis in the city is on the way to pay homage."

Niall crossed into his path. "Bookie engineered a new demon shunt. Supposed to drain them twice as fast with half the mess. Want to give it a whirl?"

"Garbagemen shouldn't care about the mess. No point when there's always more of it." Archer slid past him, careful to make no contact. "Unless Bookie has a way to send them back through the Veil forever?" When Niall stayed silent, Archer shrugged. "Maybe next time."

Zane fell into step behind him. "If there is a next time. Did I mention the end is nigh?"

"So you keep promising." Archer didn't look back— he'd learned long ago never to do that—but still the demon lights strummed his bones like a call to arms.

As ends of days went, this one looked promising, indeed.

"Damn, Sera, you look like hell. And since when do you smoke?"

Sera Littlejohn sighed and stubbed out the cigarette on the brick wall of the ambulance bay where she'd come to find a little peace and quiet. The spinning red lights and scuttling EMTs had almost done the trick before Betsy showed up. "One of your interns quit—third time this month, he said—and gave me the last of his pack."

Betsy's eyes narrowed behind her John Lennon glasses. "That drunk driver didn't finish the job, so you're finding another route to rendezvous with your maker?"

Sera reached for the cane she'd propped against the bricks. "Good to see you too, Bets."

"Chill, girl." Betsy laid a heavy hand on her shoulder. "Sorry. I was just surprised to see you."

"Supposed to be my first night back." Sera gripped the head of the cane, the ergonomic rubber cold under her fingers. She kept telling herself she'd be rid of it soon. "But Marion's sending me home again, until I'm 'stronger.' Said I looked like death warmed over and I was scaring the patients."

Betsy snickered. "Death warmed over. You're a thanatologist."

"Apparently last vigils should be presided over by someone a little perkier and better coiffed." Sera ran one hand over her simple blond braid. "I told her my lipstick was in the glove compartment, and that ended up somewhere in the trunk."

"It's been six months. You couldn't stop by the Clinique counter while you learned to walk again?" Betsy shook her head. "For being in charge of end-of-life care, Marion has all the compassion of your average vulture."

She reached into the side pocket of Sera's bag and snagged the cigarettes. Without looking behind her, she pitched them into the trash bin.

Sera raised her eyebrows. "Luckily I have friends like you."

"Lucky is right. Give me any more of that washed-out lip and I'll send you to Nutrition for a full workup." Betsy eyed her. "You get any thinner, and when old Grim Reaper Man comes for your customers, he'll think you're the ghost."

"Not a fear of yours then, huh?"

"Funny. We're so busy tonight, if Death comes looking for me, I'll triage him with the kids puking up stale Halloween candy. I swear, that club drug making the rounds is a nightmare like you would not believe, and on top of that, we've got the full moon bringing out the crazies."

Sera glanced up, although the tall buildings shut out all but a narrow slice of night. With low-hanging clouds reflecting the city lights, the sky glowed a nacreous silver. "I don't think the moon's full tonight."

Betsy huffed. "Might as well be. Everyone's got that weird sparkle in their eyes, even the ones not whacked-out on solvo, or whatever they're calling it."

"Must be the holidays coming," Sera murmured, still watching the night.

"Great. Just add salmonella, suicide, and shoveling-induced heart attacks to the mix." Betsy nudged Sera's arm. "Hey, let's get a cup of coffee."

Distracted from the sky, Sera shook her head. "I

thought you were busy. And I guess I'm spending the evening dusting off my résumé."

"Marion's a fool," Betsy said. "Somebody has to explain the big mysteries before checkout time, and you've a real gift for facing the other side."

Not the kind of gift with a return receipt, unfortunately. Sera fumbled the cane as Betsy hugged her, and they exchanged promises to lunch. She stepped out of the bright lights and relative shelter of the ambulance bay and headed for the darker street.

Yeah, the big mysteries of life and death and why some asshole with three DUIs on his record had plowed his monster SUV into her practical little sedan, putting a severe crimp in the rest of her life, along with her spine.

She was tired of asking questions when she couldn't help wondering whether there were any answers.

Which was probably why Marion had sent her home.

But home felt like a prison these days. She had spent too much time there since rehab, in a place grown too quiet.

With a twinge of pain, she aimed her steps in the other direction. Good thing Betsy had missed the prescription bottle in the bag next to the cigarettes. The ER nurse would've known in a heartbeat what those meant.

Forget the celebratory walk through the cosmetics counters. Just pop the childproof cap on the little orange bottle. She'd have to check on that drug trial the intern had mentioned. He'd said the manufacturer swore Solacin was the painkiller to end all painkillers. With that easy chemical buffer, even the sight of the short stack of job applications on Marion's desk wouldn't hurt much.

With the traffic of Upper Wacker behind her, Sera started over the bridge, ducking her head against the wind hissing across the black water.

A quarter of the way across, she noticed the man alone in the middle of the bridge.

If she hadn't been so wrapped up in her own thoughts,

she would have seen him earlier. The matte black trench coat silhouetted his height against the slash of silvery night sky. He stood braced against the wind tugging at the hem of his coat.

Born and raised in the city, she had a healthy respect for and no unreasonable fear of downtown dangers. She worked—until recently, of course—in a job with late hours in sometimes sketchy neighborhoods and had had her car broken into only twice. Even with a cane that marked her as easy pickings, she knew her trigger finger on the can of mace was limber enough.

Still, something about the man slowed her steps and ramped up her pulse.

She couldn't cross the street. She had less faith in traffic's ability to avoid her than in her own ability to avoid trouble. And running only invited chasing.

She unzipped the side pocket of her bag, where she kept the mace. Hell, if he had a mugging in mind, she could toss out the prescription bottle, and any self-respecting junkie would follow it into the river.

Despite her inner bravado, her limping steps ground to a halt.

He stood with his face half turned to the sky, heedless of the wind that couldn't ruffle his close-cropped hair. Sera expected dark shades and a lot of bling, but when he finally glanced down at her, the only spark came from the violet reflections glancing off his eyes.

Not that there were any purple lights around them— just maybe some chance fusion of red brake lights and the blue-tinged streetlamps. . . .

If she was mugged, she didn't want her description to the police to gush about the hypnotic violet lights in his dark eyes. She'd have to remember the hard edge of his jaw and the width of shoulders below the mandarin collar of his coat, which tapered to lean hips.

She jerked her gaze back to his.

He frowned in a thoughtful, not-menacing way, at

least no more menacing than was necessitated by the
austere cast to his features. "This, I did not expect."

She'd be able to ID him by his voice, if nothing
else—dark and rough, with a hint of mostly forgotten
Southern sweetness, like pralines carelessly heated past
caramelizing to burned ruination.

He drew himself up, and she thought darting into
traffic might not be completely unreasonable.

"If I told you something bad was right here, right
now," he asked, "would you listen to me?"

Sera thrust her hand into her bag. "I'd tell it to back
off." The mace canister felt sleek and cold and ridicu-
lously tiny when she held it out in front of her.

The man tilted his head. "It won't be stopped that
way. Only you can deny it."

"Consider yourself denied."

Violet flashed again in his deep-set eyes. "I am not
the threat."

"See, that's what all the homicidal schizophrenics
say."

Amusement curved his full lips in a way that made
her finger tighten on the trigger.

Danger, danger.

"Temptation is all around you," he said. "Embrace it
at your peril."

And she'd been deliberately not thinking of embracing. Peril, yes. Embracing, not any time in recent
memory.

She shook her head to clear the wayward thoughts.
"Right. There's a men's shelter on Grand. Tell them Sera
from Mercy General hospice sent you, and they'll find a
slot in their outpatient program."

He sighed. She could barely hear over the wind, but
she saw his shoulders lift and fall—under a coat far too
expensive for him to be a drug-addled street dweller.

"Sera." He pronounced it as she had said it, *Sear-ah*.
"I am not patient at all. But nothing I say will convince

you. Nothing I say will even make sense. Not yet. Just remember. For when it comes."

The wind worked its way under her coat, sending a chill up her spine. "I think it's time you moved along." She gestured with the mace canister.

He hesitated, then, with a nod, stepped past her. He stayed near the street, giving her space.

The wild wind spun by her, carrying the scent of spice and musk, a primitive blend at odds with his sleek urban look. With fickle abruptness, the wind pushed at her back, urging her toward him. And damn her weak leg, she actually stumbled a step forward.

He turned instantly, one hand reaching out.

"No." Her voice sounded too high, panicky. She swallowed. "Go on now. Git." As if he were a mongrel stray.

She waited until the darkness on the bridge swallowed him. He never looked back. Only then did she continue. On the far side, she crossed the intersection against the light, told herself she was an idiot, no one was following her, and paused anyway to make sure.

No man in a black trench coat. No mysterious threat coming her way.

Suddenly her empty apartment seemed better than roaming the city streets in the descending November night. She hailed a cab and ducked inside with only one more glance back.

"Cold out there." The cabbie's lilting English distracted her.

"Excuse me?"

"You're shaking. Shall I turn up the heat?"

She let out a pent-up breath. "Sorry. No. I'm fine."

Obviously she didn't have as much of her toughness back as she had told herself, if one crazy set her so on edge. Maybe if—no, *when* she healed, she'd take that self-defense course Betsy was always pushing on her nurses. It wouldn't protect her from drunk drivers, but who knew what else was out there?

* * *

Under the cover of deep shadow, Archer watched the woman—Sera—hurry away, her slight figure outlined in whorls of ominous light. The spectral radiance visible from the penthouse balcony had condensed and centered around her. The silver green glow reminded him of a tornado sky, when doom spiraled out of nothing. The unbound demon had chosen.

Zane joined him. "A woman? No way. All demon-ridden are male."

"The Lord works in mysterious ways. But not half so mysterious as the other guys." Archer steeled the savagery lurking inside him against her thousand weaknesses: the hesitation in her steps from the painful twist of her spine; her not-unwarranted impulse toward violence; the fear that dulled her eyes. Fear of him.

The demon didn't need a thousand weaknesses. Only one.

"Are we sure she's the target? Could the demon have gotten confused?" Zane stared across the river, where Sera had gone. The etheric lights trailed behind her like frayed gossamer wings. "She seemed nice."

The mace hadn't been pointed at him. Archer was glad he'd told the younger talya to stay out of the way. "The demon wasn't confused. It only resonates with a matching soul."

"Then why aren't we bringing her back with us? Did you tell her why we're here?"

"You can't tell them anything until the demon ascends. They won't believe you before then. Maybe not even then."

Zane peered at him. "We can't just let her go. I know we aren't sure which strain of demon wants her, but no one should go through it alone." He started forward, as if to flag down the cab.

Archer snagged Zane's arm, whipping him around. "If she's wise, she won't go through it at all."

Zane faltered. "You warned her? Is that an option?"

Archer shrugged irritably. "You can't warn any more than you can guide."

"You'd better hope Niall doesn't hear about this. Ecco and Raine were watching from the other side of the bridge."

Archer scowled, even more exasperated. "You think, if it comes to that, they want a woman joining the league? As if we didn't face madness enough."

"She'd be no worse than some," Zane muttered. Then his gaze slid away as if he'd said too much—and to the wrong person.

Archer kept a leash on his flaring temper, but since someone had stuck the tuning fork in his dreams that had him vibrating to this emergent demon, his discipline felt unreliable.

Her accusation he was a psycho killer should have struck too close to the truth. But the zest with which she delivered the line and the glint in her hazel eyes as she aimed the spray can had roused sensations he thought long dead. Dead, buried, and rotted past all unholy resurrection.

Except in the dreams that left him unwilling to sleep. Strangely attuned to the unbound demon, he'd been prepared for violence. As always. But not for this. Not for her.

He wrestled down the rage. "There's a malice in the alley back there. It followed the pyrotechnics this far. Scare it off before it gets bored and does something annoying."

Zane glanced back, distracted. "Shouldn't we drain it?"

"We won't have time for every petty malice roaming the streets tonight." Archer strode off.

"Where are you going?" Zane called.

"After more dangerous game."

Chapter 2

Sera hauled herself up two flights of stairs, clenching her teeth on the echoes of well-meaning advice.

" 'Maybe you should get a ground-floor apartment,' " she muttered. " 'Maybe you should fuse those last vertebrae.' Maybe you should just shut up."

Juggling her keys and bag at the front door, she dropped the cane. Too stiff to bend over, she left it and limped down the hall to the bathroom.

She cranked the water to hot and faced the mirror.

Six months ago, she'd draped the light fixture with a filmy scarf, telling herself she was contemplating taking up stained-glass design in her convalescence. As a mental health counselor with a certification in thanatology, guiding people through their last days, she'd seen plenty of injuries and illnesses no surgery could heal. She'd held the stump of a diabetic amputee who swore he could still feel his hands. She'd brushed the last lock of hair away from the startlingly bright eyes of a burn victim. Her own wounds had nothing on those.

She stripped naked, then yanked the scarf off the lights. Time for some hard truths by seventy-five watts.

Betsy was right. She looked like hell. Marion was

right. She looked like death warmed over. Scrawny, wan, scarred from waist to knee. If the potential rapist on the bridge had seen this, he'd have been the one to run away in terror.

She let the scarf drop. They'd stuck her father in a nursing home, something she'd promised would never happen, telling her to concentrate on getting stronger. She couldn't work, couldn't drive, could barely walk. And now she'd let herself be frightened just because a man had spoken to her.

She couldn't live like this. Wouldn't.

She thought of the pills in her bag. Maybe she'd been relying on them too much. Well, no more. And that damn cane could stay in the hallway too.

The mirror fogged as steam billowed over the shower curtain. She swiped one hand across the glass. A face stared back at her, made somehow unfamiliar by the beaded droplets of water.

She frowned at the disjointed image. She knew who she was, where she was going. She'd been thrown only a little off track. Okay, catapulted. But tomorrow, Marion was getting another visit. So was the home where her brothers had put Dad. And then she'd have lunch with Betsy and eat everything on her plate.

The fog returned, but she was done. She stepped into the shower and bowed her head under the hot water. She'd stop shivering in just a second.

Sera walked into her bedroom, still naked. Damp heat followed her out of the shower in a slowly uncoiling mist. Only the slant of streetlights through the blinds lit the room, casting deep purple shadows. And he was there, a lean, dark outline with his black trench coat buttoned tight. Spicy musk teased her senses.

She blinked. "I'm dreaming. That's why I'm wandering around my apartment naked. I never wander around naked."

"Not wandering. You were coming. For me." He stood unmoving, but the trailing edge of his long coat shifted in a draft she didn't feel. "I will make it a sweet dream."

She touched her forehead, in lieu of pinching herself and drawing his attention to her naked parts. Dripping strands of her hair tangled around her wrist. "I don't need a wet dream tonight. Go away."

He moved closer. "You called. You've called forever."

"I don't even know you . . . ," she said, trailing off when he raised a hand to brush back her hair. He had the square, blunt hands of a working man, but his thumb feathered across her temple, almost too lightly to feel. The touch sent ripples of shivery sensation through her body like a pebble in still water.

She'd been close to screaming when he faced her on the bridge. She couldn't muster the will now. It was just a dream, she reminded herself.

"So lonely," he murmured. "So lost."

"I'm sorry for you, really. But I can't help you."

"You're the only one who can. But I meant you, my love." He stroked the back of his knuckles along her cheek. "You've been alone so long, so long afraid, close to giving in, calling all the while."

"I'm not . . . I am not your love." She pulled away.

"I've breathed your soul. Whom else can I love?"

"You haven't breathed on anything of mine." Her skin prickled at the thought—a pleasure she hadn't indulged in in a long time.

From behind, his hands slid over her shoulders, down her arms, then skipped to her bare hips.

That made her shy away as nothing else had. "Don't touch me." *Not there.* The unspoken words echoed in her head.

He framed the scars with his hands. The long shadows of his fingers hid the red and white puckers of stitched flesh. "I will make you whole again, as if you'd never been broken, nothing left behind."

Speaking of dreams, everyone said she was dreaming when she'd promised herself the same after her accident. "What, you're a physical therapist?"

"Quite the opposite." .

While she pondered what that might be—as if the riddles in dreams even mattered—he eased her back against him. The leather of his coat was cool on her backside and shoulders. Her thoughts scattered.

"I will take away your loneliness, your fear," he whispered into her hair.

"I'm not afraid." And, stupidly enough, that was true.

"You will be."

His warm breath over her ear made her sigh. It had been a very long time. There'd been the accident, before that taking care of her father and his work at the church, before that raising her brothers. Why shouldn't she share the burden and the solace, if only in a dream?

"I have the answer to all your questions." His lips, brushing the curve of her ear, sent a shiver down her spine, through bones shattered and cobbled together again.

She tipped her head, whether drawing away from his lips or exposing her neck to draw his kiss, she wasn't sure. "My questions? Like why in the hell am I still talking to a dream?"

"Hell doesn't have answers." He spun her slowly in his arms. When had he undone the long row of buttons on his coat? The leather parted around his chest. "Hell doesn't have this. Oh, to feel . . ."

She braced her hands between them, holding him off with palms flat on his smooth skin.

"Sera," he whispered. "You called. I came for you. I will give you what you want."

"Man, I even went to school for this." She frowned.

"After the crappy day I've had, of course I'd dream up a big scary dude who morphs into my devoted love slave."

"Slave, yes. Only for you. I will be here for you always. I will give you what you need—"

"Right, right. Tell me more." She slipped her hand up to his neck. He'd said she was close to giving in. Well, what was wrong with that occasionally?

He matched her embrace, cradling the back of her head in one hand. "Bind me."

Between the heat of their bodies, a cold, hard knot pressed into her breastbone. She winced and peered at a pendant hanging around her neck on a black cord. The stone shone a moment, then dimmed, like a cheap opal.

"Wow, jewelry. On the first date." She tugged on the stone and the cord unraveled. She dropped the necklace to the floor. "Thanks, but I don't need to hear sweet little lies, even the ones generated by my own subconscious. But until the pills wear off . . ."

She pulled him down to her kiss.

He resisted. "Will you take me? Will you let me in?"

In answer, she opened her mouth. His lips on hers were as cool as the pendant stone; his fingers in her hair held her in place. Not that she was going anywhere. It was her damn dream, after all.

She gripped the open edges of his coat. The silvery violet mist seemed to pull closer in her tangling fingers, wrapping them in a drifting, luminous shroud. She wanted to melt into him, to swap her own frailty and uncertainties for the powerful male energy that had enthralled her on the bridge.

"Let me in," he murmured.

"Yes." Her eyes drifted shut. His mouth slanted across hers, tongue plunging deep. A shivering thrill coursed through her, rippling inward from skin to bone so her knees buckled. Only his compelling grip kept her upright against his bare chest. The faint chill of his skin made her shiver again.

A scent like cold, wet rock nagged her. Had she left the shower running? No. No pesky reality allowed. But she opened her eyes—and froze.

He was still there, arms tight around her, mouth hovering over hers.

But his eyes, locked on hers, were wrong, not the dark of the man on the bridge, nor any other human color.

White on white eyes. Ice. Ash. Ancient bone. As she stared at him, speechless, a point of blackest oblivion surfaced in the white, then another, and another, until an insectile horde of dark specks crawled across the pale sclera.

Okay, this was worth a scream.

She tried—and choked.

She woke, crouched at the bottom of the shower, spewing water from her mouth and nose. Glacial water nailed over her shoulders.

She fumbled for the spigots, hands numb. The drain had backed up into a shin-deep pool. The ceramic was frigid; the water smelled like cold lead. How long had she been under?

She crawled over the lip of the tub, shivering too hard to stand. Snatching for her towel, she curled into a ball, wracked by tremors.

"Dreams suck," she gasped.

Her hips and spine screamed in pain. Her bag, with the prescription bottle, was on the table by the front door. She could drag herself that far.

Hand on the doorknob, she hesitated.

What if he was still out there? As suddenly as the thought surfaced, she banished it. Of course he wasn't out there. He'd never been out there.

Had he even been on the bridge? Had she? Or had that been part of the dream—nightmare—too? Maybe she hadn't gotten fired from her job tonight, after all.

"Now I'm just making things up." At least the fleeting wish that Marion was a mere figment of her imagination short-circuited the frantic circling of her thoughts.

She levered herself to her feet. Her knees wobbled, and her skin was blanched cold and white as the ceramic tub. Pulling on her fleece robe, she barely felt the soft nap.

"What's worse than death warmed over? Death not warmed over."

She opened the door and gazed across the hall at the doorway to her bedroom. Streetlights through the blinds lit the room, the same as in her dream, but no tall man was silhouetted in a silvery purple mist.

Too bad, since this time she would have screamed. And then maced him. And then retrieved the cane from the landing and beaten him with it. How dare her dreams tease her with hands that hid her scars and coaxed pleasure from her bones?

She needed to get her body temp back up. Moving like one of her geriatric patients on arthritic last legs, she crept toward the kitchen and a nice cup of tea— caffeinated. She didn't want to fall asleep where her dreams could watch her, whether the eyes were dark, shot with violet, or dead white and crawling with bugs.

"Maybe I'll have an espresso," she muttered. "Heck, make it a double."

Only the soft hiss of the gas burner under the kettle broke the silence. She stared down the hallway. No one was there. If she'd heard anything else, it was only the plink of water falling into the clogged tub.

She slid a cleaver from the butcher block. She needed something sharp to unclog the drain.

She'd left the light on in the bathroom—the empty bathroom. It shone into the empty bedroom—empty, just as she'd known.

She knelt stiffly beside the tub and rolled up her sleeve. A black band looped around the drain. Had the gasket on the plug popped off? She fished her hand into the cold water, grasping the loop.

She lifted the cord and the ovoid stone pendant broke the surface with an opalescent flash, one sly vanishing wink that took with it the last of her breath.

The demon had gone to ground. The flaw where it had crossed the barrier of ensnared souls was hidden again—a last lingering link between the realms. Still, Valerius Corvus imagined the terrible bruise left by the crossing.

Perhaps the wound in the Veil evoked a peacock, tinted in violet, sapphire, and emerald. His fingers hovered over canes of glass hued just so. Then he glanced over his shoulder.

From the vermeil filigree cage, the crow watched him, jet eyes catching a flicker from the fireplace. His brow furrowed. All the other birds had slept at night—but not the crow. It kept odd hours, and the rare glint of oil-slick color in its black plumage was just as unpredictable.

He should have killed the crow and set the trap again. He thought wistfully of a pigeon with powdery gray feathers, the rainbow sheen of the breast, the neck of purest white, the brilliant orange eye. Cheese curls were cheap bait, and he still had a little time.

He removed his ring, set it carefully aside, then ran his fingers over the pliers and pinchers, blades and shears, a blowtorch. Such ugly instruments of pain, for such delicate, beautiful work.

He jostled the jewel-colored canes, searching for the black, and the rods of glass chimed against one another in warning. He forced himself to calm, but the twisting inside him made his hands shake.

He'd fancied himself up to the task, patience honed like glass drawn to spun-sugar fineness. After all, as the saying went, Rome wasn't built in a day. Nor had it fallen in a night. But Corvus had found, these days and nights, the world moved much more swiftly. His patience had suffered.

Just as well he knew all about suffering too.

A bead of liquid welled from his eye and fell. It hissed on the glass, where it left a smoky stain.

Turning away, Corvus poured himself a drink and went to the window. Below, the autumn color in the line of trees along the river had long since dulled, leaving only tattered skeletons of trunks and branches, waiting for a decent burial by snow.

He sipped the cognac. Mellow heat dampened his awareness of the petty darklings riled in the demon's wake. Any havoc the darklings conceived was nothing compared to what lay just beyond the unlit horizon, beyond narrow human perception.

A swirl of his glass set the reflected flames from the fireplace dancing in the alcohol, flickering like a phoenix on the wing. In his own depths, the demon stirred, not deceived by his enforced calm. It surged along channels in his blood and bones, seeking outlet.

Not yet. He resisted, twisting the power back upon itself, upon himself, in ways a newly emergent demon and its chosen prey could never comprehend.

A tremor of excitement passed through him, and he hissed out a single breath.

The scouring inferno, when he loosed it, would burn with abandon. In its freedom he would find his own at last. He lacked only the fuse.

How convenient that tonight's luminous trail would lead him straight to the spark that would help him ignite a conflagration that would scorch even hell itself.

Archer walked from the bridge back toward his loft to reconnoiter the neighborhood. Circling the industrial-sized blocks in Chicago's meatpacking district, with its longtime butcher shops and more-recent art galleries, took a while. With a side trip down one alley, he drained a malice that had mistakenly tried to claim the vacant territory he'd created around his place.

He left the malice's thin psychic cry to stain the bricks, a warning to the city's other resident evils. The sign might serve only to bring a feralis sniffing around for leftovers, but Archer felt cranky enough to relish a pitched battle. At least that would get his blood flowing.

He found himself little caring if it all flowed away.

Except for the unlucky malice, the block was clean— until he got through the doorway leading up the narrow stairs to his loft.

He paused, head cocked to catch the faint rustle from the landing above. "Just when I thought I'd wiped out all the pests in the neighborhood."

Niall leaned over the railing. "I wasn't going to wait out in the cold."

Archer marched up. "So, about respecting my privacy unless sweeping my place after my death . . ."

"This is more important," Niall said. "You let the talya get away."

Archer stared impassively at the other man. "Not talya yet. But I saw that somebody taped a sign to her back saying, 'Possess me.' That should do the trick."

Niall glowered. "Ecco was recording everything. Even had some of Bookie's new spectral-analysis equipment going. How often do we get to study an emergent demon? And you let its target walk away."

"Study?" Archer lifted one eyebrow. "Can you preserve a malice in formaldehyde? Will dissecting a feralis bring any of the unfortunates it consumed back to life? If only I'd known a pocket protector keeps stains off the soul."

"We need an edge, any edge in this fight." Niall paced the tight confines of the landing. Despite his agitation, he left a careful space between them. "I know you sense it, even out here on the edges. Maybe from the outside you can see all sides." He spun toward Archer, his expression stark under the black lines marring his temple. "Evil is winning."

Archer shifted. "No worse than usual."

"Much worse," Niall said, plunging on. "The djinn have always mocked the limitations of our mandate, but lately even the lesser emanations are flipping us shit. I swear, the other night a malice gave me the finger before I drained it. Last week, Jonah took out a feralis feeding on a pigeon down by the lake. And the sun was up. An old lady on a park bench told him to leave the 'poor doggie' alone. Hell, it probably would've eaten her next."

"You want confirmation e-mails of my daily demolition?" Archer asked tightly. "Not that the number of malice drained or ferales dismembered makes a damn bit of difference. There's always another load of trash."

Niall dragged a hand through his hair. "I know your counts. And, really, would it kill you to share some of those techniques? You must realize we're falling behind."

"Yes, it could kill me to share, or more likely kill your precious men, and hell yeah, we're falling behind. You think having *her* is going to change that?" Archer refused to imagine the willowy Sera pitted against Jonah's feralis.

Bad enough when the ferales just consumed cockroaches. The demonic emanations warped and mutated the ordinary chitin into battle-ready carapaces that turned aside blades and bullets with ease. He hated it when the lesser demons took wing.

"You think a woman couldn't fight beside us? It's unprecedented, I know, but Bookie's already putting together a dossier on Sera Littlejohn, and she's neither a shrinking violet nor a hothouse rose." Niall peered at him. "Or is this some sort of misplaced Southern gentlemanly honor I wouldn't know anything about? Damn it, Ferris, we're at war."

"They say honor is always the first casualty. I'm not

an idiot, Liam." He drew out the name to show he hadn't missed—or appreciated—the other man's familiarity. "And I'm not naïve. Neither are you, usually. You know she doesn't have a chance."

"But you gave her one anyway."

Archer clenched his right hand against the phantom ache. "In the end, how many resist temptation? Not enough to make the counting worthwhile, especially considering the pathetic wrecks that remain. You said it yourself, the demons are winning."

"The wrong ones," Niall muttered.

"Right or wrong? You think that matters?

Niall narrowed his eyes. "You chose. Same as the rest of us."

"Same as her. With luck"—Archer laughed, a hollow sound in his own ears—you'll have a new demon-ridden talyan fighter for your hopeless battles. If I know anything about temptation, Sera Littlejohn is already possessed."

CHAPTER 3

She drifted in a world of gray, where only a thin charcoal line marked the horizon. A cry, shrill and mournful, pierced her confusion. She blinked when the sleek monochrome shape coalesced into streaks of white, black, and powder gray—a seagull.

Sera blinked again, and the gray became heavy clouds over sullen water. The gull surfed the wind off the lake, frozen a moment before it tilted its wings and soared away over a domed building as gray as the water and sky.

She blinked a third time—third time's always the charm.

Last she remembered, she'd been hunched over a pot of black coffee, trying to decide whether to bother with a mug. Now she was freezing her ass off again, this time halfway down the spit of land that held the waterfront planetarium, one sleepwalking step away from drowning.

She took a shuddering breath and a careful step back from the water. How had she gotten here? God, what day was it? Had she taken too many happy pills when she'd sworn she wouldn't take any? Her world was being taken away one piece at a time. Her strength, her job, her poor father. Now her mind.

She backed away from the edge of the jetty and crouched in the shelter of the concave retaining wall. She passed a shaking hand over her hair. Her fingers tangled in knots. The thought that had haunted her longer than she cared to remember slipped unbidden from her tongue: "Am I trying to kill myself?"

"Too late for that."

She bolted to her feet at the low voice with its soft Southern lilt, as ill fitted to this bleak panorama as to the hard, cold features of the man who spoke.

"You," she said. "So much for third time's the charm."

"Third time?" He shook his head as if sorry for asking. "How are you feeling?"

She opened her mouth to issue a curt snubbing, then stopped. "A little odd, which you already guessed."

"I suspected."

"Your fault," she shot back. "After last night . . ." Had it been last night?

"I waited for you on the bridge to warn you." His eyes flickered between her and the jetty's edge where corrugated steel and tumbled boulders held back the gray chop of the lake.

As if he too suspected she wasn't very stable.

She took a sideways step closer to the water. "I meant later, in my bedroom." At the memory of his hands on her, a reluctant warmth flushed through her.

He stiffened. "I wasn't in your bedroom."

"Like I'm going to believe anything a stalker says." She stumbled another step toward the edge.

"Sera." Her name was a warning. "Come back from there."

"Get away from me." She let her voice rise in panic.

He held up one appeasing hand. A black tattoo marked his knuckles. "I won't hurt you."

She stepped back again, heel to the jagged steel. For good effect, she windmilled her arm.

"Sera." He leapt, reaching for her.

Sucker. She pivoted, planted a helpful palm between his shoulder blades, and launched him toward the waves.

Anyway, that was her intent. He shouted out a curse. Through his back, she felt his muscles seize, every fiber locking. He teetered impossibly over the rocks.

She fled.

She ran with the lake on one side and the head-high retaining wall on the other. People always walked around the planetarium to snap pictures across the water of the cityscape. If she could get to them before he got to her ...

The wind whipped tears from her eyes. As if she had a chance with her limp.

Then she realized she was running flat out, no hitch in her step. No pain. Fear was an awesome motivator.

Just not enough to save her.

She felt a jerk at her coat. She clawed the zipper halfway down, slithering free as she ran. But the zipper jammed. The coat slipped down to her thighs, hobbling her. He had an iron grip now, and the coat slid down to her knees.

With a shriek, she tripped and rolled, taking the brunt of the fall on her shoulder so she landed facing him. Kicking violently, she drove him back.

He leaned out of harm's way, twisting the coat around her knees to bind her legs. All her efforts barely ruffled the black shirt underneath his unbuttoned trench coat.

"Sera," he roared, "cease at once."

She landed a weak-ass punch somewhere in the vicinity of his left nipple. He jerked the coat around her knees, and she fell back, panting.

He scowled. "Are you done?"

She bared her teeth. "Come a little closer and ask me again."

He wrapped another loop of the coat around his big hand, hiding the tattoo she'd glimpsed there. "I did not come to your bedroom last night."

She kicked with both legs, though the tight binding hampered the blow. "Oh, my mistake. Must've been some other tall, dark, and handsome Southerner in exile with a bigger wardrobe budget and better taste than mine."

"Better taste? I couldn't say." His half-lidded gaze lingered on her lips.

The heat in her rose a notch—equal parts exertion, embarrassment, and improvident arousal. "You didn't say much in my bedroom either, since your tongue was in my mouth."

That brought his eyes up to hers. His grasp on her coat slackened.

They stared at each other.

"The eyes were wrong," she murmured. She couldn't suppress a shiver as she met his gaze, dark with a hint of earthy color, like a blackened bronze. "I knew it then. And fell for it anyway."

The buttoned vee of his shirt revealed a sprinkling of dark hairs. The man in her room had been smooth skinned, with unmarked hands, as if he hadn't gotten the details quite right.

"The demon takes the form of temptation." He shifted back onto his heels, dropping the coat. "That's the nature of demons."

She rallied her attention to scowl. "Demon? You mean the drugs? But I hadn't taken any." Her conscience pricked her. "Lately."

"You're an addict?" Ignoring her sputtered protest, he nodded once and rose to his feet, lithe despite his size. "That does make possession easier."

"I have a prescription." She staggered up. "I can't be charged with possession of illegal drugs."

"I don't care what you possess, but what seeks to possess you."

"Never mind the drug charges." She kicked away the traitorous coat. "Who was in my room?"

"As I said, the demon."

She sagged against the wall. The concrete leached the last of her warmth. Nothing made sense—not his words, not her sudden physical well-being, not the strange rock that had appeared out of nowhere in her shower. "Demon?"

His sigh deepened with frustration. "A circular conversation going nowhere. This is why I don't handle newly possessed talyan."

She pictured those white eyes pierced with infinity, the odd stone glowing in her palm. "Was he your twin?"

"I have no brothers. And it wasn't a he. An it. A demon escaped from hell." He angled his gaze down at her. "You thought I was with you?"

She ignored that. "Part two. Who are you?"

"Ferris Archer. I followed the emanations from the demon realm, which led me to you."

"Do you really expect me to believe any of this? That I've been possessed by a—a demon?"

"Belief is beside the point. It is true."

It was like being told she would soon be killed by a falling piano. Of course she didn't believe him. And yet she couldn't help looking up. "Demons don't exist."

"Not corporeally, not in this world. Which is why it has clothed itself in your flesh."

The lake wind swirled, and an inadvertent shudder ripped through her. She wrapped her arms around her waist, as if she might feel different. "And what if I'm not interested in sharing my flesh?"

A muscle in his jaw tensed. "You can cast it out, before it ascends, before it sets roots in your soul and its mark on your skin. But the price is high."

"Isn't it always?" She forced herself to open her clenched fingers. "Tell me Betsy sent you from AA and this is all a really bad metaphor."

"I wish I could."

"Just do," she urged him.

His lips twisted as if to hide a twinge of pain—or maybe a smile. "My sins are many, but lying is not among them."

He twitched back the edge of his trench coat and from the folds of supple leather released a blackened club the size of her forearm. With a snap of his wrist and the menacing *shhick* of sliding metal, the club telescoped to double in length. He flicked it outward, and from the thickened, studded end, a blade cascaded out in a series of glittering steel segments, like a cardsharp's precisely fanned hand almost twice as wide as her spread fingers.

From primitive club to switchblade battle-axe quicker than her stuttering heart could find its beat.

"Oh God." She cringed back against the wall.

"I never got around to naming it." He gripped the weapon just below the wickedly recurved blade and tugged up the sleeves of his coat and shirt.

The razor edge carved the cold light, sharper than the look he threw her as he laid the gleaming blade against the inside of his right arm between the inky lines of his tattoo.

"No." A sickening beat of horror skipped through her, in the same way as when she'd seen the SUV hurtling toward her, about to change her life forever.

The tattoo, neither Celtic nor tribal but even more primitive, swirled over his knuckles and spiked halfway up his arm. Against the black, the skin of his wrist looked tender, veins and tendons standing out in marbled relief.

He stilled, and despite the dread-filled thump of her heart, she found her gaze drawn to his.

"Unforgivably melodramatic," he said, "but effectively convincing."

He sliced the blade down his inner arm. Blood fountained up behind the silvery edge into a gruesome rooster tail.

With a wordless cry, she jumped forward. A sweep of her elbow knocked the axe from his grasp.

The momentum of her leap sent them both tumbling to the pavement. He swore as his back hit the ground with a jolt.

She straddled him, both hands clamped on the terrible injury, stemming the inexorable outflow of life. Her heart raced, matching each gushing pump of blood from his wrist.

"Sera."

"Are you crazy?" Was she? He'd had an *axe*, for God's sake. She tried not to wonder if the weapon was far enough from his reach, if he would use it again, this time on her. "I can't let go of you."

"If so, you would be the first."

The glimmer of old pain in his gaze ensnared her. But each heartbeat she spent wondering, another pulse of his blood eked between her fingers. "Shut up unless you're going to make sense. We have to tourniquet your arm. Damn it, why don't I have a scarf?"

"Sera, let go."

Her stomach twisted. "I feared I was trying to kill myself, but I guess you beat me to it."

"'Tis harder than you'd think." His voice was soft, and he shifted under her, his thighs hard between her knees. "Sera, please."

His tone made her pause. She was practically molesting him, something she hadn't quite gotten around to with his doppelganger. He was too big for her to restrain, too sensibly calm and level eyed for her to tell herself he was totally nuts. Adrenaline ebbed, leaving her dazed.

"I already know you're not a healer," he said. "You're

a guide. You of all people should understand release from pain can be dearer than life."

She shook her head, slowly at first, then with more vigor. "Who told you that? That's not why . . ."

"Let go."

"Damn you." She did.

Only a tracing of scar remained. The white line gleamed like pearl beneath the transecting smears of blood left by her fingers. She gasped and stumbled back.

"Easy." He reached out to steady her.

She evaded him, as if by avoiding his hand she could ignore what she'd just seen. "It's a trick."

"All demon-kind delight in trickery." He swept his hand over the scar, smearing her fingerprints into his skin, then folded the axe away and rose to his feet. "But I have not tricked you. Your possession will be hard enough without fear and doubt undermining you. Trust me on that."

He tucked the club back into the folds of his coat and held his hand down to her.

"Trust you?" She clenched her fist, sticky with his blood. If she refused to listen to him, then she couldn't believe her own senses either, which would mean she was broken in ways beyond the damage of a speeding SUV. That possibility was more frightening than anything he'd said. This time, the collision course was between what she'd known before and . . . "Possession?"

"The demon came to you. You let it in."

"I didn't know it was a demon." Just saying the word made her feel as if she were playing on the flip side of sanity. "I can't believe I'm listening to you." But she took his hand.

He drew her to her feet. He stared down at their matched bloody hands a moment, then released her. "Remember what I said about believing? You're already going through the first symptoms of possession as the demon metastasizes. Your anger and blackouts, the sensation that you've been cut off from everything you've ever known." The gray lake and sky cast a silvery pall over his eyes.

His distant, pensive expression made him seem too ... too much like her. She curled her fingers tight against the urge to touch him again, to recall his focus from the empty horizon.

He continued. "You'll tell yourself you're losing your mind, that you're embroiled in a government conspiracy, whatever makes you feel better." The silver haze hardened to bronze again as he looked back at her. "But when the demon ascends, you can reject my words and die. Or listen to me and just maybe survive."

"Survive possession."

"And what comes after. Now the demon travels this world in your flesh, and when its influence rises, you draw unnatural power through the residual link to its realm."

"That's how I knocked the axe out of your hand."

"I was momentarily distracted." He glowered at her beneath lowered brows. "It won't happen again."

She couldn't stop a quick grin at his disgruntlement. Then she thought about what he was saying, and her grin faded. "There's psychological degradation as well?"

Up went one brow. "Like homicidal schizophrenia?"

She winced to hear the accusation she'd thrown at him on the bridge tossed back like an armed grenade. "Like voices in your head, telling you to do things."

"The hierarchies in both other-realms are great believers in free will. Free, right up till you discover the price." He waved his tattooed hand dismissively. "You're still in the driver's seat. Only now you have a passenger. A silent passenger, possibly with a gun to your head, who's supercharged your vehicle for his own mysterious purpose and won't let you go. But you're not a puppet."

If she turned her focus inward, would she feel this

otherworldly passenger? The thought made her want to crawl out of her skin. But it was her skin, damn it. "You describe it like a parasite."

"Technically, symbiont. The demon doesn't just take. It gives. Technically."

The last was muttered under his breath, and she studied him, wondering whom he was trying to convince.

He shifted beneath her regard. "A weakness in your soul made you vulnerable to a demon matching itself to the emptiness in you."

"I wasn't weak or empty," she protested. "At least not until . . ."

This time, he studied her as she fell silent. Bad enough she'd sometimes felt her body, her mind, her very future, were casual stakes in a poker game where she hadn't been invited. Now it seemed her soul was in the pot too.

When she didn't speak again, he said, "The danger is greatest in the last stage of possession, during the demon's virgin ascension. Until the bond between you and the demon stabilizes, your soul might be pulled through the link to the other side."

"To hell?"

He shrugged. "No one's come back with a travelogue. But there's some reason our demons want out."

" 'Our'?" She'd been thinking only of how this strange fate applied to her.

The gray surroundings were less stark than his expression. "How else would I know all this? I am possessed too."

Archer took her for coffee. He'd seen that bewildered, undercaffeinated look often enough in his mirror, waking from mostly unremembered dreams.

Preferably unremembered.

They found a secluded table in the glass-ceiling atrium at Navy Pier, where wintry lake light gave the palm trees a surreal cast. She huddled over her frothy, butterscotch beverage, a far cry from the simple black in his own cup, but he figured she needed as much consolation as sugar and whipped cream could offer. "Did you want chocolate sprinkles too?"

At the disbelieving look she shot him, he realized he should have come up with more meaningful conversation to follow his, "I'm demon-possessed" and her mumbled, "I need a drink."

She leaned back, fingertips brushing her cup. "I'll pass on the sprinkles. I hear temptation got me into this mess."

"My demon is annihilation-class, with no special bent for enticement. I can't know you so thoroughly to tempt you as your unbound demon did."

"My demon." Her gaze wandered over him. The track of her scrutiny raised a prickle of awareness in his skin that had nothing to do with his enhanced senses. He couldn't know her—had no intention of knowing her—but some odd intimacy crackled between them all the same.

After all, the demon had come to her looking like him.

He crushed the thought. No intentions and good intentions seemed to lead to the same inevitable destination. "Is the coffee helping?"

"Making me feel human again? I guess you'll tell me if I'm not human anymore."

"You are. Mostly."

She scowled at the "mostly." "And the rest?"

"Is an other-realm emanation, latent at the moment, that matched itself to susceptible receptors in your idiopathic, perpetual etheric force." When she blinked at him, he added, "More commonly called your soul."

"Did I catch a demon or a cold?"

He slanted her a faint smile. "Our philosophers compare possession to an infection, where demonic viral code overwrites exposed portions of our humanity."

She shook her head. Her wrists, thin and pale against the black aluminum mesh table, seemed unbearably delicate, ill-suited to the fight ahead, and he wondered why the demon had chosen her. "Demon philosophy. I can't help thinking. . . ."

He made an encouraging sound, but her glance was more irate than reassured. He made a mental note that she was not a woman to be patronized. First he had to dust the cobwebs off the mental file where he kept his notes on women.

"If this is true," she continued, "I might finally get some answers."

Archer lifted one eyebrow. "To what?"

"Heaven. Hell. God. What is the soul?" Her voice picked up speed. "Does it matter if we are good people or bad? How good do you have to be? If God is good and God made everything, why would he make bad? Why can't—?"

"Is that how it lured you?" She blinked at his curtness, and he tried to modulate his tone. "It won't give you answers. You'll only have more questions."

"There's nothing wrong with wanting to know."

"Tell that to Adam."

"I didn't cause the downfall of man."

His body tightened with the remembered weight of her straddling his hips. Most often such a scuffle involved some demonic entity eager to kill him. But she'd wanted to save him, to fall under her again. . . .

He felt the shift within him, not just in the suddenly snug crotch of his jeans, but the restless demon rising at his distraction. Damn. He'd said they weren't puppets, and here he was, losing control like any newly possessed or rogue talya.

He dragged his mind back to the conversation. "Regardless, Eve didn't pass along any apples of knowledge. We have generations of historians who've filled archives with what they've learned, but they'd fill Lake Michigan with what they still can't fathom. They'd overflow the Great Lakes with what they haven't even thought to ask."

She narrowed her eyes. "Are there many like you?"

He noticed she didn't include herself. "Leagues of talyan exist in pockets around the world." When she frowned at the strange word, he explained, "One of those first scholars tagged us talyan, an unkind comparison to Aramaic sacrificial lambs."

She stared off into the middle distance, contemplating. "Aramaic? See, now I have more questions."

"You'll find no religion or science with answers. We've culled the sects of a hundred cultures to find words for what we face, but the faiths of centuries offer no solace, and the science of today provides no explanations. We are heretic and madman rolled into one." He reached across the table to take her chin in his hand, forcing her to focus on him. "Your only task now is to survive the coming days."

Her hazel eyes speared him, and his demon surfaced like a leviathan on a gaff hook. She couldn't know what lurked below. He was a fool to rile it with the touch it both longed for and feared.

He let go abruptly just as she jerked her chin up. "I've probably survived worse."

His fingertips tingled with the flush of her skin, the heat flickering up his demon's mark like ignition along black lines of gunpowder. "No doubt you have, or the demon would have chosen another."

"When I had the vision of it, it said I'd called it." She fixed her gaze on her hands wrapped around the coffee cup. "It said I was lonely. It said it loved me. How desperate is that?"

Love. The word exploded in an empty place in him,

as if that powder had burned to the end of the line. He clamped down until the echo died. "Desperate on the demon's part? Or yours?" When she glared at him, he shrugged. "It makes a bargain to fill what's missing in us and then takes what it needs."

"But why me?" She wilted a bit. "Seems a little conceited to think I've had any more tribulations than the next guy."

"Haven't you?" He waited while she considered. "But it's not about the quantity of your suffering. It's the quality. Demons are quite the connoisseurs of pain."

She grimaced. "Me too lately, I guess."

"Exactly. When the demon crosses over, it seeks a matching target, a soul that resonates with its energy. Somewhere in your past is a penance trigger. It defines the headwaters of an invisible fault line in your soul, cutting a path right to the moment when the demon breaks your life in two."

"A penance trigger?" Some memory brought a hazy glitter to the corner of her eye. "So it was because of me."

The tear never fell, but his muscles tightened as if reacting to a mortal threat. He held himself still with effort. He wouldn't reach for her again. "Whatever it was doesn't necessarily make you guilty, Sera. It just made you vulnerable."

Despite his soft tone, her instant focus pinned him. Her narrowed eyes left no room for tears. "I still can't believe any of this. I should have my head examined."

"You mean your soul."

She took a hard hit off her coffee. "I don't go to church anymore."

Her brusque dismissal cut him off as surely as he'd interrupted her list of existential questions. Well, he didn't want her to pry into his past either. He should respect those boundaries, as he would the no-touch taboo of the possessed.

"You won't struggle to believe much longer." The sleeve scratched at his right arm, and he shifted uncomfortably. The flesh might heal quick and clean, but the pain lingered. She'd find that out soon enough too. "Possession with the demon ascendant is proof enough."

She stood. "Okay then. Thanks for the coffee."

He looked up at her without rising. Niall could choke on his cracks about gentlemanly behavior. "That's it for all your questions?"

"You haven't answered any of them. I get the sense you're holding back until I make it to the other side." She smiled, barely.

He wondered whether he should try reassuring her again, but decided she'd only think worse of him. Because she was right; he was holding back.

And if for a moment he'd foolishly thought to reach out to ease the pain he'd seen in her eyes, well, she'd also been right to fend him off. Just because two lost people found each other, didn't make them less lost.

He slid a business card across the table.

She placed the tip of one finger over the terse @1 symbol on the card. " 'At One'?"

"Demonic possession twists your soul and your sense of humor. See? 'Atone.' "

"Oh. Ha." Her hazel gaze rose to his. "So tell me one thing, straight."

He inclined his head solemnly.

"Are the talyan—" She stumbled over the exotic word. "Are the demon-ridden damned?"

He hesitated. From the way she spoke, she'd had more than a flirting relationship with religion. And he'd bet his soul—had it still been his to bet—the penance trigger that made her susceptible to possession had its roots in her beliefs.

Not that evil gave a flying fuck about faith. He opened his mouth.

She shook her head. "Too late. You already answered."

He scowled. "I didn't. You're jumping ahead."

This time, her smile was genuine. "Let me know when you catch up."

She walked away. But the business card peeked out between her fingers.

Archer sat back to watch her go. Straight and steady. The sweetened coffee and her pique had given her that, at least. Once upon a time, he'd preferred more sass and sway.

But those times were dead, and she—so far—was not.

The destroyer in him quivered, a taut stretch deep in his muscles as its quarry escaped. The quiver intensified to an ache, muscles cramping, raising the hair on his arms and a black-light hunter's glow over his vision. It wanted to give chase, badly.

He held himself still as he tracked her progress out of the atrium, down the stairs. There'd be a car waiting for her. He'd taken care of that while he bought the coffee—the least he could do, and the most he thought she'd allow.

He didn't flinch when a body thumped down in the seat she'd left. "I suppose you got all that for Niall?"

"For posterity," Zane corrected. "You let her walk away again."

"She has our card this time."

"Now that she's infected." Zane drummed his fingers on the table, a tinny sound that set Archer's teeth on edge. "Did you really think she'd deny it?"

If anyone . . . "She wanted to know."

"Know what?"

"Everything."

Zane chuckled. "A gambit old as Eve. So the demons triumph again."

Archer exhaled the worst of his tension. "If you call it

a triumph when demons merge with unsuspecting conscripts to fight in a never-ending war between good and evil."

"Depends on your alternatives, I suppose."

No one knew the demons' circumstances in their own realm. The lies before possession and the metaphysical radio silence afterward guaranteed that. On their own behalf, the demon-ridden humans rarely discussed the alternatives they faced before. And there was nothing to discuss after.

Zane slid an electronic file folder across the table. "Bookie downloaded the rest of the dossier on our new recruit."

"We're not sure she's ours yet." Archer opened the slim manila-colored folder to reveal a screen of scrolling data. The league expected to market the gadget through one of their anonymous corporations. While he understood all wars had to be funded, he cared for tech in direct proportion to how well it streamlined his mission, and so far he hadn't found a digital method of slaughtering demons.

He scanned the downloading information. "Preacher's kid. No wonder she was vulnerable."

"Pop was old-fashioned fire and brimstone," Zane abridged from memory. "He's in a nursing home now. Four brothers in irregular contact. Mama disappeared from the family when Sera was ten. Still digging up dirt on that. We already knew she contracts with a hospital to provide hospice deathbed counseling, but a bad car accident this year set her back physically, professionally, and financially. Mentally too, probably."

Archer looked down at the black-and-white surveillance photo embedded in the text, the arch glance, the set of that fine-boned jaw. "Maybe."

He wondered why she'd chosen a job surrounded by the dying. Mama's abandonment hadn't been painful enough?

He'd told himself her past didn't matter, but the demon had voiced her wound when it said she was alone. How cruel then, the only companionship available to her now was a ragged band of misfit soldiers stalked by shadows and doomed to damnation.

"Bookie included a footnote," Zane said. "Turns out, female talyan may have once matched us in number. Bookie said a postscript from before the creation of the leagues references the catastrophic loss of the mated-talyan bond. The provenance on the note can't be verified—it was written just this side of antiquity—so established league archives have squat about it."

A demon-ridden couple, each missing half their soul . . . Archer's lips twisted. A Hallmark movie it wasn't.

"Anyway." Zane cleared his throat. "Some light reading while you babysit the demon's ascension. Ecco finished securing her apartment. When are you heading over?"

"When she calls me."

Zane sat back. "I know I'm the new guy and all, but do you always play so close to the chest?"

Archer closed the folder on the picture, which replaced the static monochrome with his memory of bright searching hazel eyes, a high flush across pale skin. He knew better than to be drawn to her. Her light was only a lonely traveler's campfire in the wilderness to the wolf in him. Such attraction never ended well for the traveler.

He hadn't lied to Niall when he said he'd purged his Southern gentlemanly charm. That had died with everything else. The quickening in his blood at her scent had been the thrill of the chase, the hard breathing of the scuffle, the raw intimacy of her hands over his wound. The destroyer he'd become roused to the danger of her, nothing more.

Archer rose and gathered the coffee cups, hers with

just the candy scent of butterscotch and a ring where the whipped cream had been. "We don't know which strain of demon possessed her—one of ours or one of theirs. We won't know until the mark manifests. I'll be there when it does."

"And if it's not what you want to see?"

Archer dumped the trash. "Then that's one more demon wishing it were back in hell."

CHAPTER 4

Lost in thoughts by turns too crazy or awful to indulge, Sera didn't turn when the town car honked, but the driver leaning out the window stopped her with a wave.

"I'm your ride," he said. "Guy upstairs said to take you wherever you wanted to go."

She crumpled the business card in her fist. She was tired of feeling like she was being taken for a ride. "No thanks."

Dark glasses hid the driver's eyes, an unnecessary affectation on such a gloomy day. "Hey, I'm already paid for." He leaned a little farther out, exposing the tattoo curling around the side of his neck.

She backed away. "I said no."

She'd checked her pockets on the way down from the atrium. As blackout fugues went, at least this one hadn't been terribly inconvenient. She'd lost time and memory, but she'd remembered her house keys. She supposed she could plunge a key through one of those dark lenses and see if the eye behind was brown or blue or green . . . or white.

As if he sensed the spike of violence in her, he eased back into the car and sped away.

Lots of people had tattoos, she told herself. The car squealed around a corner, out of sight, but not out of mind. Emblazoned in her memory was the same sort of archaic, arcane symbol on the man she'd left inside: Ferris Archer.

She glanced back uneasily. Questions followed close on her heels, seething and maddening and ridiculous as rabid Chihuahuas. He'd teased her that she'd come up with conspiracy theories, as if that would make more sense than legions of demons and idiopathic perpetual whatever forces and penance triggers.

Okay, a conspiracy was sounding pretty good right now.

She shivered as the cold penetrated her uncertainty. She'd ended her postaccident counseling sessions with a colleague when they'd taken her father away. Maybe she needed to rethink her impatient proclamations of health.

Even as she swore to make the next available appointment, she realized she'd walked all the way home and climbed the stairs to her apartment without cane or pain.

She stopped with her hand on the doorknob. She tilted forward to press her brow against the wood.

What was happening to her?

She prowled through her apartment as if she'd never been there, but nothing seemed out of place, nothing suggested a reason for her . . . lapse. A quick check of the television told her she'd lost only a day. She sat on the couch and rubbed her hands over her thighs, frowning absently down the dark hallway toward the bathroom.

That's where it had started, the peculiar, erotically charged dream about the man—the demon Ferris Archer. Her mind stuttered like a fingerprint-smudged CD, skipping and repeating, and she found herself standing in the bathroom doorway.

She flicked on the light. In front of the mirror, she reluctantly raised her gaze above the opalescent stone dangling from the fixture. Still just herself. No one else. She shook her head in an attempt to dispel the mist gathering in her mind. No one else in the sense that she wasn't anyone besides who she'd always been; not that no one else was standing beside her. Who else would be here, after all?

In an effort of will she banished the image of Ferris Archer that appeared in her head, if not in her mirror. Just because he was tall and ripped and carried himself as if he could stop a speeding SUV with a single scathing comment was no reason to buy into his delusional fantasies.

As if reluctant to do the job alone, her fingers were slow on the buttons of her shirt and the fly of her jeans. Finally, shirt hanging open between her breasts, she peeled down the jeans. She stepped out of the pool of denim and raised her gaze to the mirror.

Gone. Her breath caught. Almost gone anyway. Once red and puckered, all that remained of the tangle of scars over her thighs and hips were traceries almost as unremarkable as her unbleached cotton underwear.

She turned, craning her neck to look over her shoulder. The contortion was effortless, and for the last six months, impossible. Under her wondering fingertips, only faint raised ridges remained of the scars on her lower back.

"I do not believe this." She couldn't stop her smile. She twisted the other way, just because.

What had Archer said? "Don't bother trying to decide whether to believe or not. It's true."

At the thought of him, her smile faded.

And what if everything else he said was true?

"It will be one of the dark."

The man twisted his fingers as he made his pronouncement. Ten white twisting worms. Unfortunately, too large a lunch for the crow.

Corvus leaned back in his chair. "Are you certain?"

"With the solvo spreading well, the dissonance should definitely have triggered the crossing of a specimen from the more powerful strain. The crossing was so unusually violent, the Veil is still in flux, which will make our task that much easier. All signs point toward a djinn crossing, and we do have an agreement—"

"Are you certain?"

The crow stabbed its beak out between the bars to grab a paperclip off the desk. It sidled away, working the shiny metal in its beak and cackling.

"Not entirely, no."

Corvus nodded once. "Then we wait. And continue our preparations. The wound in the Veil will serve us, whether the demon will or not."

The Worm twitched, as if impatience consumed every cell of his body just as, Corvus supposed, it did all mortal creatures. "Only my work has gotten you this far. I deserve ..." Again, that twitch, accompanied by a conspicuous pallor.

Corvus let the outburst pass, as he let the thieving crow keep its little toy. "All our efforts shall be rewarded, eventually." The Worm couldn't begin to understand how long Corvus himself had waited for his chance.

The Worm nodded until Corvus thought his head would wobble off. "The demon must be djinn. I simply can't believe the teshuva could muster such force across the Veil. I've noticed the impulse toward repentance diminishes in ratio to the threat of punishment. Which explains the remorseful teshuva's mediocrity in this realm."

"You simply can't believe?" The Worm could do nothing simply, not even speak. "With the Veil isolating us from what lies beyond, our beliefs are all we have to sustain us."

Rather than endure the Worm's squirmings at the reprimand, Corvus swiveled in his chair to look out over the city. The sun burned a pale gray hole in the darker gray sky. The light raised forlorn glimmers in the delicate sculptures arrayed on the windowsill. The churches born of Rome weren't the only ones to capture peace and beauty in glass. He caressed the stone in his ring, calmed by the vista and the promise of what was—at long last—coming.

"If Sera Littlejohn is possessed by one of ours, then she will fight for the Darkness. If not, she must die."

"She's on the move."

Ecco's voice crackled in Archer's earbud, and he scowled up at the darkening sky where low clouds threatened snow. He remembered the restlessness that had driven him at his demon's ascension, but couldn't she have just done a little knitting instead?

"Wrong century," he muttered.

"What's that?" Even through the electronic connection, Ecco sounded as annoyed as Archer felt.

"I said I'm on it."

"You're not going to be able to sweet-talk her down this time, Archer," Ecco said. "If she turns djinn, you need to take her out right then before she calls in the horde-tenebrae to lick your bones. Niall, you're sure he's the man for an action job?"

"Fuck you," Archer said conversationally.

Niall was already talking over him. "Reserve this channel for the exchange of useful information, gentlemen."

"I ain't no gentleman," Ecco said. "You must mean fancy pants. Hard to believe he's got an annihilation-class demon in there at all. Just let me know where the fightin' words channel is, and maybe I'll find it—"

Archer ripped out the earpiece, ignoring Niall's tinny squawk. He left the shelter of his car just as Sera stepped out of her apartment building.

She'd dressed for the falling temps, including the scarf she'd wanted last time. She tucked her chin down into the heather wool a few shades darker than her coat, and with her blond hair contained under a matching hat, she was just another gray shadow moving through the gray city.

Until she glanced up to see him. Her hazel eyes widened, and the blush that rose under her teeth when she bit her lower lip roused an answering pulse of blood through his veins. Carnal tension and something deeper twisted in him.

"I didn't call you." She held up one gloved hand. "Not last time, not this time. Not the time when you were the demon."

"I wasn't the demon." A fine distinction at the moment.

"Whatever." She marched past him down the sidewalk. "I didn't call. In fact, I burned the business card. You're stalking me."

He fell into step beside her. "You didn't burn the card. You're not stupid. And, yes, I am stalking you."

She frowned at him. "You could at least pretend to feel bad about it." She shook her head when he drew breath to answer. "Right. No lies. No tricks. No pretending either, I assume."

"I'm here for you, Sera," he said simply. He didn't have to tell her why.

She turned to him, angling her face to make up for the difference in their height. "That's supposed to make me feel better?"

"No. It's just the truth."

She walked on. "Strangely, I do feel better."

She wouldn't, if she knew what he'd have to do if the demon possessing her wasn't one of theirs.

"Maybe just because I'm moving," she continued. "I swear, the walls were crushing me."

"The demon comes from a place of infinity. They want

to be on the move, on the hunt, stretching our senses." The rhythm of his words matched their steps, her stride matching his. He caught himself eyeing the length of her leg and scowled. "Don't indulge it too freely. Tempting a demon to run amok is a bad idea. Repentant or not, there's a reason they were damned."

She wrinkled her nose. "Never mind the demon. *I'm* happy to be on the move again. Since the accident ... Anyway, I feel almost like myself again."

For the moment. "I noticed you'd left the cane behind."

"The kids downstairs snatched it. They were riding it around like a witch's broom." She shot him a narrow glance. "Do you believe in witches too?"

"Maybe they were pretending it was a hobby horse," Archer said, still thinking of the cane.

"They're city kids. They've never even seen a horse."

He realized abruptly he was showing his age with the antiquated reference. "Just because they've never seen one doesn't mean they can't want one."

They walked in silence past houses as quiet as if the stones themselves were hunkering down for the night.

"Speaking of not seeing," she said suddenly, "my scars are all but gone."

Without a word, he rolled up his sleeve. Only a white thread of puckered flesh remained from his demonstration at the pier.

She closed her eyes, opened them again, but shifted her focus to the black. "That tattoo."

"It's my *reven*, an interrealm rift torn into my flesh to mark where the demon entered." He touched the pulse point of his wrist. A flicker of violet chased along the black lines. For a heartbeat, the surrounding skin seemed to fade to translucence, revealing not muscle and bone but some glittering void. "It's our only view into the demon realm."

"Torn?" She blinked. "That must've hurt."

"No." Honest enough. By the time the mark appeared, his torment had been too deep to notice.

"I saw a similar tattoo—*reven*—on the driver at the pier."

"The pattern identifies the class and potency of demon and its point of entry. In Ecco's case, a strong chaos-class demon." Archer smirked. "I'll be sure to let him know you made him."

"You've been watching me. You said there was no conspiracy."

"I said it wasn't a government conspiracy. We're ... private contractors. Very private. We keep watch over all demonic activity."

"You stay together?"

"More or less." Zane had mentioned an obsolete mated-talyan bond. Maybe in those days they'd taken turns taking out the demonic trash.

"Like a support group? To find a cure?"

"There is no cure."

"Funny, I don't feel doomed." She stared down at her feet. "I'd forgotten how nice a strong body is. My poor patients ... I could just keep walking forever."

He caught her arm and forced her to a halt. Forced himself to ignore her supple heat under his hand. Nice body, yeah. "You can't escape, Sera. Somewhere inside, you sense what's coming."

She strained against him, testing her strength. "And what is that, exactly? End-stage demonic infection, I know. Maybe I'll just take two aspirin and call my pastor in the morning."

Ah, he knew this moment well. He steeled himself against the pang. Just because she roused the memory of a certain idealistic, naïve young man was no reason to forget the hopeless outcome. "Too late. It's ascending already, from your soul through your body, and demons can't be destroyed. If you cast it out now, the demon will just seek a new host."

She lifted her chin. "That's easy."

"No. It came to you through your weakness—in mind, in body. In your soul."

"Not exactly fair."

"I doubt fair comes up in the demon handbook code of ethical conduct. Besides, what does it take to resist temptation when you're strong? Anybody can do that."

She pulled at him more forcefully. "I'm stronger now."

"Because of the demon. If you deny it, it will leave the way it came, through your wounds, taking what it has given you." He tightened his grip, close to bruising as his demon roused to the defiance in her stance. If he gave it free rein, she'd know the folly of questioning him. "This strong body you like so much will be gone with the demon."

"I got by before."

"And when it goes, it will take a little more than you had. Call it recompense. Most likely, you'd never walk again."

She froze. "Maybe that's the price I have to pay."

"Willing to sacrifice a chunk of your soul too? The demon burrowed into damage in your body *and* your soul. Places where it linked would be torn apart. Our theologically inclined believe your demon-mottled soul would be bound into the Veil between the realms to spend the rest of eternity waiting out the final battle in spiritual limbo."

She wasn't pulling away from him now. "Final battle?"

He ignored the question. "There's no bargaining with this devil. You stay and fight for your hold on this realm, or you are crippled, physically and spiritually, for the rest of your life. A life that the most wretched of your former patients would deem a thousand times worse than their own deaths."

Sera stared at him, eyes so wide he caught a glimpse

of the first drifting snowflakes reflected in her pupils. The demon had come to him in winter too, when old wounds ached most deeply. With all he'd lost, the prospect of spring had seemed obscene.

He would do what needed to be done if Sera's demon was djinn and not repentant teshuva. But he'd be damned—again—if he let Ecco, Niall, or anyone else force his hand.

With his grip still on her, the violet-chased *reven* he'd exposed shimmered in the lower corner of his gaze, an unspoken reminder of his compulsion. Damned indeed. As he'd told Sera, the demon-mottled soul faced, at best, oblivion upon death.

He just hadn't told her that eventually oblivion no longer seemed so dire a choice.

He didn't know what expression was on his face— grimmer than plain old death, for sure. But she put her hand over his, covering the *reven*. The unexpected heat of skin on skin flared along the demon's marking. He couldn't remember the last time he'd been touched that didn't involve blood and ichor, that felt human warm and female soft. The contact shocked him out of his reverie, as did the gentling of her gaze. "Whatever happened to you, I'm sorry."

He loosed her abruptly, pulling away from her touch, away from the perilous sensations that ricocheted through him. "Thanks for the sympathy, but I'm not one of your hospice patients. I didn't die." The way she cocked her head made him wary of more questions. "Let's go."

When he set his hand against her lower back, she twisted aside, a sinuous contraction of bone and muscle under his palm. "I'm not going anywhere. Not with you."

He took a breath, as if he could inhale patience. All he got was a lungful of cold air spiked with her faint perfume, a sweet fleeting scent even his enhanced senses couldn't quite capture. "You need to be in a safe place."

Safe for her. Or for everyone else if her demon was djinn.

She stepped out of reach. "So far, everything that has confused me most has come from your mouth." Her narrowed gaze flicked over his lips, an almost tangible touch. His skin warmed in anticipation of . . .

He shook himself as she continued. "So you won't mind if I work this out on my own."

The unexpected cravings rattled him, and he spoke more sharply than he'd intended. "You've worked things out so well on your own. Tell me, after all the long nights on death-watch, have you figured out why your father's mind has been taken? Or why your mother abandoned you?"

A violet spark bloomed in her eyes, expanding in concentric circles through the hazel irises. He had a half second to acknowledge that his insensitive remarks wouldn't make reasoning with her any easier. Without a betraying word, she leapt at him, fingers curled to gouge.

Another note to self, he ruminated as he fended off her attack. He slid to the side so her momentum carried her past him. Sensitive to aspersions cast upon her past. Well, weren't they all?

"Hey," he snapped as she whirled back. "Watch those nails."

"You watch," she growled, slashing at his eyes again.

He had to jerk back more quickly this time. She was already fiercer than he'd anticipated.

The violet spark jagged across the browns and greens of her eyes. He tamped down a twinge of alarm. If the ascension was progressing this fast . . .

"Sera." He circled her, forcing her off balance. "Come back to me, Sera."

"I didn't come for you when I was naked in my bedroom, so you can forget about it now."

This conversation wasn't helping his concentration.

He ducked her swinging fist, reluctant to engage when the violence was merely a symptom of the demon's ascension. That, and she was pissed at him. He often wondered if angelic possession was gentler.

He ducked another jab. "Sera," he said warningly.

"Never," she hissed. "Never invoke my mother with your forked tongue."

"My tongue isn't forked. That must've been the demon kissing you." Exasperated, he caught her fist, holding it tight. "I shouldn't have been so blunt, but your amateur forays into the physiology of the soul won't help you now. You have to listen to me."

Not that tussling on the sidewalk was a good way to build trust. One hand still engulfing her fist, he spun her into a tight embrace tucked against his chest.

"I know what you're going through," he murmured. Her hair, tufting out from under her hat, smelled warm with ire and that teasing perfume. He could almost, but not quite, picture the bloom, growing between the fields of his father's farm, redolent under the Southern sun.

Blindsided by wistfulness, he found himself adding, "I used to be like you, Sera. Trying to force it all to make sense, to matter. It doesn't."

As he breathed in again, she slammed the back of her head into his nose and bolted out of his grasp.

Involuntary tears flooded his vision. Through the haze, he saw her duck into the alley. He swallowed back the metallic tang of blood, swearing at his momentary weakness and her sudden strength. The demon was taking hold faster than they'd thought possible, subtly replacing the influence of the human realm; so instead of screaming for the police, she called on the nascent power within her.

He supposed he should be grateful. His task, one way or the other, would be over that much faster.

He followed into the alley, eyeing the Dumpsters and doorways that practically screamed ambush.

At a flicker from the corner of his eye, he raised a defensive arm. He caught the down-swinging slat of pallet hard against bone and winced at the crack. Just the wood, he hoped, and a helluva bruise.

"Damn it, Sera." He parried her thrust of the shorter and now-sharper plank.

"Damn you, for luring me into this." She wove a pattern in the air with the tip of her makeshift sword.

"You ran into the alley," he reminded her. "Who lured whom here?"

She snarled. "Don't be obtuse."

He heard the demon in the low thrum of her voice. Unconsciously, she was summoning it. But until the possession was complete, she couldn't sustain the attack. He could push her to the edge, but that held danger for both of them.

"The demon lured you," he amended. A strong demon, obviously, though strain and class unknown. "None of it my fault." He grabbed for the wooden weapon.

With a shout, she jumped back out of reach. And landed some twenty feet away, balanced high on the corner of a closed Dumpster.

He stared up into her shocked gaze. A very strong demon, he corrected himself.

He held his hands low at his sides, unthreatening. If she called on the other-realm energy so readily so soon, she just might be able to escape him, only to lose herself in the last stages of possession or succumb to a djinni with all the destruction that entailed.

That, either way, *would* be his fault. For carelessness, for underestimating. Enough had been lost under his watch.

He took a breath, tightening supernatural musculature not entirely his own, that did not exist in any dissectible way. His vision flickered with tracers and auras as the desire to chase, rend, consume, welled up. He channeled the surge of ravening violence and launched himself after her.

He slammed her around the middle, knocking off her hat and scarf. She shrieked, but the sound cut out as he drove her against the wall. He caught himself on the flat of his hands a hair's breadth before he crushed her into the brick.

"You'll be good," he growled. "If you survive. But you'll not be better than me."

"I'll kill you." Violet incandescence occluded the hazel in her eyes, and the demonic lows lent double octaves to her voice.

"Not yet." He tightened his grip against her straining. He couldn't loose her—wouldn't lose her.

He felt the heat rising in her, a fever out of control. The demon, invoked too soon, trailed other-realm elements leaching from her. Not yet fully anchored in the body and soul it had chosen, a demon during its virgin ascension was both stronger and more exposed, subject to the willful passions that it longed for and feared, such passions having been the downfall of angels. If he could fan those flames just a little higher, the psychic back draft would knock her senseless as her demon fled temptation.

She struggled to break free. But he anticipated every move.

"You want answers, Sera? I have them. The demon can't tell you anything anymore. It's locked inside you. Like the memory of your mother's disappearance, the fear for your father's vanishing mind. Just more questions, more pain. Until you die."

"You don't know anything about it." Blond tendrils of her hair drifted on currents not of this realm.

"I've lost more than you could ever imagine, child." But as she writhed against him, he didn't feel much like the wise elder.

He pinned his knee between her legs, dimly aware of the grinding sting of brick through his jeans. The resistance of her shoulders beneath his hands excited something in him darker and more primitive even than the demon dwelling in his own soul.

"Give up," he growled.

"I won't."

And that was the difference between them. How long since he'd felt such pure resolve? The lack sent a jealous ache through him, and a dread that he wouldn't be able to restrain her. "It's easier."

Her arch look, while still squashed against the wall, pricked him. "Even the demon wearing your face wasn't such a coward."

"You remember that moment well, do you?" He pressed her harder. "You keep mentioning it. Did possession bring you such pleasure?"

The violet wash over her eyes lightened toward amethyst. "You have no right to judge me."

Judge, jury, and executioner, if she only knew.

Still she was right. He had *no* right. His grip on her arms tightened, finding places human tender, yet coursing with demon power. She didn't flinch, only stared up, defiant, with just enough hazel left in her gaze to let him know she would always defy him, demon or not.

That remnant of her swayed him where her lithe body hadn't quite done the trick. He imagined what the demon—wearing his face, as she accused—had done to gain her compliance.

He breathed her scent again. Honeysuckle, he remembered abruptly. How had he forgotten? It had rambled every lane of his childhood. The pale flowers were touched in purple, sweetly scented but tenaciously climbing, bitten back in winter and ever more wild with the return of the sun.

A wayward lock of her hair curled around his finger, possessed of its own too-human temptation. "I wish I could save you from this. But all I have left in me is destruction."

He lowered his mouth over hers.

Chapter 5

After all she'd been through—her accident and the grueling surgeries afterward, the bizarre appearance of demonology, not to mention that unbelievable jump just now—she had thought nothing could shock her.

His kiss jolted through her as if she'd grabbed the L's third rail.

His lips parted over hers, rough and raw, nothing like the doppelganger's smooth touch. His body, hard against her, drove the thrill deeper, so her every nerve fired at his touch. She dug her fingers into his shoulders. She should push him away. She knew in the depths of her bones that she could, if she wanted.

But, oh, how she wanted.

She stretched, muscle and sinew flexing, matching his strength against her own. He growled into her mouth, and the vibration triggered aftershocks all through her. Still pinning her to the wall, he levered her arms above her head, both her wrists clasped in one of his hands, his other wrapped around her throat, driving her chin up, opening her mouth for him. She answered his growl with a moan, a throaty animal sound far too low for her own voice.

Not like her at all. None of this was like her. To throw
sense and caution to the winds, swept by primordial
needs she'd never indulged before. The ferocious pounding of blood to her belly and thighs excited and shamed
her. What was she becoming?

Her heart pulsed more frantically, and she couldn't
breathe. Her chest was on fire. She wrenched her head
to the side, sucking in chill winter air.

He swore and released her, then took a step back.
His eyes sparked with unnatural violet light. "My God.
I didn't mean . . ."

He reached out to touch her, and she flinched away
from his hand.

Just as a monstrous dark shape slammed into the
wall where they'd been. Under her shoulder, the brick
trembled at the impact. A chip exploded out, catching
her below one eye.

A bestial snarl, like a mockery of the sound she'd
made, filled the alley.

Archer grabbed her and spun her behind him. She
stumbled in a circle, trying to keep her feet under her.

Her breath froze even as her heart quadrupled its
pace. The thing was huge, half as wide again as Archer
and every bit as tall, though it slumped, one clawed foot
braced against the Dumpster, one gnarled fist on the
wall. She took in a confused impression of half-fur, half-
insectoid armor plating, and a glowing rust-orange eye.

Not pausing to be admired, it sprang at them. Its gargled cry almost drowned out the squeal of the Dumpster
shoved across the pavement.

Archer shouted in reply and leapt forward—low,
sweeping the club from under his coat. The axe blades
whirled open in a shining arc.

The creature slashed at him and jumped for the wall,
caroming off the bricks.

Straight for her.

She felt the weight of death upon her. The stink of excrement and sulfurous rot made her stomach heave. Behind the creature, half-hidden by its bulk, Archer dove forward, blade at the ready, but too far from her.

Under her hand, she found the broken slat of the pallet. She'd wrenched it up when Archer was chasing her, not even thinking that such a move should have been impossible without a crowbar.

She didn't want to think too much now either. She reached down into the empty place where she went in the moments before a patient passed, when time and chances were exhausted and nothing remained to say.

She was supposed to find peace down there, she knew—acceptance of approaching death.

What she found instead was fury.

Her vision blurred strangely, so she saw the monster trailing a stereopticon afterimage, not just where it had been, but everywhere it might go. When the demon had promised answers, she hadn't imagined such a practical application. Now she just had to guess which answer was right.

Her fingers closed over the wood, and she lunged into the trajectory outlined most brightly a split second before the monster.

One slash for every person who'd left her, starting with her mother, first when she was ten, then again at thirteen. The thing flinched back. A wild glee, not entirely her own, ripped through her. The demon. Her demon.

The monster recovered, then reached for her. But she knew, somehow, that it would, and her makeshift blade was already in motion. She chopped at its arm, batting it aside. It shrieked. The wood shattered, leaving her with less than six inches of jagged splinters in her fist.

She stepped inside the arch of raking claws and stabbed her much-shortened weapon toward the corroded eye.

The thing wailed and reared back. A glint of steel at

its throat caught her gaze. She recoiled just as the spray of black ichor exploded over her head. She threw up one hand to ward off the gruesome cascade, and a few stinging droplets scalded her skin.

A purling whine from the beast, pathetic and foul, made her stomach lurch. It kicked once with curling claws like a dead rat's clenched foot; then Archer hauled it over backward, where it lay still.

She half turned toward the wall, sinking to her haunches. The unnatural strength and surety that had buoyed her vanished, so she was left floundering on her own.

Archer plunged toward her. "Sera." The axe clattered to the pavement, and his hands were everywhere on her, searching. "Where are you hurt?"

She looked at the back of her hand where the black blood burned. She was still clutching the wooden stake. She spread her fingers, and the remaining splinters pattered to the ground. "I missed it. Geez, that close, and I still missed."

Archer sat back on his heels and raised one eyebrow. That was the last she remembered before the hollowness inside her reverberated with a cry even more terrible than the dead beast's wail, and the blackness took her.

Corvus left his tower, three leather satchels bumping against his hip with a tinkle of glass. In his wake, the whining darklings made the shadows quake. A few followed, unbidden.

On a corner lit not by a streetlamp but by flames flickering in a bullet-pierced, fifty-gallon drum, he passed a man, fidgety as the darklings.

"Hey, Jack, nice night."

Corvus slowed, then turned on his heel. "Lovely."

"You looking for somethin'? I got it."

The ancient malevolence in Corvus recognized more

holes in the man's soul than in the scudding clouds in the cold lead sky. "I seek my freedom."

The man laughed, a sound as muddy as ruined glass. "Got your freedom right here in my pocket. Wanna smoke it or shoot it?"

"Along that path lies freedom through death. Not what I seek."

The man threw up his hands. "You an idiot? A priest? Get the hell outta here."

"Why, yes. That is indeed the way to my freedom. Getting hell out." Corvus tipped his sunglasses down his nose and peered over the rim.

The dealer stiffened. "Hey, I gotta go—"

"Unbeknownst to yourself, you have been long gone, my friend." The poison burned in the back of Corvus's eyeballs. He stiffened against the pain, but the acid leak of tears spilled over, blistering his cheeks. He raised his hand. On his finger, the opalescent stone was a second icy burn against his scarred and callused skin.

The man scrambled backward, far too slowly. Corvus slashed his ringed hand like a scythe.

Following his sweeping gesture, a patchwork mist tore from the dealer's body. To Corvus's scalded eye, the severed soul glistened like a snail's broken trail.

The dealer staggered back, clutching at the drum. It tipped, and flaming debris washed across the sidewalk. The dealer fell into the embers, gagging and weeping.

Darklings swarmed around Corvus's feet like ducks flocking around a retiree bearing loaves of stale bread. Of course, they were embodiments of pure evil with needle teeth, and he threw them scraps of shredded soul.

Corvus left the darklings to their insatiable feast; not even a memory would remain to pass into eternity. He turned to the corpse sprawled on the sidewalk. The body groaned and stirred, clutching its head. Not a corpse quite yet.

Corvus hauled the dealer to his feet and brushed

away the clinging embers. "Did you fall?" he asked solicitously.

The dealer hitched up his pants. "What you want, Jack?" He recited his mantra in a muddled tone. "I got it."

"Not anymore," Corvus said softly. "But you will still be of use." He lifted one satchel over his head and settled the strap around the dealer's shoulders. "Here is the fruit of your wicked labors, the harvest of your sins. With it, you will help me sow the next—nay, the last crop."

The dealer boggled at him. Corvus sighed. "It's the hot new shit, man. Everybody's doing it."

The dealer plunged his hand into the satchel. Glass clinked when he lifted out a slim vial. Even in the smoldering light of the dying cinders, the small tablets reflected a lunar glow like unstrung pearls. "You got sol?"

"Like you would not believe." Corvus plucked the vial from the dealer's grasp and returned it to the pouch. "Don't set the price too high. Impatience and greed, my friend, will be the death of you." Already had been, in fact.

He steered the dealer's still-animate body through the pool of indifferent darklings. They already had what they wanted.

The dealer squinted at Corvus with vague suspicion. "What do I owe you, Jack?"

"Nothing. Do you know what a corvus is? No, why would you? It was an ancient naval weapon, like a gangplank with a sharp tooth on the end. The Romans dropped the corvus on enemy ships, which allowed their soldiers to rush across the bridge." At the dealer's silent confusion, Corvus rubbed wearily at his eyes. "I am a bridge, my friend."

The dealer nodded. "You giving everybody a free taste, then they come to you."

"A taste of freedom, yes, then they will come to me."

The dealer looked crafty. "If you're just the bridge for

sol, what're your masters gonna want at the other end?
I ain't paying twice."

Corvus smiled thinly. "You are wiser than I thought.
Let us just say, the masters have more pressing con-
cerns. But you, my friend, needn't pay them anything
more. And I will take my reward in the hereafter."

"You sure sound like a priest."

Corvus inclined his head. "Perhaps in a manner of
speaking."

He sent the dealer away on a drifting tide of weakness
like a plague ship. Corvus patted the remaining satchels.
Two more vessels yet to be launched into the night.

In all his centuries, only recently had enough devo-
tees of doom perceived the freedom he had sought for
so long. The Worm thought his formula was the cata-
lyst. But the hunger had come first. That emptiness had
drawn the demon through the Veil, leaving the wound
through which the rest would follow. And that craving
would never be assuaged until the world's isolation was
ended, until heaven and hell collided.

At the mouth of an alley, a few misshapen hulks,
lured by their smaller brethren's littered feast of soul,
drew back to let Corvus pass.

"Peace," he whispered. "There will be more soon.
Many more."

Awareness crept back like dawn's faint light. Sera
smelled leather and wool and something wilder. Once
again, the dream hadn't quite gotten to the point where
she had sex with Archer since they were interrupted
by . . .

As if someone had booted the sun in the ass, consciousness came blazing back. Sera jolted upright on the
unfamiliar couch.

Across from her, Archer straddled a hard-backed
chair. "Back with the living."

She remembered the eerie wail, the black monstrosity, Archer's lips on hers. It seemed more like a dream than life.

"Where are we?" She swallowed against the dryness in her throat. "What was that thing?"

"We're at a safe house. And that thing was a feralis. A lesser demon from the horde-tenebrae."

"If that was less, I'd hate to see more."

He made a noncommittal noise and pushed to his feet, spinning the chair to face her properly, as if he no longer needed its shield.

She shook her head at the strange fancy. She'd been unconscious. Why would he need a shield from her?

She tracked his path across the industrial warehouse–cum–upscale loft—spare and unpolished, just like him. "This is your place, isn't it?"

"It's both. Safe and mine." In the foyer, he tapped at the keypad. Lamps came on around the room, though the disconnected pools of light hardly brightened the darkness.

She pictured vignettes of his life in the isolated circles. The low couch of leather and steel where she was still half reclining under a wool blanket. A computer workstation against one brick wall. A weight bench on the only rug softening the concrete floor. A kitchenette with one white coffee cup turned upside down on the rack beside the sink. Shielding the bed, a freestanding accordion of white plantation shutters, as if a chunk of destroyed Tara had landed in Chicago.

She slanted a glance at him. "So I take it demon-ridden don't have girlfriends. Or interior decorators."

He gazed impassively around the room. "Do I need one?"

"Decorator? Or girlfriend?"

"You tell me."

Suddenly, lying unconscious in a strange place seemed

safer than sparring with him—definitely safer than remembering that kiss, the rough silk of his mouth, and
the raw grind of his body. . . .

She swung her feet to the bare floor. He crossed his
arms, making no attempt to stop her, so she rose and
edged away to one of the mullioned windows.

She flattened her hand against the glass. The daylight was gone, the street empty. "Why did you bring me
here?"

"To give you a chance." He stood just outside the circle of lamplight, where his black shirt and jeans melted
into the darkness. The lit half of his face was hard, his
jaw set so she almost felt the strain in his muscles.

When he'd pushed her against the wall, that tension had run all through him, ratcheting up with every
stroke of tongue. She forced away the thought. "I feel
like maybe I've run out of chances in my life," she
admitted.

He let his arms fall slack at his sides. "Where there's
life, there's—"

"Hope?"

"Another chance to die."

She choked on a laugh. "No girlfriend. No decorator.
And not a whole lot of party invitations either, I'd bet."

"Stalking demons all night cuts into my calendar."

She restrained a shiver. "That's what I have to look
forward to? Becoming a night stalker?"

"There are worse things."

"Worse than fighting monsters like that?"

"Being one." He crossed to the kitchen to fill the coffee cup from a kettle on the stove. He approached her
with the mug out.

She took the cup, sniffed. "Demons drink green
tea?"

"I drink green tea."

"You're a demon."

"No." He left her standing by the window and went

to the couch, where he pushed the blanket aside. "I'm possessed, not a demon myself."

"Right. The thing that attacked us . . ."

"Feralis. Rather than possessing humans, ferales manifest physically—very physically, as you noticed—by consuming animal substance from this realm." He rubbed at his shoulder. "You've had several following you, drawn to your demon ascending."

Where he rubbed his shoulder, the black shirt gaped, revealing paler skin. Her breath caught on a silent intake. "It got you."

He fingered the edges of the gash. "Guess so. Unless that was you."

She opened her mouth to deny . . . and couldn't speak. She had attacked him, after all. Twice, if she counted that violent kiss. Embarrassed heat rushed through her.

The corner of his mouth twisted up. "Demons have shitty tempers. Probably what got them kicked out of paradise in the first place."

"I didn't mean what I said." When he lifted one eyebrow, she clarified. "About killing you."

He shrugged. "It wasn't just you talking. But you can understand why you need to be separated from the good folk of our fair city."

The demon. How could she believe? How could she *not* believe after what she'd seen, what she'd done?

She leaned against the cold window. "What is happening to me?"

He sat back in the couch. "As the demon aligns with you, the resonating energy spikes. Your strength and quickness will increase, along with the ability to integrate sensory data. You'll heal from everything except an instantly fatal blow." His voice was clipped, as if he read from a brochure: *The Perks of Possession.* "The coldness and killing rage will get worse too, until you reach an equilibrium with the demon."

"What if I don't find a balance?" The glowing orange

eye flashed in her memory. "Will I become one of those ferales?"

He tipped his head back. "Worse."

She wrapped her hands tighter around her mug and pulled away from the chill at the window. "What's worse?"

"A demon is ascending from the depths of your soul. The question is, which of the two demonic strains chose you? A djinni, devoted to evil? Or a teshuva, a repentant demon?"

She paced across the room. "Good demons? Who knew?" She'd always fancied herself sensitive to the unknown, but a secret pitched battle had been raging with no one the wiser. What else had she been missing?

Archer rolled his head against the cushion to look at her. "Did you think good and evil were black and white?"

"Well, sort of, by definition. In the movies, you get a white hat or a black one."

A smile flickered across his lips. "The teshuva wear gray hats. Teshuva are trying to atone for their wicked ways, to earn their way back into grace. The djinn . . . aren't."

She wandered toward the weight bench. The loaded bar held more iron disks than seemed possible. "How can they atone? Why do they need us?"

His relaxed sprawl never changed, but the sudden intensity of his dark gaze speared her. She realized for the first time she'd voluntarily included herself in their little nightmare for two. But after encountering a feralis, she definitely didn't want to be alone in this madness.

"To make amends," he said, "the teshuva cleanse this realm of accumulated weaker demonic emanations like ferales and malice. The djinn rile up the lesser demons to make our realm a little more like their hell. Kind of a spiritual terra forming. But neither teshuva nor djinn can manifest fully in this realm. So they need a weapon. Us."

Speaking of weapons . . . On the back wall, her reflection broke over steel blades of all shapes and sizes. Regular honing had left faint whorls that scattered the light, the designs as intricate and menacing as the *reven* on Archer's arm.

And still nothing looked as wicked as the grotesque beast's claws. "I would think six-shooters blazing would be better."

"Attracts the wrong sort of attention, useless for close-quarters combat. And unreliable." His hand, stretched out on the back of the couch, tightened into a fist. "More importantly, our demons have to get up close to do the dirty work. It's harder to damn from a distance."

Beside the weapons, another shelf held a collection of small statues. She recoiled at the toy factory massacre. Beanbag animals had been dismembered, limbs replaced with baby-doll or action figure parts. Long blond hair and a shapely plastic leg were crudely nailed to a fast-food toy from a cartoon monster movie, while a grinning, strong-jawed manly face was stapled into the belly of a stuffed pterodactyl. Dozens of the dolls slumped against one another like half-slaughtered soldiers.

"Um," she said. "Ferales dolls?"

"Our fearless leader decided the league needed to recognize our many years of service. He made Ecco—you remember him from the town car—our morale officer. That is the result."

She eyed the carnage. "How . . . sweet?"

"Not really."

She turned her focus to the lounging male, more deadpan than the dolls. Yet for all his outward indifference, he'd kept the trinkets. "So how many ferales corpses does it take to build a ladder over the gates of heaven?"

If she'd hoped for a lightbulb joke, she was disappointed. "I'll let you know when I get them piled high enough."

Judging from the well-honed blades, the trail of dispatched demons might reach around the world. Apparently that wasn't enough. "What do we get out of this unholy alliance? Besides the opportunity to fight forever."

"Die in battle, and you get back what's left of your demon-mottled soul."

She grimaced. "Sounds like we're getting the short end of the stick."

"Just make sure the ferales get the pointy end. And take what pleasure you can in destruction, because you're saving the world along with your soul."

She shook her head. "Nobody even noticed. A half dozen town houses overlooked the alley."

"If anybody looked down, they saw some street people Dumpster diving. Or maybe a nice couple walking their bad dog." At her incredulous huff, he grinned, with a sudden flash of white teeth. "A very bad dog. People see what they think they'll see, what they want to see. And gray hats are easy to forget."

She had to admit, she might have justified away the horror. If it hadn't been drooling all over her. But willful blindness had only ever ended with her walking into walls.

She turned away from the blades. "I want to live."

"I'm told such a desire is a useful first step."

"And the next?"

"Listen to me."

She tried to keep her expression unreadable, but he cocked his head. "Why is it so hard for you to obey?"

She glared. "You ask that with a lot of arrogance for someone standing so far from his weapons."

"Even when we kissed, you would not be still under my lips."

"Excuse me," she sputtered. That was one question

she kept sliding away from. Why had she clung to him in the alley as if he were her last chance? She wished the answer were simple lust.

"It has been a while since I kissed—"

"Since the 1950s, apparently."

He shook his head. "Longer than that, I think."

"Probably never with that 'obey' crap."

"Oh, I have loved."

Even across the room, she felt the weight of his gaze on her mouth. Betrayed by the phantom sensation, she licked her lips. Could she blame the demon for that?

He closed his eyes. "You can't let even the dying go quietly, but must point and give directions. Fate's crossing guard."

She stiffened. "You make me sound like a monster."

He shook his head. "I've seen such monsters as feed on death. I don't think you're one of those."

"Don't think?" She gave a bitter laugh.

"Nothing is certain. Which is why your search for answers is doomed."

His axe couldn't have cut deeper. She walked to the kitchen area, washed her cup, dried her hands on a paper towel, and finally turned to face him. "Why are you trying so hard to convince me? Will it make this possession easier?"

He hadn't moved. "No. But what comes after might not hurt so much."

"I was told by one of my first patients that pain isn't the purpose of life, just sometimes the price."

His lips twisted in an unkind smile. "Too bad we couldn't ask him for bonus insights after he died and went to the heaven I'm sure he deserved."

"*Her* last postcard was from her third Caribbean cruise. The doctors called it a miraculous recovery." She lifted her chin. "Or are you going to tell me there are no such things as miracles?"

When he didn't answer, she wadded the paper towel

and tossed it toward the garbage can. Two points. "If I'm stuck here, where's the shower? I have demon guts in my hair."

He waved her toward a glass-blocked corner of the loft. When he flicked a switch inside, the space glowed like a candle, lit from within. She eyed the translucent glass.

"Whatever," she muttered, and marched forward.

Archer let out a long, slow breath to soothe the dangerous coiling inside him. Damn demons. Damn hers, damn his, and damn that crazed feralis, attacking in the waning daylight. Couldn't keep its damn half-rat paws off her.

No more than Archer himself, apparently.

Damn.

The water came on. A whiff of hot wetness spiked with honeysuckle snagged his breathing again. He wheeled away. The message light on his phone blinked with ever greater urgency as the number of messages increased. At its present speed, it could cause seizures. Just as well he never left the ringer on.

He'd been too preoccupied with the limp weight in his arms. Calling on the demon had shorted her out.

Until that moment, though, she'd been magnificent. The image of her lunging at the feralis, her puny weapon brandished high, was shock-locked in his brain. She should be dead, of foolishness if nothing else.

If he'd been a kinder man, perhaps he'd have let her die.

Instead, he brought her home, wiped away the blood from the nick under her eye, and watched her sleep.

Now who was the fool?

He punched SPEED DIAL on the phone. "Quit leaving messages you know I'm not going to answer."

Niall grunted. "We hauled the feralis off for decomp." He hesitated. "Any other bodies we should know about?"

At the word "bodies," Archer couldn't stop his gaze from drifting to the shower. "Not yet."

Niall let out a sigh. "I'd hate to lose her to a bad-luck encounter before her demon even had a chance to save her."

"Yeah." She'd shown no fear, no hesitation. Once she and the demon meshed, she'd be a formidable opponent.

Still no match for him, of course. Even the fierce and fearless fought to win, and that, in the bitter end, would fail against someone who fought to die.

Archer went to the dark window. "That feralis didn't just stumble into the alley. It was tracking us. It wanted her bad."

Niall was silent a moment. "Homing in on her demon?"

A lot of etheric energy had soaked the alley, and not all of it Sera's. There'd certainly been enough wide-beam annihilation-class violence, thanks to that kiss, to warn off even a stupid feralis. "Maybe."

Niall jumped on the note of reserve. "I told you this war is changing."

As if he didn't have enough to deal with. Archer cut him off. "You might also notice, I changed my security codes. Don't send anyone here. Don't contact me until this is over."

Niall clicked his tongue. "I want updates. Bookie thought he'd record the last stages of an ascension."

"Thinking and wanting just don't have much place in what's going down." Archer's breath fogged the windowpane except where the print of her hand cleared the glass.

Wanting might still be a problem.

He scowled at the imprint. "I'll call you when the possession is complete. Either way."

"Good luck." Niall's soft voice barely registered down the line.

Archer hung up without answering.

The water cranked off. In the charged silence, he realized he'd invoked his demon-boosted perceptions. Listening for the last droplets to fall. Tasting the tang of
warm, moist flesh. His heightened nerves prickled in anticipation, keen for the faintest pulse of air as she moved
through space.

Cursing even more softly than Niall's parting words,
Archer clamped down on his control. He rifled through
the armoire beside the bed for a fresh shirt.

He'd wait for his shower until she slept. God knew,
those glass blocks barely hid a damn thing even from
purely human eyes.

He stripped off his torn shirt. His twenty-four-hour
dry cleaner had commented once that pinning a note
over stains would ensure spots were properly treated.
Archer just gave him everything in a duffel bag sten-
ciled with the word "stained." The man had blanched,
but his daughter was a tidy seamstress who'd saved his
trench coat more than once.

He turned sideways to the mirror, tracking the wound
that curved around his shoulder. Only a little worse
than the bloody nose. The demon was as efficient as his
seamstress.

Sera's gaze found his in the reflection. "That was definitely the feralis's fault. I don't have claws like that."

He reached for his shirt. "Not seven in a row
anyway."

"Don't you need to bandage it?"

"It won't kill me." He should be so lucky. "Let the
demon earn its keep."

She shook her head and marched back to the bathroom, returning a moment later with a soap-bubbled
washcloth, a roll of gauze, and a bottle of hydrogen
peroxide.

She hefted the bottle. "This is all you have for first aid
supplies?"

"I use it to soak out the worst of the stains."

"Out of your skin?"

"Out of my clothes." He waggled the shirt in his hand. "My dry cleaner has convinced himself I'm a butcher." Archer started to slide into the shirt. "I guess he's right."

Sera plucked the shirt from his hands. "Not until you disinfect."

He opened his mouth to tell her off, knowing the demon's wariness of close quarters would lend its double-octave warning to keep her distance, to not distract them from its mission of atonement. But nothing came to him. He blinked. "Fine."

She sat him at the kitchen island under the pendant lights. "These gashes go right through the dermis into the subcutaneous fat." She swabbed at his shoulder with the soapy cloth. "Not that there's much fat on you."

He held himself straight, struggling not to lean into her hand despite the twanging pain. "You sound like Bookie."

She wiped away the suds. "Who's Bookie?"

"The Bookkeeper, our records keeper and historian. We call him Bookie."

"Imaginative."

"It's an honorable title, passing down centuries of study. I'm sure he could whip out a damage-infliction chart categorized by demon subtype." He hissed as she upended the bottle of peroxide over his shoulder. "Burns worse than ichor."

She caught the runoff with a towel at his elbow. "Are you always such a wimp about cleaning up?"

"Never been cleaned up before." He glanced up from the bubbling scratches and caught the momentary softening in her eyes. "Don't feel sorry for me," he warned.

"You've been hurt worse than this. I see the marks on you." She traced one finger near his spine. Though the demon lay dormant in him, still strangely undisturbed by her closeness, he couldn't stop the shiver that wracked him at her touch. "Even with preternatural healing, you must've been laid up for weeks with this one."

"I don't remember."

"How can you not remember a wound that almost filleted you?"

"It was a long time ago." At the thought of how long, he slipped out from under her hand and grabbed the roll of gauze. Might as well keep the oozing blood off his clean shirt. "Flesh heals. The scar remains, faintly. Bookie has theories why the demon can't take away the last of the scarring. Or won't."

She watched him wind the gauze awkwardly around his shoulder. "Maybe it's supposed to be a reminder."

"Not to get mauled? Thanks. Next time, send a memo."

He was glad, at least, to see the snap back in her gaze. He didn't need her pity. Or her help. He gritted his teeth as he fumbled the gauze over his shoulder.

"I meant," she said coolly, "a reminder that you aren't immortal."

"Oh, but we are."

CHAPTER 6

Sera gasped. "Immortal?"

"We can be killed, in case tonight hasn't made that obvious. But until the demon leaks out with our last drop of blood, we endure."

He knotted off the end of the gauze, and the bitter twist to his lips made the last word a curse.

"Exactly how long have you been doing this?" She waved toward the wall of weapons. "Inducting wayward women into your demon-slaying hall of maim?"

"You are the only female possessed in living memory."

Considering the immortality thing, that was saying a lot. "Are demons sexist too?"

"Bookie's working on a theory. Maybe it's just long odds. Possession by the teshuva is rare. The last man joined our league almost thirty years ago."

"Thirty—" She shook her head, bemused. "How old are you?"

"Old enough." He eased into the new shirt.

She told herself she was trying to guess his age as she let her gaze roam the hard planes of his chest, the curls of dark hair funneling down to the button fly of his jeans. A man in his prime, certainly, despite the shadowy collection of old scars. Her pulse tripped a beat for each rippled muscle in his abdomen.

The doppelganger demon had come to her as a white-washed version of this: smooth and cool, unmarked.

Apparently demons didn't know everything about perfecting temptation.

Archer turned abruptly to face her, and heat rushed to her cheeks. "So," she said to cover her embarrassment at being caught gawping. "I'm going to live forever."

"Most likely you'll be killed in one of your first fights. War's a bitch. And I'm not sure you're enough of one."

She wrinkled her nose. "Gee, thanks."

"Assuming you survive—"

"The next few days," she chimed in. "Yeah, I remember. You're taking a lot of the fun out of this."

He looked at her a long, long time, as if he had to translate her words from some foreign language. "Fun?"

Her cheeks heated again. "I was teasing."

"Teasing."

She wondered again exactly how long he *had* been at this. "I've had end-stage patients cheerier than you," she muttered.

"They got to die." He retreated to his office space, where he hunched over his computer, with his back to her.

Okay, she could take the hint.

After a restless circle of the room, she thumbed through the books stacked on the end table by the couch. Sun Tzu's *The Art of War*. Homer's *Odyssey*. A collection with *Macbeth*, *King Lear*, *Othello*.

She set them aside. No wonder he was such a grouch. She'd have to get him a few good romance novels, something to reawaken his faith in hope, his sense of humor, his desire for . . .

Her gaze strayed across the room to linger on the breadth of his shoulders. But broad shoulders weren't reason enough to fantasize about being the one to soothe his tortured soul. Other not-good-enough reasons included lean hips in fitted jeans, sculpted abs, a faded Southern drawl. . . .

Maybe romances weren't a great idea right now when her own emotions seemed so . . . aroused. Maybe later.

"Maybe if I survive the next few days," she muttered. She realized she'd been compulsively running her pendant back and forth on its cord and forced herself to calm.

She'd slipped the cord over her head before she left her apartment a million years ago. She couldn't say why. All it did was conjure up disturbing memories of the demon's pale eyes.

As she lifted the stone, a spark leapt across the inner curve. Just a trick of light. Or maybe not. She'd had enough weirdness to make her question everything, even if—especially if—her common sense said ignore it. The pendant had come from a demon, after all.

She half closed her eyes, so the darkened apartment was like a tunnel, the gleaming stone a light at the end. So easy to drift down toward it. Not like she was doing anything else.

Just waiting to be consumed by her demon.

She blinked, and the world went gray.

"Oh, damn it. Here we go again."

But this wasn't the lakeside pier. The gray was softer, vaguer. She'd been focused on the light, as she'd done in a therapy session once. "Did I just hypnotize myself?"

A low sound, half moan, half whisper, echoed back. The hair on her arms prickled.

She wasn't alone.

She turned a tight circle and caught a glimpse of some misshapen form, its outline half eaten away by the mist. Her heart thudded. A feralis? It faded back before she could tell.

No wooden stakes here. No Archer either.

"Nothing can happen to me in hypnosis that I wouldn't allow in my waking life," she reminded herself.

Of course, in waking life she'd been half paralyzed, half addicted to painkillers, more than halfway to despair. Easy pickings for a demon.

Another whisper-moan behind her. "Sera."

She whirled.

It was right behind her, pallid and gaunt. Its single weeping eye fixed on her with appalling hunger. The eye was hazel, same as her own.

Bony fingers reached for her. "Oh, Sera."

She screamed, a gurgle of terror.

"Sera! Sera, come back."

Warm hands cupped her face. Warm and wide. Not skeletal.

She pried her eyes open. Not the gray stone hanging in front of her, but a worried, blackened bronze gaze. Archer's.

She blinked. The real world stayed.

"What?" Her voice was a strained croak. "What happened?"

"The demon realm. I see the fog in your eyes. Now you know why they want out."

She shivered. "It was reaching for me. Not the demon. It was me."

He let go and sat back on the couch with a frown.

"I saw myself there," she insisted. "I was looking into the stone, and then everything went gray."

"What stone?"

She lifted the pendant. The rock, twisting at the end of the cord, winked once.

"I would have given you topaz and peridot," he said. "To match your eyes."

A flush of warmth swept through her, as potent as if he had touched her again. "You do have better taste than your doppelganger."

That sharpened his gaze. "The demon gave you this? Nothing tangible crosses the Veil."

"This did."

"Ugly." When his eyes shifted violet, she knew he'd called on his demon. "And tainted with an etheric overlay. Curiouser and curiouser." He released the pendant with a frown.

Despite the heat of his skin, the stone lay cool on her neck. "Is this the demon's link to me?"

"The demon doesn't need a physical leash."

"A mirror then." She shuddered. "When I looked into the stone, I saw myself, sick and hurting. It—I—it tried to grab me." She scrubbed her hands down her face and caught his skeptical expression. "I'm not crazy," she snapped. "And I'm not being Freudian either."

"I was thinking Jung," he murmured. "The shadow self."

She stared at him. "If you'd had some light reading, I wouldn't have been in that place."

She was being unfair, but he inclined his head. "You shouldn't be alone with all your questions. Higher mental functions like that get you into trouble every time. The demon hijacks you at the base of your ancient reptilian brain."

She blinked at him.

"Fight and feast," he explained. "And fuck."

"I know what the reptilian brain is. I'm just surprised. . . ." She stopped before she insulted him.

"Yeah. What do metaphysical garbagemen need brains for anyway?" He pushed to his feet. "Never mind the mystery stone, you need to stay anchored in this realm. Come on."

She wedged herself down in the pillows. "Where are we going?"

"To get something to eat and drink. Maybe listen to some good music. Nail you down to this world." He held out his hand, *reven*-marked and calloused but gentle on her cheek as he'd called her back.

Had she seen what she was doomed to become? What she'd *been* doomed to become, if not for the demon's tempting power? Suddenly she understood what Archer meant about the dangers of questions. She could no more stop herself from wondering than stop herself from breathing.

Except, apparently, that might be the price she paid.

She put her hand in his and he pulled her upright.

"I thought I was a menace to society in this state," she said as they gathered their coats.

"Seems you're more a hazard to yourself. I'll keep watch."

He led them out through a back hallway that took them through the adjacent building to an alley exit. "What's your favorite cocktail?"

"This feels like speed dating. I thought we had all the time in the world."

"Maybe the world doesn't have as much time as you'd think." He picked up the pace again.

"Spanish coffee. Lot of calories but oh, so tasty."

"Calorie counting is the least of your worries. Your metabolism amps up to match the demands of the demon's energy."

She huffed out a laugh. "See how you keep forgetting to mention the pluses of possession? Lose your soul, lose the weight, on the damnation diet."

The harsh curve of his mouth gentled into an almost smile. "Who knew souls were so heavy?"

"Is it a good idea to get my demon drunk?"

"Alcohol dilates the blood vessels and eases inhibitions. Simplifies the demon's ascension. At least according to our Bookkeepers." He glanced away. "Maybe it just makes it easier to forget."

Encouraged by his momentary candor, she put her hand on his arm. "How did it happen for you?"

Muscles flexed under her fingers. "Ancient history."

"As old as the stories on your end table?"

His expression hardened. "Nobody makes it that long." He slipped away from her. "Nobody'd want to."

She dragged her heels. "You mean you don't want to. So why don't you just kill yourself and get it over with?"

Her challenge echoed on the concrete and steel.

He let the reverberations fade without answering, but from the flicker of violet across his gaze, she knew she'd pricked him. "Let's save the chitchat for our drinks."

The signboard outside the club read MORTAL COIL, with a hooped snake through one letter *o* and down through the other to eat its own tail. Inside, the crowd was loud and close, the chill of night banished by body heat and laughter tinged with wild desperation. Appropriate enough, she thought.

He brought her drink, mounded with whipped cream. His own tumbler brimmed with something clear on the rocks. Black coffee, unmixed drinks, blank loft walls. The devil took the blame for any number of human excesses, but somebody certainly wasn't indulging his inner sinner.

How many years before the extras fell away, before all that remained was ... What? The demon? The stark business card he'd handed her—@1? Oh, please.

She drank deeply. The tingle of heated vodka and Kahlúa sped through her veins. Damn questions.

A thumping bass beat drowned out casual conversation. Not that they could really do casual since everything they had in common involved supernatural possession.

She took another hit off her drink with a bracing sugar-shot of cream. The crowd milled around them, too hip for their own good. She stared narrowly at a trio nearby who shook small caplets out of a glass vial. The white pills shone with startling luminosity under the black lights. Sera remembered Betsy complaining about the new club drug. What had her friend called it? Solve or something. As if they'd solve anything that way.

She wrinkled her nose. If only they knew. "I feel like the oldest thing here," she shouted over the sternum-rattling beat.

"Get used to it." The low thrum of his voice carried under the chatter, rumbling in her chest in counterpoint to the music.

She frowned at his world-weariness. She finished her drink in one long draught and licked the cream off her lips, not caring that his gaze followed the suggestive motion.

She shoved to her feet. "Let's dance."

Ha. That cracked his composure. He stared at her until she grabbed his hand.

He pulled back. "I don't dance."

"Really? I never would've guessed." She tugged. "Don't worry. I haven't danced in forever. I won't show you up like I did in the alley."

He scowled and rose. "If you'll recall, I killed the feralis."

"While I distracted it. And if I hadn't been distracted by it"—by his kiss, that was, but she squelched the thought—"I would've gotten away from you."

"To your everlasting regret."

"According to you, my regrets will be everlasting anyway."

They stepped onto the dance floor where the bass made even shouted words pointless.

Maybe once she'd been more of a funk and soul girl, but the pounding techno suited her mood tonight. Angry and insistent, the beat sunk under her skin. The stink of sweat and a drifting thread of weed pierced her senses.

She burned to the beat, letting her body move and flow, a primitive joy. Dancers bearing glow sticks whirled by like cold shooting stars.

Under the flicker of laser light off the mirror ball, she felt Archer watching her. Watching her demon?

She felt like a creature of sin. Strong, dark, vicious. It felt good. But that was the nature of sin, wasn't it?

She watched Archer now, under her lashes. He hadn't lied about not being a dancer. But she'd seen him fight, and the intense grace served him well enough. He circled her, guarded her, guided her to an open space on the crowded floor.

She stretched, arms over her head. The pendant thumped against her chest as she moved. Ah, that drew his eye, for sure.

She spun away, adding a sinuous writhe to her hips. She ran her hands down her waist, over the curve of her booty. Let him stare.

Abruptly, she was spun again, into Archer's arms. He pulled her up against his chest. She gulped down his scent, that musky spice that made her fingers curl as if to bury themselves in him. Though he'd never taken off his trench coat, only a faint slick of sweat glistened at his throat.

"Enough." Somehow, his voice reached her through the music. "You mustn't exhaust yourself."

"I'm not tired, not even close." She sounded petulant but didn't care. "I could go all night." She twisted against him, trying to pull free.

But if she'd fooled him once or twice the last few days, she must've used up all her chances. His grip only tightened.

"I think you're well enough connected to your body for now." His gaze skimmed the neckline of her T-shirt where her pendant slid on its cord, cool despite the heat.

A trickle of sweat dampened the small of her back and between her breasts. Great, she'd gotten the demon kingdom's one slacker. Oh well, a little moisture never killed anybody. Except the Wicked Witch of the West.

He gave her a shake. "Don't drift on me again."

She scowled. "I was just wondering if demons have

any supernatural weaknesses to go with their supernatural powers."

"Trying to get rid of me again? Let some of those party boys who've been sharking around finally make their move?"

She glanced past him to the other dancers. They looked so young, fresh—uncomplicated. "I'd eat them for breakfast," something inside her said.

Archer laughed once. "It's almost that time."

"For breakfast?" Another drink maybe.

"For the demon. Can you feel it?"

She shrugged, both in answer and to make him loosen his grip. After a moment, he did.

She stepped out of his arms. The crush of other bodies seemed almost overwhelmingly spacious by comparison. She pushed down a moment of vertigo and turned with a hiss when someone bumped her.

He nudged her toward the whirling edge of dancers. "Come on. Let's get you out of here."

"Not home."

He hesitated, then nodded. "Not quite yet."

Outside, the chill threat of unfallen snow made her shiver. He held her coat open for her, like any courting gentleman. She realized she couldn't remember her last date.

She narrowed her eyes against the glitter of city lights. "Looks strange out here." Each streetlamp, brake light, and lit window glowed with a hazy halo of secondary color. Archer's eyes, his skin, even the strands of his dark hair, seemed illuminated from within by some argent radiance, as if the club black lights still shone on him.

Except for his *reven*, visible where he'd pushed up his sleeves. That swallowed all light. Her attention locked on the bold, sensuous lines, like a labyrinth leading her if she had the nerve to follow. Her fingers twitched, wanting to touch. She made a fist. "Strange," she murmured again.

"You'll experience a certain amount of synesthesia until the possession is complete." He took her elbow, jolting her out of her reverie and down the street. "Even after, you'll find a cross wiring of senses when the demon ascends. That's the demon processing information you weren't aware of before."

He pointed his chin across the street. "There. Near the alley. Do you see it?"

At the entrance to another bar, garish neon cast harsh shadows. "What? That smear of—"

Two people stepped out. From the gloom oozed a darker murk. It dropped toward them. She almost recognized it, mangled and distorted, its half-seen edges bleeding out into a dark nimbus, an inverse of the lights.

Sera took half a step into the road. Archer jerked her back just as a car sped past.

"Demon or no, that would've hurt," he growled.

"What is that?" Her throat hurt, looking at the thing. She thought she saw a paw or claw, not much bigger than a city rat, and the wink of a red reflecting eye. "It looks like a dead thing flattened on the street, like I know what it used to be, but can't quite make out the shape of it anymore."

"Psychic roadkill. That's fitting. It's a malice. An unbound, incorporeal demon from the horde-tenebrae. Smaller and weaker than ferales, but more clever, if not actually intelligent."

The two men who'd left the bar stopped to light up. One man spoke, then laughed, the harsh sound carrying in a puff of cigarette smoke. The other man hunched his shoulders.

The malice crept closer.

"What's it doing?" Sera twitched. "Shouldn't you stop it?"

"They could stop it."

The hunched man waved one hand, as if to redirect

his companion. The other laughed again and punched his shoulder.

The malice dropped onto the hunched man where he'd been hit. He straightened.

Archer shrugged. "Or not."

The hunched man lunged, fist foremost. The jokester reeled back, shouting. The hunched man never spoke as he pummeled his friend.

Sera let out a painful breath as if one of those punches had landed in her gut. "Is he possessed?"

"No. See, there goes the malice, scrambling away. It'll watch, dart in, keep the turmoil going as long as it can. Others get drawn in, if the mayhem continues."

The bouncer came out from the bar and pushed the hunched man away. The jokester huddled on the wet sidewalk, neon darkening the blood on his face to inky black.

The malice was a blot above the sign, almost invisible even though she knew where to look. "Do they feed off the negative energy? Or are they produced by it?"

"Cause or effect, does it matter?"

She frowned. "Yes. If you want to stop it. If you want to destroy them all."

"Weak as it is, you can't destroy it. We can drain its energy, like emptying a balloon. But it's still there, waiting to be refilled. We're unholy garbagemen. We can take out the trash, but it never stops piling up."

"Which is no reason to let one get away with—"

"Murder? It could go there. But some people just slough them off." He clasped his hands behind his back. "Who am I to interfere?"

"You're the guy who can drain them, take them out."

"Yeah." He turned an unfathomable gaze on the trio across the street. "But I can't help thinking, if not for them, I wouldn't be losing this war."

She blinked in confusion. "If not for the malice?"

A flare of violet made her breath catch. "If not for

the humans." He shook his head. "I just wanted to show you a malice, since you've already had the pleasure of meeting the feralis."

"The horror was all mine." He took her elbow again and she glanced back. "Shouldn't we go . . . help?"

"The malice won't get more dangerous than it is right now. I'll come back for it some other night."

"So, does indifference excite it as much as anger and violence?"

When he glanced at her, his gaze was empty of demon violet. "I doubt it."

Good thing, or she'd probably see one squatting on his head right now. How could he have the power to help and yet not? How could he just walk away from such blatant evil?

Suddenly the night seemed colder than the low temperatures could account for.

He hadn't looked at her again, but he said, "You are cold. I know a place we can wait."

Wait for what? she almost asked, stupidly. Oh yes, for another version of these horrors to take her over.

The madness of what she was believing returned, made her stumble over nothing. Only Archer's hand on her arm kept her from falling.

"Almost there," he said softly.

She smelled the river, cold and dank, as they crossed the bridge. Her gaze locked on a rainbow sheen of gasoline coating the ripples.

Archer tugged at her. "Stay with me."

Why? So she could become as cold as that water, like him? She shook him off. Her vision, blurred again, seemed already filmed by that rainbow glaze, edging toward the violet.

He crossed his arms over his chest. "Gonna fight me again?"

His words sent goose bumps racing over her flesh. Not fear, but anticipation.

And for all his stance, he wasn't indifferent anymore.

The violet light gleamed in his eyes too.

"Be careful which way you jump," he warned. "You end up in the river, I won't ruin this coat for you."

"I don't want to fight you. I just want this to be over." She held up one hand when he drew breath to speak. "Not over-over. Just over for tonight."

He smiled thinly. "It's never even that over."

"What? Dawn never comes?"

"I guess we'll see."

"Good Lord, I couldn't have gotten a cheerful guru?" She stalked down the bridge. She might not know where they were going, but it wasn't as if she had another choice. Going back had never been an option, had it?

He fell into step beside her. "Cheerful gurus, like musical montages, never tell it like it really is."

"I like musical montages. 'Eye of the Tiger.' 'Highway to the Danger Zone.'"

He whirled on her. "A minute and a half of strapping into your bandoliers and greasing your muscles? They don't show you that the blood never comes out from underneath your nails and spring never comes back to your soul."

She stared back at him wordlessly.

The violet glaze had vanished from his eyes. "As for that God you so casually invoke, he won't listen to you anymore. You're playing on the dark side now."

CHAPTER 7

In silence, Archer led Sera to a cinder-block warehouse just off the river. A silver glow beamed from the roof of the building.

He punched a code into the lock, and the door unsealed with a pneumatic sigh. Warm air curled around him like welcoming arms. "Come on."

She walked beside him warily, light on her feet, head raised, nostrils flared. The atavistic stance—the distrusting demon in her—sent a pang through him.

He hadn't meant to tease or scare her with the malice sighting. He definitely hadn't meant to reveal his own dissociation so clearly. "The humans," indeed. When had he forgotten he himself was still—if not only—human?

More importantly, why had he remembered?

Almost against his will, he slanted a glance at the woman beside him.

They passed down a corridor, rounded a corner, and stepped out into the summer garden.

"Oh." Her tiny sound of surprise sent another jolt through him, of pleasure this time. "A greenhouse. That explains the light from the roof."

In the dark dreaming winter of the city, the plants

glowed with fantastical clarity under the full-spectrum lights. A trickle of water drowned out the hum of the huge fans moving the balmy air, lazily stirring the leaves. Sera stared up at the understory of a tall banana tree, its wide-bladed foliage gleaming like a jewel against the black sky above.

She lowered her wide gaze to Archer. "This is yours too? Wow, demon slaying must have excellent net take-home."

"Just no retirement plan." He walked the path between two palms, leaving her to follow.

"My mom adored miniature roses. She nursed them through the winter on our kitchen windowsill before her depression got bad." She shook her head, as if to shed the memory. "I can't keep a cactus alive, much less roses."

The twinge of her pain jolted a confession from him. "My father always said a brown thumb was the color of dung, and seeds sprout best in the richest ground."

She smiled but her glance was sharp. "Your father sounds like a wise fellow."

"He was a gentleman farmer, so he had a saying for every day of the season." He regretted the slip into shared wistfulness. Had he made a mistake bringing her here? This place had a knack for dredging up memories—sometimes the dark earth seemed to swallow long-ago sorrows, only to sprout them again like weeds—but he'd never before had cause to speak them aloud.

She eyed him somberly. "He must have loved this place."

"He never saw it. But he always aspired more toward the gentleman than the farmer part. At least he died before his only son was demoted from gentleman to garbageman." Speaking aloud gave the old memories more weight than they deserved. "Come on. There's a place to sit."

She fell into step, quiet for a moment.

The luxuriant greenery pressed closer, the grow lights barely penetrating to the tiny clearing at the garden's center. He flicked a switch at the corner of the antique Javanese daybed that dominated the space, and the strings of tea lights around the teak posters cast twinkling shadows among the orchids and ferns.

He almost missed her quick sideways glance, but he read the sudden uncertainty in the quirk of her brows and realized what the solitary bed, heaped with pillows, might look like. He tried to stifle the dull heat of a flush over his face. He'd never needed a second chair.

She crossed to the daybed. Tracing one finger across the flaking blue and red paint, she smiled up at the indolent figures engraved in the wooden canopy. Missing panels framed a view of the leaves above. "This does not look like you at all."

"Just a simple Southern farmer's son." Once, the phases of decay and growth had filled his days along with the fragrance of rich earth. Now his mind was clogged with smog and gore and nights of destruction without end. The weight of the club in his coat dragged at him.

He wondered what memories of tonight would haunt his sanctuary.

"Simple. Right." Her smile vanished. "So, why did you bring me here?"

He hesitated. The little stream coursing over pebbles out of sight murmured like a far-away crowd.

"And don't lie."

He scowled. "If tonight goes wrong, it will be easier to wash away your blood."

She blinked. "Thanks for the brutal honesty."

"You said—"

"You could've sugarcoated it a *little*."

Inexplicably, he felt his lips twitch. "Why? I bet you don't lie to your hospice patients."

"I'm not usually the agent of their destruction either."

"I don't want to be." The carved lounging figures appeared cruelly aloof, watching from on high, uncaring that his choice had been to grow things, not destroy them. "But if the demon possessing you is djinn, you wouldn't want me not to."

She took a breath. "When will we know?"

"Not until the end, when the *reven* appears."

She sunk onto the edge of the daybed, hands clasped in her lap. "How could I say yes to a bad demon?" She laughed softly. "Listen to me. Bad demon. Good demon. Does it matter?"

Hearing his scorn tossed back made him shift. "Repentant demon," he corrected. "Or not. Teshuva or djinn. And yes, it matters." At least to him.

Her gaze speared him. "Since you'll be doing the mop-up if it goes bad."

Possession offered no confirmed psychic powers. Yet she read him so easily, as if she knew all his tells; as if she knew him in ways he'd forgotten himself. "It matters to the tide of the war."

"You've mentioned this war before. And I'm going to be a soldier?"

Or cannon fodder. "On one side or the other."

She laced her fingers together and straightened. "Can I choose? You said those men at the bar could've denied the malice's influence."

"You chose. The night you let the demon in."

The memories flitted across her face, expressive even in the uncertain glimmer of the tea lights.

"I wish it hadn't come to your looking like me," he said softly.

Her chin lifted, but the faint rise of a blush in her cheeks undermined the nonchalance. "It would've promised me anything I wanted, right?"

And she'd wanted him?

The thought raced through him like the demon's battle fever, fearsome and irresistible. Without his conscious will, his body canted toward her. He couldn't even blame his teshuva, latent at the moment, for the lapse in restraint. He wrapped his arm around a palm tree—anything to hold himself back.

"Still," he said, "I would not have wanted to be part of your possession." At least not in the demonic sense. The ancient text Bookie had found referenced a talyan bond. Assassin/victim was a bond too. Sort of.

"Yeah, you must have pissed someone off to get this duty."

"No one made me." As if anyone could.

"Then why?"

"I knew it was coming. It echoed, somehow, in me so I couldn't sleep." He shrugged impatiently.

"My demon snoring kept you awake, so you get to kill me? Let me guess: no bunkmates at summer camp."

How could she tease him, when he might have to . . . "It may not come to that. Your demon may be teshuva." Then she'd only have to fight until she died, rather than die right away.

"Oh sure, get glass-half-full on me now." She leaned back. He'd memorized every angle of what she was seeing, staring up at the broken canopy or maybe the dark sky beyond the arching leaves. "If fewer pieces were missing, this box could be a coffin." She ran her hand up along one post.

Archer twitched as if each finger were tripping up his spine. "I won't let you die." He hated himself for having to add the coda, "Not from the demon."

"Our culture buries its dead," she continued as if she hadn't heard him. "Or cremates. I studied this, you know. Some cultures floated their dead out to sea. Others left the corpses exposed on raised platforms so their sky gods could claim them. Functionally, that meant carrion-eating condors."

Her voice dropped. "I've almost died twice already. After the car accident, I coded in the emergency room.

And before that, my mother ... She disappeared when I was ten, but she died when I was thirteen. She came back just long enough to try to take me with her when she committed suicide."

The word congealed the blood in his veins. A solitary violence that had rippled outward. No wonder he'd been so strangely attuned to her unbound demon. "What happened?"

"I was walking home from school. She drove up next to me and asked if I knew her. Of course I knew her. She'd been gone three years, and every day of that three years I knew she'd come back. I got into the car. We talked. And then she drove us into the river."

He couldn't stop himself. He left the shelter of the tree to move closer.

She didn't even glance at him. "The water flooded through the vents so fast. I pounded at the door. She kept grabbing at me, telling me to stay. I hit her until she let go." Finally, she tilted her face toward him, eyes bleak. "Maybe I should have let her hold on."

"No." He wanted to explain his conviction. But the breath had gone out of him as if he were stuck in that sinking car.

She gazed upward again. "I've always tried not to think about it, but maybe that was the trigger, my penance trigger. Because before she drove us into the river, she said the voices told her to do it. What if the voices were real? Like the demon. And what if they were right?"

Fists clenched, he at last dredged up his voice. "I'll make sure it won't hurt for long. Not if it's djinn." The words were ragged in his ears.

She didn't respond. The twinkling lights paled next to the violet glow in her gaze.

He swore. The end was here.

CHAPTER 8

The world wasn't gray, but silver, shot through with glittering threads, bright as lightning, elusive as snowflakes. Sera reached out to hold the threads, but they slipped through her fingers, unraveling into a darkness she couldn't bear to face.

" 'When you too long stare into the abyss . . . ,' " she quoted.

"Damn it, no Nietzsche. I'm the nihilist around here."

The darkness belled up to meet her, and she saw herself reflected in Archer's bronze eyes. "I wasn't even looking into the pendant."

"It's not the damn rock. The last stage of possession is coming to complete the link between you and the demon. When it's over, I want you on this side of the Veil. So stop drifting on me."

"I wanted to hold on." She tightened her fingers around his wrists.

He sat beside her on the daybed. He twisted his hands so he mirrored her grasp in a rescue hold. "Yes. Hold on."

"To the other side."

"No," he said with strained patience. "To this side. Not to the past, not death, not damnation. Life. Now."

"Why?"

He lifted one eyebrow.

"You're the nihilist," she reminded him.

"I thought you were unconscious. Only people who aren't thinking quote Nietzsche."

She grimaced and released him. Her palms slid past his as he let her go, his callused skin rasping on hers.

As their clasped hands parted, every molecule in her screamed as if torn asunder. She felt her essence shred like mist in the wind. The world faded again in a haze of ice on ash on starlight on cold, wet stone.

She clawed upward, icy fear swamping the air from her lungs.

Archer's hands tightened on her shoulders. "Sera?"

"I keep going and coming back." She tried to keep her tone level, but she heard the hitch in her voice, almost a sob.

"Stay with me."

"Maybe it'd be easier if I just went away." Had her mother been right all along? "You wouldn't have to—"

"Now you want easy?" His fingers dug into her flesh. When she whimpered, he loosened his grip.

And the ice crept back. She tasted ash on her tongue. The twinkle lights seemed very far away.

"Ferris," she cried out.

His arm snaked behind her shoulders, dragging her up against his chest. "Stop it." His fingers under her chin forced her gaze to his. "Stop wavering."

She clung to his solid bulk. "The last time I almost died, after the car accident, I almost wanted to." She feared the void inside her would pull him down too, unless she could fill it.

"Your soul stays here," he commanded. "Flawed maybe, but fight for it."

"Not black and white. Gray." As if she'd conjured it,

the gray crept up again. She gasped for breath as the otherworldly chill spread. If she could see her soul, would it be rimed with ice, flaking ash, winking out like an ancient star?

"Sera."

"I can't. . . ." The cold reached her heart.

Archer cradled her and whispered her name again. His breath on her skin stopped the chill. She echoed his whisper with his name.

His mouth over hers spread heat in an almost-painful wave, branching out along her nerves in sudden desire. Desire for warmth. Life. Desire for him.

The kiss the feralis interrupted had been angry, challenging. This kiss tasted of desperation.

For a heartbeat, she longed for a touch mild and sweet as spring in this pretend garden, tinted with roses and laughter. Then his lips slanted against hers, delving deep, and her thoughts upended in a violet-tinged haze.

Anything but gray.

She clutched the open edges of his coat. The row of buttons cut into her palm. With an impatient moan, she shoved at the opening.

The leather resisted, but his shirt ripped to his navel.

She blinked in surprise. She hadn't meant . . .

Hell, whatever. She reached around the width of his chest, while reveling in the heave of his breath, the shudder in his muscles, the scalding heat of his skin.

The chill lifted, burning away like fog, the dismal flavor of ash lost to the wild spark of his tongue rimming the inside of her lips and the edges of her teeth.

She should pull away—regain some space and her senses. But she felt the void all around them, between the leaves and lights. Even in this serene jungle lay shadows of death.

So she kept her gaze and hands on Archer, anything to hold on.

His hips pressed hard against hers, forcing her into

the daybed, but he reared back to look at her. He spiked his fingers through her hair to pin her in place.

"What is this?" His voice was a harsh rasp. For the first time, she saw uncertainty in his eyes.

Sure, he'd face down ferales or malice, but ask for a little foreplay. . . .

"Last hurrah." She curled her fingers into the muscles of his back and urged him closer.

He resisted. "When I may have to kill you later?"

"I've always hated that awkward, breakfast small talk."

The violet sheen she knew was the demon gleamed in his eyes. "Unfair."

She hesitated. He was right. What she was asking . . .

"If I were your lover," he added, "you wouldn't be talking the next morning. And not because I'd killed you."

An arrogant assassin. Better than an uncertain one, she supposed. She tightened her grip. This time he relented, lowering himself so that each inch of him found a resting place against her and squeezed out any place for the void.

"Don't let go," he warned.

She wouldn't, but before she could answer, he kissed her again, hard. The pendant had slipped behind her—the stone ground into her spine between the shoulder blades, the cord tight around her neck. She squirmed, and the friction of her body against his made her gasp.

She arched her back, less pressure on her neck, more on her hips. He took it as an invitation to skim her T-shirt over her head.

She wasn't well-endowed enough to always require a bra, a sometime regret of hers. But now it saved time, time she wasn't sure she had anyway.

Archer's fingers grazed her skin. She caught a deep breath, raising herself to fill his hand.

His breath left in an explosive burst. She would have laughed—if she hadn't been breathless herself.

His thumb stroked the ruched flesh around her nipple, and sensation pooled through her veins, driving back every thought of the void. Only this, now.

It had been so long. She craved the raw silk touch of skin on skin. Not cold steel flensing tissues, not impersonal latex hands describing range of motion.

She was strong and alive. At the moment anyway. She wanted this.

The cool leather of his coat draped around her, but the heat off his skin scalded her as she buried her hands in his shirt. She pushed the material back, baring his shoulders, and trapped his arms against his sides.

He wrenched back, as if reluctant to be restrained. She followed him up and pressed a kiss to the base of his throat, then flicked her tongue into the hollow. She heard his groan, felt the vibration under her mouth. She traced her hand down the crinkle of hair at his chest to the button of his jeans. With a flick of her thumb, the button popped open.

He pushed her back, eyes wide enough to fill with the gleam of little white lights.

In the second heartbeat, he was shucking out of his coat and ripped shirt, tossing both onto the ground.

For a moment, she feared the separation would leave her floating again in the demon realm. But the sight of him, all hard muscle and hot skin, seemed enough to keep the otherworldly chill at bay.

He sat back on his haunches, his expression harder than his abs, which, she thought, was saying something. "I am mad."

"Just possessed," she corrected.

His gaze swept her. Her nipples tightened under the almost-tangible sweep of his dark eyes. She stretched.

He growled and lunged forward. She didn't flinch as he buried both fists with a thud in the pillows next to her head. From the corner of her eye, the *reven* on his forearm was a black curl touched in violet. When he leaned forward to nuzzle her neck, his teeth scraped on the cord of her necklace.

"It has been so long." His low growl in her ear, the Southern drawl more pronounced with his tension, made her nerves dance. "What possessed me to . . . ?"

"Like I'd know."

"You should." His hands were busy at the fly of her jeans. He grabbed both flayed edges and yanked upward, bringing them hip to hip.

She gasped. In retaliation, she tucked her hands inside his waistband. He sucked in a harsh breath, giving her room to delve a little deeper past the top of his boxers.

His zipper parted with a resigned sigh that was lost in his groan as her fingers grazed the length of his raging erection.

His turn for revenge. Tit for tat, she thought hazily, as his mouth closed over the curve of her breast.

The damp warmth of his lips urging her nipple to a peak drew an answering moisture lower down, his big hand coaxing her. For a moment, she thought she'd drifted again, because when her senses returned, her jeans were gone, as were his.

Poltergeists or passion, she didn't care. She wanted only for him to push back the void, with that big hand, his big other parts.

With her fingers, she measured him, teased a pearl of wet from his tip. His long, inhaled gasp made her smile. She traced the pearl down his length. Hard as that part was, the rest of him trembled like the leaves above them.

She folded her legs around him. For a single instant, her spine, hips, and thighs seized, locked as if in ice, a cruel reminder of her accident. Then the hot insistence of him was burning at her core, melting the ice that froze her.

"Now," she whispered.

He hesitated.

"Right now."

Fighting and dancing, he'd been all lethal grace. Now he flowed like winter molasses, slow and sweet. She wanted to scream, but she lost her breath as he eased into her, filled her.

He started to move with sure and steady strokes. She clamped her hands around his forearms braced beside her head, her fingers digging into his flesh, distorting the lines of the *reven*. Her vision blurred, starred, and she was dazzled by half-unseen auroral lights that limned his body where they touched.

Pleasure bordering on torture radiated endlessly outward from the center of their joining. She moved as if through an illuminated hall of mirrors—each lit glass reflecting an infinite cascade of feeling back at her, completely opposite the cold, vague demon realm that beckoned her.

He plunged into her, faster and deeper now. A new abyss threatened. With each rising caress, she moved nearer the edge. And she welcomed it.

Over her own panting breath, she barely heard his chant beside her ear, speeding in time to his rhythm. Her name, a whispered endearment, a hoarse command that she come, come now.

With jackknife violence, she did.

Eyes wide, she stared up, met his dark gaze, and saw nothing of violet. There was only the brilliant bronze glaze of his desire as he followed his own suggestion, driving her into another bone-deep contraction of ferocious pleasure that curled through her pelvis and thighs, incinerating the memory of her wounds, blazing high as she reveled in every sensation, and then swept away on

Archer's half-strangled shout as he spent himself inside
her.

He rolled as he collapsed, taking her over with him
onto her side, still joined, her head nestled against his
cheek. In the shadow between their bodies, the pendant
slipped to the pillow and glimmered with faint rainbows
of color.

She closed her eyes as their heaving breaths synchro-
nized and slowed. The slick stickiness of their skin sent
fresh shivers through her with each inadvertent touch.

His hand drifted down her side, from shoulder to
waist, and came to rest on her hip.

The quiver in her skin chased the caress, and she
glanced down to follow the path.

The bleak lines on his hand lost themselves in the
demon mark that traced her body from hip bone to
thigh in whorls of deepest black.

Her possession was complete.

CHAPTER 9

Archer drifted on the rhythm of her breath, every facet of his being—plus a few the demon had loaned him—replete with male satisfaction. He couldn't hold back a regretful groan when she eased away.

The green leaves reflected in her wide eyes. "Ready to pass judgment?"

He levered himself up on one elbow. "Mind-blowing. Staggering. Really, really good."

Her lips twitched. "Thanks for the movie poster highlights, but . . ." She pointed.

He studied the quiescent *reven*. "Does it hurt?"

She shook her head. "Maybe a little. Before. But I wasn't really paying attention, since . . . Anyway, it doesn't hurt now. Should it? Would that mean bad things? Or good?"

He remembered his own agony, heard the note of hope in her voice. "I don't think pain is indicative either way. I just wondered how you felt."

"Oh. Fine. No sudden urges to desecrate holy sites or spin my head around three-sixty." She nibbled at her red lip. "Actually—who would've guessed?—this *is* more awkward than typical mornings-after. Since you're not surreptitiously groping around for your monster axe, I take it my demon is one of the reformed, and you're not going to kill me."

At the reminder of the grim promise between them, he rolled to the side. If the talyan pairing hinted at in the old text was always born from this threat of execution, no wonder the bond had been broken. "Not reformed. Repentant. And I'm not entirely certain."

She watched him warily as he gathered his boxers. "Not certain?"

"The pattern isn't djinn. But it's far more complex than any I've seen." He invited her inspection by holding out his hand. The bold lines on his skin were hardly simplistic, but they couldn't match the fractal patterning that spun out asymmetrically from the small of her back over her hips to wrap her upper thighs.

He wondered how intimately those delicate lines traced upward.

Before the thought showed up on his face, or other parts of him, he hastily added, "We'll compare your mark to others on record, but guessing by the convoluted patterning, your demon is enigma-class." That would explain her ability to confound him from the moment they'd met on the bridge with an unbound demon trailing behind her. "Enigma-class demons spawned the stories of riddlers like the Greek sphinx, who threatened to decimate a city if its question wasn't answered."

She leveled an inscrutable gaze on him, as if he weren't as good at hiding his thoughts as he hoped. "My questions, answered or not, never resulted in consequences that dire."

"Not before they didn't." He pulled on his boxers and jeans, then turned to face her. "Look at me. Tell me what you see."

She studied him. "Muscles. Chest hair."

"Look deeper."

"Sweat. And a hickey that the demon is already heal-

ing. I'll have to suck harder next time. If there is a next
time."

His breath caught. "Sera," he said warningly, "what
do you see past that?"

"A coldhearted bastard? I don't know. What am I
looking for?"

"My soul."

The gentle curve of her lips, a half smile, teased him.
"Do I get to see that along with the rest?"

"If you were djinn." That extinguished her smile.
"Djinn and angels can see souls. The teshuva lost the
ability with their eviction from both other-realms."

Her eyes narrowed. "I have no idea what's in your
soul."

"Good." He finished dressing, brushing mulch off
his trench coat. He'd tossed it aside without a single co-
herent thought. Well, *Get naked now*, might have gone
through his head, but not the head that counted. Muttering, he checked the stowed axe. No more potentially
fatal mistakes tonight.

When he turned back, Sera was also clothed, her coat
balled in her lap. "So no euthanasia?"

"You still think I would?"

The faintest hint of color rose in her cheeks. "That's
not why I said yes."

"You didn't say *yes*. You said *now*."

Her blush flared higher. "I'm liberated. Possessed,
but liberated."

"This is a good time to be alive," he said with proper
seriousness.

And surprised himself with the truth in his words.
Another decidedly lethal turn in his thoughts. If anyone
was in danger tonight, it wasn't her.

In the lazy air, the scent of sex hung close. He took a
few steps away to lean against a tree, leaving the daybed
to her. But even from that careful distance, he still saw
her swollen lips, the redness at the joining of her slender

neck and shoulder where he'd set his teeth. His fingers itched to run through the tousled blond strands, where sweat and friction had knotted curls into her hair.

What had he done?

He didn't realize he'd spoken aloud, if softly, until she speared him with a glare. Her senses were sharper, thanks to the demon. He'd have to be more careful. Now. He snorted to himself, determinedly silent.

"It's over then?" Her tone was more demand than question.

The words stung. "So it wasn't mind-blowing for you too?"

Her previous blushes paled in comparison to this one. "I meant this possession of mine."

"Ah. That."

"That. The reason we're here. The reason why we . . ." She gritted her teeth on whatever words threatened. "That was the reason we did it, right?"

He shifted. "We had to do something. I've never heard of a demon and its chosen dancing on the edge of the Veil so long and not ending up with a corpse and an unbound demon in search of another soul."

She nodded, as if eager to explain away the night. "You said the chosen has to be rooted in this realm or risk being drawn into the other when the demon ascends. What better than drinks, dancing, and sex?"

"Usually it's a lot of beer with whiskey chasers, a game of pool, and a fight in the parking lot." When she wrinkled her nose, he shrugged. "All other demon-ridden have been male. And bloody knuckles have a way of reminding you what this world is about."

"So it is done?"

He narrowed his eyes. "The *reven*, the sign you are possessed, is on you. With the demon bound to your flesh in this realm, you don't need to fear being sucked back into hell." As she'd said, only that danger had brought them together in the first place. "But you still have to master your changed senses, hone your abilities, test your limits."

She bit her lip, bringing back the color. "So, not done?"

"Did you think you'd just walk away again?" A spurt of anger sharpened his voice more than he intended. They were talking about her deal with her demon, not what had happened within the confines of the daybed. "If you had died tonight, your soul would be forfeit. That still holds true. Like your demon, only in the fight can you hope for salvation."

She flinched back with each pronouncement, and he realized he'd advanced on her, his voice rising with each step.

He rocked to a halt. Slowly, he reached out and wrapped his finger through the cord of her necklace. The stone spun, secretive and mute, as defiant as its bearer. "But the choice is yours. Just as when the demon first approached you."

She pulled away. Despite the marks of loving still on her, shadows stalked behind her hazel eyes. "And you are just another demon offering me damnation and worse."

If he hadn't checked the axe, he might have wondered if it had sprung open to jab him in the gut. Just as well the alleged talyan bonding had faded into myth. "Welcome to worse."

"Your promises have come to naught." Corvus struck the flint in front of the torch. A blue-white flame flared to life out of the invisible propane. "The demon is not djinn."

The Worm squirmed, as worms were wont to do. "Entirely unexpected. The signs all indicated—"

The sinister hiss grew louder as Corvus widened the flame. "I've grown weary of your signs. Battles fought by signs are only won in ballads. Crappy ballads."

The Worm flinched.

Corvus held the tip of his finger to the flame. The black marks peeking out from beneath both sleeves flared yellow. The Worm sucked in a breath, then gagged at the stench of burning flesh.

Just right. Corvus balanced the torch in a vise and reached for two thick glass rods. So many small acts before the final effect.

In the same way, he'd insinuated his final plan into the dreams of the pharmaceutical researcher and the executive. He'd barely called on the confusing miasma of his djinn-infused aura to charm them. With just a few suggestive words, he'd opened a path to the center of their souls and bent them to his need. One man lusted for immeasurable wealth; the other longed to be a hero. Together, they spread a spiritual plague through the city. The world would come to curse those early unwitting carriers of doom, but at least a few innocents would be spared the coming annihilation.

Well, not actually innocent, and not spared, precisely. But their deaths would be kinder than what lay ahead.

He softened both canes in the flame and spiraled the transparent black into the matte. Dark and darker, like his endless servitude. How appropriate the crow had come to him as his last work in the darkest days of all.

The Worm cleared his throat. "Actually, the strain of the demon changes nothing."

Corvus tipped his head. "True, nothing ever really changes."

"A complication only." Eagerness rose in the Worm's voice. "The league has its newest talya well guarded, but the weakness in the Veil remains. Our work doesn't require informed, or even willing, participation."

"You should know," Corvus murmured. More loudly, he said, "True again."

"My formula for the chemical *desolator numinis* performs exactly as we wanted. Soon we'll have the critical mass we need to punch through the Veil." The Worm straightened. "So our agreement still holds."

Corvus put down the glass. He took up the ring he'd laid aside and slipped it over his finger. "Why do you covet it? You cannot cozen the demon's power for yourself."

The Worm's gaze fixed on the ring. "Of course I can." His hands jerked at his sides, as if he reached for something just beyond his grasp. "The power, channeled through human flesh, is just that: power. Neither good nor evil, nor repentant."

Corvus stroked his thumb over the smooth stone. "Are there more twistings to you than I knew, my Worm?"

If the Worm even heard the name Corvus had given him, he didn't object. "Once we have the siphon through the Veil in place, we can focus the etheric energy however we wish."

Seeing the glint in the Worm's eye, Corvus tilted his head. "Such grand plans."

"Damn right," the Worm snapped.

Just as well he'd never been tempted to share his ultimate intent, Corvus thought. Seduced by the prospect of power the Worm might be, but still too small to appreciate the terrible might that, once unleashed, would free them all.

Damned indeed.

"We still need the talya and her teshuva to mark the flaw in the web of souls. And soon," Corvus warned. "My *desolator* army is nearly complete."

"And our next opportunity could be decades away." Impatience overrode the last of the Worm's trepidation, and his writhing fingers stilled into clenched fists. "I'm already working on it. She'll have no place else to go and no time to balance the demon's energies. Once we have her, I can trace the link through her teshuva to the demon realm and place the tap in that weakened point in Veil. I'll get—we'll have everything we need."

"I have faith." Corvus smiled.

The Worm smiled back.

When he had gone, Corvus returned to his glass. With each translucent layer, the disquiet in his soul sunk deeper out of his awareness, leaving him floating free of the murk. The Worm could never understand. Corvus doubted even the white-hot tip of the torch was bright enough to enlighten the man.

Meanwhile, he basked in a glow of satisfaction. He'd always known this day would come.

The playwrights of this era shied away from deus ex machina conclusions. The Greeks had loved the practice of actors, masked as the gods, descending from wires overhead to make their long-winded proclamations and neatly wrap up their complicated morality tales. Today's playwrights found such a finish too unlikely, maybe even disturbing.

They didn't believe that overwhelming, unearthly forces would come down and end their play.

Little did they know.

He found himself curious about this new demon-ridden warrior. He'd never bothered with the skulking talyan and their paltry teshuva, too fainthearted to reach for their desperately sought-after release. They should thank him for hastening their conclusion. But this one was powerful, the Worm said, and a female. Perhaps he needed to see this oddity.

He took his high spirits down from his tower into the streets. His passage rippled out in waves of frenzied darklings that would feast well before morning's light.

No sense letting the talyan get lazy now. Their teshuva hadn't much longer to repent.

Archer paused on the sidewalk in front of the refurbished old hotel, when Sera halted, staring up. "Betsy said it was almost a full moon."

In the early-morning sky, the wan moon hung between the angular spears of the hotel's Gothic crenellations, a fragile bubble over a field of needles. "Who is Betsy?"

"A nurse where I work. Worked. She told me the crazies would be out."

"Not knowing she'd be talking about you." The inadvertent cruelty of his words made him wince. "Never mind."

"Demons." Sera shook her head. "She'd probably find comfort in finally hearing an explanation for all the suckiness in the world."

"Working with humanity wasn't explanation enough?"

She dragged her gaze down from the sky. "What the hell is your problem?"

Hell. He didn't answer.

She scowled, the pale moonlight in her eyes eclipsed with violet demon glow. "I thought you brought me here so I could learn how we fight to save the world."

"We're fighting to save our souls," he reminded her. "The world is collateral damage."

"Collateral salvation, you mean."

"Guess that depends whether anybody survives."

She shook her head, blond hair sifting over her shoulders. "Are all the other demon-ridden like you?"

"God forbid."

Archer didn't turn around at the voice behind them. "Will you set her a better example, Ecco?"

Zane stepped up on the other side of them. "We're just getting off the hunt—worst ever, I gotta say—but Liam said to wait for you." He turned to Sera. "Your honor guard, ma'am. I'm Zane."

She murmured some appropriate response. Ecco did not introduce himself.

Archer put himself between Sera and the two men. "Emphasis on the guard?"

Zane ducked his head. "Niall said you weren't exactly sure. . . ."

Ecco growled. "Thought we might have to take her out. Since you couldn't."

"You might try." Sera smiled sweetly, but Archer, his demon ascending at the hinted violence, felt the sudden race of her pulse. From the curl of her fingers, he knew the fierce rush of the demon rose in her too. "Unless you're no better at the wet work than the undercover detail. Maybe you should stick to doll making."

Zane choked.

Archer smirked, his demon subsiding. "Shall we go up?"

Zane jumped forward to swipe his entry card at the door. The heavy glass etched with the @1 insignia swung open with a dull clang, and they filed in.

Archer almost bumped shoulders with Ecco as the other man tried to fall into place behind Sera. Their stares clashed. After a heartbeat, Ecco gestured him ahead, lips twisted with insincerity.

Archer narrowed his gaze, then stepped past, following Sera through the retro Metropolis lobby.

The elevator rose thirty-five floors in strained silence.

Archer glanced over at Sera. She'd been looking at him, but her gaze slipped away before he could do something—take her hand, coldcock Ecco, something—to reassure her.

Zane cleared his throat. "I remember the first time I met the league, with a mischief-class demon newly embedded in my soul." He pitched his voice as if he spoke only to Sera, although of course they all heard. "I was piss-myself scared, sorry to say."

Sera gave him a fleeting smile. "Seems reasonable."

"But you shouldn't be scared. Not of us. And the te-shuva are pretty chill too. Kinda like living in an efficiency apartment with a roommate who works days while you work nights. You share the same space and sort of help each other out, but you never even see the other guy."

"He must be the one who keeps leaving the toilet seat up," Ecco said. "Asshole."

"Anyway," Zane said, "that just leaves bad demons to worry about. And you've already racked up an assist in a feralis takedown."

She lifted an eyebrow. "You keep score?"

He flushed. "Well, not officially. The reckoning's all in the soul, I suppose."

"And the hash marks in your flesh," Ecco growled.

Sera glanced at him. "Don't you heal? I thought that's the demon's half of the deal."

Ecco smiled, full of teeth. "Doesn't stop it from hurting like hell."

When her gaze slid to him again, Archer kept his eyes fixed on the elevator doors, which thankfully opened. Ecco and Zane stepped out, but Sera balked on the threshold. Archer tried to see the room as a newcomer.

Decades ago, the league had converted the old hotel to apartments for its talyan. When Niall had taken over as leader, he'd opened the penthouse suite with its massive sunken living room as a gathering space, trying to foster community among the almost pathologically reclusive fighters. The hotel wasn't the tallest or finest in the city, but the wall of windows framed an impressive swath of skyline and morning light.

Despite the elegance of sleek modern furnishings in black and chrome highlighted with crimson, Archer didn't think any particular awe of the decorating held Sera in place, clashing violet lights in her eyes.

Maybe her reluctance had something to do with the couple dozen large, powerful men—variously scarred and *reven* marked, and at the moment liberally sprayed with ichor—rising from their scattered seats, all with violet-tinged gazes fixed on her.

When Zane had said they'd waited after rounds, he'd meant they'd *all* waited.

Archer put his hand at the small of Sera's back. He

paused while she angled herself a single degree toward him, toward the comfort—or at least the familiarity—of his touch. He noted how every man's eyes flicked to that point of contact.

Only then did he guide her forward to the man standing in the middle of the room.

"Sera Littlejohn," he said. "This is Liam Niall." He cast his gaze wider. "And the Chicago league of the teshuva, those who would repent."

The talyan fighters stood motionless, but tension lapped the room in almost visible waves.

" 'Pleased to meet you' seems a little . . . ," she responded, hesitating, then finished, "beside the point."

Niall's lips quirked up. "Hello is fine. Truth is, we're as surprised to meet you as you are to find us. A woman, with a powerful enigma-class demon. These are puzzling times indeed." He shook his head. "But we are very pleased to meet you. It isn't every day—or every decade—that we welcome a new convert to the league."

"I think that's probably a good thing." Sera's sideways glance took in the room of silent men.

"Not if we're going to stay ahead of the bad guys," Niall said.

Ecco hovered nearby, if a man with biceps the size of tree trunks could hover. "We are the bad guys. We're just not the really bad guys."

Niall shot him a quelling glance. "Don't scare her."

"Too late," Sera murmured.

At the same moment, Zane said bracingly, "She's not as nervous as I was. I about puked the first time I smelled a malice."

"Thank you, Zane," Niall said with a wry twist to his lips.

Sera shifted uneasily. "I guess I *have* already seen some of the nastiness."

"Not the worst, you haven't," Ecco said.

She slanted a glance at Archer. He folded his arms and

leaned against the column that separated the elevator entryway from the steps down into the living room. He'd done his part, shepherding her through the possession, bringing her into the fold. The camaraderie Niall and Zane dangled with their tag-team routine, even Ecco's ominous hazing, wasn't something he could offer her.

It had been a mistake to claim her so blatantly in front of the others. Just because the destroyer in him sent portents through his dreams that something—some demon, some*one*—was coming his way, didn't mean she belonged to him.

A man who lived forever—until he was brutally slaughtered by unholy minions of darkness—didn't find dating an easy proposition. Girlfriends wondered who'd left the ichor stain on the shirt collar. Wives grew suspicious when their husbands didn't grow old.

Worse, the demon's dread of compounding its burden of sin turned every touch into an inner battle that, over the years, became not worth waging.

But a female talya... Every man in the room eyed Sera as if she were the fantasy haunting his lonely dreams. If Bookie was right about the last female talya disappearing into antiquity, maybe something in their demonic DNA was waking up. The hungry stares roused a protective instinct Archer thought eradicated in his lone-wolf existence.

At least he could tell himself his unsubtle claiming would give her a bit of breathing space in this room of rogues and killers. Of course, what his mind told itself had nothing to do with the primal impulses raging through his blood.

In the face of his silence, Sera glanced uncertainly back at Niall. "I don't know what Archer told you about the feralis attacking, but I'm no fighter."

"If you survived possession, you are." Niall gestured her deeper into the room.

The other men quietly arranged themselves to points

equidistant on the other low couches and single chairs, as if too shy to approach, too fascinated to leave. Archer stayed beside his column.

Sera's gaze slid from one side to the other, keeping them all in view. She took a seat on the edge of the couch across from Niall. "Metaphorically, perhaps. But I think you all live a little more literally."

Ecco paced behind Niall. "You were a death-dealer before too. We read it in your file."

"A thanatologist." The snap in her eyes held enough hazel fire that any violet was redundant. "We offer comfort and guidance at the end of life."

Archer tried to reconcile that fierce glare with the imagined hush of a deathbed vigil. As if wondering the same, Ecco scratched his head. "So guide the poor suffering demons into oblivion at the point of a gun, or a knife, or poisoned blow darts."

Zane stepped in front of Ecco and settled himself a few cushions away from Sera. "Don't sweat the details yet. You don't even know what your demon can do."

She glanced at him. "So, how long did it take you to resign yourself to killing ferales?"

He laughed. "Are you kidding? I still want to be the next Jimi Hendrix."

She gave him an answering smile. "But duty and a demon called?"

His merry expression faded. "Duty called, all right, but instead of going to Vietnam, I headed for the border. Got caught in a poacher's snare just this side and lay there for a week with my leg half cut off at the knee. Demon came to me looking like my draft officer. For some reason, I thought I only had to serve a year."

She grew still. "Vietnam? How old are you?"

The bleakness spread, until the callow smoothness of his face looked no longer young but worn to nothing. "When was I called up? Seventy-two? This other war has made me forget."

In the silence, the sound of Zane rubbing at his jeans over the long-ago wounded leg rasped irritatingly. Out of all the gathered men, not a one breathed. Archer, fighting down his own memories, wondered if he should take a poll for pitching Zane over the balcony.

"Zane was the last to join us, before you," Niall said quietly. "Perhaps that other life still stings a bit, but it fades."

Sera frowned. "I don't want to give up my life."

"In some ways, you already had. Which is one reason the demon chose you. Just as Zane left everything to flee to Canada, so your accident separated you from what passed before."

"But I have family, friends." Sera's voice rose a half step, a plaintive note.

"You won't for long," Ecco muttered.

Archer figured he could expand the pitching over the balcony poll to include Ecco.

A stark expression tightened Sera's face, as if the rug had been pulled out from under her, along with the floor and the earth itself, leaving her to stare into a yawning abyss—or not so much into, as up from, since she was at the bottom now.

He couldn't tell her she wasn't lost, that he'd save her. She'd know it for a lie. But he found himself straightening from his post beside the column and stepping down into the room. "As Zane said, she doesn't know what her demon can do. Maybe she'll be like Bookie, working on the sidelines." He looked around for the absent historian. "Until she has balanced her demon, she's of no use to the league, with no reason to cut all her ties at once."

Niall frowned. "Since the teshuva's crossing, the Veil has been in flux and tenebrae activity through the roof. We need every man—every woman—we can get."

"Do we?" The curt question from the back of the room turned a few heads.

Archer noted who seemed unsurprised by the question.

Niall asked, "You think there aren't enough demons to go around, Jonah?"

The tawny-haired fighter's quick wits matched his brawn, but he stood inflexible now. Jonah never blabbed like Zane, but Archer had pieced together the story of how he'd picked up his demon like a particularly nasty and incurable case of malaria while serving as a missionary in Africa.

Jonah's expression pinched tight. "Bad enough we're seeing demons in daylight. Must we also face them in"—he glanced at Sera—"in our fair flowers of womanhood?"

She snorted, then turned it into a cough. Archer managed to keep his own lips from twitching.

Niall shot her a reproachful glance. "We might not understand this change in standard operating procedure yet. But the mission remains, people. Fight evil and save our souls." The *reven* at his temple was a bleak reminder as he turned slowly. "All of us."

Archer stirred. "The war will not end today, regardless."

Niall nodded reluctantly. The smile he finally turned on Sera was strained. "I must seem heartless to you. A passage through the Veil usually riles up the horde-tenebrae only until the demon is bound in flesh." He scrubbed one hand over his face. "Usually. Anyway, our resources are strained at the moment."

Archer crossed his arms over his chest. "So that's why everyone's hanging out in the clubhouse this morning."

An ozone scent spiked in the room as a few dozen demons stirred toward ascension in their irate talyan. He figured he'd better be ready to pull himself back over the balcony rail.

He held his hand out to Sera. "It's been a long night for everyone. And there's plenty more of those to come. I'll take you home." As he said "home," he realized he was thinking of his loft.

Zane stood up. "We prepared a room downstairs for you, Sera." He said her name gingerly, as if it were glass.

She smiled at him but shook her head. "I've been gone seems like forever. I want to go back to my own place."

She slanted a glance at Archer, as if she'd heard "home" in his thoughts.

Niall stood as well. "Ecco and Zane will go too. With the lesser demons out in force, your teshuva's trailing energies could prove too tempting a target. As Jonah mentioned, daylight is no guarantee of quiet anymore. We'll talk again when you are rested."

The other talyan, even Jonah, said their good nights in a low murmur of voices. Archer wondered how many would take her image to bed with them. He felt the curl of the annihilator in him, though he hadn't called on the demon, and this time he kept his hands to himself as he followed Sera to the elevator.

Crossing town in one of Niall's ubiquitous black sedans, he almost wished he'd let Ecco drive so he could have held silent watch over Sera in the backseat instead of listening to her and Zane talk softly behind him.

"Did I sound like an idiot back there?" Zane asked. "Sometimes I think the demon got lost in the woods and only picked me because there was no one else around."

"Do demons get lost? This last demon had a whole city to choose from, and it picked me."

Zane snickered a little. "If only our demons had gotten lost in the woods while picking other fair flowers."

Sera groaned. "God, how archaic was that? Jonah, right? I suppose he's been down in the belly of the whale a long time."

Zane's laughter cut out. "Too long. A lot gets stripped away."

"Sorry," Sera said. "I didn't mean . . ."

"No, geez. My demon's supposed to be the jokester.

Jonah's not a bad guy. Just set in his ways. Who'd guess fighting evil incarnate would even have a standard operating procedure?"

"And now I've mucked it up."

"Well, you being here is freaking out the lesser demons, which must be good for us."

"Yeah, I'm great at freaking out demons," she muttered. Archer swore he felt a hazel gaze boring into his skull, but he didn't look around. "Is it too late to be the next Janis Joplin instead? 'C'mon, take another little piece of my soul now, baby. . . .' "

Archer stiffened at the throaty, sultry imitation coming from the backseat.

Zane chuckled. "Not bad. I'll do 'Purple haze, all in my eyes.' " He was silent a moment. "I wish—"

Before he could say more, or, worse, sing it—and damn it, hadn't thirty-five years of death and destruction taught the boy not to bother wishing for anything?—Ecco whirled, throwing one elbow over the seat back.

"Know what I wish?" A snarl twisted his lips, and demon harmonics trembled in his voice.

In the rearview mirror, Archer watched Zane's face pale.

Sera's eyes were half lidded—hiding what, Archer didn't know. Maybe a glint of demon violet? He wondered whether he'd have to stop the car.

"What do you wish, Ecco?" she asked.

The gray light of day was pearl soft on her skin when she lifted her face to meet the other man's gaze squarely. Her hazel eyes reflected only bright compassion.

Ecco recoiled. "I wish it were quiet in here."

He got his wish. Archer drove on in silence.

CHAPTER 10

On the stairs to her apartment, flanked by three large, dangerous men—well, two large, dangerous men and one nice guy—Sera realized she hadn't had this much social life since ... ever. And all it took was giving up everything and succumbing to demonic possession.

She might have laughed, except she opened the door, flicked on the lights, and saw the devastation.

She had only a second to gape at the smashed dishes and shredded pillows spewed down the hall before Archer yanked her back.

"Ecco, Zane, check it out."

"But—" She stumbled aside as the two talyan shouldered past her.

When she would have followed, Archer gripped her elbow. "You locked the door when you left yesterday?"

"Of course."

"You sure? The demon's coils were tightening around you—"

She hissed out an impatient breath. "I set the latch to lock when it closes."

He examined the lock. "It wasn't forced. Who else has a key? Family? Ex-boyfriend?"

And she'd just been thinking about her nonexistent social life. "No one."

"It wasn't anything Niall ordered. He leaves a place neater than he found it."

Zane returned. "No one here. Judging from the crust on the spilled yogurt, it's been a few hours."

Archer urged her inside. "Pack what you need. We're going back to my place."

Ah, the downside of said social life with an immortal man suffering from supernatural possession. Always thinking he knew best. "This is my home."

Zane backed away. "Uh . . . I'll go see what Ecco's doing."

They ignored him.

Archer scowled. "You think you're a badass part of the gang now. But this isn't a malice or even a thug feralis. Breaking and entering is a human trick, and you're no match for a djinn-man. No teshuva is."

"Any crook could have done this," she argued. "At the hospital, they've been swamped with addicts on some new drug, which always means a surge in burglaries. Why would one of these djinn-men toss my apartment?"

"I don't know." His jaw flexed, as if the admission pained him. "They've never bothered with us before. We don't matter enough."

"Then why now?" She reached up to tangle her fingers in the pendant cord. "This? But it hasn't shot out a single laser beam or anything."

He didn't crack a smile. "You'd rather believe this is a random act? I don't believe in coincidences."

"Well, I don't believe in running away from a challenge." She pushed past him.

The carnage hit her as if the sharp instrument that had ripped through the curtains—why the curtains, for God's sake?—had ended its downward stroke in her belly. Where were the demon's healing powers to protect her?

She pulled the garbage can out from under the sink.

"No point in calling the cops, I suppose. Can't exactly tell them a demon tossed my place."

The pickle jar she snatched off the floor shattered in her hand. She gasped. Archer grabbed her and led her back to the sink to thrust her palm beneath the streaming water.

She stiffened against the urge to lean into the hard strength of him. "It's just a little cut. My demon will take care of it, right?"

"This will numb the sting at least." Even as he spoke, the crimson flow vanished.

She turned off the water and stared at the raw diagonal bisecting her palm. Then she glanced at Archer, her apartment in shambles behind him. "It still hurts."

He followed her gaze to the gutted couch. "Yeah."

Ecco appeared from the hallway. "They went through the whole place. Feels a little personal to me." He flashed his teeth at Sera. "Only been one of us a few hours and already you have enemies. Way to go."

Way to cheer her up. She headed to the bedroom, where dresser drawers had been upended on the floor and gutted pillows sprouted white tufts of stuffing like mold. In the bathroom, the mingled fragrances of smashed toiletries made her stomach heave. Broken mirror crunched under her shoes, and the pretty patterned scarf she'd used to dim the lights was draped in tatters over the toilet.

She rejoined the men in the living room. "It wasn't a drug burglary. My prescriptions are scattered, but they're still here."

Zane looked up from where he was tossing wreckage into the trash. "Couldn't be that easy."

"If they didn't get what they wanted," Archer said flatly, "they'll be back."

Sera pushed down the prickle of fear his words conjured. "All the more reason to lie in wait for them. Whoever 'they' are."

Ecco shrugged. "Niall said to keep an eye out for horde-tenebrae sniffing around. Makes no never-mind to me where I do that. And if it is a djinn-man . . . ," he said, trailing off with another threatening smile. "Maybe it's time to get real personal."

Sera didn't look at Archer. "I'm staying." She marched back to the bathroom. The place where it all had started.

A fragment of mirror clung to the medicine cabinet, just enough to reflect her incredulity at the wanton destruction. Not that she could have hidden anything—say, a pendant—inside the mirror. It was as if the invader had wanted to break all the connections to her old life. Like there'd been so damn many.

She knocked out the last piece of glass with her fist.

For a while, she heard the men talking in the outer rooms. She moved on to the bedroom. Knowing someone had pawed through her things, she tossed all her clothes into the closet and slammed the door, then stared at the fist-sized hole in the cheap pressboard. Somebody had wanted to put a hole in her.

Well, the feeling was mutual. Frustration welled up, prickling in the backs of her eyes. She headed for the living room to continue her work, glad the men had left her alone.

She stopped abruptly when she saw Archer wielding a broom in the kitchen. "You're still here. I didn't hear anyone."

He straightened from the dust pan. "You wouldn't have heard a dozen rampaging ferales over the commotion you were making."

She grimaced and cast her eye over the bare, gleaming counters and the four bulging bags of trash. "Thanks for the help."

Archer nodded once. "Zane said the smell of the food got to him and went to find something to eat. Ecco said he doesn't do windows and headed down to the Coil.

The club owner is a sometime associate of the league and keeps an ear out for us."

Sera sunk down on the slashed couch, trying not to feel the missing stuffing under her. Archer emptied his last load of trash and came to lean in the doorway between the kitchen and living room, arms crossed over his chest.

She stared at him.

Finally, he sighed. "I'm sorry."

"You didn't do anything except make it better. All of it."

"You have a generous spirit, Sera Littlejohn."

"If you want to believe that, don't put me in a room alone with the creep who did this." She thought for another moment. "Alone with a carving knife about the size of what did my curtains."

He smiled. "A generous spirit and a lively temper." He stepped back into the kitchen, then returned with a coffee mug, minus the handle, filled with orange juice.

"Missed the freezer, did he?" she asked sourly. "Unlike my dishes."

"No. Everything's a loss. But this was still sealed. I figured you'd take a break eventually. How are you feeling?"

The broken handle jabbed into her palm, and she raised her hand to study the almost invisible white scar. "A little achy."

He shifted from one foot to the other. "I didn't mean just your hand."

Heat rose in her cheeks. "A little achy everywhere, I guess."

A quick glance up, and she was surprised to see the answering color in his face. "If you're worried about what we did last night, you won't suffer any consequences. No diseases. And you won't get pregnant."

No consequences beyond semi-eternal damnation. "Another demon side effect?"

"The mingling of human soul and demon possession leaves males sterile. I imagine the same holds true for women, although I can't be sure, since you're the only one we know. Maybe Bookie could do some tests...."

"Let's not even go there. I don't want to explain why we're wondering." She paralleled her arms across her belly. "Anyway, after my accident, the doctors told me I shouldn't get my hopes up."

"That must've been hard to hear."

"At the time, they weren't even sure I'd walk again. I've wondered, with my mother's depression and delusions and my father's early-onset dementia, if having kids was a good idea. Sometimes, after a night at someone's vigil, it all seemed so vain and futile anyway...."

He settled at the other end of the couch. "Life isn't always madness and death."

"Said the immortal man who kills demons for a living." She quirked her lips at him to show him she appreciated his attempt—transparently halfhearted as it was.

He leaned forward, clenched hands dangling between elbows propped on his knees.

She watched him knead his thumb over the *reven*. "How did the demon come to you?"

His restless hands froze, and she regretted the impulsive question.

"Never mind," she said quickly. "That was rude. I could see everyone got very uptight when Zane shared what happened to him."

"It's awkward," he said softly.

"Right. Just because we—"

"It's awkward to have your deepest flaw inked in demon stain on your skin."

She nibbled at her lip. "I thought the demon entered through a physical wound, that the mark appeared over that injury when the demon healed it."

"The wound is just an outward manifestation." He

took a breath, then said bluntly, "Zane was a coward. He tried to run away, not because he condemned the war, not because he thought he could fight for what he believed in somewhere else. He was afraid, and rather than confront his fear, he ran."

"Then the snare caught him," she murmured. "And the demon offered to let him go."

Archer nodded. "Only to conscript him into a war that will never end. I've seen Zane hold his leg, where the wire must have cut him to the bone. I see him wondering if it was really so bad. And there's the damn *reven* flashing neon purple, a reminder he didn't have the courage to find out."

She swore she felt her own mark shift beneath her, upsetting her balance. "It takes no special bravery to die."

"You say that after all you've experienced in your work?"

She bristled. "I helped people die more peacefully, but it's not like they had a choice in the end. Zane did. We did. Sometimes it's harder to live."

"Thanks to the demon, now you'll find out how much harder it is to live forever, if a life of endless killing can be called living."

She put her hands over her ears and pushed to her feet. "This night has been bad enough. No reflection on your lovemaking skills, really."

Before she made it out of the room—and, dramatic exits aside, where exactly did she think she was going?— he said, "I tried to kill myself."

She stopped in her tracks but didn't turn around.

His weary voice sounded close, though she knew he hadn't gotten up. "I wouldn't have told you since your mother . . . But I think that's why I resonated with your demon crossing over, that echo of self-inflicted violence. I tried to shoot myself. One simple shot to the head."

She turned slowly. "The demon mark isn't on your head."

"I missed." He didn't look up. "Top rifleman in my company, and I missed."

"I wish my mother had failed too," she said.

This time he did look up, dark eyes bleak. "The pistol misfired, exploded in my hand."

"Thus the *reven*."

His chin jerked once in a reluctant nod.

"What . . ." She wanted to continue, *Rifleman in what company? When was your day?* but her historical curiosity seemed irrelevant in the face of the pain that plagued him still. "Why did you try to kill yourself?"

"I'd been wounded in one of the last battles of the war. Most of the men I'd fought beside moldered in unmarked graves. My father's farm was gone forever. My sister had remarried and moved away, taking my mother with her. My fiancée . . ." He stared down at his flexing hand. "After what happened, I didn't go back to find her again."

He opened his fist, as if he could drop the sinuous black lines that marred his skin.

"Everything slipped from my grasp. Just like my exploding pistol." A faint violet haze moved in the tarnished depths of his eyes. "The demon came to me and promised I'd have the power to hold on to something and never let it go. What it meant was, I could spend eternity throttling rampant horde-tenebrae and never erase the stain on my soul."

He shook his head. "Demons don't lie. They're fallen angels, after all. They drop just enough tidbits of the truth for you to lead yourself into damnation."

Sera leaned in the doorway, buffeted by gusts of outrage at the choice he'd tried to make. She wanted to scream at him, curse, as she hadn't been able to when she was thirteen, flailing in the water with the bubbles of the sinking car churning around her.

She struggled to keep her voice even. "Time was,

suicides weren't even buried in the churchyard. Some might say you were damned anyway."

"I didn't care. Unlike your mother, I wasn't driven by voices. There was no one left to speak." He took a long breath. "But if I'd known about your mother before last night when you told me, I would've had Niall send someone else to talk you through possession."

"Talk? How about sleep with me? Or kill me if my demon was djinn?"

"We did what we had to. I'm not asking for absolution."

Did he mean the killing, or the sex? As sudden as a flash flood ended, her anger dried up, leaving her empty. "But you think I'd condemn Zane—or you—when I've ended up in the same place."

She thought for a moment. "You said the *reven* highlights wound and flaw, both." She smoothed her hands down her hips, as if she could feel the curving lines of the mark. "I was broken in my center, body, and identity. I'm the one people turn to for answers, but really I've only ever had questions. Why didn't someone notice my mother was suffering from severe postpartum depression? Could we have prevented Dad's decline? Why did that drunk bastard have to hit me? The demon promised me explanations. Instead I've had to face realities I'd never have believed before."

His gaze had followed the path of her hands. "You catch on quickly. It took me much longer."

Once again, she wondered how long. Zane, no older than his early twenties during the Vietnam draft, should have been past fifty. And he was the most recently possessed. That would make Archer—what?—eighty years old? One hundred?

Not that it mattered. He'd proved himself spry enough. Into the weary emptiness she'd thought an improvement over the rush of troubling emotions, a flush of heat sparked along her frayed nerves.

When he lifted an eyebrow in question, she realized she'd been silent too long. She gave herself a little shake. "I need to lie down for few minutes." Just to get away.

He smiled faintly. "Have all these revelations made you stop thinking about what a bad night it's been?"

He'd shared just to distract her? "I guess my stuff doesn't seem so important when compared to ..." She waved her hand, encompassing a wider view.

"Unless the break-in is part of it." He echoed her all-inclusive gesture.

She grimaced. "At least, for once, I'm not trying to figure it out on my own."

He took a breath as if to contradict her again, but he only sighed. "Zane and Ecco will keep watch on the perimeter. And I'm not going anywhere."

She blushed. Then she was annoyed with the blush. "I didn't mean you had to stay. I can *be* alone without feeling alone."

"If the djinn-man comes back, you *won't* be alone. I'll be here." He leaned back on the couch, out of place and utterly male. "So you can stop looking for a polite way to usher me out. I won't be going." His dark eyes shuttered. "But as I said, your possession is complete. You don't have to worry about slipping into the demon realm."

He thought she was looking for a way to invite him to her bed? And for so desperate and coldhearted a reason?

Such a reason would also be completely sensible and hard for any decent man to deny, came the wicked thought. The devil himself couldn't have conjured more tempting images than the memories that scrolled through her mind.

She squashed them. "Are you sure you can't hear the demon in your head?"

"Human and demon can't communicate any more than God talks to people. Even when the demon appears to the one it intends to possess, it isn't truly speaking. Only reflecting your desires so you reach out to embrace what you so badly want." He lifted one eyebrow. "Why?"

More embracing. "Never mind."

Why did she keep imagining a connection between them? Just because a demon had usurped her abandonment issues as easily as one had hijacked his sense of loss? Most people built their relationships around common interests like travel or raising llamas, not battling incarnations of evil.

He came to his feet as she edged down the hallway. "Sera."

She halted.

"We'll figure out what the djinn-man wants with you, and we'll make him sorrier than his demon ever did."

"Is that your version of 'Sleep tight, and don't let the bedbugs bite'?"

He smiled. "Bite 'em back."

She returned the smile and disappeared down the hall.

Only after Sera had gone did Archer let some of the tension leak out of his body. Despite his best intentions, his senses tuned to her when she padded softly across the hall from bathroom to bedroom. He heard the faint rasp of sheets pulled back, the quieter sound of fabric sliding up over her skin. His own flesh prickled, as if the warmth of her hand had swept over him.

He was surprised the demon's fundamental devotion to its mission of repentance didn't send him screaming from the room, given the myriad sins he conjured in his mind.

He'd never told his story. He'd never been tempted to open that particular vein, and talyan would never ask. Of course, a thanatologist wouldn't shy away from deathbed confessions, even if no one had died in the end, at least not in the conventional sense.

He was starting to understand why the teshuva had chosen her. But she had her wounds too, and he despised himself for exploiting her weakness to absolve his. Just because she'd survived her mother's suicide with her compassion unbroken was no reason to think she'd lavish that mercy on a stranger, even if his pain echoed hers—especially a stranger who'd ushered her into an existence where what remained of her humanity was only a burden.

He closed his eyes and leaned his head back, hands tight on his thighs, to keep him from reaching for anything he couldn't keep.

If he wasn't looking for absolution, why was his every sense focused on the one woman uniquely qualified to forgive his sins?

An hour later, he heard Zane's light rap. Ecco would have busted his way in. Archer opened the door to the younger talya, letting in the scent of rain, doughnuts, and coffee. "Nothing to find, I take it?"

Zane shook his head. "Chatted up some of the neighbors on their way to work earlier. Checked the nearest businesses for security cameras. Walked the block a few times. Ecco's keeping watch from a roof across the street."

"Most likely trying to get a peek in Sera's bedroom window."

Zane sighed. "Can you blame him? The only female talya . . ." Then his eyes widened. "Not that he was peeking."

Archer shook his head. "She'd just better not catch him. Enigma-class still packs a helluva punch." He rubbed his arm where he'd almost forgotten the bone bruising she'd dealt him in the alley.

He glanced over at Zane and realized he shouldn't have mentioned Sera in bed or in battle. The expression on the younger man's face smacked a little too Knight of the Round Table as Guinevere walked by.

And look where that had gotten them.

What to do with a smitten swain? Send him off on a nice quest. "She's still recovering from possession, so she'll probably sleep until nightfall, but we'll need to keep her quiet and out of trouble when she wakes. Get Bookie to give you some of his longest histories on the teshuva."

Zane wrinkled his nose.

"Sera's a nerd. She likes books," Archer said quickly. "And getting materials out of Bookie's hands will be a trick. He won't give me the time of day."

With the swain suitably mollified and sent on his errand, Archer hacked the password on Sera's computer— as if he couldn't have guessed she'd choose Hades—to log on to his home system. He virtuously kept his digital hands to himself, ignoring her e-mail, documents, and downloaded music. Legally downloaded, he noted. God, she was such a good girl. He wondered how the demon had ever found a crack.

Oh, that's right, when her bones and the rest of her orderly world had cracked.

She'd resisted the lure of her mother's insanity, held firm against the riptide of her father's illness. Even when she was mortal, she wouldn't have had time for a worn-out soldier like him. Since he wouldn't die, he couldn't even have aspired to her professional touch at the end.

Could his soul be any more damned for the furtive, selfish gladness at her demon's coming?

The sky was darkening, barely late afternoon in a Chicago November rain, when Niall called.

"I'm sending Jonah to relieve Ecco, and Raine will bring the books Zane ordered from Bookie," Niall said. "I'll send—"

"I'm fine," Archer broke in, sensing the next replacement in juggled personnel.

Niall huffed his annoyance down the line. "You've been awake going on three days. And the possession can't have been easy."

"I'm fine," Archer repeated. He didn't want to think about her possession. He definitely wasn't going into details despite the questions he heard in Niall's voice. "I have the Bookkeeper's roll of known djinn-men and a register of angelic possessed."

"The angelic host think less of our existence than the djinn," Niall mused. "And that's saying something."

"Which is why they're both on my list."

Niall was quiet. "What is going on here, Archer? All this other-realm force, focused on our fresh talya. Why?"

"We've been the metaphysical garbagemen for centuries, taking out the tenebrae trash. Maybe it's time to think about the source of the pollution."

"Not our job," Niall cautioned.

"Says who? The demons possessing us that can't speak? A few cobbled-together treatises? You're the one who said we're losing this war." The water went on in the bathroom. "Never mind. I'm under control here. I have things under control here. Don't send anybody to replace me. We'll talk later."

"Are you stuttering?" Niall's querulous voice came down the line. "I thought you were fine."

Archer disconnected as Sera stepped barefoot into the living room, her face soft and her hair still rumpled from sleep.

He wished he hadn't said "under control" twice in a row. Made him sound out of control.

"My alarm clock is smashed." Her voice sounded husky. "What time is it?"

"Dinnertime."

She glanced past him. "Any doughnuts left?"

"That's not dinner."

"That means you ate them all without me." She pursed her lips.

He really was out of control if that tiny pout raised his pulse. "I mean we need to get some real food into you."

She plucked at her pajama bottoms. "My clothes were trashed too. I don't have anything to wear."

Ah, he wished. He let out the breath he'd been holding, then inhaled again to catch her honeysuckle scent. "Niall's sending over reinforcements. They can pick up dinner on the way."

"I feel useless. I can't even cook since I don't have dishes."

"You can still do laundry," he said helpfully. "And, with some training, destroy unholy apparitions."

"There's a career path."

"In a line of work this gory, we call it multitasking."

She blinked at him owlishly and wandered back into the bedroom.

By the time Jonah and Raine arrived with Thai food and books, Sera had shuttled a few loads of laundry to the basement with Archer as mule and escort.

She stuffed handfuls of earth-toned cotton and satin into the trash chute.

"Um," he said, not helpfully.

She glared at him. "Some creep had his hands in my underwear drawer. I'm not wearing them."

"I wasn't going to insist, really."

She shoved an empty laundry basket at him. Even setting her up with a heaping plate of pad thai and a monstrous tome while he cross-referenced his list of angels and djinn couldn't distract him from wondering what she *was* wearing under the flannel pajama bottoms and baggy T-shirt.

"I think I should go hunting with you."

That distracted him from her clothing or lack thereof. "No."

She speared the last spring roll with more than necessary force. "I heard Jonah tell Raine babysitting me is taking fighters off the streets."

"Jonah has a big mouth."

She frowned at him. "But is it true?"

"There aren't enough of us at the best of times. That's why these are the worst of times."

"Do you think these are the worst?" She pointed her chopsticks at the unbound manuscript. "Parts of the Dark Ages sound grim, and the Second World War. It says demonic activity intensifies during times of war, since incidents with strong spiritual resonance in this realm draw the other-realms. That explains Zane during Vietnam and you during . . ."

"Where do you think the phrase 'War is hell' came from?" He fixed her with a grim stare in case she thought she'd be getting a more personal explanation.

Her lips twitched to one side in irritation. "Anyway, if you need to hunt, go. I'll just watch. I'm not stupid enough to get in the way."

"You fought the feralis. You fought me—"

"That was different," she protested.

"And you wanted to go after the malice."

"But I didn't." Her triumphant tone implied she'd made her point.

"You don't have any clothes." He sighed to himself. So he hadn't been as distracted as he'd hoped if he defaulted to that argument. "No. No hunting for you." When she drew breath to keep arguing, he said with brutal finality, "I know thanatology is the study of death, but do you want someone to die to satisfy your curiosity?"

She swallowed. "Why would my going with—?"

"Leave them to fight in peace." He shook his head at the irony. "Protecting the weak and innocent is what gets a man killed."

She narrowed her eyes. "I'm neither weak nor innocent. I'm demon-ridden too, remember?"

As if he could forget. "Possessed, yes. A warrior, no."

"Not yet."

"Maybe never. We don't know what you are yet, why

you've been possessed." He gestured at the manuscript. "That's why you're studying—"

She smacked her hand on the page, lifting a puff of dust. "I've studied one of the greatest mysteries of all— up close, in person, for years—and it didn't get me any- where. Why continue down that dead-end road?" She smiled humorlessly at her own joke.

"You might as well, because I'm not taking you hunt- ing." He pushed to his feet and stalked across the room. "Excuse me a moment. I need to have a word with Jonah and his big mouth."

He'd never been one to run from a fight, so he merely walked out quickly. Why he thought he'd won just be- cause he'd had the last word, he wasn't sure. He knew she wouldn't be satisfied. So after he assigned Jonah and Raine their tasks for the evening, he returned to the apartment to mollify her with some suitably grisly tales of old hunts. If worse came to worst, he'd tear open another vein to his past. That had kept her quiet.

He stepped into the kitchen, wondering why he was so looking forward to another quiet night at home. Then the quiet really hit him.

Sera was gone.

CHAPTER II

"Stay home, cook, and clean." Sera stomped through the front door of the nursing home. "Oh, it's okay if I don't cook? Well, screw you, old fart. How ancient are you anyway? Cro-Magnon?"

"Hardly a day past ninety-ish, missy."

Sera rocked to a halt. "Mrs. Willis. I didn't see you."

"So who's the blind one around here?" The frail figure on the bench curved as if time were shaping her back into the brown ball of clay from which her maker had formed her. When Sera shut the door, a scrap of the quilting in her basket wafted to the floor.

Sera bent to retrieve it. "Lost one."

Mrs. Willis gripped her hand. "My sisters would be sad. We're all working on it together, you know." Her cataract-filmed gaze drifted. "You might not cook, but you can finish a piece for your sisters."

Sera gently untangled herself and tucked the colorful bits of material into the basket. "I only have brothers, Mrs. Willis, remember?"

The old woman shook her head. "So who's the blind one around here?"

Sera stifled a sigh as she checked in with the evening nurse, then went to her father's room.

She tapped at the open door. "Hi, Dad."

He didn't move from his seat beside the window where the square of darkness completely surrounded him. She braced herself against the jolt of pain and walked in.

She tugged another chair into place beside him. "Wendy said you liked the chocolate I brought while you were sleeping a few days ago." She hesitated. "I guess it's been more than a few days. A lot's changed lately."

She studied his face. Not much had changed here. Still the same, strong-planed features she'd watched twice a week at the pulpit for years. More gray around the temples, but far too young for this place.

"You could come live with me again," she murmured. "You'd never notice I wasn't getting older."

The unfairness twisted inside her, threshing up the anger that never really settled. She could counsel her hospice patients to peace all day long and never feel it herself. What stillness she found had only ever been some paralyzing mix of doubt and confusion.

"Oh, Dad, I never wanted to talk to you about God, about death and Mom. About boys." She lowered her face into her hands, her lashes a dry prickle against her fingertips as she closed her eyes. "And now, when I need you, I never will."

How pathetic and stupid and childish to run away from her apartment. She'd boasted to Archer that she never backed down from a challenge. But how could she join the fight to save the world? She hadn't saved her mother, couldn't save her father, and had done a downright terrible job of saving herself.

Finally she looked up. The rain had started again, the first drops streaking the window, smearing the streetlights into watery stars.

Her father stared directly into her eyes. "Who are you?" His voice was low.

"Daddy?" She forced a smile. "It's me, Sera."

"What are you?" He pushed back in his chair. "What thing are you?"

She reached out. "I'm Sera, your daughter."

He bolted from his chair, slapping her hand aside. "Don't touch me."

A stark chill swept her except where her hand burned with the shock of his blow. Her fingers curled into a fist. Like an echo, something in her turned away, resigned to the banishment. She clutched her hand against her chest as if she could hold on. "Daddy."

"Get thee away from me. Away." His voice thundered in the small room. "I cast thee out, Satan."

"I'm not . . ." Her throat locked on the words. What was she, after all?

Lost. Archer had warned her. With sudden ferocity, she longed for his uncompromising presence, to fit herself against the strength of more than just his body. Only he, who'd killed the man he'd been, could understand what moved in her now. She looked up at her father.

He met her gaze and screamed.

The cry ripped through her. She jolted, knocking over her chair with a bang. She found herself on her knees in front of her father and held out an appeasing hand.

He cowered back. "Satan, Satan, Satan."

She clamped her hands over her ears.

Wendy and an orderly burst into the room. The nurse hastened to the screaming man and folded an arm over his shoulders. He nestled against her, pointing at Sera.

"What is that light? It burns." He straightened a little, eyes widening. "Let her go."

Without warning, he lunged, gouging fingers aimed at her eyes.

The orderly hauled her to her feet and slung her toward the door. "You're making it worse. Get out of his sight."

She stumbled out with one hand on the wall. She felt more feeble than the hunched old woman standing with her quilting basket at the front door.

Mrs. Willis patted Sera's shoulder. "Your pappy remembers being a preacher, so he's still swearing fire and brimstone."

Sera dredged up a weak smile. "I just feel bad for upsetting him."

"You're a good daughter." Mrs. Willis scowled. "Your brothers visit, but they don't stop to talk quilting. Too busy, those boys. But your pappy was proud when he knew to be, and he's proud still, somewhere."

Sera tried for a slightly more sincere smile, until she saw Wendy coming toward them. Mrs. Willis disappeared into the television room. The evening news clicked on, the cheerful tone belying the description of a recent rash of addicts overdosing. "... Practically rots its victims from the inside," blared out into the hall. She knew how that felt.

Wendy gave her a hug, but Sera couldn't ease her muscles to return the embrace.

"That was bad," the nurse said. "Arnie is calming him down. Arnie's a little abrupt with visitors, but he's got a nice touch with the confused ones."

"Maybe I shouldn't come back," Sera murmured.

Wendy shook her head. "Don't get melodramatic. One bad night doesn't mean forever."

Sera couldn't help herself. She laughed. If only the other woman knew.

But Wendy smiled in answer. "See? Better already. You know there'll be bad spells. He just took a bit of a fright. But I want Arnie to walk you out. Mrs. Willis noticed that guy's been standing by the sidewalk since you came in."

Even before she turned, Sera knew whom she'd see.

The darkness of his trench coat swallowed up the light of the nursing home sign, and the flickering drops of rain made him look like something from a grainy old black-and-white movie. Probably the bad guy.

She sighed. "I know him."

Wendy's expression said she still thought she should get abrupt-with-visitors Arnie.

Sera contemplated sneaking out the back. But she'd have to ask Wendy to deactivate the alarms that kept the dementia patients from wandering. And that would oblige an explanation of why she wanted to sneak out. "Can I call you later to see how Dad settled?"

Wendy didn't drag her eyes off the figure at the street. "Call me tomorrow. I think you're busy tonight." Her gaze finally snapped to Sera and widened.

"Now who's melodramatic?" Sera stalked out the front door.

Archer waited for her at the end of the walk. "Turn left and keep walking. Do not stop."

"What—?"

When her steps slowed in confusion, he wrapped his fingers around her elbow and propelled her forward. "At least one feralis, maybe two, are closing on this position. And I count three malice on this block alone."

"Why—?"

"You're a lure for every demonic influence in the city, beaming wrath and anguish like a fucking lighthouse of doom. And that djinn-man is out here, somewhere."

"But why didn't—?"

"We placed energy sinks around your apartment." His grip tightened on her arm until she winced, but he never stopped scanning the darkness around them. "The sinks are reverse engineered from angelic artifacts and absorb the emotional output of possession."

"Stop answering my questions before I ask them," she snapped.

"Then answer one of mine," he snapped back. "What the hell did you think you were doing, leaving your secured apartment?"

"How was I supposed to know it was secured?"

"I told you we were protecting you."

"I thought you meant you, personally."

"I was." His voice was half demon snarl. "Until you left."

So much for thinking he understood her. She hunched her shoulders against the rain needling down the back of her neck. "I wanted to go out."

"I told you no."

"And just what makes you think I'd listen?" As they passed under a streetlight, it abruptly dimmed. In the sudden shadows, a blob of deeper darkness fell toward them.

She shoved Archer away, and he stumbled onto one knee. She batted the dark shape away from her face.

A biting chill enveloped her hand, spreading like a killing frost up her elbow, toward her brain and heart.

Archer was at her side in an instant. "That was stupid."

She gritted her teeth. "You're welcome."

"I haven't gotten slimed by a malice in a very long time."

Maybe she only imagined the pointed claws and prehensile tail wrapped around her elbow, but she definitely felt gnawing teeth. She gagged on the stench of rotten eggs. "Get it off."

"You wanted to hunt. Lesson one. Don't get slimed by malice. It stings."

Stung like knives of ice. And creeped her out. And stank. "Lesson learned."

He raised his head, a glint of violet in his eyes. "The feralis is circling. Drain the malice and let's go."

"Lesson two would be helpful right about now."

He gave her a thoughtful frown, as if he wanted to be

sure lesson one had really sunk in—sunk in with needle teeth.

Finally, he nodded. "Remember the man at the bar?"

"If he got slimed, he didn't seem to notice."

"Oh, he got slimed. The malice was all over him. If he'd recognized the evil, he could have driven it away. You, seeing and feeling—smelling—the malice, have the advantage."

"Great. So how do I get rid of it?" Enough theory, already.

"Wish it away."

She stared at him. "You're kidding. Do I click my heels together?"

He didn't smile. "The demon knew the name of your darkness when it chose you. Now the demon's power is yours. Know the essence of pain, fear, hatred, despair—that is the malice. Know it, and bleed it dry." He glanced over her shoulder. "Now would be a good time."

She didn't follow his glance, not quite ready to skip ahead to lesson three. She squelched the urge to run in circles and wave her arm as if she were on fire despite the hard rain. With her free hand, she reached into the darkness.

Psychic roadkill, Archer had said. Grabbing it was like reaching into a cold, dead thing, past brittle hair and flaking, scaly skin, into rotting guts and the sharp shards of broken bone. The squirm of maggots and crunch of cockroaches gave it a horrific semblance of life.

It thrashed in her grip. A tail lashed, staining the air with streamers of a strange etheric smoke.

Archer stepped closer. The warmth of his body helped dispel her chill, but his voice was colder than malice teeth. "End it."

She blinked away raindrops. End it how? Assimilate it, as her mother had been swallowed by the voices in her head? Lock it away in a part of her mind, like her father's ever-spreading forgetfulness? Or should she just deny all feeling, like Archer did, and dishearten the malice into oblivion?

Now that she had control of it, the squirming demon seemed pathetic rather than awful. The malice was wickedness given shadowy shape, but thanks to a really crappy night, she understood how easily that could happen to anyone.

"Do you have it?" Archer wrapped his big hands around hers as if they held a newborn infant.

"We were fighting and it came down on us." The rain in her eyes cast a blurred shroud over her vision. "Did we make this together?"

"What?" His body recoiled, but his hands were steady on hers. "No. It was always here. Will always be here. We just gave it a little juice." He scowled at her. "Don't go all misty-eyed sympathetic on me now."

"Sympathy means I feel sorry for you. Sympathy is cheap. To truly feel as you do, that's empathy." Could the man at the bar have fought the malice? Why did evil have to exist at all? She didn't have answers, not a one. "I want to feel it—to understand—even if it hurts."

As if her words had summoned the demon, her senses unfurled. The scene, already cast in a forbidding monochrome of black malice and silver rain on her white skin, shifted toward an otherworldly gray—the demon realm. Her grip slackened.

Archer swore and grabbed the malice. Reaching out to steady herself, she flattened her palms over his and laced their fingers tight together. The malice, snared in their joined grasp, bound them with threads of smoldering ether.

It was the first time she'd really touched him since that desperate, dangerous coupling in his garden. With her demon ascendant, the firm heat of his grasp reverberated in every molecule of her being. An unexpected jolt of need coursed through her.

At the memory of his big hands tracing patterns on her skin, she looked up at him. His gaze fixed on hers with hungry stillness. She breathed the mingled scents of leather, wet concrete, and male, and her pulse thudded hard.

Mist thickened until it obliterated the world beyond.

"How can this be?" His question was a low growl. "Demon need takes the place of all other cravings. Only the mission remains."

Heat, equal parts desire and dismay, swept her. Here she stood in the icy rain, arm half eaten by malice, but just because *he* was with her, nothing else mattered. She almost let go, to slip toward the gray.

His grasp never wavered. "Where do you think you're going? As if we don't have enough troubles in this realm." He pulled her closer, so the trailing edge of his trench coat lapped around her. His knee nudged between her legs. "Damn it, they can't have any more of you."

He meant the other demons. Where his fingers twined with hers, faint color bloomed, and she imagined that potency spilling into her. As when they'd made love, his touch drove back the shadows, drove back the demon realm that beckoned.

But he'd reminded her, they had a mission. She wanted to understand. This realm held only questions, and the malice lurked at the root of them.

"I already know the many names of the shadow," she whispered. "My question is why. You promised answers, demon."

As she had before in Archer's loft holding the pendant stone, she focused where the world went gray. She held tight to his hands, like a diver's safety line, and followed the nebulous link down into the other realm.

To her altered senses, the malice was a thin silhouette against the endless murk; Archer was a restless thundercloud shot through with scattered lightning in violet and bronze.

She felt as if she stood on a precipice, shouting into the void, with no hope of anything but an echo. But she had to ask. "Why pain? Why sorrow? Why insanity?"

From the depths sighed a mockery of her word— *Wwwhyyy?*—as if something gigantic and unseen had roused at her call and breathed out, sending up more impenetrable drifts of darkness.

"Why death? Why damnation?" She shotgunned her questions into the gloom. "And why, for God's sake, can't we end it?"

"I can end it." Archer reeled her up against his chest.

Their paired hands came together between tattered ribbons of ether. The furious raw heat of him through the rain-slicked leather of his coat jolted her from the other realm. The vastness inside her telescoped closed with an almost aural shock wave that vibrated her bones.

The malice gave a shrill cry and collapsed in upon itself with a gritty puff of sulfurous smoke, leaving nothing between them. She staggered. Only Archer's grasp kept her upright.

Another malice's squeal sounded in the night, and then yet another, farther off.

Archer's hands clenched on hers as he straightened, nearly yanking her off her feet again. "What the hell were you trying to do? And I mean literally hell." Despite the incensed grip, his face was ashen. "Enigma-class demon or not, you can't psychoanalyze a malice into oblivion."

She coughed on the lingering scent of rotten eggs. "You didn't exactly suggest a better way."

"I prefer to pop them like a balloon. Although that always leaves some shreds lying around. Where did this one go?"

"You tell me, oh popper of many demons. You squashed it."

"No. You did before I could."

"How, when you keep holding back what I'm supposed to do?"

They matched glares. In his widening eyes she saw him realize, just as she did, they were still holding hands.

They took identical long steps in opposite directions. She wiped her palms down her thighs, trying to erase the chill of malice goo. And the warmth of Archer's skin.

Between the anger and embarrassment, his expression was fiery enough. "That's not how we fight. You can't just dance down along the demon's link through the Veil into hell."

She answered, "I didn't do it alone. You followed me."

He opened his mouth, but instead, the shrilling cry of a malice pierced the night.

The scream shuddered down her spine. "I heard the others circling. Will they attack?"

He shrugged distractedly. "Saves us the trouble of hunting them down."

"And the ferales?"

"They hunt us." He refocused abruptly, the glint of violet back in his dark eyes. "I don't know what happened, but malice stain is always blood in the water to a feralis. Let's go."

He spun on his heel and slipped into the night. Staying half a step ahead, he asked, "What did you think you were doing tonight?"

"How should I know? I'm not the ancient warrior."

"I meant, why did you leave?"

She raised her face to let rain trickle down the corners of her eyes, as if mere water could wash away the remnants of the malice. "I wanted to visit my father. You said I didn't need to cut all ties yet."

"So you listen when it's convenient. I listened too, to the screaming." He glanced back, his gaze piercing.

She looked away. "He just had a bad night."

"Bad because preacher man knows his beloved only daughter sold her soul to a devil." His *reven*-marked hand was a fist. "Some people see through the mask of our flesh and glimpse the shadow underneath. The rare holy person, the mentally ill, some children, or an artist—the kind of people who are inclined to see things differently anyway. No one listens to them, so if they speak out, they aren't heard."

She bit her lip. "I didn't want to frighten him."

"Then don't return. As the dementia advances, you'll do more harm than good." His voice dropped to a rumble. "Not uncommon for the demon-ridden."

Abruptly, he halted, his hand upheld to stop her in her tracks. Violet raced along the *reven*.

"There." His voice barely carried over the hiss of tires on wet pavement. "Under the trees."

Even in November, the oaks held their kraft-paper leaves. The ground underneath was an irregular checkerboard of shadow and light from surrounding streetlamps.

Sera followed Archer's pointing finger. "God, it's bigger than the last one."

"No God here," he said grimly. "Just us."

"Oh right, we'll take care of this. So I guess it's okay he's been slacking for the last two thousand years. Anybody else we can call for backup?"

Wind rattled the wet leaves with a sound like hands rubbing in anticipation. Archer flicked her a razor-wire smile. "You wanted to hunt."

She seriously doubted a feralis popped like a balloon, unless maybe like the Hindenburg. She swallowed. "It's moving deeper into the trees. Does it know we're coming?"

"Probably. You need to learn to keep your emotions in check."

Just like him. He'd said possession compelled the deadening of feeling, but she wondered. "I thought we were going to lure it someplace."

"Remember how you said your patients didn't get to choose the time of their dying?"

Oh sure, the one time *he* decided to listen to *her* . . .

Archer kept the line of parked cars between them and the feralis as he stalked. Sera stayed low, trying to stifle her burgeoning dread. Though each step took her closer to the feralis, she couldn't keep her eyes off Archer just ahead.

He glided through the dark, his coat flaring at his heels. The axe was out, long and wicked looking to her worried eyes. After hearing how the teshuva had come to him, she understood why he didn't trust guns. But to get so close . . .

When he glanced back, lights flared violet in his eyes—the demon coming out to play.

No, not play. His expression was tight and grim. If he'd taken savage joy in destroying evil, he'd lost it along the way.

He cut between the bumpers of two cars and melted into the tiny woods. She couldn't leave him.

The dark trees closed around them.

The feralis had gone deeper. She listened for the sound of its retreat, but heard nothing over the rustle of leaves above.

"Archer," she hissed. The smell of wet, decayed earth clung in her nostrils, along with a fouler stench, like rotted meat. "Ferris, wait."

He'd pulled ahead, one more shadow among shadows. She shook her head, trying to master the fear tight on her heels.

Something was on her heels anyway.

The back of her neck prickled, and she whirled.

The feralis dropped from a tree limb overhead. The thud of its clawed feet shook the earth. It straightened until the bulging dome of its head brushed the leaves. It raised stunted wings, and its howl scattered leaves in all directions.

She spun around to run, to catch up with Archer and his suddenly too-small axe.

The second feralis appeared before she could scream.

CHAPTER 12

If he truly wanted to be alone, Archer knew he would've been grateful for the scream.

He whirled. The feralis filled the path, its chitin-armored back to him. It lunged at something out of his sight.

"Sera!" He sprang, blade low.

Not knowing where she was, he couldn't afford to flail indiscriminately. He climbed the feralis's back, like ice picking a mountain. The mutated insect flesh was as hard and uneven as any scree slope.

He wrapped one arm around its neck to get the axe in place for a throat cut. It scrabbled a multijointed limb at him, and he cursed as the barbed guard hairs clamped over his shoulder in the same spot the last feralis had wounded him. So much for preternaturally fast healing.

As he struggled to free himself, he saw Sera faced a second monster. She was trapped between the two. His heart stopped; the demon strength faltered in his muscles.

Ferales never hunted together—or they hadn't before hunting her.

She evaded the winged feralis's long arms with the same graceful twist she'd used last night at the club.

"Don't dance with it," he shouted. "Run."

She glanced up wildly and spotted him.

The feralis she faced turned as well and lifted moth-eaten wings. He knew he could keep both demons occupied while Sera escaped.

Whether he'd escape too . . .

His feralis mount bucked, but not before he caught a glimpse of her face. He groaned at the sight of her jaw set obstinately off-kilter. She wasn't going to run.

She kicked leaves at the winged feralis. "Hey, you ugly son of a bitch, no tag teaming."

The feralis crouched and spun halfway around.

"Sera, catch!"

Archer released the hidden knife from the haft of the axe and flung it toward her, counting on her demon reflexes. Time slowed as she tracked the weapon's arcing flight with an outstretched hand. Her body was already in motion, turning to confront the feralis, as the leather-wrapped handle slapped into her palm.

Time jumped to catch up, and she struck. The creature leapt back with a shriek, the retaliatory slash of its claws a many-tongued hiss in the night.

Despite his precarious position, Archer couldn't take his eyes off Sera. His heart raced, but not for himself. He wanted to toss her the axe, improve her odds, but he feared the slick of sweat on his palm would betray him. Just his luck, to end up beheading her.

"Go for the throat," he shouted. "Or the eye. Or the spine." He should've skipped ahead to lesson thirteen: Vulnerabilities of Corporeal Demon Physiology. But he'd been giving her shit about pitying the malice.

His feralis flailed more determinedly. He had to finish it before it finished him and moved on to Sera.

Suddenly, dying in the glory of battle to send his hollowed soul to its questionable reward seemed like it could wait.

The feralis lumbered in a circle as if it had an itch

it couldn't quite scratch. As it swiped at him again, he grabbed the jointed limb, avoiding the spiky protrusions. Summoning all his desperate teshuva strength, he yanked the feralis off balance.

It bellowed and twisted to reach up at him. The clawed point sliced into the back of his thigh, a piercing agony, but it lowered the shoulder pinching his weapon arm.

He laid the edge tight against the underside of its neck.

And loosed his own demon.

The axe bit deep. The feralis shrieked. The shriek died in a gurgle as the feralis came down like a mountain slide under him and pinned his injured leg. His head slammed into the hard-packed earth.

He choked on wet leaves and heaved himself up, hurling off the deadweight. His vision starred with nonexistent lights, he leapt at the feralis stalking Sera.

It turned to face him, its slavering maw opened in a cry of rage.

"No," he growled back. "She's mine."

They collided with battering-ram force, his arm driven halfway down its gullet. Its teeth razored up his arm, and he stared into the bulging eye.

He cut its throat from the inside.

It fell, taking him down in a geyser of moldering leaves. Dying spasms locked its teeth on his arm just above the elbow, and he lay in the dirt, staring into the orange eye.

As the demon fury ebbed, as the pain crept into the emptiness, he knew he had won another battle, that his teshuva had taken another step on its path to redemption. In the feralis's livid eye, he stared down that hellfire path. And saw it never ended.

Half adrift from the blow, his gaze wandered beyond the feralis and fixed on a darkness among the trees: a man, cloaked in shadows not cast by the trees, and betrayed by sulfur yellow points radiating where eyeballs should have been.

A djinn-man. Come to finish them off in their moment of weakness.

Human adrenaline and demon vigor surged and stuttered in Archer's veins. Of all the times for the djinn to finally take an interest in the chores of a teshuva garbageman.

Then, just as suddenly as the figure had coalesced among the shadows, it melted back and was gone. Wet leaves glinted with the reflected yellowish lights of streetlamps.

"Archer?"

Sera's whisper brought him back with a snap. Had he seen anything at all? No djinni would pass up such an effortless opportunity to destroy one of its traitorous, repentant brethren, would it? The jolt to his skull must have stunned him, seeing evil in every puddle of darkness.

"Ferris?" She crept closer.

"Yeah. I'm alive." Hence the pain. "Just contemplating my glorious triumph."

She crouched beside him. "How's it feel?"

"Cold and wet. And tastes like blood."

She ran her hands down his arm, exploring the trap. "Don't pull. These fangs slant backward like a shark's."

"I noticed." He hesitated. "Did you notice anything? Any other demons?"

She glanced around in alarm. "More ferales? I was sort of occupied with these two."

"No. Never mind." He gritted his teeth at the acid burn of ichor while she levered open the massive jaws. He released himself in a gush of his own blood.

"Oh God." Her hands hovered over his arm where the feralis's bite had peeled skin and muscle down to the bone.

"Don't." He clamped his arm close to his chest, molding flesh into place. "The demon will take care of it."

"It certainly did," she said tartly.

"My demon," he amended as he pushed himself to his knees. She started to help him to his feet, but he shook her off.

He cast teshuva senses outward. An annihilation-class demon came factory standard with tracking skills, but no djinn scent rode the etheric winds now.

But someone had been interested enough to toss Sera's apartment. Would that djinn-man have followed her? Then why hadn't he made his move and killed them both?

After another long moment, Archer leaned down to wipe the gory axe on wet leaves. From the corner of his eye, he saw Sera do the same with the smaller knife.

"You poked it a couple times," he said.

"Just enough to burn myself on its blood."

"It didn't gut me from behind, which it would have done if you hadn't been here."

She lowered her head. "If not for me, it wouldn't have been lurking. I just wanted to visit my dad."

"A nice quiet night? A nice quiet life?" Archer folded the axe blades and collapsed the club. He held out his good hand.

She passed the knife to him, hilt first. "Wishful thinking? Worked on the malice."

"Ferales are a little harder to do away with. As for wishing your life back the way it was . . ." He spread his hand toward the downed ferales and let her draw her own conclusions.

He saw the slump of her shoulders, started to wish something himself, and stopped it cold.

"You played your part," he said at last. "Let that be consolation enough."

At the defeat in her expression, he almost reached out to her. He knew that feeling. But what solace could he offer? "Garbagemen don't ask where all the trash comes from. They just haul it away."

She eyed the splayed beast. "Looks pretty heavy."

"It's not empty yet. I disabled the corporeal shell, but it holds the demonic energy. Look at the eye, still orange." He stood over the carcass, gathering his own energy and the teshuva's. He swayed on his pierced leg. Apparently, what energy he had to gather wouldn't fill a shot glass.

Despite his earlier brush-off, she stood beside him and threaded her arm around his waist. A whiff of honeysuckle teased past the sour stench clogging his head. A surge of desire sent the last of his blood careening around his body.

"You don't have to do it alone," she murmured.

"Yes, I do." He stiffened at her touch, summoning teshuva strength against the temptation to rest on her offered shoulder. Since the malice had disappeared between them, his control had gone sketchy, as if some other carefully maintained barrier had fallen. "Your deathbed vigils might be all kum ba yah. Out here you fight alone."

"That's been your choice. But I'm right here, right now."

When had someone last fought at his side? Keeping company with destruction left no room for another. But he needed her, at least for tonight.

Wounded arm clenched against his belly, he forced himself to step away from her. "Draining a feralis is easier than a malice, once the corpus is out of action. Locked in the husk, it can't get at you."

She wrung her hands, as if remembering the malice slime. "So, remind me what I did with the malice?"

He wasn't sure, hence his hope she'd do it again. When he'd grabbed her to get the job done, he'd fallen into her inward spiral. Just as when she'd been drawn through the Veil in the last stage of her possession. If he'd managed to stop himself from tearing her clothes off this time, he had only the malice in the way to thank. They'd touched, the malice suspended between them, and then it was gone. Not just drained, but *gone*.

When he didn't answer, she crouched beside the carcass. She wiped her palms nervously, then lifted the massive head. She tilted it to one side, staring into the hellfire eye. Ichor drooled from the slack jaws and curdled the grass with a charred stink.

"When the malice got me," she said, "I was thinking the man at the bar never had a chance. The malice goaded him; he attacked. Where was hope when he needed it? Compassion? Where was peace?"

"Just as there are angels to balance the djinn, some say the horde-tenebrae are countered by smaller lights, called blessings." Pain reverberated from shoulder to thigh when he shrugged. "I've never seen one. Just more figments of wishful thinking, I think."

"Why would you think that? Why would you *want* to think that?" As she half cradled the throat-slashed feralis like some perverse pietà, her eyes gleamed, not with holy benediction, but with violet challenge.

He glared back, blood seeping from his tight-clenched fist. How could she ask why with the monstrosity still staining her hands? All her questions served only to stir up memories and trouble. He resented the memories more than the trouble.

Light-headed with exsanguination and fury, he stalked forward, lashing up his demon. He leaned down and grabbed her, to pull her away, and do the last dirty deed himself.

His blood spattered her cheek, the tear-shaped drop crimson on her pale skin. He froze, aghast at the violence in his touch, which leapt from him like embers from an inferno. He couldn't even blame the brutality on his demon, interrupted mid-ascension within him.

She faced him as boldly as she had the evils of the

dark, as fierce as when she'd rolled him across the bed in his garden while knowing the night might end with his assassin's blade, as if death and damnation held no terror for her. With all she'd been through, maybe they didn't.

So what chance was there that one battered, filthy, pissy male would faze her? With the edge of his thumb, he wiped the blood from her cheek.

The droplet fused his skin to hers for a heartbeat, slick like the sweat of passion, a hint of salt—his demon senses rousing unbidden—like the balm that had welled from her body on their joining. His breathing grew ragged.

He saw her lips part, and her wordless exhalation feathered across his palm. He wanted to follow her down to that place she conjured, where the empathy in her hazel eyes softened barren winter shadows to spring.

He yearned to gather her close, to fit those deliberately forgotten fragments back into the tattered remnants of his soul, to let her shine into his darkness and find those pieces he'd thought long lost—light, life, desire.

He leaned down, set his lips softly on hers, prelude to all he wanted, the first step that would change the world around him. The salty sting in the back of his throat tasted not of blood, but tears.

He recoiled. The yearning in him tore free, with an unvoiced cry. She fell back onto her haunches. The feralis husk rolled off her lap.

"Fucking teshuva," he whispered, staggering back from her. "No touching." Had the destroyer in him forgotten the risks of temptation? Had *he* forgotten the agony of wanting what he couldn't hold on to? As if damnation weren't bad enough without the mockery of what he'd lost thrown back in his face. "You are an innocent fool."

"And you are bumming me out." She gave the husk a halfhearted kick that waggled the lolling tongue. "Why'd you freak? I thought you were going to let me exorcise it this time."

"I didn't do anything to the feralis." It could go to hell for all he cared. She'd certainly taken him halfway there. "And I did not freak."

"But it's gone."

She was right. The feralis's eye had grayed, empty and cold as his heart. He would have thanked God, but he doubted the Almighty wanted credit for either the feralis or his heart.

He glanced at the other carcass, opening his teshuva senses for the inevitable scraps of ether. Nothing. All the demonic energy was gone. And she'd never even touched it. She'd just touched him. His blood still thrummed urgently through him, as if he'd escaped a fate in her eyes every bit as damning.

"But I didn't do anything either," she said, as if she'd heard his thoughts. "I don't think."

He certainly hadn't been thinking, lost in his pointless craving. Still, the demons were gone. What more could he want?

He told himself not to answer that question.

But her touch, his yearning, and the demons' fate seemed fatally intertwined. His mind reeled at the implication. Whatever they'd done, they'd done together—just as she accused. Now the malice and ferales were gone.

The headlights of a passing car swept over them, catching on the feralis's fogged eyes. Sera jumped away from the husk with a muffled curse.

He dredged up a smile, trying to keep the twist of his lips more toward the wry side than the bitter. "So the world goes on without us. We keep the battle in the shadows for their sake."

And maybe for his own sake too. He steeled himself against the glimpse of light in her eyes that tempted him to reach out of his darkness. Why did he have the feeling that temptation could be the end of him as surely as she had somehow banished the feralis?

Sera prowled a wary circle around the downed demons. "I read that demons are solitary hunters."

"We are. They are." An unease he couldn't pin down played along his spine. "These two must've honed in on you and found each other."

"It's nice to be wanted. By someone." Her low tone required no reply.

She didn't touch him again, but his skin ached for her, his bones yearned. His blood heated, a thousand times more scorching than his wounds.

If once some strange bond had joined possessed lovers, some wise talya had probably torn it out by the roots. Hell, he felt torn in two. He'd lived with pain a very long time, he reminded himself. But somehow, this time, it hurt worse.

He took her back to his loft. Sera kept silent as he slammed the door behind her and coded the lock.

She'd nearly gotten them killed. She thought she knew how to handle the stark reality of death. The pockmark freckles of demon spatter were healing even as she watched, but her hands still shook. So much for handling anything.

She cut a glance at Archer. In the cab, he'd called Jonah about the attack, using not particularly subtle code words such as "accident in the park" and "hazmat disposal." He'd also called Liam and tersely recapped the night's events. Without looking at her, he'd added, "She's fine, untouched. Unless I kill her."

Now he stood in the middle of the unlit room as if he'd forgotten she existed.

She hesitated to remind him. "Maybe I should stay at the league hotel. Liam said he had a room for me."

"This place has energy sinks too. You won't lure any more demons here."

That hadn't been why she suggested it. She wondered whether he emoted enough to leave a drip mark in those energy sinks. "All right. Your arm ..."

"I got it. Help yourself to some clean clothes." Without a backward glance, he left her standing there.

She waited until steam fogged the glass-block bathroom before exploring. The incongruous plantation shutters concealing the low-framed bed from the rest of the room also hid an armoire and dresser.

Keeping her gaze off the bed, she rifled through the drawers. A pair of cotton flannel pants and a T-shirt soft with wear seemed like the fabric equivalent of a consoling hug.

She cleaned up at the kitchen sink. Other than her mud-spattered jeans and faintly scarred hands, she'd escaped the evening unscathed, if she didn't count the memory of her father's screams, the sickening stench as the feralis dropped from the tree, or Archer's bleak stare as he wiped away the gore.

The last of the suds swirled down the drain, and she wished she could purge her thoughts as easily.

The shower gurgled to silence. Her heartbeat ramping up for no reason, she quickly pulled on the fresh clothes, inhaling the whiff of cedar from the too-large T-shirt. On the couch, she tucked her bare feet underneath her. She pulled a pillow onto her lap, realized it didn't make much of a shield, but held on to it anyway.

The lights in the bathroom went out. Archer appeared, a darker shadow in the doorway.

His clothing matched hers. She felt the weight of his glance, but he made no comment as he padded across the living room.

With the two blades they'd used on the ferales in hand, he pulled up a chair across from her, took up a rag and a bottle of fluid, and began to clean the axe. Head bent over his task, his wet hair glistened like the steel.

Her fingers itched to smooth the hint of damp curl. Instead, she pushed the pillow aside and took the smaller knife. She rummaged through the case at his side for a second rag.

After a long minute of silence, he said, "For a first hunt, that didn't go badly."

She raised one eyebrow.

"You didn't die," he amended. "Eventually, that might not sound like much, but for now . . ." He held his blade to the light, then wiped along its length. "So, what did you learn tonight?"

"I suck as a killer?"

"You didn't die," he reminded her. "You learned not to get slimed by malice. You learned ferales are weak at their throats, eyes, and spines, and almost impervious anywhere else. You learned how to bleed out demonic emanations."

"But I'm still not sure what happened," she interrupted. "When you grabbed me—"

As if she hadn't spoken, he continued implacably, "You learned to leave your old life alone." He raised his gaze to hers.

She said nothing.

He went back to the knife. "Once you let the demon reflexes take over, the rest is simple."

She didn't think he meant just during the fighting. She couldn't restrain a shiver—which she knew he saw, so felt obliged to explain. "You threw me the knife, and I didn't have to think. I was so angry at being frightened, I just . . ." She pressed her thumb lightly to the knife's edge, creasing her skin. "And then I was so frightened at being so angry, I couldn't . . ." Once again, the words failed her. Blood welled out of the furrow in her thumb.

Archer eased the knife from her grasp, while the tiny wound in her thumb faded to just another line bisecting the loops of her thumbprint.

She glanced at Archer's arm where the feralis's jaws had clamped like a bear trap. With a touch she told herself was cool and clinical, she lifted his hand to study the wound. The flesh was raw and tender looking but nowhere near the gruesome maiming she'd seen. She traced the black line of the *reven* where feralis teeth had slashed complicated new patterns. Violet sparked behind the stroke of her finger.

He sat unmoving, but the muscle in his forearm jumped into sharp relief.

She flushed and released him. "Sorry. I don't know why I'm still shocked by it. It's been—what?—three whole days now since I first heard of demons."

He eased enough to smile faintly. "Seems like centuries." He gave the blades a final coat of oil and returned them to the wall of weapons.

She raised her voice to carry across the room. "Has it been? For you?"

"What?" He didn't turn to look at her.

"Centuries?"

"At least." He said it so easily, she wasn't sure if he was being sardonic or truthful. Or both.

"When will it end?"

"When I am killed."

She grimaced. "Not you. The fighting. Will it end with the last malice and feralis? Will that be peace on earth?"

He shrugged, broad shoulders shedding her questions like rainwater. "We'll never know. Because it'll never happen."

"Why not?"

Finally, he turned to her, bracing his shredded arm on the weight bench. "The teshuva and djinn that cross the Veil between the realms can't exist here without our flesh to clothe them. The horde-tenebrae thrive on the wickedness done in this world, feeding on sin, spawning evil. They won't be gone until we are."

"We could teach people not to let them take hold.

That man at the bar wouldn't have wanted the malice on him if he knew he had a choice."

"He knew he was furious. He knew he had fists." Archer pushed away from the bench. "Would he have believed a fiend he couldn't see drove both fury and fists? Would believing have stopped him, or made him think he had no option but to succumb? Or would it have emboldened him?" He straightened, managing to look down on her from across the room. "And unlike you, he wouldn't have enhanced senses or speed or healing to help him, even if he wanted to resist."

She bit her lip at the criticism. "Then how do we win?"

"Who said we'd win? We fight."

"Forever?"

He let the word hang. "Until the end."

She didn't ask for a definition of end.

"Meanwhile, there's a djinn-man out there somewhere who needs a name and a face and a severe ass-whooping." He moved to the office area and flicked on the computer. "I have more of our histories and case studies in my bedroom. Make yourself at home." He gave her another long look that lingered over her borrowed clothing until the cotton seemed to wear thin. "I'll sleep on the couch tonight, and we'll move you to Niall's quarters in the morning. You'll meet Bookie, and maybe he'll have an idea what to do with you."

How he managed to banish her so completely in a room with no walls she wasn't sure.

She took a glass of water with her and sat cross-legged on the bed with a dusty-smelling manuscript in her lap. It listed those possessed around the world who'd banded together in leagues like the one headed by Liam Niall. All were men's names, she noted, tracing her finger down the roll call. She stifled a pang of loneliness. Not for herself, but for those centuries of solitary warriors. "The world goes on without us," Archer had said. Or had he just pushed it away? Not that she blamed him, considering.

Beyond the screens, she caught a glimpse of the tumbled dolls. For all his declarations of holding himself apart, he kept the league's horrible little trophies, the only adornment in the otherwise empty loft. Did he really want to be so removed?

Suddenly she wondered if the tortured, mismatched dolls represented the defeated ferales ... or the talyan themselves.

The thought made her wince. As if defending Archer's detachment, the next pages warned of rogue possessed, talyan who refused to temper their possession so the demon ran always ascendant. Despite the lurid topic, she fought the heaviness of her eyelids. When Archer finished up, she'd insist on taking the couch since she'd already caused trouble enough.

She switched to a book on fighting techniques, hoping it would keep her alive, maybe even awake.

On the page about mitigating damage from highly corrosive feralis ichor when using explosives during husk demolition, she stretched out at the foot of the bed, propped on one elbow. *Might as well get comfortable while reviewing such mayhem*, she thought.

Somewhere in the part explaining the impossibility of removing the last of the psychic stains left after draining a malice, she laid her head down on her forearm, just for a moment.

The glistening snow lay so deep, she had to jump. Each bound took her higher, skimming the moon-bright earth. Her footsteps, farther and farther apart, left dark imprints in the snow, like lonely islands in a silver sea.

She spread her arms and pointed her toes, aloft like a ballerina. Her heart pounded with delight. And fear. If she fell, her feet were not under her.

She tried not to look down, but she did. Her shadow cast a hazy violet cross on the snow.

On her back in the snow, thrashing her arms and legs, she almost frightened herself with the violent waving, but then she realized she was making snow angels. She hadn't made snow angels in forever.

She laughed, looking up at . . .

"Ferris," she whispered.

He was seated on the edge of the bed, his hip near her curled knees. "I heard you. I thought it was a nightmare."

She turned her head, knocking her nose on the book's cracked leather spine. "I fell asleep."

"Counting sheep instead of ways to eviscerate ferales?"

"With bedtime stories like yours, who needs nightmares?" She rubbed at her eyes. "I was going to tell you I'd sleep on the couch."

He stroked the back of his knuckles through her hair. "You remind me of things." His voice was a murmur, as if he hadn't meant to speak aloud. "Things I'd forgotten. How do you smell of flowers here, in the middle of winter?"

She glanced away, keenly aware of every molecule of space between them. If she pushed upright, she'd be sitting as if ready to kiss him. If she rolled the other way, onto her back . . .

"What time is it?" Distraction seemed like a good idea.

He didn't bother checking the clock or his watch. "Very late. Or very early." His gaze fixed on her. So much for distraction. "I was getting ready for bed. I heard you." His voice, already low, trailed off.

Apparently, since he'd lost his T-shirt, getting ready for bed meant getting at least half naked. The dark hair across his chest and the demon mark on his arm stood out in bold relief against his skin. At least he still had the flannel pants. She forced herself not to look, to see if anything there stood in bold relief.

"I didn't mean to bother you," she said.

"I can't stop myself from listening. I can't stop this thing between us." Violet hazed his eyes, as if he were ready for an attack. From her?

She didn't understand the depths of his agitation, but she sensed its source. At the hot musk of aroused male, her heartbeat ramped up again, and her skin tingled as if thawing after hours of playing in the snow. Jumping off a cliff might be fine in a dream, but she knew better in real life.

Didn't she?

"It was just one night." Was she trying to convince him? Or herself? "We did what we had to."

She eased up onto her elbow, a half step to scooting away from him. He tensed, eyes sparked brighter as when he'd plunged into the wood after the feralis. The tightening of his every muscle echoed in her own.

If she ran, he'd chase. If she stayed utterly still, he'd say something, probably something she didn't want to hear.

On one of the pages flattened under her hand, she'd read about taking the initiative, pressing the advantage, never letting the opposition catch his breath.

So she coiled her knees against him, threaded her fingers behind his nape, and pulled him down to her kiss.

It was doubtful this was what those stuffy old historians had meant. She shoved the books off the bed.

"Sera," he said against her mouth, "I don't think—"

"I just read, upon the twenty-first repetition, an attack sequence becomes rote muscle memory." She traced the upper line of his lip with her tongue. "Don't think."

He groaned and pulled her tight against his bare chest so she sprawled half across his lap. His body was hot enough to melt snow angels through concrete. She closed her eyes and let her head tip back so he could run his teeth up the column of her neck.

She wrapped her fingers around the iron-honed muscles of his arms and held on against the sensations threatening to send her out of her body. He'd pulled so far away after the last time, she wanted to remember his every touch, forget the chill of her father's rejection, forget the terror of the feralis fight, think only of the warmth of breath on skin.

She'd gotten the impression, for all Archer's talk of sin, that the pleasures of the flesh were few and far between.

She let her hands roam up his shoulders, reveling in the strength. The faint tremble at her touch became a shudder as her hands drifted back down his narrowing flanks to his hips.

He sank his fingers into her hair, thumbs at her temples, and almost painfully drew her upward to meet his gaze. "Sera, what are you doing?"

His voice was harsher even than his touch.

"I can draw you a diagram," she said. "Hold on. I've got a notebook here."

His eyes narrowed, searching hers. "You'd mock me now?"

She stared him down. "I would kiss you now."

His eyes widened. She knocked his grip away and set her lips hard against his. He breathed faster than he had after the fight, his hands fisted in the hem of her T-shirt. The salty musk of his arousal filled her head. She tasted him deep in her mouth.

When she rose up onto her knees, he skimmed his hands inside her shirt, grasping her waist when she rocked on the mattress. He looked up at her, fingers pressed against her hip bones, neither reeling her in nor pushing her away.

She'd seen that wary look from him before, as if he couldn't quite grasp what he wanted. He reached for her without flinching only when he wanted her to destroy a demon.

She bent over him, so that his head hovered near her breast. The pendant stone swung over him, but she wasn't interested in that particular mystery at the moment. "Touch me," she whispered in his ear as she trailed her fingers down his back. The muscles beneath her palms flexed and jumped. "That's why you came over here, isn't it?"

"You cried out."

"You told me you don't lie."

"You made a sound."

"It wasn't a nightmare."

He was silent a moment. "You laughed in your sleep. I wanted to see . . ."

The prowling huntress in her faltered. The bold talyan warrior quivered at her touch. She should have exulted at the thought. Instead, she felt as if she held something fragile in her grasp, a delicate crystal that might shiver apart.

She leaned back a fraction. His hands dropped to her hips, and though she kept her gaze on his, at the bottom of her vision she saw the sinuous lines of the *reven*.

Violet haze scudded across his eyes like eerie storm clouds.

She leaned over again and pressed her lips, gently, to his forehead. "I dreamed of flying, and of snow angels."

"Angels don't fly," he said with great seriousness. "Not in this realm."

"Maybe in their dreams too."

"Maybe." He enclosed both her hands between his big palms. He raised their clasped hands to his lips. His breath fanned over her knuckles, sending a shiver down to her knees.

When he looked up, his eyes were dark and half hooded. "I'm sorry I woke you. Go back to sleep."

The shiver went deep freeze. She slipped her hands out of his. "But—"

"I brought you through the possession, which no doubt rouses feelings of connection—"

"Couldn't have been the great sex that did that." She jumped off the bed.

"But any lasting bond could be our doom." He still sat with his hands folded penitently. "I almost got you killed tonight. I knew the feralis was hunting us, and still I was thinking about you."

About her? A treacherous warmth softened the stiffness in her spine. "No harm done. And you said together we banished the demons so thoroughly, we didn't leave any pieces."

"I don't know exactly what you—what we did, but it was more dangerous than any tenebrae I've fought."

The nascent warmth in her snuffed out. "It didn't feel dangerous. When you touched me, I knew everything bad about the malice and the ferales didn't have to be that way, didn't have to *be* at all, and then it was gone. It felt . . . right."

"You think right makes it harmless?"

She lifted her chin in challenge. "You felt it too."

His pupils constricted, lost in a sudden flare of violet, as if she'd struck some terrible blow. "If I die in battle with a demon, the stain on my soul is at least lightened. But if I take you with me . . . I am already damned, but I won't be twice damned."

"My life and my soul have nothing to do with yours." She wanted to stamp her foot, but he was already treating her like a child. "You'd fight with a man, with Zane or Ecco."

"I hunt alone. I always have."

"Which doesn't mean you always have to."

"Yes, it does." He stood. The thin flannel made it obvious he wasn't impassive to her touch, but from his expression, harder yet, she knew he'd never give in.

"Don't put me aside like you did your fiancée. You

didn't even give her a chance to accept what you'd become."

"No one should have to accept."

"No, you clearly haven't. After how many years?"

The violet deepened toward black, merging with his pupils as he roused the demon in him. "If there ever was a mated-talyan bond, it died out for a reason."

From that flat, threatening tone, she thought he was desperate to do some convincing of his own. "What bond?"

"Nothing. It's only a story in one of Bookie's old books. There's no mystical fate holding us together; just blood and demon gore."

Apparently rejecting her for personal reasons wasn't enough; he'd had to find something in the demon-ridden employee manual to make it official. "Since you're kicking me to the curb, I'll call Liam and make sure that room is available."

His hands clenched at his sides. "I said I'd take you in the morning."

"Never mind. Zane will let me in."

"Zane's too young to be your partner." The words seemed torn from him.

She frowned. "I just need his key card to open the door."

He paced a few steps. "Ecco is the strongest fighter, but he's reckless. Maybe—"

"I'll find someone." Her tone rang harsher than she'd intended, with more nuance than she really meant. She saw it hit home in the way he straightened. If only she took more pleasure in his pain. "What's the phone number to the hotel?"

He grabbed the phone, punched a button, and tossed it across the bed. She turned away, listening to the ring, so she didn't have to look at the rumpled covers and he couldn't see the bleakness she knew was in her eyes.

CHAPTER 13

She'd planned to sneak into the league hotel under cover of darkness, but Zane met her at the door and said Liam had asked for her.

The penthouse suite was quiet—with most of the talyan out demolishing demons, she supposed. A couple of the men nodded to her, but none approached. She remembered how Archer had run his hand down her back, claiming her.

At the time, she'd been too nervous to pay attention. Now she wished she'd smacked him, since he didn't have the guts to hold on to what he claimed.

Annoyed, she circled the room as she waited for Liam. She paused before a collection of black-and-white giclee prints. The stark abstracts entranced her. Desert landscapes, she thought, or close-ups of the human body leached of context, but somehow they were familiar. . . . With a jolt radiating out along her teshuva's marking, she recognized the empty, flowing lines of the demon realm.

"Compelling, aren't they?" Liam stepped up beside her. "Who'd guess a demon-ridden could have an artist's eye?"

"Slaughter would be easier without a lot of refined sensibilities."

He was silent a moment, as if contemplating who in particular might've led her to that insight. "Archer said you helped take out two ferales tonight."

Apparently Archer hadn't explained the odd circumstances. She tucked her hands inside the sleeves of her sweater, warding off the phantom sensation of Archer's fingers laced in hers. "A distraction, at least."

"Still, he seems to think you'd be more valuable in some other capacity."

She lifted one eyebrow. "Like what?"

"No idea. We don't have any purpose besides offing demons." He ran a hand over his hair. "Since we found you, our Bookkeeper has been searching our records for any modern precedent for a female talya. I've asked him to meet with us."

"It's not too late?"

"Despite what Archer says, I have to believe it's not too late to make a difference. . . . Oh, you meant too late in the evening to meet." He flashed her a boyish grin. "We're busy when the horde-tenebrae are, and since the last Veil crossing, they've been very busy."

"Which I'm told has been my fault."

"Your demon's fault, which is not quite the same as yours."

She took a last look at the prints. She should make time to meet a talya who'd found beauty in hell. "I'm glad to talk to your Bookkeeper. I've been studying the collections he sent over. Grim stuff."

"And dull. We're men of action. And woman." He inclined his head. "Which is why we bring in Bookkeepers from outside the demon-ridden. Somebody has to keep their hands clean enough to take notes."

"I suppose you can't post Bookkeeper job openings at the local coffeehouse."

"We start the search in seminaries, military colleges, and head shops."

She lifted an eyebrow. "How open-minded."

"That's the point." He gestured toward the elevator. "I've set up a room downstairs to talk."

The parlor had a warmer ambience than the penthouse, with taupe highlighted in moss green to replace the black–and-white and crimson. The man who waited there was similarly less stark than the talyan, his ruddy coloring and slight build a marked contrast to the powerful and austere warriors.

Liam waved him forward. "Sera, this is Bookie, our Bookkeeper for the last seven years. His father held the post before him."

Bookie pushed his glasses higher on his nose. "I'm excited to meet a female possessed." He peered at her, as if she might do something noteworthy right then.

She smiled. "Is Bookie your title, or should I call you by your name?"

He blinked. "Yes, it's my title. And my name."

She let it go. Everyone else was possessed; why shouldn't he be *obsessed* at least? "I'm glad to meet you too. I'm fascinated by your collation of accelerating timelines in cyclical demonic activity. Although I guess by the dates on the paper, your father worked on that report too."

He straightened. "You read that?"

"Your hypothesis that demonic disturbances are becoming more common certainly calls for investigation."

Bookie straightened. "I've been trying to get reliable figures for contact with malice and ferales, since teshuva-djinn interactions aren't feasible, but . . ." He slanted a glance at Liam.

The league leader dusted his hands. "Well, you two have a lot to talk about, and I have evil to destroy."

Bookie muttered as Liam escaped.

Sera raised an eyebrow. "Men of action don't take kindly to gathering stats?"

Bookie glared after the retreating talya, then shrugged. "It's not as if I have a peer review journal waiting for the article."

"Chicago isn't the only place with demons and talyan. Don't you share your studies with them?"

"League enclaves with supporting historians exist in many of the world's bigger cities. Wherever enough people gather, they attract the horde-tenebrae. But the leagues focus more on putting out fires than . . ."

"Than discovering the source of fire?"

He gave her a considering look. "Well, we won't change their minds anytime soon. One of the downsides of immortality."

"Stubborn, are they?" Sera tried to tell herself she didn't care.

"Also arrogant, violent, and borderline suicidal." He hesitated. "Present company excepted, I'm sure."

"I'm sure," she murmured. The way Archer had thrown off her touch as if she were poison, he'd certainly excluded her from his bad ol' boys' club.

But Bookie turned away as if embarrassed by his candor. "I'm interested in running some tests, if you're agreeable. None of the others will sit still long enough."

She was suddenly wary. "What are the tests exactly?"

The overhead light glinted off his glasses as he tipped his head back. "Nothing that will kill you."

After the immortality crack, that didn't exactly reassure her. But she wanted to make a place for herself in this new life. Not that she had a choice anymore. She'd never been content with more of the same. If she could advance this war against evil, what had happened to her might be worth something.

How much *was* a soul worth anyway?

Bookie took her downstairs. He explained how the

league had converted the old hotel to their private retreat. Past generations of talyan, she was informed, had made sound investments during their long, ascetic lives.

In the basement, the lab was a clutter of hardware, steel cabinets and glistening glass pipettes, sheaves of papers and a bottle of red wine.

He saw her roving gaze land. "Would you like a glass?"

"Are the tests going to be that bad?"

"Ironically, considering that intoxication lends itself to many sins, I've never seen a talya drunk. The demon-quickened metabolism never falls behind."

Again, that didn't exactly answer her question. But when he patted an exam table, she hopped up. He photographed her eyes and showed her the pictures of her enlarged irises. Then he showed her a second set.

"Under ultraviolet," he said. "Flowers must look beautiful to you when the demon is ascendant, like they do to a butterfly."

"I haven't seen any flowers since my possession." The last flowers she'd seen had been in Archer's greenhouse. And she'd been otherwise occupied.

She wrenched her wayward thoughts back as Bookie continued. "It's an endless source of amazement to me, all the ways demonic energy shows itself in our realm, right down to the changed structure of your bodily tissues."

"There are other changes too," she murmured.

He cocked his head, then turned away to gather the materials for a blood draw. "Yes. The immortality, the aptitude for violence."

She'd meant the weary, wary eyes, the hesitation at every touch, the loss of faith in hope itself. But she supposed those didn't show up in blood work.

"Liam thought you might have some insight into why this demon chose me, a woman, and what that might mean . . . ," she said, hesitating, then finished, "to the league, to the war between good and evil. And repentant evil, I guess."

He didn't look up from threading a large-bore needle. "I couldn't really say. I'm little more than a secretary around here. Roll up your sleeve."

She dragged her sweater back. "Liam values your opinion. And Archer also suggested I talk to you."

"Archer? He's one of the few who sends me his demon depletion counts with any regularity, although he's always stingy on the details."

"Maybe he's not the sort to brag." She managed not to snort since then she'd have to explain herself.

Bookie pressed the needle against her skin. "That's right, you've fought with him. Twice."

More than that. Of course, Bookie was talking only about demons. She grimaced as he drove the needle in.

"I'll be glad to share my experiences," she told him in some desperation. She needed guidance here.

He huffed out an aggrieved sigh. "Then I'll share my thoughts. Mostly that I don't have any. No idea why the demon chose you. No idea what you will offer the never-ending battle. If I knew ... maybe I'd finally make the talyan pay attention."

In silence, they watched her blood pour into the syringe.

"I want to get a biopsy of muscle tissue too," he said at last. "Take off your sweater." She hesitated, but he turned away to stow the syringe, saying, "I'd give you a local anesthetic, but the demon would neutralize it as fast as the alcohol. You'll just have to tough it out this time."

This time, right. Because so far possession had been such a cakewalk. She stripped off her sweater, sitting in just Archer's T-shirt.

Bookie turned back with an even larger needle—and froze, his gaze fixed on her chest.

Somehow, she didn't think the unflappable historian

acted this way around Ecco's chest. "Something wrong?" Annoyance flickered through her, and the room wavered toward a black-light tinge.

She fought back the rise of irritation since demonic intervention seemed somewhat extreme. Until Bookie reached out to touch her. She caught his wrist, arresting the stereoscopic possibilities where he touched her, and then she broke his arm.

The possibilities collapsed into one when he finally looked into her eyes. He went limp. "I don't—"

"Definitely don't." She forced herself to release him.

"That stone. I've never seen another—" He drew back, rubbing his wrist. "Where did you get it?"

She narrowed her eyes, demon-fueled suspicion warring with her customary yearning for answers. "It came with the teshuva. Why?"

"It's dangerous. You shouldn't go waving it around."

She hadn't been waving it. "What is it?"

"Desolator numinis." He clutched the biopsy needle. "A djinn weapon."

The stone burned icily against her skin. "Djinn? Why do I have it?"

His gaze shifted away.

"I am not evil," she said softly.

"Good and evil are such subjective terms."

She couldn't help herself. She laughed.

Bookie didn't. "The league would laugh at me too. Right before they tore you to pieces as a djinn traitor."

That shut her up. "But I don't even know what it is."

"Most talyan don't." He scowled as if he resented the need to enlighten her. "It's in our league records, from long ago, if they'd read. The stone is fluorspar, common in old hydrothermal vents. Lots of occlusions in this sample, more like the material used in fluxes than the refined stuff used in making glass."

"Demons wear jewelry made from ancient volcanic

events. Explains why people thought hell was in the bowels of the earth."

He gave her an approving nod. "Underground was the closest our ancestors could come to envisioning the tenebraeternum, the eternal shadow that is the demon-realm."

She remembered what Archer had said. "So it's ugly, yes, but that doesn't make it evil."

"When saturated in your demonic emanations, it undergoes an etheric mutation. It becomes a *desolator numinis*, a soul cleaver, a metaphysical solvent that dissolves the link between body and soul."

Okay, that was definitely evil. She would have ripped the pendant from around her neck, but she didn't want to touch it. "Should I tell . . . ?" Whom? Archer had already separated himself as far as he could from her. No cleaver necessary.

"What? Tell them to read the archives they've had for the past two thousand years?" Bookie let out a long-suffering sigh. "Let me find out what this means first." He hesitated. "Do you want me to keep it here?"

She grasped the stone, cold and oily slick. In her years of work, she'd presided over a great many spirits set free from failed flesh. To cut a soul from the still-living body . . . She swallowed back a flash of sick horror. "No. I understand you owe your loyalty to the league, but will you come to me first?"

He nodded. "Meanwhile, let's get that biopsy done."

His touch stayed as professional as any she'd endured during her surgeries and therapy, but she felt the weight of his gaze on the stone.

"Speaking of long-ago stories," she said, "Archer mentioned a—a mated-talyan bond."

He smoothly extracted a core of her flesh. "Bond? Hmm, yes, it's around here somewhere. Bookkeeper archives have more old stories than anyone can remember."

She tried to quell the twinge of disappointment that Bookie didn't think it was important either. Why was she so eager to find yet another place where her life had become not her own? Archer had told her the demon dwelled in the emptiness of the talyan soul. Apparently there wasn't room for anything else these days.

Bookie added the biopsy to his rack of samples, more bits of her lost to this change. "I have enough here. I'll get back to you on the rest."

Clearly dismissed, she rode the elevator back up-stairs. At least Bookie must think she wasn't an imme-diate threat if he let her walk out. Unless he was even now calling the firing squad. She rubbed her arms at a chill she hadn't noticed before, wincing when her hand scraped the needle hole.

He hadn't even offered her a bandage. Stupid complaint, since the wound would heal before she looked at it again. She closed her eyes, trying to sum-mon the memory of a motherly kiss and unnecessary Band-Aid.

To get there, though, she had to claw past the last vi-sion of her mother and the black lapping water. Had her mother's soul floated out in that last moment? And where had it gone? She knew what her father's religion would say. She sighed and opened her eyes with the el-evator doors.

Without the large restless men, command central al-most echoed with emptiness. She stepped out onto the balcony. The wind seemed colder, the night blacker, her spirit lower than a couple of vials of missing blood could justify.

She leaned over the railing, remembering her dream of flight. If she launched off the balcony, she wouldn't be making snow angels; she'd be making a mess, a mess she doubted even the demon could clean up.

Could possession have saved her mother? Certainly the demon of depression that led to her fatal choice could have predisposed her to accept a teshuva's alternative, the same as Archer.

Sera tightened her grip on the rail. Would she have wished this fate on her soft-eyed mother? In her fury and confusion after her mother's death, she'd told her father she would never set foot in his church again, not when his faith consigned suicides to hell. He'd accepted her decision, always thinking, she knew, that she would relent.

Relent. Repent. She'd believed in her father's sermons just as she'd believed her mother could love her family enough to get out of bed, even on the bad days. Once the questions started, they didn't stop.

Now she was finally going to get some answers on the really big questions of death, salvation, the fate of innocence. She touched the pendant. Maybe even know the shape and heft of a soul.

She rolled back her sleeve. Tiny knives of wind pricked her skin, but the hole in her arm was gone, except for the ache.

She hoped her answers wouldn't prove as ephemeral.

He moved through the night, painting himself with the psychic screams of drained malice, swallowing down his own screams. Unraveled ether curled in his wake like a dread banner.

Even humans who considered themselves dangerous, who eyed him from their own gloom, melted away when he passed. Only the ferales hunted him, and they hunted with vengeance in their gleaming rust eyes.

Somewhere beyond the endless waves of evil, he sensed a presence, darker yet, that he could not reach, though he hacked his way through demon after demon. He slogged through the destruction of his own making until caked ichor welded the blades to his hands. But the darkness casting the deepest shadows eluded him with a whisper of mocking laughter that even the howls of the ferales could not disguise.

Dawn came. Washed of hue like a faded malice eye, the sun glinted a moment as it rose above the lake horizon. Then a bank of gray clouds swallowed it.

Still, that momentary gleam diverted the rage in him. He walked out onto the pier and stripped off his gore-spattered clothes.

He stared impassively at the ichor dried into the creases of his hands. Then he leapt, letting the demon-powered shove of his thighs thrust him beyond the boulders at the base of the pier.

He was flying.

Then falling. The freezing water shocked through him, jolting his heart as if it hadn't been beating before. He flailed through the slap of wind-pushed waves, back toward shore.

Free of tenebrae stench and scum and sting, Archer hauled himself up onto the rocks. He huddled for a moment beside his filthy clothes, wracked with shivers.

A jogger and her dog passed above him on the sidewalk. The dog caught his scent, yelped, and bolted ahead, the oblivious jogger swearing and staggering to keep up.

He held his breath as he donned his clothes again. His cleaning service was going to double their fees again. Or maybe this time they'd just lock the doors when they saw him. He wouldn't blame them.

He'd been drawn, against his will, to stand outside the hotel. He'd looked up and seen the golden beacon of her hair.

His heart stopped then, as he watched her lean dangerously over the void. He would catch her; that's why he had come, why he'd been drawn back, why he'd been put on this earth for so many years with a strength he used only for annihilation. . . . Then she pulled back out of view, never noticing him so many stories below her.

He went out to destroy.

That, he reminded himself, was truly why he was here.

He trudged back to the sidewalk. He wouldn't ask any cab to pick him up, and he wasn't in the mood to call Zane for a ride. The league hotel was closer than his loft, and he kept a change of clothes there.

So despite his best intentions, he found his weary steps turning toward the one place he'd decided was off-limits.

He knew the league had been out in force the night before, having encountered other lingering shreds of etheric energy. Only Haji, a closemouthed talya whose blinding speed with the enormous curved blade did his boasting for him, walked the otherwise quiet halls on the residence floor.

They nodded as they crossed paths. Archer turned at his private room, fumbling for his key. Then he hesitated.

He glanced over his shoulder. Haji had disappeared into the elevator. He glanced in the other direction down the hall.

He closed his eyes. His enhanced senses, battered and raw as his flesh, prickled.

When he opened his eyes, he was standing in front of a door not his own. He knocked.

He stood there, hearing nothing but the shush of blood through his veins. He swayed a little on his feet, half asleep. Finally, the door opened.

"You weren't going to answer," he said.

"My first reaction." Sera blocked the entrance with one arm braced across the opening, her stance forced casual. "Was that the right one?"

"Probably."

"I didn't think you'd leave."

"Probably not." He studied her through heavy-lidded eyes. From her soft yoga togs, he couldn't tell if she'd just gotten up or was getting ready for bed. His pulse kicked up a notch, and he stopped himself from thinking any more about her bed. "Can I come in?"

"I suppose we don't need more gossip with you standing outside my bedroom door."

"Technically, it's a suite, not just a bedroom. So this could be league business. And technically, manly warriors don't gossip; they relay information."

She stepped back. "Just so the information they're relaying is not that you're fucking me."

He winced as he stepped inside. The outer room looked hotel generic except for a blanket thrown over the couch beside a haphazard pile of books. "I came to apologize for that."

"For not fucking me?"

"Can you not," he said with great dignity, "use that word now."

She raised her eyebrow. "Squeamish?"

He raised his arms, mutely displaying the spatters and stains.

She sighed. "Fine. Apology accepted. Go take a bath."

Images kaleidoscoped through his mind, raising more than his pulse this time. "I am out of practice with relations between men and women. I didn't mean to hurt you."

"Our relations were fine. Twice fine, as I recall. I wasn't hurt."

He managed not to grit his teeth. "I didn't mean physically."

She rubbed her forehead. "When I accepted your apology, that meant we don't have to talk about it anymore. I know office romances never work out."

He frowned. "Since when does evil keep office hours?"

She waved her hand dismissively. "Naïve young apprentice falls for sexy older mentor. Seduces him. Ruins his chance for tenure. Sacrifices her chance to learn who she is on her own."

Despite the sexy-mentor remark, he was regretting the impulse that led him here. "You wouldn't have survived the possession without me. And I'm no league sycophant."

She crossed her arms, her expression blank as any battle-trained talya. "Right. That would be just a little too much like a relationship."

He backed toward the door. "I should go. I wanted you to know that Lenore, my fiancée, would not have wanted me back."

She let her arms fall slack at her sides. "You can't know that. You didn't see her again."

Sera was nothing like Lenore. Lenore had been a vivacious brunette who'd made clear that while she might marry a well-to-do farmer's son, she would never pluck her own chickens. At the time, his going off to war had been terribly romantic to both of them.

He just shook his head and caught a flicker of emotion as Sera's eyebrows drew together. Mostly bewilderment, he decided, recognizing the uncertainty he felt himself.

"You run like storm clouds," she murmured. "Sometimes I see the light hidden behind, but mostly you freeze everyone out. Does winter ever end with you?"

His face felt encased in ice. "Not so far."

She shook her head. "This isn't why I let you in." She lifted the pendant hanging around her neck. "I wanted to tell you, Bookie identified it. The stone is a weapon. A soul cleaver."

"Never heard of such a thing." He'd had his nose against it, with his mouth on her nipple. He'd been cleaved, all right, of his instinct for self-preservation. Heat washed through him, and he struggled to focus on the stone, not the enticing curves behind it.

"You wouldn't know it. It's djinn."

That focused him.

She lifted her chin with a hint of desperate bravado. "Aren't you even happier you rejected me last night?"

He fixed his gaze on the pendant and stepped closer. She stood unresisting as he cupped his hand behind hers, the gray stone suspended in their nested hands.

"Bookie thinks it's dangerous," she murmured. "Maybe the djinn-man knows I should be playing on his team."

"*We* are dangerous. But you aren't djinn-ridden."

She glanced up at him, uneasy hazel eyes glinting with demon light, green and brown and violet in a mesmerizing swirl. "After you saw the *reven* on me, you said you weren't sure."

"I am now." He overrode the question forming on her lips. "If you worry, your demon is teshuva. You think a djinni would choose someone who frets about being evil? If half the wickedness in the world arises from not caring, the other half definitely comes from not questioning."

"Oh, I have questions," she said fervently. "How about some answers finally? What should I do with it?"

"Bookie had no suggestions?"

She hesitated. "Not really. Other than not becoming a traitor."

Archer tightened his grasp. The stone stayed cold, but her skin warmed under his. "Maybe the difference between teshuva and djinn is not so clear-cut as we'd like to believe. More a continuum."

"You're saying one wrong step and I could slip over to the dark side?"

"I'm saying maybe the shadows are relative." In some strange way, the thought was a relief. It left room for improvement, for options.

For hope.

He let a touch of Southern cadence soften his words. "If ever I turned away from you, Sera Littlejohn, I'd do so not in hatred, but because I'd want no one else at my back."

The curve of her collarbone brushed his fingers as she slowly exhaled. The innocent contact pained him. He released the stone, and with it her hand.

"Thank you for that," she said softly.

"Thank you for forgiving me for last night."

"I didn't go quite that far." She tucked the stone under her sweater, and he sighed to himself. "I'm no saint to offer forgiveness."

"No saint. Demon-ridden. And demons don't lay blame for anything. It's the other side that withholds absolution."

"Since we're both demon-ridden," she said, "maybe we should just let it go already."

He inclined his head. "The naïve apprentice surpasses the master."

"I said mentor," she reminded him. "Not master."

He smiled. "My mistake."

"You won't make it again. Zane is teaching my first lesson in fighting this afternoon."

He tried to look solemn. "I shall be duly afraid."

She narrowed her eyes. "Weren't you leaving?"

He bowed and left.

Despite years of sporadic residence, his room was barer than hers. He imagined the tart comment on her lips and fell into bed, the stench of destruction lost in the lingering perfume of honeysuckle.

Archer woke hours later, showered, and e-mailed his night's counts to Bookie, then headed down to the kitchen where Niall stocked a gourmet larder, though the copper-bottomed cookware shone from lack of use.

There'd been a lot of broken dishes in Sera's apartment. He wondered if he had the cojones to ask her if she actually knew how to cook.

Maybe if she hadn't joined Zane's fight club yet. He grimaced and poured himself a glass of organic orange juice.

Niall had once tried to engage him on the topic of sustainable agriculture, but Archer had looked him hard in the eye and reminded him he wasn't a farmer anymore. That shut Niall up, though it hadn't stopped his sighs at the mountains of empty wrappers of decidedly nonorganic doughnuts, nachos, and things that could be microwaved in his otherwise-pristine kitchen.

Archer settled at the counter just as Ecco sauntered in, rubbing the back of his neck. The talya grunted something unintelligible. Archer nodded coolly.

Ecco grabbed the juice from the fridge and sat at the far end of the bar. He took a swig from the carton.

Archer raised one eyebrow. "We have glasses."

Ecco swallowed another deep draft. "I'm going to drink it all. Why bother?"

"Because a feralis wouldn't."

Ecco stared at him.

Archer sighed and elaborated. "Because we're civilized human beings."

Ecco laughed. "I saw the laundry you left for pickup. You had to double-bag it. Obviously you spent a very civilized night." Suspicion brightened his eyes. "After you peeled that veneer a little too close to the bone, did you come home and put that boner to good use? Did our sweet new talya make you feel like a gentleman again?"

Archer put his glass down gently—or gently was his intent. The glass shattered. Shards pointed up from the circular base like a screaming malice mouth.

"Never," he said softly. And he did speak softly, though the annihilation-class harmonics raised shivers in the broken glass so the jagged teeth sang discordantly. "Never speak of her again."

Ecco sat back. "That'll be tough. She's part of the league now."

Archer reined in his cold fury. "Then treat her with respect, as you would any of us."

"Do I respect any of you? But anyway, she's not like us." Ecco's expression clouded. "Everything's changing. A female possessed. Ferales hunt in packs now. Malice leaving the shadows. I smell djinn on every quarter of the winds, and it drives me mad. Are we truly losing this war?"

"At least no one will make you use a clean glass."

Ecco glared. "You go out as furious as any of us. More. So quit pretending you don't care."

"I've lost wars before. It's not as hard as you think."

Ecco crumpled the OJ carton and pitched it. The container bounced off the wall into the recycle bin. "You call us garbagemen, right? Hard to charge into the apocalypse when you're hip deep in your own trash."

He rose and sauntered toward the door.

Archer lifted a hand to halt him. He'd never thought of the brutish Ecco as prescient or even particularly lucid, but the talya's conviction struck him hard. "I've seen you at least knee-deep in ferales guts, and you didn't use the word 'apocalypse' then."

"Knee-deep? Oh yeah, I remember that. Good times." Ecco shook his head. "This is different."

Archer let him go. Interrogating Ecco worked no better than asking a woolly caterpillar how it knew to grow a woollier coat when the coming winter would be harsh. He grimaced at the homespun analogy that came so easily to his mind after years of denial. Yet another change.

He'd talk to Bookie about the stone, about Sera, about the never-ending battle that seemed balanced at a turning point. And on his way to the lab, maybe he'd stop by the ballroom and contemplate the source of Ecco's unease.

CHAPTER 14

In the hotel ballroom, Sera eyed a pair of fencing foils crossed on the wall. "I wouldn't want to face even a malice with just those."

"Once upon a time, those were the weapon of choice," Zane said. "They say ferales weren't so large as today."

Sera blinked in the misty daylight bouncing off the wall of mirrors. "Demons evolve? Fascinating."

"Before my time. I've only seen them big and scary as shit."

"I'd still rather have this." She walked down to the machine gun display. "Doesn't quite go with the theme of the room, but feels more reassuring."

"The theme of the room is 'Save your ass.'" Zane grinned. "The league teaches combat skills from the martial arts, swordsmanship and marksmanship, wrestling and tumbling. But possession gives you all the raw fundamentals of gutter fighting."

Sera wrinkled her nose. "Gutter fighting?"

"Anything goes and there are no style points, because in the world of demon destruction—Hey, what's that?"

From the corner of her eye, she saw him swing a closed fist. Her pulse ramped into overdrive, and her heart picked up a strange syncopated beat, as if assimilating another rhythm. His fist seemed to slow, trailing an afterimage.

She threw up her elbow and deflected the blow, then spun on the ball of her foot, put herself behind him, and shoved him away. "What are you doing?"

"Testing." He rubbed at his forearm. "You pass."

She scowled. "No more pop quizzes."

He turned her toward the mirror, urging her with a smile when she resisted. "Did you feel the demon ascend?"

She stared into her own violet-flecked eyes. "Maybe."

"You'll learn to call on it, to use the power of evil for good." He brushed one fist over the ragged hem of his cutoff sweats. The *reven* below his knee was a simple geometric wave—it lacked the intricacies of her mark or the raw boldness of Archer's. "Sometimes, you won't want to turn it off. It's just easier to let the teshuva run rampant."

She shifted uneasily. "Sounds a little too much like the kind of demons the preachers warn against." She tried not to remember the sound of her father's cry—anger, fear, and hatred like a writhing ball of biblical serpents.

"No doubt. Let's try some moves. The teshuva may win the night, but training can save you some flesh and scars."

When she'd contemplated taking Betsy's self-defense class, she's never imagined needing it to slay demons. Probably that went without saying. She'd thought it would build strength and confidence, be a good workout. Now, she had all the strength she could need and had lost confidence in anything she ever knew. At least it was still a good workout.

She panted through a third cycle of the stylized routine. "Any reason the demon couldn't give me buns of steel along with immortality?"

Zane ogled. "Why mess with perfection?"

She rolled her eyes back. "You know what I mean."

"You're still human, mostly. And your life isn't in danger, so the demon stays latent." He drummed his fingers against his thigh. "Maybe it's not supposed to be too easy."

She dropped into a lunge and tried not to topple over. "Trust me, it's not."

"I mean redemption. Doing the wrong thing seems easier."

"Stagnation and decay are inevitable." She slowed to let the routine seep into her muscles. "Entropy is the fate of the universe."

Zane scowled. "Bummer."

"All else being equal," she amended. "Our presence infuses fresh energy into the system."

"But we can never give up or rest, or the other side—chaos—wins." He stared down. "We'll never win."

"The hardest moment in my old job with hospice patients was accepting the moment there was nothing left to do."

"Then they died," he reminded her. "We don't do that. Not easily, anyway."

"Point being," she said with exaggerated patience, "I had to be satisfied with just being present, that being there was all I was meant to do, and it was enough."

He glanced up. "And were you satisfied?"

She wondered when she'd decided that her old job was just that—old, in the past. And that it hadn't really been enough. She wrinkled her nose. "At least you get to kick the ass of the things that annoy you."

"Now so do you." He raised his fists. "Let's fight."

"Enough."

The voice from above brought them up short. In one of the balconies overlooking the ballroom floor, Sera caught a glimpse of a darker shape.

"Archer." Zane tipped his head back with a ready smile. "What do you think?"

To her disgust, she found herself holding her breath to hear the answer.

"She drops her guard on left-side attacks." Archer stepped to the front of the balcony. The weak sunlight left shadows to curl down his arms into the demon mark.

He jumped over the balcony railing and, before Sera could scream, had dropped the two stories into a neat crouch a few steps away.

"Don't try that at home, kiddies," Zane muttered. "Not unless you can call on your teshuva at will."

"Don't ever do that again," Sera said, much louder. She wanted to yell over the pounding of her heart in her ears. "You scared the life out of me."

Archer lifted one eyebrow. "The demon won't let you go that easily."

Then he attacked.

Silent and so swift she didn't see him move, much less catch the afterimage. He pinned her right hand behind her back. He didn't guide or suggest. He just held her tight.

Her skin tingled at his touch, her muscles wanted to yield before his greater strength. Like an inexorable time-lapse tide, desire lapped over her. Only fury at her own lack of self-control kept her afloat on the relentless flow of craving.

She pivoted on the ball of her foot, not fast or strong enough to break his grip. But she caught a glimpse of the violet sheen in his eyes.

Oh, *now* he wanted to play for keeps. And how pathetically needy was she to soften just because he'd said a few nice words about how she probably wasn't unutterably evil?

She feinted right again, since he expected it. When he started to follow, she wrenched left. She ignored the grinding pop in her right shoulder as she aimed her left elbow for his temple.

He ducked to avoid the blow and she was free. She danced away a step, then pounced.

Let him make all the snide comments he wanted about her weak left side. Her only desire was to throttle him with both hands. But her right arm wouldn't move.

He grabbed her left wrist. "Hold, Sera."

"Oh sure, stop the fight when you're losing. Again." He'd walked away quick enough last time.

His lips twisted, amusement or annoyance, she wasn't sure. "Your shoulder."

As soon as he spoke, the radiating pain made her gasp. She glanced down at the unnatural wrench of her arm.

"Out of joint," Zane said. "You got her?"

"Wait," she said.

Archer reeled her in. Zane took her elbow in one hand and held her upper arm with the other. "Take a deep breath and let it out while I count down. Three. Two . . ."

In one steady pull, he slid her shoulder back into place.

She yelped and rocketed away. Her flight carried her halfway across the room. Her gaze locked on the mounted machine gun a long moment before she turned to glare at the men.

"Now, Sera." Zane held up both hands.

She rubbed her shoulder. "Don't even."

Zane slanted a glance at Archer. "We could've worked on the left side tomorrow."

"And if she met another feralis tonight? I tell you, she encounters them with unnerving frequency."

She bristled. "I've walked away fine from every en-counter. Except when I'm fighting you."

She caught a glimpse of regret in the half-mast of his dark eyes before he turned back to Zane. "Make her work both sides every time. No sense setting her up for failure."

"Standing right here." She waved. "And not deaf."

"Just a newbie on the fight scene," Zane said soothingly.

She scowled. "Not so new. One malice dispatch and three feralis assists."

Archer rolled his eyes. "And learning fast."

"You're not the only teacher around," she shot back.

"But I'll be one of them." He made it sound like a threat.

Zane brightened. "You're sticking close for a while? Jonah said I should ask you for some pointers."

"Are you sure you don't need to get back to the bat cave?" Sera muttered.

Archer didn't even glance in her direction. "I want to go through some archives."

Zane pursed his lips. "Those old things? Looking for something in particular?"

Archer shrugged.

Sera stifled her own spurt of curiosity. Whatever he did was his business. He'd made that clear enough. "Ready to try again, Zane? I think I'm starting to feel my demon ascend."

Archer shook his head. "You need a chance to heal. You and I will go a round tonight." Before she could protest, he said to Zane, "Shall we spar while I wait for Bookie?"

Zane's face lit up. She figured as playmates went, she fell somewhere below frogs and mud pies when the big boys showed up. With a huff, she turned to go.

"Sera." A rueful note in Archer's voice stopped her. "I didn't mean to hurt you. I should've known you wouldn't accept the demonstration meekly."

She raised one eyebrow. "Thanks."

He frowned. "That wasn't a compliment."

"Wasn't much of an apology either."

His scowl deepened. "I wasn't apologizing. I told you before I'd do what it takes to keep you alive."

He'd walked away, saying she'd be better off without him. And he'd really meant he'd be better off without her. Oh, but he did admit he regretted it. Too damn bad—for both of them.

"Then I'll return the favor. Zane, when Archer attacks, he overcommits and goes too far. So long as he's faster and stronger, his strategy wins. But he holds nothing back for the next step. I suppose an annihilation-class demon doesn't think it needs a next step, what with the annihilation and all." Archer's half-lidded stare weighed on her. "Maybe you can help him with that."

Zane nodded eagerly. "I'll see what I can do."

She contemplated sneaking up to the balcony to watch. But she doubted Zane was the fighter to adjust that Archer attitude. And she knew he'd know she was up there. She didn't want to guess what motivation he'd ascribe to her staying.

She wasn't sure she knew herself.

The subtle shift of air when he leaned toward her as she walked past all but drew sparks along her skin and shivered down the marking over her spine and thighs.

Maybe the demon wanted that rematch now. Unresolved tension settled deep, making her bones itch.

She paced in the lobby, staring out at the hazy daylight, unwilling to do anything stupid, such as make herself a target, just because she feared she would jump her drill instructor's bones—and not in the approved gutter-fighting sense.

Still, hours remained before the deeper dangers of night. What was the worst that could happen? Despite the gruesome answers that kaleidoscoped through her mind, the twisting inside her drove her outside.

The chill sunk into her core and lulled the edgy demon. Or maybe it was just distance from Archer. When a sharp rumble attracted her attention, she hopped the next train to wherever.

The city flashed by—like her life lately, zipping past

at half-blurred speed. She'd been possessed by a demon, slept with a man who should've been dead, been rejected as a bad bet by a should've-been-dead man possessed by a demon. . . . No, that was unfair. Rejection implied far more emotional connection than he allowed.

She'd had rejection enough to last a lifetime the day her mother left. Mom coming back had only sealed the deal. Her therapy studies had convinced her, intellectually, her mother's abandonment had nothing to do with her. But that didn't change the fact she'd been left alone to care for four angry brothers and a devastated father.

And then her mother had returned. In a broken whisper barely louder than the car engine, she'd told how the voices in her head had driven her away, how they were driving her now thirteen-year-old daughter in tow, toward the river. Her cry had risen, in counterpoint to the straining engine as they roared up the bridge. "Now they won't get us," she'd screamed, just as the car smashed the concrete railing into gray dust.

Sera steeled herself against the memory. She was just brooding because her father, through no fault of his own, and Archer, definitely to be faulted, had each come to the same conclusion about her: Not worth holding on to.

At least Mom had wanted her around, at the end.

Her own wallowing drove her out of her seat. When the train doors opened, she followed the wave of exiting commuters.

The wave broke around a thin man in the center of the platform. Only the thatch of his muddy brown hair was visible as he hunched over, shaking a glass vial urgently over his hand, though nothing came out.

"Ah, it hurts again," he murmured. "It hurts."

Sera, carried past him by the crowd, turned at the chiming tinkle of breaking glass. The man stood in a pool of shards, his body slumped, as if he'd dropped something precious, but he didn't bend down to retrieve any pieces.

She frowned, remembering the kids at the dance club, popping pills. No wonder Betsy was complaining about the drug's potency if people jonesed this bad.

She swung around a cement column, avoiding the last commuters, but when she took a few steps back along her path, the man was gone. Only the glittering circle of glass remained.

She looked in all directions. A wind swept past, ruffling posters taped to the column. Her gaze locked on the glossy neon blue of one flyer.

Tent revival. Faith healing.

She almost laughed. See what thinking of a preacher father and demon-ridden lover predisposed the eye to notice? If only she could've taken the poor addict.

She started back toward the platform, then stopped. She considered the street name of the train stop and returned to the flyer. The revival was only a few blocks up.

No other place to be, she reminded herself.

Revival conjured up images of billowing white canvas and a balmy Southern afternoon. Instead, she found a church of concrete blocks that seemed grayer in the Chicago wind. She joined the straggling line of people entering the building.

An usher gestured her down an empty aisle in one of the dozen semicircles of folding chairs. "I pray you find what you are seeking tonight."

She ignored the handbills—all invitations to join the church—and watched the small choir file haphazardly onto the stage. They opened with a hymn just out of tune enough to make her wince. A faint nimbus of light glowed around the stage lights, and she blinked. The choir wasn't so off-key that it brought tears to her eyes. But the halo remained.

A flicker of awareness rose in her. She knew anyone looking would see her eyes glinting violet.

She edged forward on her seat. Was a demon sneaking in? Besides hers, of course. She scanned the room. The spotlights left no shadows for even a scrawny malice to hide.

The choir shifted into a processional. A man stepped toward the stage, his silver-tinted hair reflecting the lights, but Sera's gaze arrowed to the short, red-haired woman in practical flats behind him.

Her head was bowed, but when she glanced up to take the stairs, her eyes glinted an otherworldly gold.

Sera eased back, her heart knocking counterpoint to the thud of footsteps on the stage. The choir hit a more or less high note on "Yahweh" just as realization hit her.

"An angel." If the toughest part of angelic possession was suffering through tone-deaf singers, she wondered whether she could still trade up.

The silver-haired preacher launched into a sermon on the nearness of heaven.

"Closer than he knows," she muttered. "Unfortunately, so's the other side."

The crowd stilled when he lowered the microphone and let his gaze roam the room. Slowly, he lifted the mike. "Someone is hurting, and no aspirin out of the bathroom cabinet, no solvo out of the alleys is going to cure it. Let the Spirit in. Who is hurting here?"

An older woman stood with a slight wobble, and Sera almost heard the grinding pain of hips gone bad. Two ushers flanked the woman's progress toward the preacher, who stood with one hand outstretched. As the woman stepped up to the stage, her forehead connected with his hand. The choir burst into song. The woman fell backward into the ushers' arms.

Sera squinted against the aura that blazed up, not around the preacher, but off to one side.

The redhead stood, hands clasped. Around her, fragile, scintillating whorls of gold sparked and glowed. The otherworldly light expanded, like a blown bubble. The aura engulfed the first row of seats, then the next, spreading toward Sera.

She stood, uncertain how angelic energy would interact with the demon. She didn't think it would leap out of her chest like some horror-movie alien. Neither did she particularly want to test her theory.

"Are you hurting?" The preacher pointed at her. "Come forward and receive the Spirit."

Hadn't she learned anything by falling for the demon's promise to answer all her questions? She'd been folded into a deeper layer of mysteries, only to find another, still-deeper stratum beyond that.

She stepped into the aisle. Apparently she hadn't learned a damn thing. She walked through the ring of angelic light, hand over her chest. Just in case.

The redhead swayed. Did she sense a disturbance in the force? Sera wondered wryly.

The preacher smiled, capped teeth almost as big as a feralis's, if not quite so scary. "My dear, does your heart pain you?"

An usher thrust a second microphone at her.

"What?" She dropped her hand. "No. It's my . . ." Actually, the demon had done a lovely job. Even the dull ache in her shoulder was mostly gone. "It's my soul, I suppose."

The red-haired woman lifted her head. Her eyes shone gold.

Suddenly, tempting her to a game of possessed chicken—whose otherworldly passenger would flinch first?—seemed colossally stupid. Could she tell Sera carried a teshuva and not a djinni? Would it matter to her possessing angel?

"Isn't it always the soul?" The preacher beamed. "Come closer, child."

She realized she'd taken a half step back. Maybe her demon was trying to tell her something—or was it a lingering, childhood resentment of the God who'd taken her father's time, yet hadn't saved her mother?

She shook off her uncertainty and stepped forward. His hand touched her forehead. She couldn't help herself; she closed her eyes.

And staggered back as the choir launched into another bombastic hymn, the bass cabinets under the stage thudding in her chest.

"Be healed," the preacher cried, "of all that afflicts you."

Since she didn't want to add ruptured eardrums to the list, she reeled away. But not before she'd looked hard into the blank, gold eyes of the angel-ridden woman.

A few-dozen people advanced up the aisle. Sera threaded between them out the back door to cool her head, which spun with possibilities.

The clouds had consumed the last of the day's sun. In the charcoal light, she rubbed her eyes, as if she could smear away the violet tint she knew was there.

The revival carried on into the night. Finally, the crowd trickled out, all smiles and eyes reddened with human tears. Sera slipped back inside.

The angel woman stood next to the preacher. Gold light still glimmered, now closer around her, as if the evening's work had sapped her. But when he put an arm around her and kissed her forehead, the glow brightened.

A call from the other side of the stage drew him away, and the woman looked up to meet Sera's gaze. They met at the front of the stage.

The woman fumbled in her pocket. "Have you come for your money back?"

Sera shook her head. "Why would I want my money back?"

"Since we couldn't heal you. Your soul is still divided."

"As was noted earlier in this very spot, isn't it always?"

"Sometimes more than others," the woman murmured. "A complicated philosophical point I don't feel like arguing right now."

Sera took a leap. "So I take it your husband doesn't know you are angel-ridden."

The woman touched the wedding band on her finger. "We call it hosting."

"Does sound less invasive that way," Sera agreed.

The woman smiled faintly. She sat and patted the chair beside her. "I'm Nanette, and I don't want a crick in my neck. Unlike the teshuva, my angel won't mend every bump and bruise."

She sounded more envious than condemning, so Sera joined her. "I'm Sera, and I apparently had a crick in my soul. How long have you hosted an angel?"

"Since my miraculous recovery from leukemia at age seven." The woman wrinkled her nose. "When my aunts talked about angels watching over me, they had no idea." She studied Sera. "You haven't had yours long. I see remnants of hell still popping off you like sparks from a firecracker."

"Tell me I don't stink of brimstone."

Nanette smiled. "No. But you shouldn't look anyone in the eye when the demon is active. The purple is too intense even for colored contacts, although people will try to explain it that way."

Sera remembered the glint in Archer's eyes when he confronted her on the bridge before the demon had come to her. She'd thought it beautiful.

"I've never seen your kind here before," Nanette said.

"Maybe they're smart enough to hide."

"I wouldn't have missed them. They just don't come. Neither do the angel hosts. Most possessed think they've learned enough about the battle between good and evil."

"But you've stayed connected with . . ." Sera thought a moment. "I was going to say the real world. Maybe I should just say oblivious."

Nanette gave her a ghost of a smile. "I was young when I married Daniel. He was a good man, for no reason other than goodness' sake. I needed that."

Sera frowned. "He doesn't know what you are, but he's taking credit for your work."

Nanette bristled. "I bet we help more people with our after-school program and soup kitchen than you with all your demon slaying."

Sera held up one hand. "I'm not criticizing what you have." A job she loved. A man who loved her. To smooth the other woman's ire, she added, "My father was a pastor. He's why I came tonight when I saw your flyer."

Nanette nodded, still a little stiff. "I don't mean to be defensive. Honestly, the angel hosts are more judgmental than you. As if the war can only be fought with flaming swords."

"Your swords flame?" Sera smiled. "I bet that's tidier, not to mention way cool."

Nanette smiled back. "Wouldn't know. They apparently only issue weapons in the 'Soldier of God' swag bag, not the 'church mouse' parting gift."

Sera hesitated, reluctant to offend again. "Do you really heal people?"

"The power comes and goes. Yesterday at the convenience store, I was counting out change when it hit. The cashier got excited because he could pick up all the coins I dropped. Said his copper bracelets were finally working on his arthritis." Nanette held out her hands. "People seem happier, anyway, after they've been here."

"That's good." Sera's thoughts raced ahead to possibilities she was almost afraid to contemplate.

"I'm surprised to see a woman possessed," Nanette said. "Demons seem to gravitate toward large, scary-looking males."

Sera grimaced. "Yeah, those large, scary-looking males were pretty surprised too. I take it angels aren't so sexist."

"They choose all ages, physical types, mental capacities. Angel hosts can sicken, grow old, and die as other humans."

"I suppose angels have nothing to prove."

Nanette eyed her. "Did you? Is that how the demon tempted you?"

No wonder the talyan had squirmed when Zane talked of his possession. Archer was right. Sera didn't want to reveal the weakness that made her an agreeable victim to the demon. That was probably why they said pride often went-eth before a fall.

She shrugged. That was all the answer she was going to give.

Nanette folded her hands on her lap. "So why did you wait for me?"

"If I need to understand this war you all say we're fighting, maybe I just wanted to meet our only ally."

"Angels don't fight alongside the teshuva. In fact, beware of those who think the only good demon is a hellbound demon. They'd kill you and leave your teshuva to repent on its own."

Sera rolled her eyes. "How very pious of them."

"Don't scoff. The hosts to mighty angels would not be stopped by the doubts of a church mouse like me."

"Maybe a demon-backed slap upside the head would make them less inclined to judge."

"Your eyes are purple," Nanette said.

Sera let her irritation over a hypothetical encounter fade. "You'd think they'd appreciate the help. Says something about the opposition that our two armies fighting on separate fronts still haven't met in the middle."

"It says that the battle will never be won."

Sera sat back. How could an angel echo Archer's pessimism?

Nanette lifted both hands, palms up, as if revealing something obvious. "How could you ever win?"

"Drain every malice. Butcher every feralis. Lock this realm against every invading djinni."

"But you can't go where the real battles are."

"The demon realm?" Sera's pulse sped, ramping toward demon double time. "I've been there, during my possession. And I had another glimpse when Archer and I—"

"Not the tenebraeternum." A glint of gold brightened Nanette's eyes. "Where the true war between good and evil is fought every day. In the human heart."

Sera blinked. "Oh. That."

The gold glint morphed into simple amusement. "Yes, that. Why do you think angels and demons don't war outright? Their only battlefield is in us. As long as there is one of us tempted by evil, the war continues."

Sera pursed her lips. "That does complicate things."

"Salvation is a path, not a stake with a feralis impaled on it."

"With a couple candles in their eyeless skulls, they'd make lovely tiki torches along the path." Sera sighed. "I hear you."

"You just don't agree."

"Your interpretation dooms me to an eternity of fighting without victory." Sera pictured the hard edges of Archer's face, etched by pain and weariness sharper than his blades. Her heart ached for him, but she felt a flare of wonder at his endurance. He would never falter.

Nanette shook her head. "Eternity itself is too short to make a difference."

Sera was silent a moment. "Then why?"

"Because to do otherwise is unquestionably a defeat."

"The angels teach you that?"

"My aunts. I thank God for them every day." When

her name was called across the room, Nanette stood. "Will you come back so we can talk more?"

Sera stood also, not answering. She glanced across the room to where the preacher was waving. "He's lucky, to have an angel for a wife."

"Oh, he prays every day too. Mostly for the strength to put up with my lousy housekeeping." Nanette smiled, a dimple in her cheek. "He loves me. I love him."

She said nothing more, as if that were enough.

When Sera held out her hand, Nanette ignored it and hugged her. "You will come again?"

"There's so much I want to know. Like, since demons and angels should be matter and antimatter, why aren't we exploding right now?"

Nanette drew back. "I'm glad you didn't say that before I hugged you. We'll add you to our prayers."

"Don't bother. I'll never be a housekeeper."

"I think we should aim for something a little more significant anyway."

"A flaming sword?"

Nanette wrinkled her nose. "Peace."

Daniel walked toward them, stage smile forming. Sera spun on her heel. She didn't want to make small talk with a man so unaware of the dangers around him, however pure his intentions.

It would be too hard to decide whether she more pitied him . . . or envied him.

Chapter 15

Corvus Valerius stared at the crow. So many shades of black, touched with prismatic color. For all the bird's commonness, its insignificance and transience, the demon realm had nothing to compare to those delicate layers of light and shadow.

He closed his hand gently around it, savoring the warmth that suffused his palm despite the unrelenting chill of the ring around his finger.

He dashed it to the ground.

Shards of glass flew—which was more than he could say for the lamp-work bird.

In the filigree cage, the living crow flapped its wings.

"Flawed," Corvus hissed. Under their black markings, his arms ached with the memory of old pain.

The glass bird would never fly, of course. But it should look as if it perched on his windowsill only because it had not yet taken the notion to flee.

His latest work, despite its glistening transparency, felt leaden, dead. He should slag it down as an ashtray.

The crow stuck its beak between the bars, angling toward one of the chunks of glass that had landed nearby. It purled to itself when it couldn't quite reach.

Corvus turned his glare on the living bird, snatched a velvet cape from his desk, and draped it over the cage. "Sleep well," he growled. "I have night work, but tomorrow . . ."

Darklings gathered around him in a greedy tide as he made his way through the city. He did not slow to indulge their begging whispers for a sundered soul. Not much longer and then they would feast to satiate them for all eternity.

The darklings followed him up a shallow flight of steps, past a stylized dragon, and under a set of paper lanterns that swung fitfully in the wind. He opened the door, and they boiled through after him.

The hostess recoiled, eyes wide. For a moment, Corvus thought she was one of the rare humans who saw the darklings clearly. But her gaze fixed on his face, and he realized his own hungry expression caused her unease.

He smoothed his features, as much as possible. "Good evening. I believe my friends are already here."

She didn't answer, just bowed as he passed. He made his way to a booth near the back where two men waited.

One, clutching a bottle of sake, stared across a huge platter of sushi at the man opposite him. "Geoff, how can you gorge like that?"

"I eat when I'm hungry. You should try it."

"You're always hungry these days."

"So I am, Matty, m' boy. So I am. You going to drink all that yourself?"

Corvus, noting the blotched aura flaking off Geoffrey, wasn't surprised at the man's gluttony. Shedding his soul like gangrenous skin, he probably felt empty all the time. The drug dealer on the corner had more substance than this one.

"Gentlemen." He pulled up an extra chair at the end of the booth. "I'm late. Forgive me."

Geoffrey waved his chopsticks, scattering blistered

flecks of his soul. The darklings swarmed close. But rather than attacking, they flinched back in a smoky wave.

"Thank you for coming." Matthew sat stiffly, knuckles white around the sake bottle. "I know it's late."

The darklings milled around Geoffrey—crawling under the table, climbing the back of the booth, clinging to the red globe lantern hanging over them. The chorus of their aggrieved hissing raised a chill draft that set the votive candle dancing.

Matthew let go of the sake to wrap his arms around himself. "I called you both here to tell you first." He took a breath. "There's a board meeting tomorrow, and I'm going to recommend pulling the plug on Solacin."

Geoffrey dropped his chopsticks, sputtering. A gobbet of his soul spewed from his mouth as he cleared his throat. The darkling on the lamp lunged for the morsel . . . then dropped it with a psychic shriek that spiderwebbed the candleholder with fine cracks. It fled, its shady brethren close behind.

Corvus raised his eyebrows. "And why would you abandon such a wonderfully effective discovery as Solacin?"

"When it's going to make us all a shitload of money," Geoffrey growled.

Matthew glared across the table. "You must've heard. The cops and public health are screaming about this new addiction. They're calling it solvo." He sloshed sake into his thin-walled cup. "Solvo? Solacin? Get it? It's ours. Somehow, it's on the street." He tossed back the drink, then looked at them, inviting them to share his horror.

They stared back at him. After a moment, Geoffrey returned to his sushi.

Matthew lowered his cup, wide eyes glistening. "You already know," he whispered. "Did you know it's killing people? They say it feels great, makes all the pain go away, just like we hoped. But then they say you stop feeling anything; you go numb. They say you turn into a fucking zombie."

"Zombie? Oh please," Geoffrey said testily. "Not at therapeutic dosage levels. At least, not in the same numbers they're getting among recreational users."

"Not the same ... You're saying you've had fatalities in the clinical trials?"

Geoffrey shrugged. "Nothing we can't pass off. And not fatalities. Not exactly."

Matthew reeled. "Our psychiatric pharmaceuticals are supposed to help people!"

"We are helping." Corvus put his hand on Matthew's clenched fist. His ring glinted in the crazed light from the broken votive holder. "Sometimes you have to hurt to help. And not everyone can be helped. Sometimes it's better to let those people—"

"No." Matthew pulled away. "When you brought us the Solacin formula and helped Geoff find a way to manufacture it in bulk, you didn't mention all these caveats and fine print."

"Don't be an idiot," Geoffrey said. "We make drugs. Of course there's fine print. Anyway, life comes with even finer print. Why do you want to bother people with the gory details?"

Corvus slanted him a curious glance. "Were the details starting to bother you, Geoffrey? Is that why you're taking Solacin?"

Geoffrey startled. "I'm fine. You can see I'm not a zombie."

Considering how the darklings had fled from the moldering wreckage of his leaking soul ... Corvus pursed his lips. The Worm hadn't mentioned this side effect of the chemical *desolator numinis*—leaving the soul tainted beyond even the ferocious hunger of the darklings. Geoffrey's shriveled and sour soul had been no feast before, but the stone in the ring would've left it intact. Not that the disposal of the souls mattered.

Corvus needed only the leftover bodies, emptied of their resolve and troublesome morality, pliant to any suggestion that promised to fill the aching void within them.

Matthew smacked his palm on the table. "This is completely unethical. You're probably sneaking Solacin out the back door and pushing it on the corner as solvo yourself."

"No," Geoffrey said. "But he is." He smirked at Corvus, payback for the revelation of his addiction.

Corvus sighed. He'd regretted the need to bring in outsiders for mass production. He preferred the personal touch, his ringed hand hovering in benediction over a suffering soul. No true priest, as the corner drug dealer had named him, guaranteed such effortless salvation as a tablet on the tongue.

But he'd needed more followers emptied of their souls than he alone could convert. Only that accumulated weight of impious blanks would complete the destruction of the Veil.

"Jesus," Matthew moaned. "You're both insane. Solacin was supposed to release thousands imprisoned by depression, PTSD, phobias—"

"You gonna read the ads back to me?" Geoffrey snarled.

"Do not fret, dear Matthew," Corvus said. "The weight of their souls will be lifted, that at least is true. And with their sacrifice, we all will be freed from our chains."

Matthew stood. "The board will hear about this. It ends, now." He strode away, his righteous wrath a shining shield around him.

Geoffrey reached for the abandoned sake bottle. "Well, that's that."

Corvus grimaced. The problem with zombies, of course, was that for all their many useful qualities, they lacked initiative. But Geoffrey had already served his purpose. Matthew, however, could still be a problem.

"It will be over soon, but not yet." Corvus pushed to his feet. "I'll talk to him."

"Just talk, hmm? That's why you're cracking your knuckles?" Geoffrey laughed. A bit more of his soul flaked away.

Corvus let his hands fall to his sides. The ring still burned coldly on his finger. "There is much poor Matthew does not want to understand."

But he would, since unfortunately for Matthew, the shield of his righteous wrath was only a metaphor.

Archer waited in the cold light of the hotel door, contemplating his shadow cast onto the sidewalk before him.

Sera hunched her shoulders when she saw him but came on steadily to stand on his shadow. From the glint in her eyes, he thought probably she wanted to put her foot through his corporeal self.

He didn't move. "I don't want to hunt you down."

"Then don't. You're good at letting go."

"We said we'd meet." He kept his voice neutral, though the effort revived some of the warmth he'd been missing.

"Actually, you told me to show up." She rubbed a hand over her eyes. "Look, I don't want to fight with you. Not verbally, not physically. Not anything."

When he still didn't move, she reached past him to punch the summons on the key pad.

He didn't flinch away to stop her from touching him. He never flinched, even though touching her—thinking of touching her—burned worse than ichor. He just sucked in his breath to avoid her.

And inadvertently breathed honeysuckle. His body tightened, all senses—man and demon—coming alert.

He kept his voice even. "No one's home tonight to let you in. They're on rounds, killing the horde-tenebrae riled up by your coming."

"My demon's coming," she corrected.

He ignored the interruption, just as he'd ignore the promptings of his lust. "At least you'll learn how to do your part."

"You told Liam you don't know what my part is," she said. "And you didn't seem interested in learning anything more."

That stopped him. She was still angry—no, hurt he'd turned away from her. Didn't she understand how dangerous their intimacy, that uncontrolled spiral going God knew where, had become?

He could deny his temptation; he might refuse any further role in molding her to Liam Niall's little army of the damned. But the simmering pain in her gaze was too much. He'd take claws over tears any day.

He drew himself up. "I know damn well you can't go off sulking."

"I wasn't sulking," she flared.

"Where were you?"

She shook her head. "I don't answer to you. Open the damn door already. I changed my mind. I do feel like fighting with you."

Just as he'd wanted, he reminded himself when she arrived at the ballroom ten minutes later, her hair in a severe braid, her slender curves defined under slim-fit yoga pants and workout bra.

She stood in front of the windows, her fair skin and hair bright against the blackness of the night. As if his mind needed a frame for the maddening loop of images from their night together.

He swallowed past his dry throat. The destroyer in him offered no subliminal suggestions while he contemplated where he'd put his hands on her. He'd planned to show her all the places a fight could go wrong. She'd already shown him one he hadn't considered.

Her hazel eyes snapped. "Well?"

"Follow my lead."

She snorted, but softly, so he didn't have to respond.

She mirrored him through the tai chi poses, not touching. A little of the ancient harmony flowed through him.

He feinted at her. She blocked him, harder than necessary. He sent the same attack in the other direction. She faltered, stiffening.

"Easy," he murmured. "Same as before."

They sparred until her cheeks were bright with color and her hair a wild corona with the tie long gone.

When he paused, she shook the sweat-darkened strands back from her face. "I'll have to get a cut like yours."

"That would be a sin." His fingers twitched with a visceral memory of blond silk wound between his fingers. Shaking off the sensation was harder than sublimating the demon. His body ached even where she'd never landed a blow.

She settled her hands on her hips. "You told me someone else would teach me this."

"I changed my mind too . . . ," he said, hesitating, then added, "about some things."

Her expression was shuttered. "Why?"

She didn't ask what, he noticed. Just as well.

"This shift in demonic activity since you—since your demon arrived. I wanted to talk to Bookie tonight, about the tests he's doing with you, about some of the history leading up to this crossing. He knew, from the tear it left in the Veil, that the demon was strong, although he had guessed it would be djinn. Maybe the pendant stone threw off his readings. But if he was wrong about that, we might have to rethink our strategy against this upsurge."

She took a few steps toward the mirror, as if looking for the demon inside her. "Maybe you can convince him I'm not evil."

"It would be safer for you if you were. The djinn are damn hard to kill."

"More than the teshuva?"

"By orders of magnitude. Maybe teshuva are weakened by their repentance, or maybe they repent because they are weak. Whichever, we're at a disadvantage and always have been, just left to pick up the pieces." He fell silent until she turned from the mirror to meet his gaze. "Until you."

She blinked.

"Even before your possession was complete, the demon was strong and your link to it impressive. What you'll be with time and training . . ." He watched as she turned to pace across the room. "When your demon roamed the city, Zane said the end was nigh. He might've been right."

She spun to face him. "How can there be an end? I thought you said good and evil are endemic to the human heart?"

He hesitated. "But must they be eternally, inescapably bound? Think of other diseases that have been cured."

"Evil is like chicken pox?"

He grimaced. "Maybe more like smallpox. Something deadly to be eradicated. When you drained that first malice, and later the ferales, something strange happened. They vanished."

"Isn't that the point?"

"But they were gone. No shards. No echo. Nothing left in this realm." He took a slow breath. "Sera, millennia of talyan have just been hopelessly holding back the tide of evil. With that one malice, those two ferales, you turned it."

She tipped her head to one side. She had hold of the pendant and ran the pale stone along the cord as she considered. He could almost see the gears ticking over in her brain. A sense of calm stole over him. He'd never met as serious and intense a questioner. Her response could only deepen his understanding.

How long had it been since he'd done anything besides destroy? And long for his own destruction? When had he last had an inkling of possibility for an end to his pain?

Sera was his hope.

Her devotion to the last moments, when even loved ones gave up, had given her a clear-eyed resilience of spirit, the opposite of everything he feared he'd become. The realization shifted something inside him, something he didn't want to examine too closely.

Hope could be crippling in ways beyond mere feralis claws and malice slime. The wounds left by shattered hope plunged deeper than the healing power of the strongest teshuva.

He would've sneered at the exaggeration if he hadn't carried the scars.

She shook her head. "I just don't know. Dark and light. Evil and good. The dichotomies started with the big bang and somebody thinking to write it all down in a best seller called the Bible and about a thousand other storybooks since."

Had he thought she'd agree with him so easily? In a way, he was glad she hadn't. If he could convince her, maybe he could convince himself. "Then we'll just have to go back to the big bang and do it again. Without evil this time."

She smiled. "You don't want much, do you?"

"Oh, I do," he said softly.

Her smile faded.

He gave himself a shake. "I think we're done here for the night."

"You bring up a host of mysteries and then disappear? Lovely."

He cocked his head. "Did you want something else?"

"Answers," she snapped.

"I left a message for Bookie with some suggestions to jump-start his research, and I borrowed a history on—"

"I was thinking of something a little more today, now, this instant."

"You are young and impatient, grasshopper," he said, just to watch her scowl. "I also asked Ecco to bring back a malice. I want Bookie to record you draining it. He finished his father's work on an etheric shunt to drain demonic emanations, which rather than metaphysical garbagemen, makes us metaphysical waste-treatment specialists. Not really progress. But what you do . . ." He shook his head.

She rubbed at her arm where the malice had fastened its teeth. "Yeah, it was interesting, all right."

"You wanted blood-and-guts action."

She grimaced. "Not my own."

His amusement faded. "I hope it won't come to that. For the sake of both our souls."

"You do what needs to be done, and so will I. You'll just have to let go of the rest."

He contemplated all that had slipped away from him over the years. "My soul?"

"Your hurt."

The accusation rankled, unfair, not to mention pointless. "I thought you'd have figured out by now that the demon heals the wound but not the pain."

"I'm not talking about the battle scars."

Neither was he. "When you've fought as long as I have, see if you still feel the same."

She raised her chin. "Who's got that kind of time?"

"I'm not going anywhere." The thought should have depressed him, being far too true. But somehow the snap in her eyes made him glad the nights were long.

Sera made him go another bout, retribution for that crack about their respective ages. If he wanted to play the wise old man, at least he could wheeze a little.

Too bad he was in such damn fine shape. But they were both breathing hard at the end.

"We're through." A glint of respect shone in his eye. "Save something for the malice."

She rubbed her shoulder, wincing at the twinge. "How is Ecco supposed to catch one?"

"Oddly enough, or maybe not, he has a way with them." From behind, Archer splayed his fingers over her shoulder. "Where does it hurt?"

Her breath, which had eased, jumped again at the contact. "It's not bad. The teshuva is taking care of it."

"Just checking." His voice was soft, at odds with his firm hands.

She forced herself not to lean into him. "You were saying, about Ecco and his malice."

"I found him once, covered in slime. They kept coming to their slaughter. I thought he might cry. He said it was like drowning kittens. Evil kittens, but still."

She shivered, telling herself it was his story, not his touch. "I shouldn't think poor malice, but somehow I do."

"Hate the sin, not the sinner."

"I think you mean, 'Love the sinner, not the sin.' "

His hands fell away. "Same thing."

"No," she said patiently. "One is negative and one is positive."

"I suppose, if you want to split hairs and not malice." He stretched, a roll of muscle and sinew that made something inside of her leap in answering reflex. "The talyan won't be back until early morning. You should get some rest before then."

She wasn't sure she wanted to. Who knew what her dreams would be? Temptation, no doubt. "Let me know when you need me."

The faint breathlessness in her voice made her squirm. Just the workout, she told herself. *Any*body would have been breathless. It wasn't just *his* body having that effect on *her* body.

Without waiting for his confirmation, she escaped to her suite.

Despite the long day, she couldn't sleep. The talk with Nanette and the sparring—physical and verbal—with Archer had her brain in a whirl. She called and left a message for her physical therapist, canceling her appointments, saying she felt much better lately. It was too late to call her brothers or Wendy at the nursing home. She lay on the couch and wondered if, from now on, it would always be too late.

She must have fallen asleep, because when the knock came at her door, she was dreaming about an assembly line full of pie shells. À la *I Love Lucy*, she sealed squirming malice into the pies. But the pie shells were glass and she sliced her thumb. Suddenly, on the conveyor belt sat a huge, hulking feralis, its orange eyes fixed on her, drool from its overhung jaw burning holes in the crusts.

She staggered up at the second knock.

Zane waited at the door. "Archer said meet him in Bookie's lab."

She gathered a sweater, her bag, and a notebook—not sure what else one took to a malice execution—and followed him. "Will you be there?"

He shook his head. "I'm beat, literally, figuratively, you name it, it's beat. You'll be okay?"

"Just not sure what to expect."

"You've done it already. Do it again."

And again. And again. " 'Four and twenty blackbirds baked in a pie,' " she sang under her breath.

Zane picked up the next line. " 'When the pie was opened, the birds began to sing.' " He shook his head. "I'd be pissed if my dinner started talking back. Speaking of dinner . . ." He gave her a wave and broke off at the kitchen.

Daylight gleamed through the windows, but the halls were quiet, the talyan having returned from their night's work and now recovering for the next. As she headed down to the lab, the silence thickened, until she found herself holding her breath.

So she heard the low murmur of the men's voices, then a thin blackboard screech that raised her hackles. The malice.

"You're jumping to conclusions," Bookie was saying.

"I got slimed for nothing?" Ecco's petulant complaint was almost lost in Archer's brusque reply.

"Testing a hypothesis is not jumping to a conclusion. You should know that."

Bookie gave a sharp laugh. "I do, since I'm the one supposed to be creating the hypothesis."

"Who cares?" Something rattled, and Sera imagined Ecco slapping his hand down on a tray of obscure implements.

"Easy for you to say," Bookie snapped. "No one wants your job."

Archer's soft voice carried all the more clearly for its intensity. "Your rank is safe, Bookkeeper, always has been. If your father made you feel unwelcome in his studies, perhaps he wanted more for you than a lifetime down here."

Sera winced, picturing Bookie's expression. No one liked their familial failures laid out on the exam table. She should know.

She scuffed her feet and whisked around the corner, already talking. "Sorry I'm late."

The three men moved away from the stiff stances they'd held. Archer nodded at her as she dropped her bag on the counter.

Between the men, a beaker topped with a gold seal held a flowing, inky substance of half liquid, half gas. She leaned closer, then recoiled with a gasp when a red eye spun across the inner surface of the glass.

"Don't knock it over," Ecco warned. "They're a bitch to get out of the ductwork, and they always end up in my shower."

She swallowed. "I didn't realize you could fold them so small."

"They're like rats. They go wherever that eyeball fits. Still a pain getting them into the bottle, even with the etheric dissonance generator and the rogue-priest blessing on the glass."

"I already have papers on malice morphology," Bookie said impatiently.

"That's not why we're here." Archer leaned his hip against the counter. "I want you to take an ESF and ion reading as Sera drains the malice."

"Seems kind of unsporting at the moment," she said.

"Like shooting fish in a barrel?" Ecco grinned. "We could let it out and you can try to drain it before it ends up in your shower. I'd hate to have to come after it."

She grimaced. "I guess I'll work up the nerve then."

Bookie crossed his arms. "I have papers on malice dispatching too. Adding footnotes to studies already done is all very interesting, but—"

Archer straightened from his lazy stance.

Bookie fell silent. Even Ecco studied his fingernails with sudden attention.

Sera leaned over the beaker again. "I don't know how I did it before."

"Don't think about it," Archer said. "Just do what comes naturally."

"Supernaturally," Echo said. When they glared at him, he waved one hand. "Continue, please."

Archer glanced at Bookie. "Do you have the equipment set up?"

Bookie gave a curt nod. "As you requested last night." He wheeled a squat cabinet closer to the table. Sera was reminded of a hospital crash cart, only in this case, they were offing something, not saving it.

Bookie saw her attention and despite his pique, seemed unable to prevent himself from explaining. "The ether-spectral field detector will record emanations from you and the malice. Probably fairly consistent with readings we've taken before." He glared at Archer. "In our realm, lesser demons manifest as an etheric shell, if you will, containing spectral energy. When a talya captures a malice or incapacitates a feralis, the teshuva's emanations overwhelm the lesser-demonic field, altering its pattern. Once closely enough aligned, the lesser energy is subsumed within the teshuva energy, leaving only the exhausted etheric shell—drained."

"Like sucking down a beer bong and tossing the can over your shoulder," Ecco murmured. "Without the burp." No one looked his way.

"That's why you don't tangle with the djinn, only horde-tenebrae," Bookie continued. "The teshuva can't overcome the stronger emanations of the djinn."

Sera pictured Nanette hefting a beer bong. "How do angels fare against the djinn?"

"God's chosen warriors share nothing with us," Archer said tightly.

For once, Ecco and Bookie muttered in annoyed agreement.

Sera shifted as Bookie aimed a palm-sized satellite dish at her. "So where does that energy go?"

"Anecdotal evidence from sensitive talyan"—Bookie's scornful look eliminated the men in the room—"and untested theory indicate the matched demonic vibrations rejuvenate the teshuva and help maintain the human form over many years and otherwise fatal wounds. If improperly balanced, the energy could destabilize the teshuva, leading to unpredictable behavior in the possessed talya." Another scornful, if carefully unfocused, look.

"Definitely seems like more research is needed." Sera tried a smile on Bookie.

He stared back. "I suppose that's why we're here." Amidst the reflected stainless steel in his glasses, the inky bottle of malice roiled like a second pair of pupils.

Her stomach followed the uneasy motion. "Okay then."

She reached for the beaker. From the corner of her eye, she saw Ecco straighten, then subside when Archer shook his head.

She grasped the seal, half expecting it to burn or freeze or shock her. But the thin gold foil just flaked away under her fingers.

Behind the red eyeball, the malice boiled out like greasy smoke. The room filled with the stench of rotten eggs and worse gone putrid. Ecco swore. Bookie gagged.

Sera sunk her fingers into the writhing loops.

It never regained the vaguely animalistic shape of a roving malice. It only mewled. She couldn't decide if pity or disgust moved her more.

She thought of her conversation with Nanette and remembered how Archer had accused her of talking the malice into oblivion. "Somebody told me that good and evil might be hopelessly intertwined." She twisted the malice between her fingers, then glanced at Archer. "And somebody else hoped maybe they aren't."

Archer's half-lidded gaze glimmered with a barely suppressed hunger, as if only they two stood in the room. He'd accused her of trying to psychoanalyze the demon, but whom was she trying to heal?

She folded the malice in on itself. "If terror and torture roam free as malice and ferales, where are the parallel shapes of beauty, joy, compassion?" Ether compressed like oily cobwebs under her hands. At most she could make a spit wad, not even a paper airplane. "How can I reshape one malice into a thousand origami cranes to make a wish come true?"

She'd heard the wary hope in his voice before, wondering if there might be an end to his fighting. That *she* might be the end.

But her past told her she could have hope or she

could have the end; the agony of hope unrequited or the peace of inevitable death. Not both.

The moment spooled out, the room fading to sketched monochrome lines, except for the violet streaks in Archer's tarnished bronze eyes. In his clenched hand, tendons stood stark under the black of his *reven*, as if he could smash ether under his fist. With his demon's help, he'd bound hope and death into one convoluted and ruinous wish.

In the empty, echoing space that linked them, she said to him, "I'm sorry, but I will not be your end."

She spread her hands.

"Quit mooning at him," Ecco snapped. He jumped forward to grab at the malice, jolting her. "You're going to lose it."

Before she could even flinch, Archer caught her. He pulled her close, his big body steady and unsettling at the same time.

His breath against her temple raised shivers down her spine, through the unseen marks encircling her thighs. "You trying to lose me again?"

He wrapped his fingers possessively around her arms, brushing her breasts. The shock she always felt at his touch leapt between them, and the fragile bubble where she'd spoken just to him imploded. Rocked on her feet, she held him fast.

The malice unraveled in a cascade of pitchy streamers until only the stench remained.

Bookie cleared his throat. "Very pretty."

"Where did it go?" Ecco turned a tight circle.

Archer straightened with a growl. "I told you to let her do it."

"She tried to let it go." Ecco dragged in a deep breath, as if he could sniff out the malice through the stink. "If you hadn't stopped her . . ."

Sera ducked away from Archer to stand on her own. "It's gone, all right."

Ecco blinked. "But there's nothing left."

She pinned Ecco with a gimlet stare. "If I'd known you *like* malice in your shower . . ."

Archer studied Bookie expectantly. The Bookkeeper fiddled with the dials on his machine, his brow furrowed. He muttered.

"Well," Archer prompted.

"It happened so fast." Bookie straightened his glasses, a faint tremor in his hand. "I can't quite believe—"

Archer frowned. "Didn't you get it?"

Ecco pulled out a pack of cigarettes and lit up. Cloves masked the sulfur stench. "I'm not getting slimed again just because you forgot to push 'record.' "

Bookie whirled on him. "It's not that simple."

"Demon here. Demon gone. Gone where?" Ecco peered over Bookie's shoulder. "What's this braid of light?" He pointed with the cigarette, the glowing cherry tracing the readout. "Here's where the malice is draining, like usual. But here looks like the inverse, as if somebody wove it back together, except light instead of dark." His brow furrowed. "When Archer grabbed Sera."

Sera took a step around Archer's big frame to see the screen. The spirograph pattern could have been the exploding malice's good twin, the splintered strands winding back toward some bright, elusive center.

"Yes, it's unusual," Bookie said with cool reluctance. "I need time to decode and match against previous readings. Unless you can figure it out by yourself."

"Whatever." Ecco took a hard drag off the cigarette. "As always with you people, been fun."

Archer waited until the talya's footsteps faded down the hall. "About Sera's necklace."

Bookie jerked his head up. "She told you?" He frowned at Sera. "I thought we agreed to wait until I could convince the league not to kill you out of hand."

"I've pissed him off once or twice, but I took a chance Archer wouldn't slay me without better cause."

Bookie didn't smile. "Possession of the *desolator numinis* is more damning than you know."

"So explain," Archer said. "Is the stone how she destroys the malice?"

Bookie hesitated. "From what I've read, the *desolator numinis* is like the energy sinks we use to ward league dwellings from the negative emotions that attract horde-tenebrae. Except the matrix seizes the emanations we call souls." He glanced at the spirograph. "It seems likely she's doing the same with demonic ethers."

Sera's skin prickled as if the pendant squirmed against her neck. She resisted the urge to tear it off.

Archer let out a slow breath. If she hadn't spent the last few days as his living shadow, she might have missed the carefully buried disappointment in his voice. "Then it's just a kinder and gentler garbage can for dumping demonic trash, not a one-way ticket back to the demon realm."

Bookie laid one hand on the spirograph machine as if steadying himself. "Is that what you hoped for?" His tone rose incredulously. "An opening into the tenebraeternum?"

Archer's expression blanked. "And why not?"

"You can't just rip through the Veil as if it were some petty malice." The historian sputtered, as close to a laugh as Sera had heard from him. "It'd be chaos. Actual chaos."

From Archer's predatory stillness, Sera didn't think he was particularly amused, especially when he asked softly, "Are we not teetering on that edge already?"

Any semblance of laughter fled Bookie's face. "Not that close, as far as most of us are concerned. Bringing on the apocalypse for your own sense of closure seems arrogant, even for a talya."

Hoping to ease the spiking tension, Sera cleared her throat. "The *desolator numinis* might be just another prison, but it could still hold a hint."

"What hint?" Bookie's lip curled, nothing like a smile but not quite a sneer.

If anyone was arrogant . . . From Bookie's sudden pallor, she knew her eyes flared violet. "The hint inherent in all prisons. A way to escape."

She remembered Zane's comment about the temptation of calling on the demon, and shame pricked her. Bookie, acerbic comments and all, was part of the league, not the enemy.

"A way out might be a way back in. If the stone holds demons, just like the demon realm, what we learn from one could apply to the other." She relaxed her fingers, fisted around the pendant. "Who besides you can tell us what other hints the Bookkeeper archive holds?"

Bookie inclined his head in grudging agreement. "More than one person could discover in a lifetime. A mortal lifetime, anyway. But I'll let you know what I find." He clicked off the spirograph device, and the machine powered down with a descending hum.

"On that note . . . ," Archer murmured.

Sera grabbed her things and followed him out. "I thought nerds were charming these days."

Archer propelled her down the hall with a hand at the small of her back. "He is not the man his father was. I suppose that is true of us all."

In the elevator, she turned to him. "What did you think you'd find today?"

"Something, anything we didn't know before. Which is plenty." His gaze rested on her with a hint of the unruly need that kept flaring between them. "But I think you're even more rare than the secrets in Bookkeeper histories."

She wanted to kick herself for the hiccup in her heartbeat. Rare indeed. Two-headed calves and meteor strikes were rare too. Rare didn't always mean desirable.

When the elevator stopped on her floor, he held her back. "I want to show you something. Come up to my room."

Actually, meteor showers were beautiful, awe inspiring, and only very rarely killed people. And who wouldn't want a two-headed calf?

She followed him up.

CHAPTER 16

His room had a better view of the city than hers, but about the same level of personality—which was to say, none. She wished she hadn't made fun of his Spartan loft. She could've saved those zingers for now.

He must've seen her expression. "I don't stay here often. This way." On his desk, a computer idled, the league's @1 insignia scrolling randomly. "I want to show you what Bookie won't acknowledge."

She leaned over the laptop beside him, inadvertently bumping his wide shoulder. "But I've finished less of the Bookkeeper backlist than I have malice and ferales."

"I don't need indoctrination. Bookie won't look past what he already knows. His father was a brilliant researcher and historian, but our current Bookkeeper doesn't seem confident enough to follow the tradition."

Sera thought him more frustrated than unsure, but she didn't really know the man. "What can I do?"

"You have a good mind. I need that."

He'd brought her up to his room for her good mind. With effort, she focused on the computer screen, trying to ignore the hot bulk of his body, the memory of how he'd pulled her close as the malice unraveled. "So show me."

He took a breath that ruffled her hair. "When we first registered the distortion in the Veil that meant a demon was crossing over, we also began recording an upswing in horde-tenebrae activity in this realm. The intensity of activity surpassed anything we'd seen before." He opened a graph that showed the abrupt spike. A few more clicks opened demon-fighting strategies, historic battles, ancient prophecies, and oracular folklore. "Bookie believed a djinni was crossing. He said we should stay out of its way if we wanted to survive."

"Sounds like reasonable advice."

"I said we should destroy it before the possessed came fully into his power."

She pursed her lips. "Sounds like your sort of advice."

"Niall agreed with me, conditionally."

"You threatened to do it without him."

"I'm sure I phrased it more tactfully."

"No doubt. So then I enter the picture."

"Unexpectedly, a woman." He ticked off on his fingers. "A repentant demon, but potent. Undiminished post-crossing activity." He closed his hand into a fist, his gaze fixed on her. "And an unusually thorough technique for banishing demons."

The coiled tension in him made her restless. "Which all means what, exactly?"

"I couldn't understand why you seemed to be slipping back into the most dangerous hour of your possession when you drained that first malice. You were sinking into the demon realm. And then with the ferales, I almost followed you down. It seemed so peaceful, I almost . . ." He straightened, putting a short step between them. "Anyway, I hoped Bookie would confirm the technique, but I think your demon isn't simply draining the malice or locking them away in a stone matrix. I think it's sending them back through the Veil."

"How can that be?" If she'd been immersed in a beaker, the water around her would be boiling from the concentration in his eyes. "Everything I've been told so far involves the demons invading us, not the other way around."

"You have a unique connection to the other side. What if the teshuva chose you for that?"

She grimaced. "I was demon fodder from the start? So my mom was right; they were after me."

His gaze softened. "Or she was the start, your penance trigger. Ever since she took you for that last car ride, you've flirted with death and damnation. Is it surprising you wore a path to the demon realm that led the teshuva back to your door?"

She stiffened against the unfurling anger and wondered whether her eyes glinted violet anyway. "Don't blame her. Or are you saying I brought this on myself?"

"What good is blame? I gave that up along with everything else a long time ago." He paced the length of the room. "I'd rather think about a half dozen djinn crammed back-assward into one of Bookie's beakers. We could take the war where it belongs."

"And maybe you can ditch your demon while you're there."

He froze in midstride, anguish sharpening the lines of his face.

She cringed at the sting of cruelty in her words, but she couldn't stop needling him for the self-immolation that lurked at the heart of his craving. "If my demon can uproot a malice from our realm, why not another teshuva? A cure for possession."

"There is no cure. Possession is a terminal case. Except for the part where you never die."

She wrapped her arms around herself—since no one else would. "You've said things are changing."

"But we still don't know how. Or why."

"Well, that's why you were testing me tonight," she reminded him. "And why you told Liam you wanted to take on the next djinni instead of fighting horde-tenebrae on the sidelines as usual. Why are you so afraid of hearing you might be right?"

"Because what if I'm not?" His voice was low.

"Is hope that hard to grasp?"

"I can't remember. It's been so long since I reached for it."

As a grim silence fell, she sensed the demon settle within her and wished she hadn't provoked him or it. "Which battle was it, Archer, that began this war for you?"

His gaze strayed toward the window, the gray light bleak in his dark eyes. "The War Between the States." His lips twisted. "Everyone notes the irony of the term 'civil war.' War is never civil. Of course, the Latin meant citizen. One citizen against another. The teshuva against the other legions of hell."

She processed the time. A hundred and fifty years of fighting. "No wonder," she murmured.

"I tried not to."

"You really think a demon can open the Veil between the realms, that we can banish all the wayward evils that plague our world and end this war?"

He met her gaze, jaw flexing on words he wouldn't say.

Her cell phone rang, and she almost jumped out of her skin. She ignored the muffled tone in her bag.

The ringing cut out as her voice mail picked up. After a moment, the phone rang again.

Archer lifted one eyebrow. "You going to answer that?"

"You going to answer me?"

He shrugged. The ringing stopped and started again.

With a curse, she grabbed her bag and dug out the

phone. What could possibly matter more than her role in the existential dimorphism of good versus evil?

"Hello?"

"Sera. Thank God you're all right."

For a second, she struggled to align the words with her life at the moment. She really wasn't all right, and God didn't have anything to do with it.

"Jackson?" Her oldest brother never called beyond confirming mealtimes for major holidays. "What's wrong?"

"We just heard about your apartment. You hadn't called us, so we didn't know what to think."

She frowned at his tone of mingled reproach and relief. "We got it all cleaned up."

"Cleaned up? They said the building was a total loss. And all the dead . . ."

Her skin chilled as all the blood rushed to her pounding heart. "I'm sorry, what?" She nudged Archer away from the computer, found his Internet icon, and entered her keywords.

The picture bloomed on the screen. For a moment, disbelief and vertigo left her stomach roiling.

Flames engulfed the building, spreading *downward*. The two silhouetted firefighters looked small and helpless against the inferno.

SEVEN DEAD—THREE CHILDREN—IN FREAK APARTMENT BLAZE.

"Oh my God." Her knees gave out at a nudge from behind, and she collapsed into the chair Archer had pulled out for her. With a quietly exhaled curse, he leaned closer to read the article.

"You didn't know?" Jackson's voice was incredulous. "Where have you been?"

"My apartment was broken into. I've been staying with a friend." Her attention drifted as she scanned the article in shock and she reminded herself to guard her tongue. No sense blurting out something even more disturbing.

"You could've stayed with me," Jackson said.

She grimaced. She hadn't moved in with her brothers even after the car accident. She loved them, but their mother's fate had left them with an aggressive head-in-the-sand philosophy of life. Their father's decline had focused them even more myopically on their ambitious careers, vigorous social climbing, and high-profile philanthropic projects. She was proud of them, and they drove her nuts with their single-minded attention to mundane matters.

"I told you it was a bad neighborhood," her brother fretted. "Break-ins. Arson."

Her world spun again. "Arson?"

Archer tapped the screen over the words "possible arson."

"At least you're safe." Jackson paused. "Where did you say you're staying now?"

"With a friend."

"That Betsy has just been trouble, getting you that job—"

"Not Betsy," she said. "No one you know."

"Well, bring her over for dinner, as thanks for saving you."

She slanted a glance at Archer. "I don't think he's ready for dinner with the family yet."

Jackson was quiet. "He?"

"My sometime lover, Jackson." She rubbed her forehead at the sputtering she heard on the other end of the phone. The room on her end was deathly silent. "I can put him on the phone if you want to thank him now."

Archer backed away.

She imagined Jackson doing much the same. "Geez, Ser, some stuff I'm still too young to know."

"Prude." Affection for her brother welled up, as if the

images of fire had burned a hole through a lifetime of daily dross to pure emotion underneath.

"Nut. If you need anything . . ."

"I know." Her gaze strayed to Archer, who stood looking out the window, legs braced, arms crossed.

A hundred and fifty years since he'd heard the voices of his family. No wonder he hadn't let himself care for anyone since, knowing the people he came to love would die while he went on.

Assuming she survived so long, would she be the same? Were the mysteries that the demon had promised to reveal as important as seeing her father through his last days, as watching her nieces and nephews grow up?

For once, the answer didn't matter. How could she willfully narrow her worldview again to birthdays and Christmasses, even the solemn rites of deathbed vigils, knowing a war raged in the shadows without her?

"I love you, Jackson," she said softly. "Talk to you later."

"Yeah. Sera, would Dad have liked him?"

She closed her eyes, Archer's silhouette etched starkly on the back of her eyelids. "Probably. Before."

Before her father lost his mind. Before Archer's possession.

Jackson sighed. "Just keep being safe, okay?"

A little late for that. "Okay."

As she disconnected, an updated photo showed blackened stalagmites, all that was left of the building. She could almost smell the sour stench of burned insulation and electrical wiring. The article said no definitive cause for the deadly blaze had been found.

The chill that had briefly left as she talked to her brother crept in again. "What are you thinking?"

Archer turned from the window. "That it's a good thing you were here."

"Was it my fault?"

"Did you set the fire?"

She pushed herself up from the desk. "You know what I mean."

"It's a long step from breaking and entering to fatal arson." He hesitated. "Unless you're a djinn-man. Then it's as easy as breathing. The pattern of the fire in the photo isn't natural."

"Seven people," she whispered.

"I'm concerned about the security hardware we installed in your unit."

She looked up in horror. "You think it short-circuited and started the fire?"

"No, but it should have triggered an alarm here." He ran a hand over his head. "Something else to talk to Bookie about."

"I should have called the police about the break-in." She rose to pace.

He watched her, expression shuttered. "There's nothing they could do against a djinni."

"What can *we* do? We have to stop him. How can we—?" She raised her head. "What's that smell?"

He shook his head. "You're just . . ." Then he sniffed and must have caught the same drifting scent of smoke. "Fuck."

He raced to the door and threw it open without checking the handle for heat. The demon's healing powers gave him leeway, but she couldn't help thinking of the people in her building who hadn't had that luxury.

She followed him into the hall just as he slammed the glass on the fire alarm. At the piercing shriek, she clamped her palms over her ears.

He grabbed her wrist and hauled her toward the stairs. He flung open the door and shoved her in. "Go. Get out of the building."

She clung to the railing and whirled around when he started up the stairs. "Where are you going?"

"Remember that picture of the fire? The flames dripped down. I need to check the roof."

"You think he's still up there?" Without another word, she started up the stairs, three at a time.

He jumped half the flight above her, eyes whirling violet with his ascendant demon. "No heroic-buddy-movie-of-the-week shit."

"Heroic, my ass. First my apartment. Now here." She passed him. "It's only paranoia if someone isn't after you."

They raced for the roof. Archer burst through the access door with a squeal of torn hinges.

The vast roof was an asphalt wasteland broken only by knee-high vents. One, missing its cover, sent up a curl of yellowish smoke.

Sera's gaze skipped across the surface, drawn by another movement. "There. Behind the AC unit."

Archer bolted across the roof, leaving her heart in a tailspin. They'd been sparring unarmed; she knew he didn't have his axe.

A commotion arose farther down the stairwell as the other talyan reacted to the alarm. She shouted back through the doorway, "Up here."

Archer was halfway across the roof, in pursuit of a figure clad in charcoal gray, almost invisible against the asphalt.

The gothic crenellations that decorated the roofline were only steps away.

The intruder reached the edge and clambered into the open space between the merlons—and jumped.

Sera gasped as the intruder disappeared from sight. It was a certain death fall. Even with a demon, she'd known that last night standing on the penthouse balcony.

Archer must have known the same. He skidded to a halt at the edge and peered down.

Just as two winged ferales burst over the crenellations.

The demons were smaller than the ones she and Archer had faced in the oak glade, with atrophied, catlike lower bodies and skeletal arms, but their wings were fully functional. The intruder dangled below the ferales, clinging to a chain that harnessed the winged monsters together, part aerial chariot, part demonic attack helicopter.

The ferales screeched in frenzy as they struggled to escape the vertical pull of air alongside the building. The stench of filthy feathers reached Sera.

The intruder hung a dozen feet out from the side of the building, exposed on the chain.

"Archer, no." She read in the set of his shoulders the moment he made his decision.

He jumped after the intruder—they slammed together in midair.

The added weight was too much for the ferales. They plummeted out of sight, screaming.

As Sera leaned over the edge, horror choked her.

Just below and to one side, the ferales beat the air with their wings, thrashing to regain altitude. Between the flailing feathers, Sera caught a glimpse of Archer and the intruder grappling. Neither seemed to have the upper hand, or much effect at all, in their precarious position tangled in the chain.

If only she could get Archer a weapon. A scuffle behind her made her straighten. "Tell me you brought a gun—"

She turned to face a half dozen more flight-ready ferales. End to end, they were eerily similar down to the snubbed fleshy beaks in their otherwise humanoid faces. They spread their wings, and stinking feathers blocked what was left of the sun.

Over the hiss of their breathing, she heard a shout from the access door. A few of the ferales turned to face the new threat of arriving talyan fighters, but the remainder advanced on her.

"See what happens when you aren't paranoid enough?" she muttered.

No league brothers, no weapon, no Archer. And the hellfire glint in the ferales' eyes vowed payback.

She wedged herself between the merlons, fingers scrabbling at the molded cement. The wind whistling up the building traced a frigid finger along her spine. The ferales crept closer. Once they were done with her, Archer wouldn't have a chance against their united effort.

She had only one shot. And she had it only with him.

Without looking around, she threw herself backward. The muscles in her thighs burned with sudden desperate strength. She twisted through the thin air, calling on the demon's sinuous power.

She collided hard with Archer and the intruder. But she knew instantly the broad chest under her grasping hands, and all her senses flared with awareness. The struggling ferales shrieked as the pendulum momentum of her leap swung them wide away from the building.

"On the arc back, let go," she cried.

She couldn't see; she could only cling to Archer. Her stomach churned as they reached the apogee and started to swing back. The ferales fought to hold their position. And then she was in free fall, Archer's arms tight around her.

They hit the side of the building and skidded down the concrete. She reached out blindly with one hand, still clutching him with the other. A railing slammed against her forearm, and she screamed.

But they wrenched to a halt. She focused her wind- and tear-blurred eyes. Archer had grabbed the railing. They hung thirty stories above the street. The black lines of his *reven* writhed in the clenched muscles of his arm.

His face stark with the strain of stopping their fall, he peered upward at the leashed ferales hovering several stories up. "You know how much I hate letting go."

"Well, don't do it again, really." She grimaced at the grinding agony in her arm. "I don't think I can reach over."

He flexed, pulling them up. Violet sparks raced along the *reven*, skin lucent with the ascendance of his demon. He hauled them over the railing onto the balcony, where they collapsed in a sprawl.

"We have to get back up there," she said. "Talyan are pinned down by the ferales."

A rattle of gunfire interrupted her, and a half dozen dark shapes launched from the roof. They circled around the demonborne intruder, riding the high-rise updrafts.

"Flying monkeys," Archer growled. "I hate flying monkeys."

"They were after me." Sera pulled herself upright. "I saw it in their beady little eyes. You told me ferales don't pack."

"Must be they're stupid and didn't read the handbook." His gaze followed the ferales with furious intensity. "Either that, or somebody—say a djinn-man with evil on his mind—brought them together. Did you notice the structural similarities? Those weren't back-alley ferales forming off scrap flesh. Those were bred and fed to a purpose."

She shuddered. "They had human faces."

"They could've plucked you right off the streets when we left the building. But we surprised the djinn-man."

"Yeah, I bet he was way surprised when you jumped him."

Archer bent his gimlet stare from the retreating intruder to her. "Not as surprised as when you did it." He pushed open the balcony door into an empty suite. "Get inside."

He stripped off his shirt and made a rough sling. She winced as he cradled her arm.

"Broken," he said. "Give the demon a few hours before your next crazy stunt."

"Oh, it's crazy when *I* do it."

"I had him in my fist." Archer's violet-shot eyes closed to slits. "He was after you. He won't get his way."

Bruises blossomed and faded on his bare torso—his teshuva dealing with the damage. She brushed her fingers along the clear mark of a large hand spanning his neck, with a darker imprint where a band like a ring had scored his skin.

He shuddered and closed his eyes.

"You are not to die for me," she said softly.

When he opened his eyes again, only tarnished bronze remained. "Not your call."

He wheeled away, leaving her to follow.

The hotel lobby swarmed with agitated talyan in various states of undress and even more varied states of armament. No one was leaving despite the thickening stink of sulfurous smoke.

"Where's the fire department?" The image of her burned-out apartment flashed through Sera's mind.

"I pulled an internal alarm," Archer said. "The authorities won't be alerted unless absolutely necessary."

She eyed him. "There's a fine line between secret society and mass delusional psychosis."

"How convenient that talyan make excellent tight-rope walkers." He waited until Liam was free, then slipped in among the gathered talyan. "Sera's apartment building was torched late last night. Looks like we're the djinn-man's second hit."

Liam spiked his fingers through his hair. "Haji found birnenston leaked down from the roof. We stopped it in the vents. For now."

Archer's expression turned grimmer yet. "Who's trying to douse it?"

"Perrin and Lex have the knack, but this might be more than they can handle. I gave them ten minutes. Then I'm calling the fire department."

"Won't help," Archer warned.

"They'll keep secondary fires from spreading to the neighbors." Liam ran a hand through his hair. "This djinn-man leached out enough birnenston to poison two buildings in less than twenty-four hours. He might be more than all of us can handle."

A talya ran up, gesturing for Liam. They left together. The rest waited tensely, poised to escape with the league's treasures.

She caught Archer's eye. "Birnenston?"

"An incendiary substance left behind in tenebrae lairs. They foul a place just by existing in this realm. Chemically, it's hydrofluoric acid with an etheric mutation. The more potent the demonic emanations, the nastier the birnenston."

"I had a hospice patient who died after an industrial acid accident." She shuddered at the memory of the fatal blistering.

"Hydrofluoric acid is the worst. It seeps into the body without surface burns and melts the victim from the inside. Birnenston is literally burn-stone, but the stone is human bone. And with the etheric mutation, the damage can go soul deep."

"Birnenston." She rolled the word on her tongue. "Brimstone? As in 'fire and . . .'?"

He nodded. "Impossible to extinguish through mortal means. Only a bane-class teshuva can burn it out."

Ten minutes passed, although to Sera's mind, it felt more like hours. Liam returned, looking grim. He commanded attention without a word, the talyan radiating out from him like a wheel.

"The birnenston is contained." His low voice carried in the still room. "But it exceeds the definition of unholy mess. Judging from the virulence, we're dealing with one tough djinni. And now he's targeting us."

"Let's make that mutual," Ecco growled.

Liam kept talking. "We need time to isolate and extinguish the birnenston. Until then, I'm closing the building."

Archer leaned close to her ear. "Birnenston acts like a slow poison. It doesn't kill, but it saps demonic power.

Bookkeepers think chronic birnenston toxicity helps contain demons in hell. Out here, it weakens our teshuva, which can get us killed by the next feralis we take on."

"Demons have kryptonite," she murmured. "The more you know."

Liam continued. "Zane has the list of safe houses and will be assigning teams. Take charge of your inventory and let's get going."

Archer took her arm as if she were part of his inventory. "We move on when our cover is compromised among the human population. Doesn't happen often, especially in a city this size. We've never been forced out by djinn." He scowled. "They haven't cared enough about us to bother."

"One cares now," she said.

As if he'd overheard them, Ecco pressed his point. "The djinn-man. What are we going to do about him?"

Liam shook his head. "Once we're secure—"

"I smell defense," Ecco said. "I hate playing defense."

"We need a base of operations," Liam said.

"For what? Screwing with malice?" Ecco paced around the outer edges of the crowd. "Time's past for that."

A few murmured as the agitated talya passed them—whether in agreement or annoyance, Sera couldn't tell.

"That's our calling," Liam said. "We—the teshuva—fight against the tenebraeternum for our souls."

"Djinn are eternally shadowed too," Ecco pointed out.

Sera glanced up at Archer's expressionless face.

"That's for the angelic—," someone started.

"Fuck the angels," Ecco growled. "They haven't gotten anywhere in two thousand years. It's our turn."

"That's not the way it's done," Zane said.

Ecco spun to face him. "Things are different now." He

pointed across the room at Sera. "I saw her extinguish a demon. Not just bleed it off. Destroy it."

She stiffened as every eye turned to her.

Ecco pressed his point. "She wasn't taking out the trash just to do it again tomorrow. She snatched that malice out of the ether and sent it back to oblivion where it belonged." He grinned toothily at Sera. "Who puts the repo back in repentin'?"

Archer stirred. "You're a poet, Ecco. But we're not sure what she did, or how."

She wanted to elbow him, but her broken arm refused to twitch. It hadn't been her alone. Only together had they banished the malice and the two ferales. Was he so determined to keep her at a distance that he'd deny what they'd done?

"Djinn-stuffed bastard wants to make this war personal," Ecco said. "I say let's man up. Or woman."

Liam shifted, glancing at Archer. "Does he make any sense to you?"

Archer shrugged. "What happened was odd. Bookie's working on it."

"Now this," Liam said.

Ecco stepped inside the circle. "We have to—"

Liam silenced him with a look. "We're evacuating this building. We're checking in at our new assignments. We hunt tonight. Same as always."

Ecco scowled.

Liam continued. "Whatever new wrinkle we find, the old wrinkles don't go away. We're still the hottest iron in the fire to smooth it out." He rubbed his forehead. "Analogy fails me. Get going, people, before the birnenston makes us all as foolish as Ecco. If he's right and the apocalypse is now, I'll be sure to page you."

There was a general chuckle, and the talyan started to move. Sera listened to them make plans to rendezvous with their assigned partners.

She started when Archer's hand fell on her shoulder. "Ready?"

"To go where? My place is gone. This place is ruined." And he wasn't even willing to acknowledge this monstrous force between them.

He steered her toward the door. "At least you're traveling light, like a good talya."

"Not funny." She balked on the sidewalk. He guided her to one side, out of the way of the stream of men. "What do they expect me to do?" she whispered, catching the sidelong glances.

"Nothing. They've learned not to expect."

"They're hoping."

"Definitely not that."

But she knew he was wrong.

She waited while he retrieved his league belongings and, for lack of a better plan, climbed into the box-laden SUV when he held the door for her.

She stared out the tinted window that turned the already-dreary day to twilight. "Who is he?"

"A powerful djinn-man who knows what you are."

She wasn't surprised that he could follow her thoughts. "Which is what, exactly?"

"Something equally powerful, judging by his reaction."

"Trying to kill me."

Archer shook his head. "He hasn't tried to kill you."

She looked at him in dismay. "He burned my house down."

"Which isn't the same as trying to kill you."

"Killed others," she murmured.

"And their souls went up or down as destined."

"No consolation," she snapped. "It never was, even when it was just my day job and not my life, like it is now." She laughed harshly. "My life, however long that may be."

"The djinn-man could kill you," Archer said flatly.

"He hasn't. He's got you—all of us—off balance, on the run. He wants something else." He ticked his finger on the steering wheel. "Also no consolation, I suppose."

She stared at him a moment. "Not really, no." Then she turned her attention back to the road. "Where are we going?"

"My place. We'll drop this load and get my system synced with Bookie's updates. We need to know why this djinn-man wants you."

"Nothing good," she muttered.

"We're demon-ridden. Good was never an option."

CHAPTER 17

At his loft, they unloaded the truck. Despite the ache in her healed arm, she found relief in the mindless task of ferrying boxes. He never let her out of his sight—nice to know when she was the target of some supremely bad-ass demon.

While he messed with his computer, she steeped a pot of tea. As if unseen forces flowed around it, the bed drew her gaze.

He'd excused himself for rejecting her because he'd almost gotten her killed on the hunt. But if a djinn-man was gunning for her, did getting accidentally dismembered by a raging feralis even count as a worry?

Archer dumped a laptop into her hands, startling her out of her daze. "This has the annotated library of Bookkeeper studies over the last few-hundred years. Find everything on demon crossings and the effect on the Veil."

"What am I looking for?"

He gave her a hard look. "Everything."

She settled in the chair on the other side of the couch, so she didn't have to face the bed, and buried herself in the small screen. When he brought her a cup of the tea she'd forgotten, the water was stained dark as the sky outside.

She blinked and started to get up. "What time is it?"

"Time for me to go out on rounds." His hand kept her pinned to the chair. "You stay here. Don't leave. Don't let anyone in. I'm setting the perimeter alarm. Someone will be close by."

She lifted her chin. "I'm not afraid. Cautious, yes."

"Then maybe you'll stay alive." His fingers tightened. "We'll find him."

"We have forever," she reminded him.

He took a step back. "Call if you need me."

She watched him go from the window, knowing he could see her but not caring.

The loft, with its isolated pools of lamplight, felt vast and cold. She heated the tea again, managed only to make it bitter, and went back to the computer.

Her search yielded little in the way of Veil crossings. Demonic emanations seemed unidirectional. Djinn and teshuva crossed into the human realm and stayed. Though horde-tenebrae energy could be dispersed and took time to regenerate, if a djinn and teshuva host was killed, the higher strains of demon simply possessed another soul and continued on their heretofore separate paths of wickedness or repentance.

The only interesting note was a centuries-old meditation describing the Veil as woven from atoning souls. Such souls formed a natural—or supernatural—barrier between the realms.

Sera shuddered to think of such never-ending suspension. That her demon had breached the Veil to send the malice and ferales back seemed unprecedented.

The hours passed, and she fell asleep on the couch. Archer returned just after dawn.

"Sera." Weariness roughened his voice and brought out the lingering Southern jangle. "Just me. I'll sleep like the dead, so make all the noise you want. Don't leave."

Without waiting for a reply, he'd headed for the bathroom. He didn't even turn on the lights.

That didn't stop her imagination from supplying the pictures. She lay back, listening to the water. He hadn't walked as if he'd been wounded during the night's fighting, but no doubt he'd keep his shoulders square, whatever the maiming.

Thoughts of his shoulders led naturally down his arms to the demon mark. Thinking of his *reven* made her think of her own, framing her hips, which—of course—made her think of his hips, grinding against hers under the spray of warm water....

She took a deep breath. When she heard him collapse into bed, she waited long enough for him to fall asleep before she got up.

She continued her work from the evening before, but somehow ended up searching Civil War firearms. She learned he'd been cruel with himself about his poor aim. It hadn't been uncommon for powder-packed guns to backfire, though she supposed the demon was an unexpected addendum.

After a quick glance toward the bedroom, she turned her search to Civil War–era Archers. He'd said his father was a farmer. She hit on a note for a James Archer of Louisiana, owner of a thousand-acre cotton plantation and father of Ferris and Emily. Then she saw it was a death notice. Though the man had been in his grave a hundred and fifty years, she had to fight back a welling sadness for the tormented son he'd left behind.

She scanned for files on Emily. Maybe there'd been children. Then she stopped herself.

She remembered how Archer accused her of butting into her patients' most vulnerable moments. Only this time, instead of trying to reconcile people to death, she'd have to explain someone who hadn't died. Even if she found descendants, how exactly would Archer introduce himself? *Hello, I'm your great-great-grandmother's brother. Why, yes, I am looking spry for my age. Aren't you glad you got these genes?*

She shook herself. Demons weren't genetic. Then she thought of her depressed mother, her father's dementia. Different kinds of demons.

She shut the laptop. People and history, long dead, all of it. When he'd said he'd lost everything, she hadn't quite imagined how much he'd *had* to lose.

She leaned back and closed her eyes. How long ago, how much, none of it mattered, because it hurt just as much. Even the demon couldn't take away that pain. Why did she imagine she could?

"Did I get you up too early this morning?"

Though his sleep-softened voice sent her heart racing, she held herself still, glad she had folded the screen down. She cracked one eye open. "Just taking a break."

He was barefoot, still in his flannel pajama bottoms. Two buttons held a wrinkled oxford closed around his navel, revealing a long, open vee of chest.

With a mental shrug, she opened her other eye. "Good hunting?"

"Too good. But not good enough. No dead djinn." He wandered to the kitchen. "We're out of tea."

So he sent her shopping with Zane, in charge of supply for the safe houses. She wrinkled her nose at the addition of Ecco as bodyguard, and Archer warned, "The djinn-man wants you, Sera. We don't know why, but we know we don't want him or any snacking feralis to have you."

When it came to snacking, she discovered the terrible talyan junk-food habit that filled up cart after cart. When Ecco groused about the length of the checkout line and the lack of good magazines, she just about lost it.

"Then quit eating so many doughnuts."

"I'm supposed to save the world on yogurt and baby carrots?" He looked appalled. "Must be a woman thing."

She glowered. "Go wait in the car."

He crossed his arms. "And shirk my duty, risking my soul? Assuming Archer didn't just shred me for compost."

"Then I'll wait for you." She marched for the door.

"Go with her," Zane said softly to Ecco, as if she might explode if he jostled her with loud words. "I'll finish here."

She plunked herself down in the driver's seat and stared at the first flakes of snow whipped in the wind.

Ecco disappeared into the back. After a few minutes, he cleared his throat. "Do you think you and Archer are compatible outside the bedroom?"

She glared into the rearview mirror. "Excuse me?"

"Does he listen to your dreams? Do you like his friends? You're a cute couple and all, but that trick you did together with the malice in Bookie's lab seemed a little kinky as the basis for a long and loving relationship."

She twisted around. "Are you smoking something back there?"

"You gotta have things in common besides the zing, you know?"

Before she could answer, Zane emerged with his conga line of shopping carts. They made their deliveries in a heavier snowfall, the flakes curdled by the wind into tiny stinging shards.

"That's it," Zane said. "I'll drop you off at Archer's."

"I have one more thing to do." Since her time was ticking away toward death, doom, and probably more damn deliveries.

Zane pursed his lips.

"And don't give me any fear-of-Archer crap," she said. "I'm dangerous too."

Zane shot Ecco a hard look. "Why'd you let her drive?"

"I had my magazine." Ecco waved the glossy pages

with the voluptuous brunette on the cover promising TEN WAYS *HE* CAN PLEASE *YOU* IN BED.

Zane looked disgusted. "Shoplifting?"

"Hey, I'm possessed by evil incarnate."

Sera scowled and headed to the outskirts of the city. The Good Faith Baptist Church looked even more pitiable without the neon blue flyers to brighten the cement blocks.

She glared at Ecco. "You. Stay. And for God's sake, don't do any more of the quizzes." She speared Zane with a glance. "You coming?"

She marched inside, Zane dogging her heels, and left behind Ecco like a Rottweiler who hopefully wouldn't eat the steering wheel.

Nanette smiled when Sera entered the office. "Sera. I wasn't sure you'd come to visit. And you brought a friend. Did our talk help you?"

Zane lifted his head as if he tested a nonexistent breeze. "Angel?"

Sera ignored both questions. "I actually hope you can help someone else."

Zane darted a glance at her. "Ecco? Really, Sera, all the saints in heaven couldn't help him, much less one earth-bound angelic possessed." Suddenly, he recoiled. "Not Archer? He'll kill you. In the metaphorical sense." He glanced at Nanette. "Her, maybe not so metaphorical."

Sera held her flattened palm out to him. "It's my father. Can you heal him?"

Archer woke from a dead sleep.

Despite the hours of the teshuva's restorations, his body screamed a protest when he sat up. The slashed muscle and broken ribs were healing, but every night he went out, the malice seemed more numerous and clever, the ferales bigger and bolder.

And without a partner at his back, the shadows crept

far closer. It was enough to make a man want to dive under the covers again and wait till the sun came up—except the sun didn't banish these demons anymore.

And the covers weren't so welcoming in an empty bed.

He listened for Sera. Despite his avowal that he never heard her, despite her disbelief that kept her quiet as a ghost, he was attuned to her comings and goings. She'd gone out with Zane and Ecco as guards, but still he listened.

Wouldn't do to jump out of bed in front of her with a raging hard-on.

He sighed, his nearly ever-present erection when he thought of her just one more pain in his wracked body. Unfortunately, not one the teshuva could do anything about.

He rose, dressed, and went to the kitchen. As he waited for his tea to steep, he paced the room to ease the tension from his torn muscles. Out the windows, the tall buildings cast the streets into gloom, and wayward swirls of snow caught the streetlights' glare. He'd slept nearly the entire day, but his weary body could've gone longer. Still, if he took it easy, he'd be fine for the night's rounds.

Mostly fine. Good enough, anyway. Still safer than proximity to his studious roommate after they'd shared the same bed, same breath, same slick of sweat . . .

So much for easing the tension in his body.

He retrieved his tea but couldn't stop pacing. One circuit took him past his cell phone. He listened to the message that he had no messages.

The panic button on Zane's phone linked to Archer's. If anything went down, Zane would need only a split second and the barest flick of a finger to call for backup.

After the night he'd had, Archer wondered if a split second was too long a grace period to expect.

He called Zane. The call went to voice mail. Ecco

didn't carry a cell phone—said it made him feel wussie. As a last resort, Archer called Sera's cell.

"Hi." At her calm voice, relief coursed through him. Then she went on. "Insert clever outgoing message here." The tone beeped.

He hung up.

All his senses prickled, worse than when the echo of the unbound demon hunting its chosen had haunted his dreams.

Grabbing his coat, hefting it against the weight of the axe nestled inside, he headed for the door. He took the car, cruising the city, hunting he knew not what.

His phone rang. He snatched it up before the first tone faded.

"Archer." The gasp reached him through the stuttering line. "I need—"

"Sera." He gripped the phone, as if he could hold the broken signal together with his bare hands. If ever there was a time for that fabled mated-talyan bond . . . "Where are you?"

"Hurry. Ecco is down—" The interference was like nothing he'd heard before. In the static, faint whispers mocked him, making his skin crawl. "Nanette can't hold them alone."

"Where are you?"

"The nursing home. Hurry."

He cranked the wheel, sending the car into a two-lane skid across the road. A horn blared behind him. "Stay inside, Sera. Stay on the line." Even as he spoke, he knew it was futile. He heard the click and pictured her rushing into the fray.

He called Niall and gave directions to the nursing home.

Niall didn't bother asking questions Archer couldn't answer. "Raine and Valjean are almost as close as you. Watch for them. Don't lose her, Archer."

He wouldn't answer that either.

Less than ten minutes passed, but the last of the iffy light had failed as he double-parked outside the nursing home. Before the car rocked to a halt, he was running across the lawn.

The picket fence leaned askew; the ground was raked into vicious furrows of dark frozen earth and dead grass. Blood, crimson fresh, glistened through the thin haze of snow. A meaty scent hung in the chill air.

His heart thudded heavily in his chest. No Sera.

"Ferris Archer?"

He ripped his gaze from the signs of struggle.

A woman he didn't know waved from the front door. "We're here. Inside."

Sera had actually listened to him? He tried to ignore the curdling in his gut.

He headed up the walk warily, one eye on the woman, scanning the shadows all around.

"Hurry," the woman said. "They won't come close while I'm here, but I don't know if that will last."

He narrowed his eyes against the coruscating shivers of golden light that emanated from her. "I didn't think angels bothered with the lesser demons."

"They started it." She held her hand out to him. "Please. Get inside."

"Where is Sera? Is she . . . ?" His throat closed around the words as he followed her in.

"She wanted to go after them, but I stopped her." She lifted her nose when Archer cut a glance at her. "I do have the Almighty on my side."

"Is that all it takes?" he murmured.

"I'm afraid your man, Ecco, didn't fare so well. Sera is helping him, and preventing the nurse here from helping too much."

"Humans." He grimaced.

The woman pursed her lips reprovingly. "The innocent. The ones we protect."

He paced her down a hall. "Is that your duty? I've

only seen your kind taking on the djinn, and damn whoever is in the way."

"I believe damning is your specialty." She paused just
beyond an open door and lowered her voice. "The nurse,
Wendy, has convinced herself that a gang drug war went
down in her front yard, and we were coincidentally
caught in the crossfire as we arrived. She wanted to call
the police, so Sera told her you're a detective with the
city."

"Do I look like a cop?"

"I believe Sera said undercover vice."

He smiled humorlessly as they stepped into the room.
Then even the illusion of amusement left him.

Ecco was sprawled facedown on a table. Blood
soaked the creamy eyelet of the tablecloth under him.
He'd been laid open to the bone in a dozen places. Sera
stood piecing him together.

Another woman, visibly shaking, staunched the
blood flow with a handful of towels. She glanced up
wildly as Archer entered. "Who are you? You're not
the paramedics." Her voice rose shrilly. "Where are the
paramedics?"

Sera met his gaze, her eyes wide and desperate. A
shock jumped between them, almost a physical thing, as
if she'd thrown herself into his arms, as if he'd pulled her
so close he'd never let her go again.

He tightened his hands into fists, but she never moved.
She turned back to the other woman. "Wendy, this is the
police officer I told you about."

"There was another shooting just down the street,"
Archer lied smoothly. "Same gang, we think. The paramedics had to stop. I'm making sure it's safe. Then I'll
take the patient to them."

Wendy glanced down. "He can't be moved. We need
a stretcher, an IV, oxygen...."

"I'm sure it looks worse than it is," Archer said.

The three women stared at him.

He shrugged. "Wounds like those often bleed a lot."

"Like these?" Wendy's voice was slightly calmer. "You mean the kind that go all the way through?"

Ecco had the good sense to groan then and push himself partway up on his elbows.

Sera steadied him. "Don't move. You'll spring another leak." She glanced at the third woman. "Nanette, is there any chance you could . . ."

Nanette shook her head. "I can't help him because of his . . . condition."

Wendy frowned. "Sera, she's a faith healer, not a miracle worker." Then she laughed, the hysteria edging back into her tone. "Faith. Miracle."

Nanette put her hand on the woman's shoulder. Wendy let out a sob.

Archer scowled as well. They didn't have time for miracles. They needed something a little more immediate. He took Sera's arm and dragged her away. He steeled himself against the urge to touch her everywhere, reassure himself that not a single drop of the blood he'd seen was hers. "Are you all right?"

She nodded, swaying in his grip. "They took Zane. Ecco couldn't stop it. I had just stepped inside with Nanette and was talking to Wendy. I heard the shouting, and I ran back out, but—"

"Who, Sera? Who took Zane?"

"The ferales."

He straightened. "Ferales don't—"

She shook him off. "I know, I know. Ferales don't pack. Tell that to the ones that flocked over the hotel too. This was worse. Ecco tried to follow. They tore him apart and just vanished."

The pool of blood in the yard swamped Archer's vision for a heartbeat. "I want us out of here."

"We can't leave Wendy—"

"She's in more danger with you here." He watched coldly as her expression blanked.

He dialed Niall and curtly explained the situation. "Have Raine and Valjean secure a tight perimeter. We're coming out."

He heard Niall talking into another line, a moment of silence, then return. "Done. They say there's nothing in the vicinity. Valjean wants to start tracking."

"No. He and Raine will bring Sera and Ecco back. I'm going after Zane."

"Negative." Niall's tone brooked no opposition. "Get her back here, now. I want her safe. Then you can find Zane."

Archer ground his teeth together. "Fine. Loose Valjean. I don't want the trail to go cold. The djinn-man was here."

He disconnected and turned back to the women. "I'm taking these witnesses into protective custody." He prodded Ecco and ignored the welling of blood. "Sir, can you walk?"

Ecco grunted something like an affirmative. Wendy stared openmouthed as he pulled himself to his feet.

Sera put her shoulder under Ecco's arm. "I'll help you out to the car. Nanette?" The smaller woman stood on Ecco's other side. Sera looked back at Wendy. "I'm so sorry. I'll call you."

Archer gestured them toward the door. "Ma'am, if I can ask you not to speak with anyone about this . . ."

Wendy shook her head. "I'm not going to upset my residents."

"Exactly." He blocked the door as Wendy started to follow them. "I can recommend a good cleaning service."

She blinked at him. "Oh. That would be good."

He eased her aside with the distraction of writing down the name of his cleaners. Sera led the small group out, Ecco limping along. He closed the door on the curious woman and followed them. Just beyond the fence line, he glimpsed two prowling figures, Raine and Valjean, keeping watch.

He levered Ecco into the SUV. "Try not to stain the seats."

The "Fuck you" he got in return lacked strength but not sincerity.

He glanced at Nanette. "I'm afraid we're going to have to keep you a little longer. Then we'll send you back to your faithful."

"Archer." Sera's voice was edged. "I asked for her help."

"That'll teach her." He went to the driver's side. Out on the street, he saw Raine take over the idling car he'd abandoned. Valjean, his gaze fixed on some sign at his feet, melted into the darkness.

Then their short and somber procession headed into the night.

Chapter 18

Niall met them at the front door of the central safe house. He took in the sight of them, then directed his gaze upward. "I'm not going to like this story, am I?"

"It gets worse," Archer said grimly.

Sera tried not to cringe as she walked past Niall. She'd lost one of his fighters.

They brought Ecco to a room too bland and clinical to be called a hospital room. Nanette looked around. "And I thought our church was ugly."

Niall pursed his lips. "I take it you aren't host to a seraphim?"

Sera gestured from one to the other. "Nanette, this is Liam Niall, leader of the Chicago league of teshuva. Liam, Nanette is a faith healer." She took a breath. "I wanted her to help my father."

"Angelic possessed can't aim their healing," Niall said.

"I told her," Nanette said over Sera's "I had to try."

Niall dragged a hand over his head. "Not that it matters. What happened?"

Ecco, laid out on the bed, stirred. "I was escorting Sera and Nanette to the door of the nursing home, Zane behind me. They came out of nowhere. Seven, maybe nine ferales. They were huge, biggest I've ever fought, quick too."

Archer studied him. "You took a helluva beating."

"I've never seen anything like it. They attacked in concert and kicked my ass like my teshuva was getting its nails done. Three of them cut between my group and Zane, forcing us up the walk. The rest went after Zane."

Archer frowned. "Why Zane?"

"Hell if I know."

"He was certainly the easiest to take," Nanette offered. "Even I could see his demon was weakest."

"But to what purpose?" Niall paced the edges of the room. "Ferales devour on the spot. They don't take leftovers, much less prisoners."

"Things are different now," Ecco said grimly. "I told you."

Sera shivered. "My fault."

"How?" Archer demanded. "Because you didn't get taken yourself?"

She met Archer's violet-tinged gaze. "You warned me. You said he wanted me."

"Not bad enough to make a feralis smart," Ecco said. "They grabbed the wrong person."

"If they were sent for small and weak," Nanette said, "they wouldn't understand their master wanted female. They would only sense Sera's strong demon and think, 'Not that one.' "

Sera's blood congealed in her veins. "We have to find him. We should all be out there."

Niall shook his head. "No one gets between Valjean and the tracks. Once he's on the scent, I'll throw everything we have into finding Zane."

"I may not rank in the upper echelons of the celestial hierarchy," Nanette said, "but perhaps the heavenly host can be of assistance."

"They never have before," Ecco said.

Nanette steepled her fingers. "Since there's a djinni involved, playing some deeper game, they might be more open to alliance."

Niall sighed. "Ma'am, I think you'll find your kind are hard-hearted when it comes to us."

" 'Love the sinner,' " Nanette said piously.

"So I've heard," Archer growled. "But we are the sin."

"We need to get Nanette home," Sera said. "Will she be safe?"

Niall lifted one empty hand. "You said the djinn-man wants you."

"Haji will take her," Archer said. "He can watch her place overnight."

"I have my own protections." Nanette took Sera's hands. "Tell Wendy I'll be back to visit your father. I can reassure her everything is fine."

Sera slanted a glance at Archer. "Just in case that impressive tangle of lies didn't do it."

He folded his arms over his chest. "It was for her own good."

So, the man who said fallen angels didn't lie could make an exception for the good of others. Although she supposed he'd never claimed to be any kind of angel.

Nanette sighed. "I can't promise the power will rise in me for your father's sake, but I can at least pray."

Ecco sputtered.

Sera didn't even glance at him. "I'm sorry I dragged you into this. I didn't intend—" She held a flat palm out toward Ecco. "Nothing from you about paving the road with intentions." She sighed. "Pray for Zane as well."

Nanette nodded.

Ecco groaned. "All of you, get out. Give me an hour's sleep and I'll be back on my feet. Then I'll be wanting me some ferales screaming."

After a hug between the women, Niall escorted Nanette out to find Haji.

Archer lingered near Ecco. "An hour won't be enough to get you sitting upright, much less off your knees. And you know your teshuva didn't desert you, so you might want to spend this time contemplating why you weren't on your game."

Ecco turned violet-tinged eyes on him. "I ain't got no death wish, pretty boy, unless it's dead ferales. Unlike some others I could mention. Even if I did, I would never sacrifice anyone else to reach my glory day."

Sera put her hand on Archer's arm. "He did everything he could. There were just too many."

Archer shrugged her off. "Fine. We'll see how many references Bookie can find to ferales' pack behavior under djinn control."

"No." Up her spine, the demon mark burned until she straightened. "No more research."

"Valjean is looking for a trail, and our contact at the Coil knows—"

"We have to *do* something to find Zane." She took a breath. "After all, we have the bait they want."

Archer glared at her, violet swirling brighter in his dark eyes. "What?"

Ecco pursed his lips. "I get it. We set a trap, and she's the bait. Sounds like a good idea to me."

Archer rounded on him. "Since when are you the strategist?"

Ecco gave him the middle finger and rolled over.

Archer dragged Sera out into the hall and slammed the door on Ecco's room. "You think if you read a few histories, learn a few moves, you can turn the tide of battle?"

She gritted her teeth. "You said I was different."

His tone edged toward a sneer. "And I've always been wrong."

"I have to find Zane." She tried to keep her voice hard against the quiver that threatened. "I lost him."

"He's a fighter, not your baby boy."

"You've never lost one before, have you? They've been killed, yes. But lost?"

"We're all lost," he said.

She snarled. "Don't get metaphysical on me."

"Fine," he snapped back. "You want to be realistic now? Then stop trying to find a loophole out of madness and death."

She recoiled.

He stepped into her space to loom over her. "You want us to save Zane. You want Nanette to save your father. You want to save the world. Hell, I think you even want to save me."

The scorn in his voice raised her hackles even as something else in her withered. "A few of those, at least, are worth saving. Which is more than I can say about giving up your life and soul for a slaver's ill-fated cotton farm."

He went utterly still.

As soon as the words were out of her mouth, she regretted them. Why was she fighting him? What was the point? "That was a hateful thing to say."

"You've been doing more research than I realized." He took a step back. "Hateful but true. My father owned slaves. I would have if I'd managed to keep the farm, if the South had won the war. And you're right; it was stupid to sacrifice my soul when the battle I was fighting was already lost. Which is why I won't let you make yourself bait."

Wouldn't let? She bristled, remorse morphing to anger. She echoed his words back at him. "Not your call. You've kept yourself an outsider in the league. If Niall, like Ecco, thinks it's a good idea, I'll do it."

He shook his head. "Always pushing. The universe probably crushed your spine just to make you sit down and shut up for a minute. No wonder the demon was able to tempt you so easily with the promise you could just keep pushing."

Her throat tightened. She clenched her fists as if she could shift the tension away from the threatening tears. "You're asking me to just give up?"

He shook his head. "Nobody has to ask. Sometimes you don't have a choice."

She stood in the hall and watched him walk away.

Towers these days didn't have dungeons, which puzzled Corvus, since this world hadn't lost the taste for dungeons. But the towers did have basements, and sub-basements, which served just as well. Enough levels down and, even within the thick concrete and rebar walls, the smells were the same—cold, damp, and inescapable decay.

He brought his second set of tools down there: the torch with the slightly askew propane stream; the pliers and tongs that didn't quite meet straight anymore; the dulled shears that didn't cut so much as crush.

He'd also brought the slivers of ruined glass.

The splinters glittered in the harsh light—but not so bright as the corroded eyes skittering in what shadows they could find.

He sighed as he contemplated the darklings' trophy. Despite his less-than-gentle tutelage—and it wasn't as if they didn't eat the brains he gave them—they'd still managed to snatch the wrong talya. He should have risked getting closer. But the last time had been too close.

He slapped the talya's cheek lightly. The man jerked, head lolling. With another sigh, Corvus threw the remains of his glass of cognac in the man's face.

He sputtered, yanking against the birnenston-soaked bonds. Corvus waited while the talya's gaze shuttled around the barren room, taking in the shifting kaleidoscope of lesser demons, the table of tools, and finally returned to Corvus himself.

Corvus nodded at the sudden, fearful constriction of the talya's pupils. "I am djinn."

"I am so not surprised."

Corvus smiled sourly at the impudence. "No need for your name, rank, and serial number. Your league brothers call you Zane. Your petty-mischief demon came from one of the shallowest circles of hell. And your number is up."

Zane shook his head, spraying cognac. "Your insults have broken me already."

"Oh, I don't need words for that." Corvus stretched his empty, bare hands. "Even your puny teshuva will heal your wounds again and again. The screaming will go on for a very long time."

"So what do you want to know? I'll sing like a bird."

"Nothing really. I know everything I need." Corvus surveyed the table of tools. "Except how to extract a demon." He turned back with a pair of pliers in his hand. "I shall set you free."

"By killing me."

Corvus inclined his head. "An unfortunate corollary."

For a moment, Zane's expression calmed. "To let it go . . ."

Corvus pressed the back of his hand against his forehead, shielding his eyes from the harsh lights as he felt the tightening of the demon's rising. "You have fought long enough. Not so long as I, but as a courtesy, I will not add your corpse to my army."

Zane pulled back as far as the bonds would let him. "Yeah, thanks for not much."

"Perhaps your soul, once free, will thank me."

" 'Charity begins at home.' "

In Zane's widening eyes, Corvus saw the reflection of his own yellow gaze, the acid tears that burned furrows down his cheeks. "I would, you know. If I could."

"Please don't let me stop you."

"Oh, you won't." He brought the pliers up against Zane's cheek. "Hell itself can't stop me now."

Sera wished Niall's safe house were bigger, if only to give her more room to pace. Bigger would have put more space between her and Archer too.

He was always deep in conversation with another talya or on his phone. He never even glanced up. She knew this because she was staring angry holes in him. She could help if he'd stop being such a stubborn, patriarchal throwback.

The scornful voice in her head told her she'd done entirely enough. She sunk to her haunches in the hallway. At the other end, she saw Archer on yet another phone call. If she hadn't been off the reservation pursuing her own hopeless fantasies . . .

"Whenever the djinn-man tried to snatch you again, he might've gotten someone else."

She glanced up at Niall. "You reading my mind?"

He shook his head. "Just looking at your face."

"Nice to be transparent."

He followed the earlier path of her gaze down the hall toward Archer. "It's only obvious if someone knows what they're looking at."

She watched him with a slight frown.

He shook his head. "Archer said he's going to tie you to a bedpost to stop you from making a terrible mistake."

As if Archer, beds, and she hadn't already been a terrible mistake. She dragged her mind back to the conversation at hand. "Did he explain why I think it would work?"

"He didn't have to. I told him I'd set you free to try it."

She pushed to her feet. "Then let's—"

Niall put a hand on her shoulder. "If I thought it would work."

"It will."

"Sera, this djinn bastard is already two steps ahead of us. If he got you, he'd be light-years ahead."

She frowned. "But light-years closer to what?"

"We still don't know. Bookie sent me a message saying that your research has him thinking. He wanted to meet with you, but then this—"

A flurry of activity down the hall attracted their attention.

Archer was shouting into the phone. "We're on our way," he said, urging the talyan around him toward the door.

Niall and Sera ran to join the exodus.

Despite her night-long avoidance, she found herself in the SUV Archer commanded, crammed in the backseat between Jonah and another talya.

Archer met her gaze in the rearview mirror as he careened through the early-morning streets. "You're coming because I didn't have time to lock you in your room. Don't get caught. Don't get dead."

She scowled and said nothing.

Wind-blown snow snaked across the pavement in hypnotic patterns before them and whipped into spume behind. She felt just as helplessly thrown into chaos.

Archer's voice in the phone was cold as he organized the attack with fighters in the other vehicles. "I told Valjean to try the sewers. He caught a scent down there, followed it up, and Haji has the schematics on the building. He's downloading them to your GPS units now. Raine has the area under surveillance. No one's been in or out, but we don't know how many humans are inside or their relationships to the djinn-man." His tone hardened. "Valjean says the place is crawling with demon sign, so innocence is unlikely. Still, if you encounter humans, try not to kill them until we have cause. And we want the djinni contained."

He disconnected. Sera tugged nervously at her necklace.

Beside her, Jonah shifted. "Can we hold a djinni?"

Arched didn't look back. "We will."

The two talyan glanced at each other over her head. Uncertainty radiated off them like a chill.

They closed on the gaunt, ugly structure in a rush of dark vehicles. The street in front was empty.

"Too much available parking," Jonah muttered. "Never a good sign."

Out of the cars sped a dozen talyan, silent and swift.

Sera half thought Archer would lock the doors on her, maybe leave the windows cracked open if she was lucky. But he didn't say a word as she ran with them.

Later, she wondered if he'd guessed what they would find.

Jonah in the lead smashed through the glass front doors without slowing. The rest followed.

A wall of malice, black and frothing as a standing wave of oil-fouled water, met them.

She flinched at a painful grasp on her arm.

"Let us take care of it." Archer took her hand and laid the haft of his smaller knife across her palm. "Don't reveal yourself here."

She gripped the knife. "Don't touch me, and the thing between us won't happen." He stiffened as if she'd raised the weapon against him.

The other fighters weren't waiting for them anyway. Instead, they ripped through like superheated scythes, steaming away malice in wide swathes.

The talyan pressed forward. Sera heard a whoop of satisfaction at the easy progress. Before the malice had been entirely dispersed, a tide of ferales swept forward.

But they were small and halfhearted in their attack, almost clumsy. One stumbled past the talya ahead of her, and she put Archer's knife through it. It collapsed without even a groan and only a thin trickle of ichor.

The fighters mowed through the ferales as easily as the malice, some pressing toward the center of the building and the basement access, some hanging back to guard the territory they'd taken.

"Birnenston has weakened these demons," Archer said. "This must've been a nest for years and we never knew."

She realized he'd been sticking close, but not close enough to touch, even as he contributed his share of the decimation. Making sure she didn't screw up, she guessed.

She frowned. "Why would the djinn-man stay here if it poisons his demon?"

"Maybe we can ask him this time."

She glanced at him, caught by the note of reservation in his voice.

By then, they were making their way down the stairs, a few scattered malice fleeing ahead of them.

She heard one of the warriors give a single cry, then fall silent. Her blood froze.

Archer shouldered her aside. "Wait here."

For once, she didn't argue. The rest of the talyan cleared the stairs around her, leaving her in the dim, dank space. A lone malice skittered aimlessly in the dark corner at the bottom landing, like an autumn leaf caught up in a swirl of wind.

A sob echoed through the basement door. All else was silent. She couldn't stop herself.

She crept down the last few stairs and stared in.

Framed in the open doorway, head bowed, Zane was tied naked to a chair.

If all the malice and all the ferales they'd battled on their way down had bled like humans, still the flood would have been a drop compared to the pool of crimson surrounding the chair.

With a choked cry, Sera broke through the ring of waiting talyan, though Liam tried to catch her. "Someone untie him. Oh God, Zane."

He raised his head to meet her gaze—except his eyes were gone.

Archer wrenched her back. "We can't untie him. The bindings are acting as tourniquets. Until the teshuva gets its act together and starts healing the worst of the wounds, we don't dare loosen them." He lowered his voice. "It's all that's holding him together."

Sera swallowed hard, until she had herself under control. "Let me go."

With each step sliding or sticking in the insane spill of blood, she went to Zane's side and crouched beside him.

"You guys found me." Blood trickled from his mouth. Behind the broken and missing teeth, his tongue was split, whether from blows, his own teeth, or from the heavy shears on the floor just in her line of vision, she didn't want to know. "Not a second too soon."

"We were gonna stop for coffee, but . . ." She tried to keep her tone light, but she heard the quaver in her voice.

A few talyan in the circle, including Liam, turned away.

"I've got a theory," Zane said. "When the teshuva came to me, I was so afraid to die, I would've agreed to anything. I'm not afraid anymore."

"Hmm. Where's the theory part?"

His breath rattled wetly in his lungs. "I think the demon is finally gone."

"The djinn-man? Yes, he's gone."

"I meant my demon."

Stillness rippled out from her to the listening talyan.

"It's not death that frees you from the demon," Zane said. "It's the end of the fear of death. That's peace. I knew you'd understand." His voice trailed off.

Archer pulled her back. "Leave him be. Let the te-shuva work."

She bit her lip. "What if his demon is gone?"

Archer crossed his arms. "You think he wouldn't be dead already with those wounds?"

She didn't doubt Archer knew death intimately, but he didn't know the knife-edge between life and death like she did. Years of hospice work had shown her both the precious fragility and the monstrous tenacity of life. "Demon or no, we can't stay here. It reeks of evil."

Archer nodded. "The birnenston. Probably why Zane's teshuva hasn't been much help."

Unwilling to question him again about the demon's continued presence, she let it pass. "I know you don't think much of first aid, and we're way past that now, but somebody should look at Zane."

His lip curled. "Your faith healer?"

"I was thinking a little more practical."

When the slow leakage from Zane's body congealed, they gingerly cut his bonds. Only his rasping breaths told them he was still alive.

The transport back to the safe house might have been a funeral procession. Liam arrived a few minutes after them, the task Sera had set him complete.

Sera met Betsy outside Zane's room. "This is awful," she warned. "But I didn't know whom else to call."

The nurse clutched her small duffel, still blinking the early-morning sleep from her eyes. "I've done three mercy tours following two civil wars and a genocide. You can't shock me."

Sera gestured her in.

After one small gasp at the sight of the battered, raw meat that had been the talyan warrior, Betsy upended the duffel on the table beside the bed. Zane flinched at the clatter of glass vials.

"You're awake?" Betsy slanted a glance at Sera, eyes wide with disbelief. "I'm a nurse. If I hurt you, tell me."

Zane chuckled, little more than a gurgle. "I sort of doubt I'll notice."

"Ah, a funny guy," Betsy said. "Those kind pinch my ass."

The bare twist of a smile on his cut lips faded. "No pinching, I promise."

"Just to be safe, I'm putting you out again. You won't feel a thing."

"Good," he whispered.

Sera set her hand on his shoulder while Betsy emptied a syringe in his arm. He went slack, and she reassured herself that his chest still rose.

Betsy started cleaning and suturing. "I could lose my license for this."

"We know all about risk." Archer laid a hefty stack of bills beside Betsy's duffel. "For your next civil war."

Betsy glanced at Sera. "Is he for real?"

Sera shook her head, no.

"It helps to think of it all as a bad dream," Archer agreed.

Betsy grunted. "You say this guy can't go to the hospital, but we don't know what internal damage he's suffering. And you can be sure he's suffering."

"Yeah, we're sure," Archer said. "We just needed you to stabilize him."

"He's still capsized," Betsy said. "We're just keeping him from sinking any more. Barely."

"That's enough."

"Probably not." Betsy unrolled an arm's length of gauze. "Whoever did this was a monster."

Sera bowed her head.

"We'll catch him." Archer hovered just behind her. The warmth of his big body took a bit of the chill off hers.

Betsy eyed them. "You vigilantes? That why you won't go to the police?"

Sera sighed. "Remember that self-defense course you wanted me to take? Consider it taken."

"You're gonna save the whole city from bad guys now?"

Sera looked at her hard. "How many gunshot wounds, rapes, and finger-shaped bruises on kids have you seen? If you could stop it, wouldn't you?"

Betsy stared back. "No one can stop it."

Sera let her intensity bleed away. "Slow it, then, even if you're not sure what you're doing matters in the end, even if nobody else thinks you're right."

Finally, Betsy shrugged. "Guess that's why I came here."

Wrapped in gauze, Zane at least looked tidy. Sera gave Betsy a hug. "Liam will take you home. Use the money to refill your black bag. We might need you again."

Betsy's lips twisted. "Fine. But don't you forget, no one can fix dead."

Sera nodded—but death just wasn't the scariest of her fears anymore.

CHAPTER 19

Archer slumped on the chair outside Zane's door, a weary bookend with the talya across from him, listening to the rasp and hitch of breath from within the room.

Perversely, bright sunlight gleamed through the window at the end of the hall, low in the winter sky but undaunted. Archer would've poked it out had he a knife long enough.

It was the least he could do for the man inside.

Why had he allowed anyone else to guard her? He'd known what stalked her and had been painfully aware of her innocence of what unholy evil could be done to her. But edgy with the longings she aroused in him, he'd let someone else take his place.

And Zane bore the consequences of his dereliction.

His own chest wrenched with every labored breath he heard. He welcomed the pain as penance, wishing he could truly take the other man's wounds upon himself.

The scuff of footsteps down the hall made him raise his head, though the other talya never even glanced up.

The silhouette approaching was backlit by the sun, the head haloed in a golden corona, the outline carved

away by gleaming light until all that was left was a slender, ethereal darkness that burned into his brain.

The figure raised its arms, and for a heart-stopping
moment, Archer thought flowing wings would surely
follow, arch up to shatter the too-small corridor, while a
fiery sword pierced his heart. . . .

Another step closer, and the shadow fell over his face.
He squinted.

Sera thumped her arms down, her expression twisted
in frustration. "What are you doing out here? Go sit
with him. And lose the long faces."

Archer pulled his scattered thoughts together. Not a
seraphim come to slay him as he so richly deserved, but
just Sera, demon-ridden, coming to tongue-lash him.

The other talya rose uneasily. "He's still unconscious.
And he couldn't see us anyway."

She sighed. "Even unconscious, he'll know you're
there, that you care. And he doesn't need to sense your
doom."

"Is there some reason to hope?" Archer murmured.

Sera turned the blast of her hazel eyes on him. Freed
from her ire, the talya slunk down the hall, out of sight.
"With that attitude, you just stay out of here." She
marched into the room.

Despite her injunction, Archer followed to lean in
the doorway.

She tidied the bedside table where Betsy had left an-
tibiotics and extra bandages—as if the teshuva needed
those. The league didn't even stock aspirin.

If the teshuva had gone . . . He drained the thought
as thoroughly as any malice. But the shards remained.

Sera talked softly about the sunlight outside, the
wind clearing the clouds, the contrast of sun's warmth
and wind's bite that made it hard to decide whether to
stay in or go out.

"Have to put up with the one to enjoy the other, I

suppose." She pulled up a chair to the bed and brushed her fingers over Zane's forehead. The rest of him had disappeared behind a shroud of bandages.

Archer's fingers closed into fists so hard the muscles ached all the way up his arms.

She glanced up at him, then gestured to the chair opposite her. He shook his head. She scowled, but he noticed that the light caress of her hand never changed.

"Archer's here too, Zane," she said. "He feels terrible that you're hurt. But not as terrible as I do."

Archer drew a breath to refute her on a few key points, but on the sheet, Zane's hand twitched. Archer caught the movement and straightened. "Is he coming around?"

Sera took the slack fingers in her own. "You don't have to wake up yet. When you're ready."

Archer shifted from one foot to the other. "He might be able to tell us more about the djinn-man."

"You have Valjean and everyone else with an ounce of tracking sense roaming the city. You sent one team with Bookie's mobile spectral tracking machine, even though you're not sure it works. The only useful thing you haven't done is stuck me out as bait . . ." She took a calming breath. "Anyway, what more can Zane tell you?"

"Not the where," Archer acknowledged, "but the why."

She lifted Zane's hand as if he were evidence. "Does that matter at the moment?"

"You, the constant seeker, ask me that? Why's the biggest question."

"I meant the djinn-man's plans won't change just because Zane finishes his rest. We'll know soon enough."

That sounded a little too much like "The end is nigh" for Archer's comfort. He scowled. Since when had the thought of the end become something to be feared instead of welcomed?

He stared at her in dismay and slowly backed into the hall.

She couldn't make him afraid to die. He wouldn't allow it. That fear would make him useless. Everything he'd lost would have been lost in vain.

The hallway was dark. The sun had succumbed to the clouds again. So much for her theory about taking the bad with the good. It was all bad, and to forget that, even for a second, only made the rediscovery more painful.

If spring came back around, it wouldn't touch him. He'd have to blame his momentary hope on the teshuva within him that still thought it would win its way back into grace.

Idiot demon.

Wrapping the fury of betrayal around him like a fine trench coat, he stalked down the hall.

If Zane was twitching now, his teshuva would have him awake in another hour. They'd get their answers then, and the end they'd bring on would be like nothing the djinn-man could ever have imagined.

"You were almost caught." The Worm paced, wringing his hands with such frenzy, Corvus wondered he didn't tear them off.

Perhaps his next sculpture should be a carrion bird, some great-winged, soaring beast that descended to earth only to thrust its naked beak into the soft flesh of the welcoming dead.

But the thought of those feathers, more black on black on black, made him shudder. The damn crow was hard enough—so hard that for the first time since he'd stolen the techniques of colored glass from his Roman masters, he'd thought of giving up.

He was glad there would be no next time.

"If you get caught," the Worm was shrieking, wriggling closer, "they'll know—"

With a lazy snap of his wrist, Corvus reached out and

wrapped his fingers around the man's throat. "Worms serve a useful function, but they turn up in multitudes wherever there is dirty work to be done. So a wise worm keeps a low profile."

The Worm pried at the fingers around his neck, eyes bulging even more than usual.

Corvus loosened his grip. "Don't test my patience. I find my grasp on it tenuous of late."

The Worm stumbled back out of reach, rubbing his throat. He croaked, "Is that why you killed the talya?"

"I freed him." Corvus turned to the window to look at his sculptures. The seagull in flight, his first, was still his best, he thought. Ever since, he'd tried to recapture that abandon of line and wildness of raw material. The faintest touch of blue threaded through its belly had been an inspired act, as if the bird launched itself toward the wide-open ocean, the pure waters reflected in its white feathers. He almost heard its mournful cry.

The annoying chuckle of the crow interrupted his reverie. The wretched bird had stuffed itself into its water dish and was flinging up a spray as it bathed and gargled.

He stalked toward the cage.

The bird cocked its head toward him, feathers fluffed to twice its size.

Just beyond the cage, the Worm watched him as warily.

Corvus glanced over at the man. "The darklings misunderstood my command. I've neglected their breeding since my army has changed. But I still need Sera Littlejohn. The solvo blanks must be near to punch through the weak point in the Veil when her teshuva ascends."

The Worm shrugged, obviously trying for detachment, as if he could shed his anger and fear like the crow's feathers shed water. "It's too late. The league will be alert now, watching for you."

Corvus waved his hand. "I have aeries all over the

city. The miserable talyan never look up from their desperate grubbing."

"After that attempt on the hotel, they'll know this wasn't some anomalous ferales attack. If they have their noses to the ground, it's only to pick up your scent."

"That is why I have worms to muddle the way." Corvus eyed the other man. "And now I think you will help me again."

The Worm backed away. "This is getting too risky. I never thought—"

"Because you are a Worm," Corvus said patiently. "My ferales failed, but you can bring me Sera Littlejohn."

The Worm stiffened. "Me? How can I—"

"You will have to bring your squirmings out of the shadows, of course." Corvus touched the ring, the stone cool and smooth under his caress. "After the last talya, I have learned something of extracting demons from their mask of flesh. Bring me Sera Littlejohn, and you will finally have your reward."

The Worm's gaze fixed on the ring. "You'll do it?" His voice rose again with barely suppressed glee. "You'll strip her demon and give it to me?"

Corvus bowed his head. "I promised. You will know intimately the power of the Darkness."

Archer woke at a hand on his shoulder. He'd know that gentle touch anywhere.

"Sera." His voice sounded rusty, as if he were some penitent monk who hadn't spoken for years. He cleared his throat. "What's wrong?"

He'd taken the couch in the safe house's common room as his command post, collating reports from the haunt- and reaper-class talyan trackers in the field. Now his time sense told him it was the deepest part of night.

"It's Zane. He's . . ." Her breath caught on the next words. She tried again, substituting, "He's not doing well."

Archer surged off the couch. "The teshuva should have—"

"It's gone."

From a few steps away, he turned to glare at her. "A demon doesn't just wander off."

"I don't know where the hell it went. But his wounds haven't healed at all. In fact, there's a new one. In his leg. The djinn-man hadn't gotten that far."

Archer's blood ran cold.

The halls were dark and empty except for the two talyan in chairs flanking the door to Zane's room.

Sera's brows drew down in angry bewilderment. "No one would go in to sit with him."

Archer slowed, looked closer at her. Just as the teshuva could take away the wound, but not the pain, it couldn't erase her sorrow, though the lines of grief would never etch her face. "Have you been here all day?"

She nodded mutely.

The bedside light cast a soft glow over Zane. Other than that, his skin had bleached the same color as the bandages.

Archer sat heavily on the chair beside the bed. Carefully, he peeled back the lower half of the sheet and the gauze Sera had laid over Zane's leg.

The slice in his white flesh wasn't worse than what had already been done to that battered body. But Archer felt the last of his hope drain away with that slow welling of blood.

Sera murmured in surprise. "His *reven* is almost gone. You can barely see the shadow on his skin."

Archer nodded wearily. "The demon took its mark with it."

She stilled. "It's gone?"

He didn't repeat himself.

She spun for the door. "Then we'll take him to a hospital. They'll heal him the human way."

"Sera." The harshness of his voice stopped her in her tracks. "There's nothing anyone can do for him."

"But . . ."

A chill stole over him, as if his blood pooled on the floor to mingle with Zane's. "His initial wound, the one that brought the demon on him, is back, along with a lifetime of damage done while fighting for the teshuva."

She hesitated. "So every wound he ever took . . ."

"Will now bleed him dry. He's a walking battlefield of wounded in one man."

"My God, the agony . . ."

"That, at least, is spared him. Since the teshuva couldn't take away the pain when the wound was inflicted, Zane lived through it then, so it doesn't come back now. As if that's any consolation." The coldness in him flared to fury. "Cowardly, useless fucking demon to leave now."

"We can't do anything?" Sera's voice was small.

The fury faded as hope had. The cold remained. "Wait."

"I always hated that part of my old job," she said softly. "The waiting."

"You don't have to."

"Yes, I do."

He didn't answer.

The shuffle of bare feet separated them. Ecco stood in the doorway, his face expressionless.

Archer gave up his seat, and Ecco took it—a measure, Archer knew, of the damage done.

Ecco crossed his arms. "He's dying?"

Sera took a breath and nodded.

"Just when I was starting to like him."

She frowned. "You've been living and fighting together for almost forty years."

"The fighting part got in the way of the living part. Well, both are over for him now."

Sera closed her eyes with a "God, give me strength" sigh. Archer almost smiled.

Ecco studied the comatose man. "Aren't you going to play the harp or something?"

"After a patient told me dying would be sweet release from my attempts, I gave up the harp. Plus, the music always sounds a little depressing, don't you think?" She took a breath. "I usually just sang."

Ecco voiced Archer's surprise. "You sing?"

"A little. I haven't killed anybody yet."

"So sing us something."

Quietly, so at first Archer thought she was only humming, she began. He retreated to the back of the room.

She segued into familiar notes that had lulled him more than once on the front porch of his home, where he'd lazed with evening heat and the childhood conviction that summer would never end.

" 'Through many dangers, toils and snares, I have already come. / 'Tis grace hath brought me safe thus far, and grace will lead me home.' "

How old had he been? How many years before the war that would take everything? The voices singing had been lower and far wearier than Sera's, rich with the slow cadences that had all but deserted him. As the verses of "Amazing Grace" rolled over him, he swore he caught the drifting scent of sun-warmed honeysuckle. He rested his head back against the wall.

" 'Yes, when this flesh and heart shall fail, and mortal life shall cease, / I shall possess, within the veil, a life of joy and peace.' "

The last note faded, and Archer straightened. He sensed the change in the room and glanced at Sera. Her head was bowed. She'd dropped her hands into her lap, and from the tension in her laced fingers, he knew she felt it.

Death had come.

On the bed, as if he knew too, Zane stirred. "Mom?"

"Just us," Ecco said. "Sera and me. And Archer." He glanced over his shoulder where the hall had filled with silent talyan. "And everybody else."

Zane tilted his head from side to side, though what he was looking for, Archer couldn't guess. "I'm tired."

Sera touched his forehead. "Then rest. You've worked hard, for a long time."

Zane let out a sigh, too long for the air that must have been in his lungs. Archer held his breath as if he could stop the last exhalation.

But Zane wasn't quite ready to go. "Archer?"

"I'm here."

"Someone came in after my eyes . . . I heard some-one call him Corvus."

"So we have a name," Archer said. "Good. Don't wear yourself out."

"I am worn-out." Zane sighed again, even deeper. "I think Corvus is too. He's old, older than any of us. He said he wanted it to end."

"Any time," Ecco growled. "The minute we find him, he'll be over."

"His djinni is too powerful. It stole . . ." Zane's hands flailed on the sheet, as if in remembered shock. "It stole my teshuva. I felt the demon ripped from me, and then it was gone. Just gone."

Silence spread in waves from his words.

"But there's no way out for Corvus, no one to stop him," Zane said softly. "He's found a way to rip through the Veil where the teshuva's crossing weakened it, to free all the demons of hell."

"My God," Sera whispered.

Zane nodded once. "God will have no choice but to open the gates and send forth his armies of heavenly host in response."

Archer rubbed his hand over his face. "Yeah, that would pretty much be the end."

"He said his army of corpses is massing against the

Veil, but he only liked to talk when he was hurting me, so it was hard to pay attention."

From the talyan in the hallway, ripples of questions came back. "How can he do that?" "Rip open the Veil?" And louder, "What can the dead do? No one reaches across the Veil from this side."

Archer stiffened. Across the room, Sera lifted her head, awareness a violet tint in her eyes. "Actually, maybe we can."

Chapter 20

Sera supposed there was a measure of relief in having some clue what the djinn-man intended. Bad enough that her demon had weakened the barrier between the realms, but now whatever wicked quirk or misplaced kindness allowed the teshuva to send others back through the Veil, Corvus wanted to use it for his own ends.

Well, all their ends, apparently.

She pushed the frightening knowledge away. She'd panic later, when she had a free moment.

She stroked Zane's brow, ignoring the seep of blood from all his wounds as his body quit holding itself together.

Teshuva and cellular cohesion gone, only his spirit and the memory of pain remained.

"That's it," Zane whispered. "Will you sing again?"

She took a breath and watched him inhale with her.

Now comes the nighttime, little bird, be done.
To the nest with feathers soft, come home.
Bright eye, close. Let the moon keep her watch,
Guide your dreams through the dark hours.

She went through the verses, remembering her mother singing to her youngest brother in the womb. By the time he'd been born, her depression had been full-blown and she never sang again. Sera refused to let the memory tighten her throat, not now.

> *Sleep, my nestling, in the quiet boughs.*
> *One last sigh now, settle you down.*
> *Sleep deep, my child, fuss no more.*
> *And my kiss shall wake you in the morn.*

She held on to the last note. Finally, the limits of her still-too-human lungs faded her to silence.

Despite the muscled bulk of talyan who'd crept close, the air felt too light, the room empty. Sera pressed the back of her hand to her eyes a moment, then laid her fingers against Zane's neck.

The slow seep of his wounds had stopped with his heart.

"He's dead," Ecco said.

As one, the men straightened. A murmur swept through them. Surprise, sadness, anger? Sera couldn't tell. She'd felt all of those emotions herself. Once upon a time, her job had been to sit with the family after the death, guide them the first steps down the path to acceptance and, eventually, joyful memory.

Not this time. Not when the path out of the death-watch led toward the end of the world. She stood too quickly and swayed on her feet. A hand at her elbow steadied her.

Archer, of course.

"Come on," he said. "Time for somebody to sleep, anyway. Plain old sleep, though, nothing metaphorical."

She tried to dredge up a smile, but he was having none of it.

"This way." He steered her past the talyan.

"What will happen to him now?"

"We have a place outside the city. Used to be a farm when land was the core of the league's wealth, but Niall returned it to a native prairie reserve. Zane will be buried there." He stopped outside the door to an empty bedroom. "It's peaceful."

Sera looked up into his dark eyes, haunted with remembered losses. "Are many buried there?"

"The graves are unmarked, and talyan cadavers decompose quickly once the demon leaves. Who knows how many fighters have been lost in a battle most people don't even know about and wouldn't believe anyway?" Rage curled around him, sparking violet.

She touched his sleeve. Underneath, she knew the demon mark ran rampant. She took a step backward into the room. "Come inside."

The violet in his eyes flickered out behind a cloud of confusion. "What?"

She took another step back. "I don't want to be alone."

She thought he would run. Technically, according to the stages of grief, denial came before anger.

He didn't move. "What will this solve?"

"Nothing. It's not a problem or a question. I just won't be alone tonight, and neither will you."

"It's not tonight anymore. It's almost morning." He sighed, longer even than Zane's last breath, followed her inside, and locked the door.

He took off her clothes as if he'd never had the chance before, unbuttoning and unzipping with rapt concentration. He pressed his lips over each uncovered inch with exquisite gentleness.

She shoved at his shirt with impatient hands and bared his chest. But when she reached for the fly of his jeans, he captured her wrists.

"Slowly," he murmured. "We have forever."

They might not even have the rest of the dark hours. But his lingering caresses stole her breath, made her forget what she was going to say, banished even the thought of later.

He led her to the bathroom and finally shucked his jeans. With the light still off, he started the shower, and steam curled through the little room. To her demon-enhanced vision in the unrelieved blackness, an aura outlined him with scintillating lights of smoky, silvery green.

Where they touched, as he led her under the spray of water, the lights shot through with gold.

"How do you see me?" she asked wonderingly.

"As a mystery I'll never understand."

"I meant the colors. Is this part of the talyan bond?"

He stilled. "I don't know. I don't even know what the bond is, what it's doing to us." He turned her, back to front, and pulled her close against his chest, letting the water tumble over both of them.

She nestled against the insistent nudge of his erection, but he didn't try an answering grope. Instead, he slicked his hands over her hair, then drew the warm, wet strands down over her breasts, barely grazing her nipples. Despite the heat, she shivered.

"I want to thank you," he murmured against her cheek, "for what you did with Zane."

The hot water, or maybe Archer's looming presence behind her, kept the worst of the coldness at bay as she considered. "It was my fault. We shouldn't have been there."

"Taking out the horde-tenebrae was his job. And the only way to redeem himself."

"Then the least I could do was my job. My old job." She closed her eyes when he brushed his lips over her temple. "Do you think it mattered to him?"

He was silent a moment, which made her realize that she trusted him to tell her the truth. "We can't know what it was like for him. But you made a difference for everyone else in that room. They all hoped they might someday go as gently into that dark night."

"I suppose that has to be enough."

His slick hands skimmed over her shoulders. She leaned back as he dug his thumbs into tight muscles.

"It's hard work, isn't it?"

"Harder because Zane didn't have to die." She shrugged, lifting his hands. "In a way, I was glad to leave it behind. I want to *do* more."

He didn't answer. He moved in front of her, and knelt. She stared at his bowed head as he ran his hands down her legs.

"Why don't you sing outside the vigils?"

She shifted. "How do you know I don't? This last week hasn't exactly been much to sing about."

He looked up at her, not blinking despite the droplets of water beading his face. His eyes shone silver.

Those eyes would burn through her if she didn't answer. "I sang with my mother in my father's choir at church. When she got too sick to go, I led the group. After she disappeared, I gave it up. I didn't start again until I heard how severely I sucked on harp. But singing got tangled up with death."

He reached up toward her belly. "You have a beautiful voice."

"Thank you," she said, a little breathless as his hands stroked over her hips.

"Beautiful like the rest of you." His hands framed her pelvis, thumbs brushing the points of the *reven* curling over her hip bones. The mark gleamed a brilliant amethyst in the nimbus of demon light. "Even this is beautiful. So graceful and intricate."

She thought the bold, powerful lines of his *reven* suited him perfectly. She took his arms and pulled him upright. Where she touched him, silver pinwheels struck off his skin.

"I see why you left the lights off," she murmured.

He shook his head. "I didn't know. I just thought. . . ."

She waited a moment. "That I'm shy?"

"Maybe I am."

"We'll see." She turned off the water and stepped out of the shower. He followed as she padded, dripping wet, to the bed.

He yanked the blanket half off the bed, but she avoided the wrap he tried to make. "You'll get cold."

"You'll warm me." She stepped into him. Silver sparked before she even touched him.

His arms closed around her, tentatively, as if she might break.

She threaded her fingers through his short hair and pulled him down to her kiss. He breathed out against her mouth, and his arms tightened around her, pulling her up onto her toes.

They fell backward onto the already-rumpled bed, mouths locked.

When he lifted himself above her, he was breathing hard. "Why did you invite me in? You aren't afraid to be alone."

She stared up at him. "Not afraid, no. I wanted life. I want you."

He stilled. "The two aren't necessarily the same."

She slipped her hand between their bodies to press against the base of his erection. "You're not dead."

He groaned, half laughter, half desire. "Not yet."

"I won't hurt you." She stroked her fingers down the length of him.

"Make me feel. . . ."

"What?"

"Just make me feel."

She adjusted her hand, cradling the heft of him in her palm, burnishing her thumb over the hot flesh. "Good?"

"Yes."

"Alive?"

"Very." His breath caught as her grip tightened sensuously. Then he caught her hands. "Too much."

"No such thing as too alive."

"Too good, then." He stretched her arms over her head.

In retaliation, she locked her heels behind his back. Her thighs slicked wet over his flanks. His cock pointed at her, shining with his aura like a burning brand.

He put a hand under the curve of her behind and pulled her up hard against him. She gasped at the friction of him sliding into the shadow space between her legs, grazing the pulsing nub at her core. He held her there, his heat radiating through her, silver whorls spiraling over his skin.

She writhed against him, driving herself toward the brand that would mark her yet again. She had other marks. Accident victim. Demon possessed. This, Archer's brand, she chose for herself.

And that would mark her as what, exactly?

She didn't care. Alive was enough, wasn't it?

She slid, wet skin on wet skin, impaling herself. Sweet heat soaked her from the inside out. She rocked against him, taught him the rhythm singing in her veins.

He loosed her wrists so she filled her hands with him, his shoulders, the taut muscles of his back, his buttocks clenching as he drove into her.

The impatient, rising sounds of his desire flared along her nerves, brighter than the aurora surrounding them. "I can't wait," he groaned.

"Don't wait," she whispered. "Now. Now."

The heat and light and life she'd longed for spilled from him, rolling through her, vast and devastating as a tidal wave, carrying with it her own orgasm. Just when she thought she was doomed, it washed her up onto the safe shore of Archer's chest and receded.

He was still gasping where he'd collapsed beside her. The storm of their racing heartbeats calmed.

"So, are we dead now?" he murmured against her neck.

"I could die happy."

His arm tightened around her. "What just happened?"

"Classic life-affirming behavior after a catastrophe."

"So you're saying you do this for all your patients?"

"Don't piss me off when I'm afterglowing." She glanced down at their tangled limbs. "Actually, we're not glowing anymore."

"The sun's coming up."

She hadn't noticed the square of the window beginning to lighten. With the mundane light and no threat in sight, her demon-enhanced vision faded, unneeded.

Now that they'd slacked their desire, what else was fading?

She sighed and sat up, finger-combing her hair. "We should get ready for the funeral."

Archer pushed himself up onto one elbow. "No funeral. I told you, a talyan cadaver won't last long once the demon's gone. We're lucky to get it in the ground."

She twisted to look at him. "Doesn't someone say a few words, something?"

"What is there to say?" Faint Southern sweetness in his low voice, he sang back to her, " 'Sleep deep, my child, and fuss no more.' "

Her fingers tangled in the knots of her hair. "What about good-bye?"

"It's not a journey that needs your good-byes." He captured her hands and smoothed the snarls she'd made. "It's over, Sera."

Of course it was. She went to the bathroom to splash cold water on her face.

When she returned to find her clothes, he was on his phone, his expression grim. Speaking of cold water . . .

She dressed and waited until he'd put his jeans on to ask. "That call didn't look good."

"Just getting messages. Nothing new on the search for the djinn-man. But Bookie has some results from the malice draining. He said considering what Zane reported, he wants to run a few more tests with you."

"Tests." She grimaced. "But maybe Zane didn't die in vain."

"It's always in vain." He pulled on his shirt and rolled back the sleeves, exposing the wild, dark lines of his *reven*. "Bookie said the hotel still reeks of birnenston, but he needs only a few minutes with you in his lab, so you'll be fine."

She frowned. "We don't care *how* Corvus plans to rip the Veil. We just need to stop him. And to stop him, we need to find him. Isn't it time to think about my trap idea?"

"With you as bait?" He shook his head. "We don't necessarily need to find him. We just need to make sure he doesn't find you."

"But what about the next talya whose teshuva can do what mine does? If he finds another . . ."

"He won't. You're unique."

"You can't know that."

He looked down at her. "I know."

He took her hand and raised it toward his heart. She hesitated, surprised at the gesture.

Then he locked a bracelet around her wrist.

The dull metal weighed heavy. "Gee. A present."

"No uglier than your necklace." He shrugged at her scowl. "It's a tracking bracelet. Niall asked me to put it on you earlier, but Zane kept you occupied. Don't go outside or it'll set off alarms. Every talya has orders to jump you."

"You're the only talya who jumps me. And I'm officially rescinding that privilege." She thrust out her arm. "Take it off. I'm not your prisoner."

"Don't think of it like that. Think of it like . . ." He cocked his head. "No, go ahead and think about it like that."

She slammed her palm down on her thigh. "What about my meeting with Bookie?"

"I decided you're right. Tests aren't important enough

to risk your life. And baited traps definitely aren't worth it."

"It's not your life," she said between gritted teeth.

"It is now."

She sputtered. "What sort of throwback, slave-owning arrogance—"

He took her jaw gently in his hand. "I don't think your situation compares, do you?" When she flushed and shook her head, he released her.

She folded her manacled arm against her belly, the bracelet chilling her through her T-shirt. The lover who had warmed her from the inside out was gone, leaving only the talyan male, cold and hard. "You said you wanted me at your back. This is not much of an alliance."

"I said if anyone, you." His throat moved, as if he swallowed back more words. "But my first promise was to keep you alive."

"That was before we knew the fate of the world hung in the balance."

He stilled, except for a single spark of violet that arced across his eyes, a reminder that once his demon had counted the destruction of worlds as nothing. She held her breath until he shifted, breaking the spell. "Just until we get this under control."

"You're the one who believes the war will never end," she reminded him.

"But the battles do. Ask Zane." He opened the door and frowned at her when she didn't move. "You're not confined to this room. Just this house."

"I'm going to stay here for a while." She kept her expression utterly neutral.

His frown deepened. "Fine." He took a half step into the hall. "The bracelet is a titanium alloy. Ferales can't break it. The lock can't be picked, and Niall has the only key. You asked me about the mated-talyan bond. This is the best I can do."

She looked him hard in the eye. "Get out."

He took another step back, and she indulged in a monstrous door slam that barely missed his nose. Never mind the talyan sleeping down the hall. They'd apparently agreed to jump her.

She didn't hear footsteps, but the pressure eased from her chest, so she knew he'd gone.

She retreated to the bed, found it rumpled, damp, and scented of sex. With a muttered curse, she threw herself into the desk chair.

She nudged aside the curtains. The gray light of dawn wasn't going to get any brighter, considering the weight of the clouds. The hazy light was the same color as the manacle around her wrist, though not as muted and bitter as her pendant—or Archer's blasted heart.

Maybe she could get Bookie to come to the safe house with his tests. She could call or e-mail him, assuming Archer hadn't cut off her communications too.

She twisted the bracelet around her wrist. For sure she should cut off communications with him. How unsurprising that he hadn't mentioned locking her up *before* they made love.

Not that she'd given him much chance to talk.

The urge to connect was classically life affirming, never mind his sardonic response. The connection didn't have to be physical, of course, so why had she chosen that? Why with someone who courted death so exclusively, he left no room for any other courtship? And why was she even thinking courtship when she'd only needed the release of another body against hers?

Considering she fancied herself a seeker, she shied away from those questions with hypocritical quickness.

She didn't have to explain herself, not even *to* herself. No one would call her on it, certainly not the entity within her. It had less than nothing to say.

She pushed to her feet. Archer'd had time to get out of her way. She'd find a laptop or phone and contact Bookie.

It sure would be nice to have some answers from somebody.

Walking into the hotel lobby behind Niall and Ecco, Archer gagged as the scorched miasma of birnenston assaulted his demon senses. The teshuva scuttled deeper out of his awareness, away from the unholy poison. "I thought it was getting better."

Niall coughed. "Bookie said so. But since unadulterated humans hardly get worse than a headache, what does he care?"

"It'll never be clean again," Ecco said. "Let it burn, or sell it to the angel crowd. They're always, 'Brimstone this and hellfire that.'"

Niall grimaced. "We won't be here long. I want to see how Lex and Perrin are coming with the cleanup. And this still feels less grim than the safe house."

Archer couldn't disagree—Sera was probably vibrating the walls with her fury by now.

In the lobby, a half dozen talyan waited. Niall didn't waste time with niceties. "Tell me what we have."

Valjean stepped forward. The talya's face was lined with weariness, so tired his teshuva hadn't been able to keep up with the damage. "I've been all over the city. Twice. I can't pick up the djinn-man's sign anywhere." He paused. "No, that's not quite true. I get whiffs of him everywhere, but when I follow, I end up trailing some clueless human."

Archer shifted restlessly. "Djinn accomplices?" Just as the league had the assistance of human Bookkeepers, so the djinn and angels had their spheres of influence in the worldly realm. "Corvus told Zane he was mustering an army."

Valjean shook his head. "I talked to a few, but Corvus said an army of corpses, and they weren't dead." He grimaced. "Although one woman said I looked like I was working too hard and offered to help me forget my troubles with a few of her pills. She smiled the whole time. Wouldn't be much of a soldier for the tenebraeternum."

"Corvus is powerful, but he's still a man wrapped around that demon. He didn't just disappear." Niall bracketed his temples with his spread fingers, his thumb pressing against the stark lines of the demon mark around his eye. "How far out have you gone?"

Valjean slumped. "I'll go farther."

"Good." Niall turned to the next talya. "Jonah?"

"Horde-tenebrae activity is up across the city. Their stench is probably interfering with Val's tracking. Can't tell if what's going down is making them desperate or incredibly cocky." The fighter laid his hand over the vicious puckered wound running down his face and neck. "I was rear guard, three brothers in front of me, and a feralis tried to grab me from behind. Thing had to know we'd take it, but it wanted to kill me first."

Archer calculated a scant half inch to one side and Brother Jonah would have spewed his lifeblood from his carotid before his teshuva could intervene.

Shifting his gaze from the half-decapitated fighter to the tracker swaying on his feet, Archer realized they were losing this battle.

Niall's gaze grew distant as he listened to more reports. Archer knew he was piecing all the information together in search of patterns and possibilities. Having barely escaped the Irish famine, he hungered now for the details that let him lead a ragtag band of demon slayers toward the glory to save their souls.

His expression said their prospects were about as appealing as the last potato collapsing into black rot. "Bookie, what have you found out about this Corvus?"

Bookie looked as road-worn as the rest, ruddy features blanched. "The league register has one possible match: a Corvus Valerius, possessed back in Nero's day."

A murmur swept the room. Such a long possession indicated a demon of incredible power. The demon would need to keep human flesh alive through centuries of cellular decay and the inevitable madness of isolation brought on by such unnatural longevity. And, of course, win every battle with every angelic host it encountered.

How dark must the djinni be to never release its stranglehold on one man? And how twisted must that man be? Archer's own heart withered at the thought.

Bookie went on. "The register says Corvus was an arena slave who fought his way to gladiator rank. On the verge of earning his freedom, he was pitted against three cannibal savages, a lion and a bear, and an alleged Amazon—at the same time. He lost. League chronicles from then on repeat variations on the Corvus name."

"Why the bid for apocalypse now?" Archer wondered aloud.

Bookie shrugged. "Because he can?"

"There's never been a better time," Jonah said. "Or should I say, a worse time. Today, one bomb maims hundreds, one disease wipes out thousands, one dictator dooms millions to poverty and terror." In his vehemence, blood trickled from his barely knit flesh. "Evil isn't just beating us. It's pointing and laughing and racking up frequent-flier miles too."

"Well, statistically," Bookie said, "there are more people on the planet, so of course more people bleed, suffer, and die."

Niall rubbed a hand over his face. "So now God is a numbers runner? If anybody's running, it's us, out of options."

"Not really," Bookie said. "Do what you've always done. Just keep playing along."

Ecco stiffened. "Excuse me?"

"The angels and djinn fight a holy war that can never be won. The teshuva fight for a redemption they can never earn. And you all are just along for the beating."

Bookie tapped the papers against his leg. "Keep up the good work and nothing has to change."

Archer's gut twisted at Bookie's interpretation, even though he'd come to the same revelation a long time ago—though not so long ago as Corvus, who'd apparently decided to end the stalemate.

In some sick way, he understood. As Sera had said, empathy meant feeling, truly feeling, another's pain. He had less than two centuries to Corvus's two millennia. Now that she'd brought his emotions back to life, reminded him what it was to fear, he could only dread what Corvus was capable of, having lived ten times the agony.

Bookie cleared his throat. "I've also finished the workup on the most recent possessed."

Archer lifted one eyebrow. "Sera."

Bookie shrugged indifferently. "Her technique for dispatching malice brought up some disturbing questions—"

"Skip to the point, man," Jonah said.

Bookie glowered over the rim of his glasses. "The continued tenebrae activity is due to persistent damage in the Veil. And she is the one preventing the Veil from sealing."

"The Veil is always in flux after a crossing," Ecco said. "Although not so long, usually. Her teshuva—"

"Not her teshuva," Bookie snapped. "She." His gaze narrowed on Archer. "Sera."

Archer felt a chill go through him. "How? She's human. Demon-ridden, yes, but still human." Suddenly, the distinction seemed terribly elemental to him.

Bookie frowned. "In the ESF reading, Sera's soul force radiates outward into our realm, conjoined with the demon, just like any talya/teshuva possession. But her soul force also cascades *backward* along her teshuva's remaining umbilical. Through the Veil. Into the tenebraeternum." He gave a little shrug, with an expression like reluctant admiration. "You could almost say that instead of the demon possessing her, she is riding the demon."

Archer stiffened. "No one would choose to be possessed."

"That's your occupational myopia. If you'd look around, you'd see people are capable of more than you suppose, all on their own."

Reluctantly, Archer considered Sera's history. Between her mother's suicide, her career in death, her accident, her relentless delving into mysteries with no answers, maybe she hadn't chosen to bargain her soul, but a conspiracy of circumstances had cut off any other path.

Niall asked, "What does this mean to Corvus's plan?"

The pages in Bookie's hand crinkled as he clenched them. "I can't say. I just thought it was interesting. Has to make one question Sera's intent, unconscious or not. And, actually, the true strain of her demon since it apparently crossed over in response to Corvus's tweaking the Veil."

Valjean straightened. "You think we've been harboring a djinn all along?"

Archer took a step forward. "No."

"Djinn or teshuva, the flaw in the Veil remains," Bookie said, "so it doesn't really matter either way."

Jonah sputtered. "She's conspiring to free all the denizens of hell, and you don't think that matters?"

Archer spun on the other man. "Sera does not want to destroy the Veil. She fights for us."

Jonah scowled. "I won't risk losing my soul just because you've lost your head fucking a djinn whore—"

Archer punched him. He aimed the short, vicious blow for the neck wound. Fragile, new flesh parted under his knuckles, and blood sprayed. Jonah reeled back, falling to his knees.

With a harmonized shout, the other talyan piled on

Archer, pinning his arms. He braced his legs against their weight so they couldn't take him down but stood unresisting.

He stared at Jonah through narrowed eyes as Niall helped the other man to his feet, hand clamped over the reopened wound.

Niall scowled at Archer reprovingly. "He wasn't hurt enough?"

Archer cocked his head, assessing. "I could punch a hole in the other side, even him up, since he's such a stickler for appearances."

Jonah croaked something unintelligible. Niall led him to the lobby chairs and handed the bleeding talya a decorative pillow. "Hold that against your neck until it clots."

Ecco chortled. "Now we see how our fine gent here is part of her connection to the demon realm."

Bookie, who'd put half the room between himself and the scuffle, halted his retreat. "What do you mean?"

"You said you saw the link to the demon realm in the spectrograph. What I saw on the ESF recorder down in the lab were three strands. The thin umbilical of Sera's demon, and piggybacked on that, Sera's bright soul line. And then the third line, stronger and darker than the others. Archer."

Archer remembered the braid of light pictured on the screen, the three strands in an intricate weaving dance. "The third strand would be the malice."

Ecco shook his head. "No way would the emanations from a single malice show up as such a high-amplitude wavelength. And it's the amps that get you. Sound like anyone we know?" He hooked his thumb meaningfully at Archer.

Everyone stared at Ecco. He shrugged. "Shit, guys. I'm not just a pretty face, and I do know my malice."

Bookie wrinkled his lip toward a sneer. "And you think *he* is linked too?"

"The bond between them is damn strong, emphasis on 'damned,' " Ecco said. "Just ask Jonah. When he stops foaming blood."

"Ecco," Archer said softly without turning to look at the man, "I don't want to hurt you too." But he would. He figured that part went without saying.

"You're an arrogant asshole," Ecco said, "but you don't lie to yourself. If Sera is the bow, you're the arrow. The power and the point. She held the fissure in the Veil, and you rammed the malice back through." He secured his grip on Archer's arm. "Kinda like the aforementioned fucking that's got you wound so tight around her."

A bone-deep tremor shook Archer—every atom of his being coursed with demonic fury. He held himself stone-still, though the room around him glimmered with the black-light effect of hunter's sight.

"I suppose there is historical precedence," Bookie said grudgingly. "If you consider that women have always been in charge of life and death. And, anecdotally at least, a woman had first dealings with a devil and suborned her mate later."

Ecco laughed. "I so dare you to say that to Sera's face." The big talya tightened his grip another notch, as if he feared his next words would be even less well received than the last. "She might have the soul connection to the dark side, but when Archer saw she was in trouble with the malice, he jumped in with annihilation on his mind. If Eve had him around, farmer boy here would've made her apple pie."

Valjean, hanging off Archer's other arm, grunted. "Explains why we've never seen this phenomenon. No female talya."

Ecco nodded. "And no way was I going to have sex with any of you lot."

"When was the last time I thanked God?" Valjean let go of Archer. "This is all very titillating, but we're no closer to finding the djinn-man. How Archer and Sera send demons back through the Veil won't save us if all the demons come pouring over to our side first."

Niall glanced over the tense group, his gaze narrowing on Archer. "We'll find Corvus and stop him. We're going to trap him."

"Liam." Despite the arcing demon energy, Archer's blood froze. "No."

"Trap him?" Valjean perked up. "Have to admit, it'd be easier if he'd come to us. Why would he—?"

"Not Sera."

Archer stiffened, hearing the words screaming in his head spoken aloud. He glanced over at Bookie.

The historian shook his head. "You can't use her as bait. We can't risk Corvus taking her from us."

From his chair, Jonah snorted, spurting blood.

Niall frowned at him. "I said hold that pillow tight." He turned his attention to Bookie. "Corvus wants to exploit her teshuva's connection to the tenebraeternum. He doesn't realize he'd be stealing half a weapon that could destroy him." His expression remained impassive, as if he weren't discussing sending Sera to her likely doom.

Archer spurred his demon, felt the ripple through his body, and fixed his gaze on Niall. The league leader should know the other half of his new weapon wouldn't be passively aimed. "I won't let you sacrifice her."

"It's what we do, who we are." Niall's gaze never flickered, his demon latent as he spoke the cold truth. "And it's all our souls at stake."

Into the tension, Bookie said, "The probability of catastrophe halved is still fifty percent too high. Why hand Sera to Corvus on a silver platter now? Give me time to finish my work."

Archer knew what Sera would say to that idea. He wrenched out of Ecco's grasp and stalked toward the door.

Niall called out, "Where are you going?"

"The birnenston is making me crazy. I'm leaving before I do something I might regret." He glanced at Jonah on the way past. "Which is not you, by the way."

Jonah flicked him off with vigor, and Archer was grudgingly glad he hadn't killed the man.

He had enough undying regrets. But if the only way out for him had to be paid with Sera's gold head on a silver platter, he would live with those regrets. However long—or short—that might be.

CHAPTER 21

When Archer slammed through the safe house door, he left a glimmering violet outline of his palm embedded in the wood. He must be radiating on all wavelengths, overwhelming the house energy sinks, to leave such blatant demon sign in his wake, but he refused to name the emotions that narrowed his vision to the woman before him.

He curled his hands into fists, wanting to reach for her, but fearful of what marks he'd leave this time.

Sera, focused on her laptop, didn't even glance up.

He towered over her. "Get up. We're going."

She pecked a single key on the keyboard. Still looking at the screen, she said, "Can't," and held up her arm with the tracking bracelet.

He slipped his fingers between the manacle and her wrist. The contrast between the slick coolness of metal and fine silk of her skin hummed in his senses. He snapped the bracelet in two.

The halves fell to the floor with echoing thuds.

"Oh dear, my unbreakable titanium alloy." She lifted her gaze from her bare arm, still cradled in his grasp. "Bad day?"

"Getting worse," he growled. But the warmth of her penetrated his icy rage. The tug that lifted her to her feet was only as abrupt as simple male arrogance required. "Come on."

"I was in the middle of something."

"Yeah, you are. What do you think's making it worse?"

A flicker of alarm crossed her features. She stopped being a deadweight. "Where are we going?"

"Away."

"Let me get my bag."

"Now." He'd made clear to Niall he wasn't okay with the baited-trap idea. It wouldn't take long for Niall to figure out that "wasn't okay with" meant "was going to stop it."

Luckily, the house was almost empty, and he'd yanked the telephone landline on the way in. By the time Niall connected with a talya close by, Sera would be safely away.

Archer didn't want to hurt anyone else today. And he didn't want to wonder why he was willing to kill for this blond wisp of a demon-ridden woman at his side—just because his experience with demons and her link to the other side combined into a weapon unlike any found in talyan archives. . . .

More than two millennia of league knowledge—not to mention his almost two centuries of numbing annihilation—had been thrown into utter confusion, and all because of her.

Two cab rides and a fast walk with several doubling backs brought them to the greenhouse. Sera glanced over her shoulder as he unlocked the door. "So whom am I watching out for here?"

"Anybody who looks like a bad guy. Or a bad guy pretending to be a good guy."

"Right. That about covers it. Except for the good guy pretending to be a bad guy."

"We don't have any of those."

"Yeah, we do."

When he glanced down, she was looking at him. He pushed her into the building and locked the door behind them.

She rubbed her hands up over her arms, and he realized he'd dragged her out of the house without her coat. Preoccupied with his suspicions, he hadn't even offered his.

"Let's get you something warm to drink."

She waited while he made tea, then turned to go out to the greenhouse. "You coming?"

Their night in the garden flashed before his eyes. He'd brought them here because this place had always been his refuge. Jonah might've been right about the losing-his-mind part.

As for Ecco's theory ... The talya's crude comparison of offing demons to sleeping with Sera struck him as wrong. Not just borderline sacrilegious, but missing some vital aspect. Rather than trying to think it through, he followed her.

She took one of the wandering paths. He waited until the tension across her shoulders eased before he spoke. "I'd shackle you again to protect you."

"I know you're old-fashioned—really old—but that's not your call."

He tightened his hands around the teacup. "What was I supposed to do? Until I destroy Corvus—"

"You can talk to me. Tell me what you're thinking."

He noticed distracting her wasn't on the list. Too bad. "Even Bookie thought the baited-trap idea was bad."

She frowned. "Did you see him today? He didn't answer my e-mail. But Liam seemed to think my idea had merit."

Archer didn't want to discuss how the meeting had gone down. He certainly wasn't going to correct her mistaken notion that everyone else was against her self-destruction too. "I just need a little more time before you sacrifice yourself."

She trailed her fingers across the leaves. The hazy light leached the color from her eyes so they gleamed as silver as when they'd made love under the showering water. "And I just want what's happened to me to *matter*, to know it isn't all pointless."

"Oh, it matters," he murmured.

"Before, you didn't think anything mattered."

He turned his face to the sky—so he didn't have to meet that probing stare. "Maybe you've changed things for me."

Like the fact he would never be allowed to return to the league.

Attacking another talya, it happened. Angry, hurting men with superhuman powers sometimes got cranky. As long as no one died, no harm, no foul. And they were hard to kill.

But to betray the purpose of the league, the mission of the teshuva to seek redemption . . . A demon not repenting was a djinni, its possessed just another djinni-man to be hunted into a better-late-than-never grave.

And all because he couldn't forget the feel of her beneath him, beside him; couldn't forget, again, how to feel.

He slugged back the rest of his tea. "Warm?"

She nodded, a faint frown creasing her brow.

"Good." He didn't want to guess whether the heat in his own skin was the memory of hers or the unholy promise of hellfire to come.

"You have changed," she said. "The demon rides you hard. Ever since Zane's death."

He stiffened. "Of course, I'm keeping the teshuva on simmer. In case you forgot, we're under siege."

"You've always been under attack. Something else is wrong."

A hint of violet played at the corners of her eyes. He

knew she was calling on other-realm senses to monitor his response. The demon might not confer mind-reading powers, but the constriction of pupils, the dilation of blood vessels, the tinge of nervous sweat, could be every bit as damning.

She studied him. "You told me once you had no brothers. But all the talyan are your brothers now." She took a breath. "Zane's body might be dust already, but you don't have to forget him. You're still allowed to mourn."

"I don't have time to mourn." Honest enough, although maybe he should convince her he needed time alone—with her—to work through Zane's death. Maybe a couple weeks immersed in her welcoming body, how had she put it?—affirming life.

But she shook her head. "It's not about time. You said you wanted me to help you feel."

So much for distracting her with his needs. "I know what loss feels like," he snapped. "I learned a long time ago."

"The war . . ."

He glowered. He was supposed to be playing the wing-wounded bird, leading the hunter astray. So why did the ache seem real? "War is all about loss. What happened to Zane was a terrible reminder, but it's nothing I've ever forgotten."

"What have you tried to forget?" Her words, soft but relentless, stalked him. "What did you lose—or whom—that made you afraid to ever lose again? The farm? Your father?"

"Frederick." The answer burst out against his will, startled like the bird into flight, never mind what was revealed to the hunter.

Sera was silent.

"A friend. A boyhood friend." He raised his head to glare at her. "A house slave boy my age. For a few summers, we had a secret fort in the lowlands. Sometimes he did my lessons on the sly while I ran wild. All I had to do in return was chop wood for him."

The swirl of green, brown, and violet in her gaze reminded him not so much of bright honeysuckle now as an orchid deep in the labyrinthine swamps he and Frederick had explored, rot turned to exotic flowers in the gloom.

"My father found out Frederick's mother had taught him to read. He sold them in town, since what point having field hands who could read, and sent me away to school up North, since what good was an heir who chopped wood." He clamped his teeth closed on the urge to tell her how, even then, his father had rubbed at the pains in his chest when working the cotton, and how rumors of war bubbled like foul swamp gases from the white fields. "When I returned, the bayou had been drained to make way for more crops. And I found out Frederick had tried to run. He was caught about twenty miles from my school and taken back. Somewhere along the way, they beat him to death."

He fell silent, and the violet in her eyes faded. "That's why you hold yourself apart from the other talyan? As penance? But you weren't responsible for Frederick's running, or his death."

He raked her with a scathing glance. "I know that."

"If you won't risk the pain of losing, you'll never know the joy of holding, either."

"I know that too. But it's not just me at risk."

They faced each other, the whisper of leaves overhead like a watchful crowd taking bets.

Whose wound bled more freely? Was this the twisted trail that had led them to each other across two realms, human and demon? But what hope had they of healing each other, the woman who'd been abandoned and the man with a penchant for losing everything?

She dropped her gaze first, and he knew he should

feel like crowing with victory. Instead, he felt as if he'd lost—again.

Her voice was softer yet in defeat. "So how long are we hiding out?"

Corvus was going on two thousand years old. How much longer could he last? "Just a few days."

By then, she'd be suspicious. And he'd need to find a safer place for her while he hunted Corvus. He'd never mentioned the greenhouse to the others, but he hadn't hid the place either. Bookie could uncover his financial tracks easily enough. Good thing Bookie was on his side, at least as far as the Sera–baited trap went.

"A few days." She walked on, leaving him a few steps behind. "Do you serve umbrella drinks out of that kitchen? I always wanted to take a tropical paradise vacation." The meandering path brought them to the center of the garden. She lifted her head to stare at the daybed. "What will we do to fill the time?" She glanced over her shoulder at him.

He felt the dull heat in his face and tried to keep his voice level. "I have to run out." Run away. "You'll be hungry later, and green tea won't hold us forever."

"Forever?"

"A few days," he amended. "I won't be gone long. Will you stay here and wait for me?"

She looked at him.

This time he let the strain come through in his voice. "Please?"

Finally, she nodded. "I'll stay."

The crow shrilled, a high, thin shriek, and threw itself against the bars of the cage.

"Be still," Corvus growled, and reached for it again.

Just one stinking feather was all he needed. If he could look at the subtle shades up close, he might finally capture the spirit of the creature. This would be his last chance.

The phone rang. The crow flapped into the peaked point of the cage. With a vicious curse, Corvus slammed the cage away, rocking it on its stand.

He grabbed the phone. "What?"

"I set it up."

The Worm. Corvus closed his eyes, calming his breath. "When? Where?"

"Actually, she contacted me. She had some questions about her demon. I told her to meet me tomorrow night at the lab." There was a hesitation on the other end of the line. "She hasn't responded yet."

"She'll come." Corvus paced the edges of the room. "You're the league's Bookkeeper. Of course, you'll have her answers for her."

Frustration leaked out in his voice, but he didn't bother to hide it. The Bookworm would suffer any indignity gladly in pursuit of his very own demon.

"I've found something else you should know." The Bookworm's voice shifted, a note of sly satisfaction hardening his tone.

"Oh?" A warning rang in Corvus's head. With a city between them, had his Worm grown a spine?

"The wound in the Veil where Sera's demon crossed is still raw." The Worm paused. "Because of an unusual side effect when she is the presence of her talya lover."

Corvus stilled. "Her lover."

"Ferris Archer. The djinn may not think much of the teshuva, but this one talya alone has destroyed a legion of your lesser brethren. Through Sera's link, the two of them have forced tenebrae back across the Veil."

The stillness in Corvus turned to ice. "How can that be?"

"Demons come out. Why shouldn't the reverse be true?"

"Because . . ." Words failed Corvus.

The Worm huffed out an impatient breath. "I've explained before. The Veil is nothing more than an energy barrier. A meta-seraphic barrier fueled by the suffering of bound souls, true, but still merely energy itself in the end. To be harnessed by those with the knowledge and the proper tools." Even distance couldn't conceal his sneer. "That power isn't constrained by the convoluted mythology that binds you."

Corvus tightened his grip on the phone. "You said the solvo blanks would draw a djinn. But the demon was teshuva. You said the female talya would be unbalanced. Instead, this talyan pair could be a hindrance." Could they even be a threat? Impossible. Nothing had ever stood against his demon. "You swore through your studies you had found a way to finally part the Veil."

"And I have," the Worm snapped. "With the solvo blanks, I set up a potent, dark resonance. Those soul-emptied husks of undead damned should have attracted an answering darkness that would leave a breach we could exploit. Sera's analogous penance trigger made her the demon's target, but her lifelong refusal to yield to death and damnation twisted the resonance back on itself. The mirror of the other-realms coughed up exactly what we sought: a way through the Veil. I just didn't realize the reflection would be so . . . bright."

"And what other reflections have you missed, Bookkeeper?"

The Worm was silent a moment. "It won't matter. Archer and Sera don't grasp what they have between them. Most of the time, they're fighting against it and each other. Besides, they are only two people. Just keep them apart. Once we tap the Veil and cull the energy we need, two talyan—hell, all the leagues in the world—won't matter in the end."

Corvus pictured the peacock-bright hues of the bruised Veil torn asunder—not at all the businesslike venture the Worm envisioned, he knew. He closed his eyes against the rising acid sting. "True. Hell won't matter in the end." Birnenston leaked under his lashes, burning on his cheeks.

"I've done my part. You can't cut me out now." The Bookworm's voice rose eagerly. "How do I prepare for the demon?"

Corvus realized he'd left the door on the cage open. He turned. The crow was still inside, too frightened to fly out.

Weren't they all?

When he spoke, his tone was soft at last. "Stop here on your way to the meeting with Sera Littlejohn. I will make you ready for your reward."

Archer's agitation grew with every minute gone. Would she wait?

He couldn't go back to his loft. Niall had staked out the place. Archer had almost stumbled on Valjean before he sensed the other talya. If Valjean was tracking him instead of Corvus, Niall must have decided his best bet to find the djinn-man was using Sera.

With an urgency thrumming in his blood, the chill of coming night energized him. He shook his head. Feeling lighthearted just because he was on the lam? How sad was that? Although he supposed ditching garbageman duty was a plus to becoming an unrepentant demon.

At the greenhouse door, Sera met him with the point of a five-foot bamboo stake.

He reared back, hefting one of the plastic bags. "I brought Thai food. I see you have the skewers."

"I wasn't sure it was you." She eased her grip. "In the past few seconds, I managed to invent a lot of monsters fumbling around out there."

"My hands were full." He edged past her. "Re-arm the door. Code's SOLO-2-10."

In the garden's heart, he laid out a little feast. Sera filled two plates, wafting the aroma of peanut sauce and limes. "Starving," she mumbled around her first mouthful.

"I didn't mean to take so long." He started to explain, then stopped himself, cursing the sense of partnership that almost made him slip. She didn't need to know they were being hunted by both sides now. "Lots to do."

"I've been thinking, since *I've* had nothing else to do." She gave him a flat look, then continued. "I want to try a few experiments with the pendant stone, the *desolator*—"

"*Numinis*. 'That which makes the gods lonely.' " He pushed his plate away, his stomach tightening. Great, the one time she was willing to stay home and indulge her academic side. No Bunsen burners for her, no nitro or C-4. Oh no, she wanted to play with hellfire.

"If it can trap other-realm emanations, I bet it does make them lonely. Probably scared shitless too." She shrugged. "Not that gods shit. Presumably. But if we can find the key to accessing the matrix, we might have a clue how Corvus intends to break through the Veil."

Which was worse? Letting her play with fire, or telling her that she might burn down the world? So he explained Bookie's discovery of the reason behind the persistent opening in the Veil.

He left off Ecco's corollary and finished with, "So, I'd say we have a pretty good sense why Corvus wants you."

"I'm doing it?" The chopstick clattered out of her hands. "Me personally? I can't even blame my demon."

She could blame him. "It's just another symptom of possession you'll need to master. You already look like a natural with a spear."

She rose to pace. "You say that as if I might not usher in the end of three realms."

He stepped in front of her and ran his hands over her arms, as if he could banish the chill dread in her eyes. "You aren't going to make anything bad happen." Not without him, anyway, and he wouldn't let anything bad happen. That's why he'd brought her here.

She looked up at him bleakly. "Not meaning to doesn't necessarily stop it. I can tell you that."

He paused, fingers wrapped around her arms. The feel of her was a distraction. No wonder the demon shied away from touch. It was hard to concentrate on salvation when sin felt so good. "I thought you wanted a few days of paradise vacation, and here you are talking shop."

"Right. End of the world. Same old, same old."

"It is. We'll ask Corvus. He's seen two thousand years of this."

She pulled back against his hands. "Two thousand years?"

Archer sighed and released her. Why did he keep revealing things she didn't need to know? He'd get himself in trouble one of these times. "He was a Roman gladiator before the djinni possessed him."

She shook her head. "God, imagine all he's seen and done in two thousand years."

"Mostly spawning unimaginable evils, I'd guess."

"Why don't we have that kind of power on our side?"

He definitely wasn't going to tell her nobody was on their side anymore. "Only the good die young."

She wrinkled her nose. "Tell me everything you learned."

He didn't. But he told her some. He avoided all mention of Ecco's theory. How could he explain it when he didn't understand it—didn't believe it—himself? How could the heat between them mean anything against hellfire?

Not to mention she'd want to know how the league planned to make use of their united effort when he'd just proved himself the worst sort of team player. After he killed Corvus, and she was safe, he'd figure out how this partnership thing worked. Sacrificing his solitary hunter cred was a small price to pay for the chance to rid the world of darkness.

And, hell, didn't even the lone wolf sometimes take a mate?

He lured her back with a dark chocolate bar and pomegranate. She stopped her endless questions long enough to frown at the dessert. "Odd."

"I don't have even two hundred years under my belt, but I've tried some things." Thinking about what was under his belt made him shift awkwardly. He leaned back against the daybed and held a wedge of the pomegranate out to her.

She eyed him, then took the fruit and a square of chocolate. She copied his lounging position, leaving a space between them.

He handed over a plastic shopping bag. "I brought you some other things too."

She rifled through the contents. "A toothbrush. Jasmine tea." She paused. "Underwear? Just my size. You thought of everything."

"Yeah." Oh, he'd been thinking.

He'd gone predator-still he realized when she glanced away, looking up at the little white lights and the black sky beyond, anywhere but at him. "Is it going to snow?"

"Not in here. This is paradise." And because he was possessed and couldn't leave paradise well enough alone, he leaned forward through that carefully made empty space between them and kissed her.

He breathed the heat of chilies and the pineapple sweetness, tasting bitter chocolate and tart pomegranate. Had there been a time when he couldn't feel anything?

Touch was still agony, though irresistible, the hot tension in his body almost more than he could bear. His fingertips ached for her. He filled his hands with the fall of her hair to cradle her head as he kissed her. The rush of blood through his veins held a single, sustained note

of desire. That keening note morphed into his name on
her kiss-bruised lips.

"Ferris." Her hand in the middle of his chest was a
gentle restraint.

He dredged up some last semblance of sanity to ease
back.

She nibbled at her lower lip. "Are you all right?"

He thought a moment. "Why do you ask?"

"I'm so used to seeing at least a few purple sparks in
your eyes." She raised her hand to his cheek. "All I see
now is you."

"The demon is here. I'll never be free of it." It had
just been pushed to a way-back burner by the entirely
earthly urge that possessed him now.

"Just as well," she murmured. "You couldn't be here
now without it."

He inclined his head in acknowledgment, resting
against her palm.

Her hazel eyes half closed. "What excuse shall we use
this time? Our first time, you saved my life. The second
time, we celebrated life after a death. And now?"

"How about making my life worth living? For the
night at least."

He saw the flare behind her lashes. Not the violet
flash of demon light, but a quick shine of something else;
it was gone too fast for him to name. Then her thumb
brushing his mouth sidetracked him.

He lifted her, laid her back, and pressed between her
thighs to admire her sprawled across his bed. He leaned
down to kiss her navel, where her shirt had ridden up.
The warmth of her under his mouth was like the promise of spring, and he had only to coax the blooming blush
from her skin.

"Come here," she murmured.

"In a second." A minute. An hour. A life. Since his
possession, the thought of how long his lifetime lasted
had horrified him. But now . . .

Just below his lips, he knew the first tendril of her demon mark waited, inscribed on her skin. He eased back.

"Ferris?"

He unzipped her jeans, hooked his fingers through her belt loops, and tugged. The black *reven* uncoiled across her pale skin, a winding path that had led him from the restless dreams of an unbound demon to where he knelt now.

"Yet again indebted to a demon," he muttered.

"What?"

Always with the questions. He ran one hand up inside her shirt and splayed his fingers wide to press her flat. His thumb circled her nipple, and she caught her breath. "Have I mentioned that a side effect of immortality is staying power?"

Another tug on her jeans and he was feasting again.

Her hips rose under his questing mouth. Her breath grew ragged, each stuttering gasp twanging through his body so that his own desire strained to the breaking point as he pursued his quarry.

She tangled her fingers in his hair. "Be with me now."

Demonic intervention couldn't have gotten him out of his jeans any faster. She locked her heels behind his thighs and guided him in.

He groaned as she closed around him, hot and tight. "Oh God."

"Really?" Her eyes sparkled up at him. "Is this a good time for that?"

He growled and buried himself deep, bringing himself as close as skin would allow. She arched her back as he eased out again, a torment at leaving her. He held her on the edge, relishing the challenge. She never dropped her gaze.

He remembered her staring at him, defiant with the feralis's carcass in her lap in the moments before the demon vanished. He remembered how, covered in blood and ichor, he'd yearned to surrender to her clear-eyed compassion, to follow where she led, even into hell.

Suddenly, he realized why Ecco's comparison of fucking and their trick of piercing the Veil didn't quite ring true. Sera in his arms made his blood rush and his senses sharpen as if the demon in him rose to some terrible threat, but nothing compared to the dangerous intimacy of her smile, of falling into her gaze. The old archive record had intimated that the mated-talyan bond had changed the world, which—call him a selfish bastard—wasn't anywhere near as terrifying as what it was doing to him.

She touched his cheek. "Don't stop now."

"Wouldn't dream of it."

If it wasn't lust that had opened a path through the Veil to banish demons forever . . . His heart raced as if it would find a way out.

Maybe it was love.

CHAPTER 22

Sera woke to a sweet perfume. When she rolled her head to the side she saw Archer, his face looking unbearably young in sleep. Just over his shoulder nodded the curved petals of a lily.

A florist, who made almost as many trips to hospice as Sera, had once told her that lilies symbolized death and resurrection, hence their popularity at funerals. Sera eyed the smooth ivory flower. If she were the sort to believe, such a foreboding portent might make her nervous.

As it was, the weight of Archer's arm on her belly just made her have to pee.

She eased out from under him. He snuffled lightly in his sleep, reached for her, and contented himself with the warmth of the pillow.

She touched the hint of a wayward curl at his brow, the only suggestion of disobedience in his otherwise-brusque haircut. He didn't move.

After his efforts last night, she couldn't blame him. He'd kept her wild with wanting, his excruciating restraint almost driving her mad before his control had finally broken.

And when it had, his fierce desire might have frightened her—if it hadn't matched her own so perfectly. Thrust for thrust, raking nails against taut skin, each gasp had driven them closer together until, in the darkest part of the night, on the edge of exhaustion, they'd come one last time with an intensity that eclipsed even the fireworks of their demon-streaked auras. It might have been just the twinkle lights, but she was pretty sure she saw stars.

The marks of his passion were still imprinted on her, his scent on her skin. The violence of their joining hadn't fazed her, but the sense of possession made her heart trip treacherously close to dangerous thoughts.

She was being forced to give up her past; her future was murky at best. She had no business thinking beyond the glorious release from today.

She leaned forward to press her lips to his forehead. No thoughts of more, she warned herself, just a bit of sweet revenge that he might be as invisibly marked by their night as she was.

He murmured against the pillow and let out a sigh. She fought off the reluctance to leave him. She'd be back in a moment.

She might be in paradise, but padding naked through the garden felt too weird, not to mention chilly without him beside her. She pulled on her clothes—including fresh underwear; he'd judged her size exactly right, so perhaps demon-enhanced powers of perception were good for more than hunting evil—took a square of chocolate, and headed for the office area.

After taking care of nature's call, she returned to the kitchenette. She heated two mugs of water in the microwave and threw in tea bags to steep. She wasn't sure what Archer had planned for the day—although his more lurid whispers last night gave her some ideas—but she figured she'd go mad if she sat twiddling her thumbs again. Apparently, a paradise vacation wasn't her cup of tea.

She eyed the computer at his desk. At least she could check her e-mail, see if Bookie had replied. She nudged the cups away from the keyboard. The system didn't require a password, so she logged in to her account.

A red exclamation point flagged Bookie's message.

She opened it and scanned the message: *Tonight at the lab?* Archer wouldn't be thrilled with the location. He'd said the hotel still stunk of birnenston—not that the demon-free Bookie would care.

She wondered if Archer would give her a hard time about going. He hadn't checked in with the league last night, hadn't even called for an update on the search for Corvus. But if he didn't want to take her, she knew the way. Just as well he'd removed the tracking bracelet.

She e-mailed Bookie to confirm.

Before she shut down, the reply pinged back in a chat box: *Sera, are you all right? Where are you? Where is Archer?*

She sat back in the chair. Suddenly, Archer's not being in contact with the league seemed ominous.

Her pointer hovered over the little x in the upper corner.

Instead, she typed: *I'm fine. Archer is fine. Why?*

He kidnapped you.

"Nobody tells me anything," she murmured. She typed: *No, he didn't.*

Niall wanted to try your baited-trap idea. Archer refused. And then you were gone. Bookie outlined the meeting Archer had told her about. Except he'd told her almost nothing.

She bit her lip. Bookie explained that they'd all—all but Archer, apparently—agreed she was strong enough and clever enough to take her place as a talyan warrior. They trusted her not to get herself killed unnecessarily.

Don't know what Archer planned, Bookie sent. *Since he never fights alongside the league, maybe he didn't think they'd be there for you. Doesn't seem to realize he's the one who's never around.*

And if Bookie had sounded a bit obsequious—strong and clever enough, indeed—he knew Archer painfully well.

How could a man who fought alone submit to a tactic that involved making himself helpless, trusting in someone else to save him? No one had been around to save Archer before. Could a man who'd lived into his second century change?

But Bookie was wrong to think Archer didn't know the name of his pain. She'd seen his grief and guilt at Zane's death, knew he blamed himself for not being in harm's way. She also knew he'd be infinitely more determined not to let it happen again. Never mind what hung in the balance.

Say, the fate of the world.

He was so used to losing, he'd sacrifice himself every time, even if his pain wasn't the price to be paid. She knew it only hurt him more that his suffering wasn't enough.

The demon had promised her answers to the philosophical questions of life and death, salvation and damnation, good and evil. As it turned out, death, damnation, and evil were a little less theoretical and a lot better armed than she'd anticipated. Fighting for life, salvation, and good meant leaving her old life behind but brought her to Archer.

And Archer really wasn't going to appreciate the irony that he was the one who'd taught her not to let a battle go by without making her mark.

She typed one last message. The dark letters burned on the white screen: *Set the trap. I'll be there.*

She sat, lost in churning thoughts going nowhere. Finally, she rose. She turned away from the path into the garden and went instead down the cinder-block corridor to the front door. She punched in the code Archer had given her.

Just hours ago, he had explained the code came from the *Song of Solomon*, a passage his farmer father often quoted: *"For, lo, the winter is passed. The rain is over and gone. The flowers appear on the earth, and the time of the singing of birds is come."*

The latch released under her thumb, letting in the stinging Chicago wind. She slipped out quickly.

The real problem with suddenly acquiring the knowledge of good and evil wasn't simply the knowing part. It was deciding what to do about it.

If she wanted to fight, wanted to matter, she had to go.

She'd just kicked herself out of the garden.

A touch of cold roused Archer. He reached for Sera, but his arm closed around empty air.

He rolled onto his back, staring up at the canopy. She'd be back in a moment and he'd have to decide what to tell her about his revelation in the night.

Love conquers evil. How simple that was. Not easy necessarily, but simple. God knew, it still took a sharp blade, not Air Supply ballads alone, to subdue a rampaging feralis.

All this time, he'd held himself apart, dealing death and refusing to lose again, when only partnership with the woman he'd come to trust and admire could make a difference.

Eager to share his insight, he called her name. Water murmured over rocks in the little stream, and leaves rustled gently.

But no answer.

He slid out of bed. Without pausing to gather his clothes, he circled the paths. Empty.

Kitchen and bathroom. Empty.

In the doorway, he stopped, backpedaled, looked at the two brimming cups of tea beside the computer.

When he jostled the mouse, the black monitor brightened. He reviewed the history. Within a minute, he'd read everything she'd typed.

Fury pulsed through him, pushing back the chill gathered on his skin. Damn Bookie. That wasn't how it had gone down. The historian hadn't liked the baited-trap idea either; he must've caved in.

Of course, his own version had missed some key points too. And she'd obviously decided who was to be believed. And where she wanted to be.

He crossed his arms against the chill.

She'd rejected the kidnapping charge, but now she knew he'd tried to keep her from a path she'd chosen. He, the great talyan warrior, was afraid of death—not his own, but hers.

What use was a talya afraid of death? Sera, always the guide, had shown him the answer.

The e-mail time stamps said she'd been gone almost an hour, but he imagined the frost she'd let in still lingered. He returned to the garden's center to yank on his jeans. The scent of lily, sex, and Sera drifted around him.

She'd made him no promises—nor he to her. How could he before, knowing his immortal life was not his own, when eternity had been given to him only so long as he waged the teshuva's war.

And how could he now, knowing she didn't feel the same. The bond between them when they banished the demons had been an illusion as fleeting as a Chicago spring.

He'd forgotten the only way the garden could survive in this harsh place was behind thick walls and iron restraint. Letting someone in had been a mistake, one he wouldn't make again.

*   *   *

Sera walked until the falling snow stopped melting on her bare arms. Let the demon keep her from freezing if it wanted. She couldn't go to the league hotel before her appointment with Bookie. She didn't want to answer their questions about Archer.

She wondered how much trouble he was in. The talyan were independent and wayward souls, and Liam steered them with a light hand. But even his relaxed management style couldn't allow outright revolt.

Her willing return might take the sting out of Archer's mutiny, especially when they needed all the fighters they could get. She had more reason to be angry with Archer than the league did. She was the one lured away under false pretenses.

A rebellious part of her mind asked, what pretense? She knew he hadn't wanted to see her broken like Zane. Whether his motivation was guilt, simple humanity, or . . . something else, didn't change the fact she almost welcomed his intervention.

Archer would confront Corvus without hesitation. She'd just have to keep that boldness in mind when her turn came. Of course, it'd be easier if she had his death wish too.

Her aimless steps brought her to the nursing home. She stood across the street, half hiding behind a parked truck. Two days ago—only that long?—she'd called Wendy to say Nanette would check on her father, but she'd never heard how the encounter had gone.

Lights on the porch gleamed warm and welcoming, but Sera didn't approach. If her father had sensed the repentant demon in her and wanted her banished, she could only imagine how he'd feel about her releasing all the demons of hell. Not exactly a distinction to make a papa proud.

She pictured the honor student bumper sticker peeling off under a bloodred scrawl: MY CHILD IS IGNITING THE APOCALYPSE.

She turned and kept walking.

By the time she'd fully tested whether the demon would let her die of exposure, or only *wish* hypothermia would stop her shivering, she found herself outside the hospital. The emergency room offered heat and a seat. Unless she was spurting copious amounts of some bodily fluid, nobody would look twice.

As a place to contemplate her possible demise, with the gray linoleum tiles, beige plastic chairs, and the stench coming from the vending-area coffee machine, it could double for purgatory any day.

"Sera?"

For a heartbeat, her world felt surreally normal, as if this were the start of another workday in her old life— her old, old life.

"Betsy." She stood up too fast and swayed as the blood rushed out of her head.

"Whoa." Betsy put a hand under her elbow. "Damn, girl, you're freezing, and you're whiter than . . . You're always white. Where's your coat?"

"I lost it." She realized she sounded vague and shook her head.

Betsy steered her toward the admitting area. "Are you in trouble?"

"Hey." One of the waiting patients held up his hand. "I was next."

Betsy scowled over her shoulder. "Yeah? What's the problem?"

"I was putting up my Christmas lights, and the hammer tacker put a staple through my thumb." He waved the digit in question.

"Right. Give me a minute to set up an OR for amputation." Betsy pushed Sera into the nurses' lounge. "We finally get a break from all the solvo crazies—it's weird, they just disappeared; are they all getting high together somewhere?—and back come the normal crazies to fill the gap. Now, tell me what's going on. How's my patient?"

Sera dropped onto the worn couch. "Buried in an unmarked grave somewhere in Southern Illinois."

Betsy let out a long breath. "It's that one big guy you were with, the one with the scary eyes. He looked like trouble incarnate, and now he's got you mixed up in it."

Sera couldn't argue with the physical description. But she shook her head. "I mixed myself up in it. And those guys will help me make it right." Just not the one big guy.

Betsy sat down beside her. "Honey, I know you never believed this, but the weight of the world isn't on your shoulders."

"It wasn't before." She could admit that, now that she knew what the real weight of the world felt like.

"You need to get out, save yourself."

Sera bit her lip. "It's complicated. I didn't mean to bother you. I didn't know you were on today."

"I'm always on."

Had she subconsciously remembered her friend's schedule? Sera wondered what she'd hoped to find here. "You've seen the worst that people do to one another. Do you think . . ." She remembered the two men lit by the neon bar sign, the shadow of the malice darkening them. "Do you think they mean to do it?"

"What's my other choice? Every shooter, beater, and user is clinically and legally insane?"

"Maybe they are driven to it by . . . ," Sera said, hesitating again, then finished, "by their demons."

"We all have demons. The trick is not listening to them. That's what I think."

The nurse wasn't speaking literally, Sera knew. She wondered what the other woman would say if she found out that she was right.

She had an advantage, seeing what everyone else

thought was allegory, if they bothered thinking about it at all. Wouldn't everyone fight evil if they saw what she'd seen?

She rose. "I have to go."

"You're not going to listen to me, are you?"

"I did listen. I'm going to fight my demons."

She just wished she knew which were the most dangerous.

When she left, Betsy insisted on handing over her coat. Sera wanted to promise she'd bring it back. But she didn't like to lie. Now seemed a good time to start keeping her soul as pure as possible. She remembered Archer's insistence on the truth. Right up until he didn't like the truth, of course.

On her way, she stopped by the hospital chapel, a non-denominational room with a lone stained-glass panel ripping off Monet's water lilies. The orange throats of the lilies looked like a drained feralis's fading sulfurous eyeball. That mental image probably didn't haunt most visitors to the chapel, but she knew she'd find no peace, regardless.

If she was honest, she'd admit she never really sought peace in her faith. After her mother's disappearance, she'd wanted answers, which wasn't the same thing at all.

Looking around at the conscientious trappings of watered-down spirituality, she knew she still wasn't ready. She didn't want to be consoled or calmed. She didn't want a conviction someone else handed her, however prettily or practically it might be packaged, like a bouquet. She wanted it to grow from within. Until it did, she'd go without.

Outside, the snowfall had thickened, and the low, heavy clouds hushed the city night. Whirling flakes glittered in streetlights come on early in the gathering darkness. She arrived at the league hotel a little before the hour and thought she'd wait in the doorway until Bookie came looking for her. But when she rattled the door, it opened.

She frowned at the lax security. But they'd moved everything out to avoid birnenston contamination, so maybe there was no reason to lock up, especially since Bookie knew she was coming.

In the lobby, only the low night lighting was on, leaving the ceilings all but invisible. She eyed the shadows and remembered the swarms of malice in the building where they'd found Zane. Shaking off her unease, she headed downstairs to the lab.

The lower halls were entirely unlit, leaving indirect light from a few office windows to spread in pools along her path. Only Bookie's lab at the end of the hall stood open and bright.

She took a few steps toward it, then slowed, her senses tightening.

She knew the violet flicker was in her eyes as the hallway took on a black-light cast, reflecting energy signatures her human eyes couldn't see. The birnenston stench had dissipated, but faint smudges on the walls remained like smoke stains. She held her breath, listening, and heard nothing.

Nothing to see, nothing to hear, but all her senses, and the demon's too, thrummed a warning.

She didn't call out for Bookie. Soundlessly, she backed away, wishing she'd been quieter going through the stairwell door. She turned to run.

A man stepped out from a dark doorway she'd passed, blocking her return to the stairs. He faced her, a black silhouette. He took a step forward, and to her demon-pitched hearing, the step boomed with other-realm power, reverberating in her bones until her teeth rattled. Another thunderous step brought him within reach of one of the lighted rooms.

And still he was a black silhouette. Her enhanced vision couldn't penetrate the unrelieved darkness that devoured him.

Now she knew why he'd taken the name Corvus—Latin for blackbird.

She bolted. Not Bookie's office, obviously a trap. Was the historian there, wounded or dead? The next door down the hall wasn't locked. She ducked in, then cursed when she flicked on the light and realized there was no lock on what was clearly a catch-all room and small at that.

She hauled a battered desk in front of the door. It wouldn't stop Corvus, she knew. He wasn't relying on his ferales anymore.

In the hall, each step boomed with etheric shock waves that sent her demon, trapped within her, fleeing in helpless circles until she reeled with vertigo. Her hypersensitive hearing faltered, so one moment her ears rang with the relentless footsteps, and in the next, only an eerie, lying silence.

No wonder teshuva didn't fight the djinn. Her demon obviously thought they were doomed. Great. Abandoned once again.

Screw that. She pushed another desk in front of the first, then spun it ninety degrees lengthwise so that only a few inches separated it from the far wall. If he pushed open the door, the door would shove the desks into the wall.

That wouldn't stop him either. Nothing would.

She cast around the small space, looking for something, anything, to defend herself. A box of file folders. A rolling chair. A shelf with a row of glass beakers. Maybe the acoustic tiles overhead hid a false ceiling where she could escape.

The door exploded inward, crushing the corner of the first desk. Splinters and a strip of metal blew through the room. The rebound sent the second desk spinning crazily. It knocked her to the ground.

She tried to roll and screamed at the pain in her leg.

Broken. She knew that physical sensation of sound, of bone grating on bone. The right femur was snapped in half. She wouldn't be able to stand until her teshuva healed her.

From outside, Corvus shoved at the debris, all that was keeping him from entering.

She clawed through the wreckage, avoiding the chair that rolled toward her as he crashed through. Glass from the shattered beakers cut her palms.

Her fingers closed around the metal strip.

She rolled to her back, saw him looming over her, and lashed out with the thin metal.

He recoiled, but the tip grazed diagonally across his face. Blood sprayed. Before she could attack again, he lunged, pinning her wrist under his boot, grinding her hand into the broken glass. On either side of the bloody line, his eyes narrowed.

Okay, yeah, they were doomed.

He plucked the measly weapon from her grasp, slicing her fingers. She bit into her lip rather than cry out.

Without the teshuva focused on the djinni, she finally could see the man. Blunt features, thick neck, shaved bullet head. He looked like a gladiator. The scratch she'd given him was healing, almost lost among the myriad faint scars on his face.

But his eyes . . . She'd expected anything—crimson red, jaundiced orange, deep black, or blank white— besides this shimmering, celestial blue.

He wrapped his fingers around her neck and straightened, pulling her upright, up to her toes, then off her feet entirely. The ring on his finger cut into her throat. He held her aloft without straining.

"Where is your demon?" He gave her a little shake, as if she might be hiding it in her pocket. "Teshuva coward, where are you? You'd abandon your woman to fight your battles alone?"

She clawed at his fingers around her neck, prying at the large-stoned ring she could feel but not see. She kicked, but the agony in her leg almost made her vomit, not good while being choked.

Her all-too-human vision darkened. She supposed she should be glad for a relatively painless death, compared to poor Zane's.

On the other hand, she finally understood Archer's desire to go out in a blaze of demon-shredding glory.

She'd add her own demon to the ass kicking. The te-shuva had promised her strength, and she was dying from want of air.

As the blackness closed around her, her last sight was those heavenly eyes, and her last thought that heaven should be pissed.

CHAPTER 23

Half buried in leaves beside the daybed, Archer's cell phone buzzed. He glared at it balefully. Wouldn't be good news. When was it ever?

Because he feared whom the bad news might be about, he answered on the last ring before the call went to voice mail.

The voice on the other end was tentative. "This is Nanette. Sera's friend. I don't know if you remember me."

"The faith healer." A prickle of unease went through him. "Is Sera all right?"

A pause on the other end. "She's not with you? I had the impression . . . Sorry to bother you."

"Wait." He gripped the phone. "What's wrong?"

"Someone needs to talk to her, rather urgently, and I can't reach her. I remembered you gave Wendy, the nursing home director, the name of your cleaning service. I called them—who needs a twenty-four-hour dry cleaner?—and they agreed to give me your phone number if I promised to tell you not to send them any more business like yours. I said I would, and I have."

Archer closed his eyes, struggling for patience. "Can we get to the 'rather urgently' part?"

"Do you know where she is?"

"Not at the moment." Likely never again.

"We have to find her. She's in terrible danger."

"She's possessed by a demon. Of course she's in danger." He tensed at the thought of what the angelic host would do to her if they discovered she could open a path into the demon realm.

"Not just danger to her soul. Real danger. I mean, her soul being in danger is real danger—"

"Urgently," Archer reminded her.

"Sorry. I've just never seen anything like this. All he keeps saying is he needs Sera."

"He?" Archer's blood froze. "Nanette, listen. You may be dealing with a djinn-possessed man. And he is most definitely dangerous."

"No, this is just a man. And he's hurt."

"He could be disguising what he is, to gain your trust."

"Mr. Archer," Nanette said briskly, "I am host to an angel, a lesser angel, but even I'd smell a djinni this close."

"He's with you now?" Archer was already pulling on his boots.

"Yes. He knew Sera came to me, but he says he needs Sera too, to be healed."

Archer automatically checked the weight of the axe in his coat. "What does he think Sera can do?"

"I have no idea. I don't think even the highest seraph could help."

"Is he dying?"

"I don't know what will happen if he does. This man doesn't have a soul."

Archer, with the club out but the blade retracted, ghosted through the dark cinder-block church, demon senses ranging out around him like a pack of leashed hunting dogs. No djinn.

He recognized Nanette in the doorway of the main office. She wrung her hands, but her distress seemed contained. His concern that she had called him under duress faded.

"This way," she called.

He stepped cautiously into the smaller room—and froze when he saw Bookie splayed on the couch.

The historian lifted his head and groaned. "You're not Sera."

"No." Archer circled toward the couch. "What the hell's going on, Bookie? Where's Sera? She was supposed to be meeting with you."

"I need her. I have to find her."

Nanette sighed. "He won't say anything else. I almost called my husband, but then I noticed his"—she waved one hand helplessly—"his lack."

"His missing soul."

She nodded, her face ashen. "I know the teshuva lost the vision for what lies within, but my angel sees the brightness of someone's soul." Her gaze slid away from him. "Or darkness. But there's always *something* there. With him, nothing." She lowered her voice. "It sickens me to see. Like falling into a well. I can't imagine what it's doing to him."

Archer watched Bookie through narrowed eyes. "I don't see how losing your soul suddenly makes you stupid."

Nanette gazed at him reprovingly. "I think he's gone a bit mad."

"I have no problem with mad. He just has to share the details." Archer loomed over him. "Bookie, where's your soul? And what's Sera supposed to do about it?"

From behind his glasses, the man's gaze flicked over him, incuriously. That, more than anything, made Archer believe something was wrong. Bookie had never been able to look at any of them without at least a hint of frustrated superiority. "I need Sera."

"Right. For what?"

"I have to drive her away, destroy her havens, make you doubt her. I have to give her to him."

A chill spidered down Archer's spine. Bookie had tossed Sera's apartment, keeping her on the run from . . . ? "Who's 'he,' Bookie?" The freeze all but stopped his heart as bitter logic supplied the name. "Corvus."

"He said I had to make an opening, make a place for it, in me."

More questions without answers for the first ones. "Make a place for what?"

"He stole it from me. Now he'll steal hers. Steal it and set them all free." He muttered in Latin.

Archer grabbed the man's shoulders and shook him. "All what, Bookie?"

"The demons," Bookie shrieked. "All the demons. He'll free all the demons." His shriek rose to a glass-shattering pitch. "I wanted a demon. She took it, and it was supposed to be mine."

Archer recoiled. Bookie began to cry. The gut-wrenching sobs shook him harder than Archer had.

"Why would anyone want to be possessed?" Nanette whispered.

"Only a fool." Archer stared down at the weeping man.

Bookie had betrayed them.

The man looked up, tears speckling the inside of his glasses. "Don't let him eat her demon. It's mine."

Everything came together in Archer's head. Bookie e-mailing Sera for a meeting time. Sera slipping out. She'd gone to the meeting . . . with Corvus. Only hours ago.

He hauled Bookie upright with such violence his glasses flew off. "Where did he take her? Damn you, Bookkeeper. Where?"

"Mine," Bookie mumbled. "I helped make the hole in the Veil, and he made a hole in me, so it's mine. I need it."

Archer cursed and spun away, grabbing his cell phone. He punched in Niall's number, and was speaking almost before the other man could answer. "Corvus has Sera. Bookie sold us out. Retrace Bookie's movements for the last forty-eight hours. He's been in Corvus's presence within that period. We need the djinn-man's lair."

He hung up, grabbed Bookie again, and headed for the door. "You, take me to your leader."

"Wait," Nanette cried. "I'm going with you."

Archer didn't slow. "This could get messy."

"I might be able to help. If I see the wandering soul . . ."

"You'd help him?"

She bit her lip. "I told you, I don't think I can. But the soul might lead us to this Corvus. And Sera. And if he is trying to unlock the demon realm, you need all the help you can get."

Archer stared at her. He'd traded the deadliest force of talyan fighters for a soulless traitor and a bottom-rung angelic possessed.

Hell of a way to save the world.

Corvus paced in front of the talya bound on the floor, small and pale as the exotic gazelle that had once been thrown into the arena with him. That had been an absurd match, his hacking sword against the delicate, curving horns that weren't even aimed at him. He'd slaughtered the beast with blood-soaked thoroughness, to the crowd's screaming delight. His soul had withered.

And that had been before the djinni came to him.

He crouched, nostrils flaring to catch the scent of blood still seeping from her wounds.

Where was the demon? Why did it let her bleed? Unease swept through him.

The crow cheeped, a ridiculous sound, and poked noisily through the empty shells in the bottom of its cage. He hadn't remembered to feed it, distracted as he was by the destruction he was about to unleash.

But the key to unlocking the door to the demon realm was still unconscious. He'd almost killed her once already in his impatience.

The crow squalled. To shut it up, he threw a handful of seeds at the cage. Ungrateful wretch.

When he turned back, the talya was still slumped on the ground but was watching him.

He strode across the room to tower over her.

She stared up, no violet in her eyes.

He grabbed the waistband of her jeans and ripped. The sound of tearing denim was lost in her scream as the pant leg snagged around her broken thigh.

Pinning her down with his foot when she flailed at him, he stripped her pants. He gripped the bruised flesh of her thigh and squeezed. Her scream cut off in a sob-choked gasp.

He traced one finger along the curving lines of her demon mark. Such perfect arcs, like the gentle bend of heated black glass, spun finer and finer toward the juncture of soft skin between her legs.

His hand resting on the triangle of silk left covering her, he met her tear-bright gaze. "Summon it."

"I must've left it in my other pants pocket." Her voice rasped through her strained throat. "Just let me run home and get it."

"I am through waiting."

"Two thousand years finally enough?"

He backhanded her, not so hard as to break her slender neck, and settled to his haunches. "Why do you talyan delight in needling me? I just feel better about hurting you."

"Zane teased you, so you tortured him? And Bookie

too, I suppose?" Her voice cracked. "What's your excuse for loosing demons on the world?"

He rolled up his sleeves, revealing the jagged black marks climbing like ancient thorny vines upward from both elbows. "The world welcomes its demons with open arms, just like your Bookworm. He came to me, you know, tracked me down through Bookkeeper archives. He thought he could drill through the Veil and tap the energy on the other side. He envied you talyan your power, and wanted his own." He held out his hands, palms up in mock helplessness. "Maybe everyone should have a chance to face their demons, and I am only midwife to the inevitable."

She snorted, triggering a coughing jag. "Whatever Bookie wanted, I didn't agree to play mother to the coming horde."

"How convenient that I don't require your cooperation." He walked away.

He didn't need her willingness, but he did need her demon ascendant. Only its energy coursing through its link to the demon realm would reveal the weakness in the Veil. And the cowardly teshuva was nowhere to be found.

He smoothed his palms over the clamps and shears and jagged rods of glass—the tools he'd arranged so carefully on his desk in preparation for their discussion. Without the demon, she wouldn't survive five minutes of his most gentle techniques.

He glanced back at the woman. She'd taken a possessed as her lover, Bookie had said, and with him found a way to cast out evil.

For a moment, Corvus wondered.

But no. A djinni was no paltry darkling to be shooed back to the Darkness that did not fade. Unbidden, his breath quickened. The acid sting of his demon scoured the backs of his eyes.

Sometimes even demons wouldn't forgive temptation.

He focused his burning gaze on the talya. In her present condition, the brute darklings that lurked in the basement would find no sport with her. But their smaller brethren. . . .

He jerked her up onto her good leg. She paled around the red imprint of his knuckles, but didn't cry out. Her strength wouldn't save her, but would only keep her around long enough for his plans to reach their inescapable conclusion.

He hauled her downstairs, dragging her behind like a broken marionette when she stumbled.

He'd chosen the tower because the riverside location opened on soaring views over the city, views that brought him some measure of quietude. Only later had he discovered the dank basement with its river access.

Over time, his presence lured a plague of darklings to the passageways. The noxious morass of birnenston seeping from them had fueled his research into odd weapons that had hooked politicians, generals, and terrorists in many countries. They'd thought they were using him for their own ends. In a manner of speaking, they were right.

If contact with the poison sometimes forced his djinni into hiding deep within him, it always seemed to recover.

Even with their violence subjugated to his energy and the birnenston, the darklings were a malevolent flock. The occasional stink of corpse wafted from the basement when they snagged the homeless mumblers, the young runaways, the overdosed prostitutes. Sometimes he threw them a proverbial bone—or a not-so-proverbial bone.

Lucky darklings, this was one of those times.

CHAPTER 24

Through waves of pain, Sera grasped at consciousness. A tiny voice told her coming awake wasn't going to make the nightmare go away. But not knowing was worse.

She gritted her teeth and pulled herself into awareness—cold, damp, stinking awareness. She coughed on the mingled stenches of stagnant water, rot, and sulfur. Yeah, sometimes knowing was worse.

"You're free."

She pushed herself up. The stone under her hands was slick with mold and other things she didn't want to identify. Too dark to see, anyway, without her demon's help, since only torches lit the cavernous room.

"Honest to God," she said hoarsely. "Who uses torches anymore?"

"It makes the darklings feel at home."

Sorry she'd asked, she rubbed her wrists. Embedded glass stung, but he hadn't lied. He'd left her unbound. "Free at last, free at last."

Corvus stood between the torches. "You can run for the stairs. I won't stop you." He swept his hand one way, and the torchlight shadows jumped on the old iron door that guarded the stairs. "Or you can swim." He pointed toward the waterside dock. "It is more than was ever offered me."

The dark around him winked with tiny crimson stars. Malice eyes. How unfair. Once she knew what to look for, even with her defenses stripped, she could still see them.

Then she saw the others.

They stood unmoving, facing her, eyes clouded and unseeing. Something about that wall of empty eyes—human-colored in mixtures of brown, blue, green, but blank stares—made her flesh crawl.

She kept her voice from trembling. "Friends of yours?"

"They are nothing. Quite literally. Pay them no mind. They can't help you any more than they could help themselves, but they won't stop you either. They wanted their freedom too."

She raised her chin. "I wouldn't think a slave would keep prisoners."

He crossed his arms over his chest, muscles rippling. "I won my own way out."

"Funny. Rumor has it you lost your last bout." She studied him. "Judging by the *reven*, your arms were—what?—both broken? What did the demon promise you? The chance to take up arms again?"

"No." The torch flames made the marks writhe. "It said I could lay down my sword forever. It gave me deadlier weapons instead." He straightened, as if regretting his words. "They aren't prisoners of mine. They took the chains upon themselves. I loosed them. And now, with you, I'll free the rest of hell, and my struggle will be done."

Her teshuva had been right to make itself scarce. If Corvus wanted it, she couldn't let it out.

She dug her nails into the stone wall behind her. Clenching her jaw until her teeth just added another pain in the chorus, she forced herself to stand. "I won't open the Veil. The demons stay."

His face twisted, old scars contorting. "You want us to fight for them, angels and demons, forever? Let them suffer and die if they are so inclined."

She swayed, trying to make sense of his anguish. "Did Bookie even understand what you wanted? Do the demons? Or are you still the gladiator, thrown into the ring by his masters? Alone?"

His expression settled into something like calm. "If hell fancies burning, then let it truly burn. As for God and his judgment, let us see how he fares on his own against the devils at his gate."

Slowly, so she didn't knock herself over in dizzy pain, she shook her head. "I won't sacrifice the world just to teach God and hell a lesson."

"Then go." Corvus spread his hands.

"Right. Run or swim. No bicycle portion of this triathlon? Oh wait. My leg's broken."

A poison yellow gleam brightened his eyes. "Ah. True. This would be a good time for your demon to make an appearance. Before the rest of the darklings get home for dinner."

She contemplated the djinn-man, the shifting mass of malice, and the blank-eyed watchers against her MIA demon. She just had to make sure the teshuva stayed lost. "Damn," she muttered.

"If you do or if you don't," Corvus agreed.

She glanced at the rank, black water and shivered, remembering the lapping tongue of river against cracked windshield glass. That was out. She wouldn't want to drown before she was brutally killed.

She wheeled toward the iron door and started to run—or hobble.

She wasn't even halfway there when the malice descended.

Of course. He'd said he wouldn't stop her. He just hadn't mentioned anything about his pets.

She fell, and the malice swarmed over her.

They bit deep, latching on to her hands and glass-cut wrist, one ankle, her neck, and cheek. They snapped at one another when they couldn't reach her.

With each ravenous pull of malice mouths, terrible images played through her head, as if the vile little monsters sucked every ugliness to the surface for their feast. Her mother's waxen skin. Her father's screaming mouth, opened wide. Her own body, mangled after the car accident. Every dark and dreadful thought brought back to life, to haunt the heart like ghosts or zombies.

The sick weight of the malice made her wish she'd chosen to jump into the water, after all. Maybe she could drown them, float them away—as her mother finally had.

A low moan raised tremors down her spine. For an awful moment, she thought the sound came from her.

She twisted her head and met the vacant stares of Corvus's prisoners. From the black holes of their slack, gaping mouths came the whispering groan, despair or hunger or both.

They'd wanted freedom from this, she realized, from the torment that fed the malice so richly.

The watchers grew dim as her vision grayed, like shades of her hospice patients. Had guiding them to quiet grace been a terrible deception, only to assuage her own fear of the end they were all coming to someday? Was grace an illusion, peace a myth?

She was going to die with her questions unanswered. Or maybe only in her death would she have her answers.

At least she was about to find out.

Niall rattled off his report. "At five o'clock this evening, Bookie took a cab over to River North. He was dropped off near the Mart. That's the last location we can confirm until he showed up at Nanette's church."

"We're close," Archer said. "Maybe Bookie will give himself away if he sees the place." He glanced at the man slouched in the passenger seat. "You going to help us, Bookkeeper?"

"I need Sera," the historian muttered.

Archer shifted the phone to his other ear. "Yeah, he's going to help."

"I'll send everyone I can," Niall said. "But this storm is closing down fast. And I'm getting strange reports. On the way to meet the cabbie, Jonah saw ferales herding people. I think Corvus's army is on the move. They weren't corpses yet, but if they're with ferales, they soon will be."

Archer glared out at the thickening snow. "If we don't stop Corvus before he forces Sera to open the Veil, a few oddball ferales will be the least of our problems."

"And the people with them?"

Archer hesitated. "They're fucked." He hung up to manhandle the SUV through snow soft and heavy as a burial shroud. "We're all fucked."

The water was a dark slash through the white as they crossed the bridge. They quartered the streets until Archer finally slammed his fist on the steering wheel. "He can't just disappear."

"The high tower," Bookie whispered. His breath fogged the side window where he'd angled his pale face.

Archer ran a hand through his hair. "They're all towers."

In the middle of the next block, from behind a parked truck, a pedestrian stepped out into the street. Archer slammed on the brakes, and the SUV slewed sideways.

The homeless man, his coat hung awkwardly from one shoulder, never looked around, his gaze fixed upward.

Archer tightened his grip on the wheel as another

oblivious walker—a girl in stiletto heels still not high enough to keep her out of the snow—followed the man into the street, her face turned toward the sky as if drawn by a hook in her lip.

Archer glanced at Bookie, then back at the pedestrians. Zane had said Corvus commanded an army of corpses. "Nanette. Those people. Tell me what you see."

"What? Nothing." Her voice rose with excitement. "Nothing. Just like Bookie."

The odd couple cut between the parked cars, following a line only they sensed, and disappeared into a park. Archer pulled over, his hand on the door handle, ready to give chase.

"Over there," Nanette said. "Three more of them." The enthusiasm in her tone wavered. "Whatever they are."

They followed slowly until Bookie clawed at his door, whining, "It's here."

"My God," Nanette whispered.

Archer glanced in the rearview mirror. Nanette had her cheek pressed to the glass, as rapt as their unwitting guides.

He peered out at the dark high-rise. "What?"

"Don't you see them? Stop the car."

He hauled the wheel over, bouncing onto the curb. "What is it? Bookie's soul?"

"No. It's like . . . but not a soul." She tumbled out before he could turn off the car. He got out, hand on his axe.

She stood, eyes bright, mouth agape like a child catching snowflakes on her tongue.

He followed her gaze.

High up, white and drifting, the birds, brighter than the clouds, flew through the storm.

They soared on other-realm winds that didn't disturb the endless fall of snow. The trailing edges of their ethereal wings flickered with light as if from a distant dawn.

They looped around the building's crown in graceful patterns that almost reminded him of something, if he could only trace their flight with a pen.

"Bookie said tower," Nanette murmured. "I looked up, and they were there."

After a moment, Archer found his voice. "I see them too." He followed the intricate dance, the patterns sketching ever-more complicated fractals into infinity, like Sera's *reven*. His breath caught. "This is the place."

He hit Niall on speed dial, handed Nanette the phone, and ran for the door.

"You don't have to die, Sera."

Nothing existed outside the evil movies in her head, but the voice snaked through.

"Everybody has to die," she murmured.

"Not now you don't. Just call on me."

The demon. Her teshuva.

Or maybe the other demon. Corvus.

Either way, the voice was right. Her demon could save her.

She just had to damn the world.

Shouldn't everyone fight the demons with her? Her wounds of abandonment would never heal, even if the teshuva came raging back. She sighed, a breath that felt like her last. She would not call on the demon. She wouldn't make the world face its demons.

Not peace, but resignation.

Until the iron door exploded and her name came howling through.

In flash-frozen images worse than anything the malice visions had conjured, Archer crashed in, engulfed by a dozen ferales.

His flaring, violet gaze caught hers. As always, his glance blazed over her skin, slammed through her bones. Then he was fighting his way toward her.

The ferales raged out of control, in a melee of clashing claws and jaws, rending one another as often as Archer. A handful of the malice on her squealed and scrambled away.

Corvus dodged for the stairs, out of the fray.

The fanned blade of Archer's axe spun through the air, its shining edge shedding ichor. In his off hand, the smaller knife flashed and pierced, but always another mutation of evil barred his way.

She dragged herself up, then stumbled a step toward him. Malice weighed on her, draining her spirit like bloated ticks. No way could she reach him; far too many monsters were between them.

Her broken leg twisted, and she sunk to the floor. A malice dropped back on its smoky coil of a tail and wailed.

Archer's answering shout of defiance echoed across the stones. He rose up, scattering ferales. He stood, stark and alone, black coat in tatters around bare skin and crimson rivulets of blood.

"Sera!"

He reached out, as if he could hold her across the cavern, against the death and damnation that threatened.

The ferales swept in. Archer brought up his blades, winking fierce and fragile against the darkness. One hideous fiend towered over him, its slavering maw open to crooked rows of serrated teeth. The feralis roared and fell upon him.

Sera screamed, the cry ripped from her body and soul. She held out her hand, straining toward him. She needed to go to him. He needed her. She toppled forward, her body weak, her will failing.

But her soul, the other half of her soul . . .

"Ferris!"

The demon, roused at her cry, burst across her senses. The dark cavern flared to eerie black-light incandescence, demon sign smeared across the walls. The wild power drew down to her core and swirled in the mark over her hips and thighs. Between the violet-shot lines of the *reven*, her bare skin faded to other-realm translucence.

The etheric supernova rose, exploding through her in a shock wave that shook the shadows and reached between the realms.

Desperate, dying, she fell toward the Veil.

CHAPTER 25

Corvus climbed the stairs three at a time, cursing with each crash of his foot against the treads.

Igniting the apocalypse was proving more troublesome than he'd anticipated.

He supposed he should be grateful to the male talya intruder, since his appearance had triggered the resurgence of Sera Littlejohn's teshuva. But so much for enjoying the end of the world in peace and quiet.

He swept his hand over the glass-working tools on his desk. Where was the stone? He'd removed his ring as he always did before his rougher work. He didn't see the cold silver glint among the dark steel and iron.

With another curse for the woman who'd distracted him, he shoved all the tools off the desk, almost knocking over the gilt cage.

The crow cackled. The batting of its wings sounded like airy laughter.

Corvus turned.

The crow stilled. It took one slow, sidling step.

Corvus lunged, then swung open the cage door. The thieving crow shrieked and pecked at his fingers.

He wrapped his fingers around its neck and dragged

it out. He didn't notice when the black talons stopped tearing at his hand.

He sighed and reached for the sullen gleam half hidden in the discarded sunflower hulls.

Archer thought she was dead. Her eyes were closed, shutting him out. Ice congealed around his heart. The ferales piled over him, slashing through flesh to bone.

In that numb moment where even piercing fangs couldn't reach, he realized death would bring him silence and stillness, but peace wasn't what he wanted.

He wanted Sera.

And he'd fight through hell itself to find her.

Crying her name, he burst out from under the ferales in a spray of blood and fury. He reached for her as if all the space between them were no obstacle to his need.

She lay crumpled on the floor, her skin shocking white against the purple panties he'd given her.

He knew the moment she reached through the Veil. As her physical weakness loosened her hold on the world, she followed her demon's link to its realm and turned her vulnerability into preternatural power.

The walls of the basement seemed to bell outward, rippling into other realms. The ring of soulless let out a collective moan that raised his hackles. They held out their empty arms, as if they wanted to follow her down—down through the Veil, that tangled web of disembodied souls. . . .

Suddenly, he understood what Corvus had wrought. The soulless army—like a fire's backdraft—would implode against the Veil, weakened where Sera's demon had so recently crossed, sucking down the souls that imprisoned all the demons of hell.

All the remaining demons, that is. Archer summoned his own and tore through the ring around Sera.

But they were too many, their hungry need too great.

He took only three steps toward her before the ground between them cracked.

From the corpses' gaping mouths, a groan shivered the air, rising toward a gasping yowl. The patchwork brick and cement of the cavern floor broke apart. Thin tendrils of fog snaked out.

Archer caught himself on the edge of the crack. The hem of his coat fluttered forward, drawn as if by a breath.

The ferales pounded toward him, his blood already in their teeth.

Still too far away, Sera lay swamped in malice. Surrounded by rings of evil, she couldn't even see him. The soulless army would swallow the Veil and crack open the demon realm upon the world, and he couldn't do a damn thing.

By himself.

"Sera," he roared, "I won't lose you."

Through the shifting morass of malice, a glint of blond shone.

"I can't do this alone."

The last was merely a whisper as time warped between the realms, but he caught a hint of hazel as Sera lifted her head. He wanted to scream at the dark bruise high on her cheek and the raw welts left by hungry malice mouths.

With a hiss of retribution, the crack in the floor raced thin and jagged halfway across the room toward her, and sucked down a malice.

The demon squealed and was gone.

The other malice sprang in all directions with a dissonant chorus of shrieks. An other-realm vortex, like the winds that held the spirit birds aloft, spun up. Malice were swept into the air, like red-eyed bats in a cyclone, screaming as they were drawn toward the maw. Archer staggered with its force, though the torches burned steadily on.

A feralis, turning to flee, reeled into one vein of the gray fog. It bawled as its substance unraveled and poured into the void.

With each step he took toward Sera, the frenzy of the vortex increased. More gray tendrils reached out from the rift. The ferales hunched under the invisible inhalation of energy. A handful of the soulless slumped as if their bones had turned to jelly.

One of the torches leapt toward the ceiling, then extinguished itself. The rift glowed with a nacreous, mesmerizing energy.

When he'd danced this dance with her before for the lone malice and the two ferales, they'd broken free of each other easily. Now, the link between them had taken on a dangerous power of its own, just as he'd always known it would.

Without turning away from her, he deflected the attack of another feralis. A strand of the rift engulfed it. The continuing arc of the axe sunk into another feralis leaping out of the shadows.

The demon split apart in a noisome collapse of rat bones and roach shells. Archer jumped back and released his hold as the blade was sucked through the vortex in a glittering trail of particles.

The rift wasn't consuming just demonic energy.

Avoiding the tendrils, at last he dropped to his knees next to Sera. The malice were gone, the bruise already fading from her cheek.

"Rise and shine," he murmured when she blinked as if waking from a dream—or nightmare. "I guess you're already shining."

Brilliant amethyst winked at him as she took in the whirling gray fog. "This looks bad. The Veil . . ."

"You gave us a chance. I took it."

"A chance? I should have died rather than risk—"

"No." He gripped her shoulders hard. "Risk."

What wouldn't he risk for her? His life? Of course.

His soul? In a heartbeat. Ah, yes, his heart . . . He lifted her to her feet. "But the Veil is breached, just as Corvus planned."

Her gaze shifted to the ring of Corvus's soulless army, their mouths slack in unvoiced screams. "Do we kill them? Will that stop it?" Her tone was bleak.

"Too late. Corvus said they were dead. He knew death wouldn't save them. We need to stop him from calling any other demons through."

"Call them? How?"

"Those spirit birds circling." He knelt in front of her, hands gentle on her thigh, making sure her teshuva was setting bone and muscle straight.

Through gritted teeth, she asked, "You could see the sculptures from the street?"

"We saw the spirits. We thought they were Bookie's soul at first."

Her expression darkened. "Corvus stripped the essences of the birds like he did Bookie, bound them to the glass. Why?"

"Birds have always been associated with the soul. The soulless that Corvus created homed in on them. Unbound demons crossing the Veil, seeking vulnerable spirits, will be lured too. Can you walk?"

"Hurts. But I can move." She raised her hand to his cheek. "How can you?"

"Head wounds bleed." So did all the other ones, but the teshuva was getting to them. He just had to ignore the pain. Even harder, he had to ignore the desire to rest against her touch. She'd rejected that—rejected him—to continue the fight. Well, fight he could give her. He lifted her to her feet. "Let's go before Blackbird flies the coop."

They took the steps at a staggering run. Frantic cawing echoed down the hall as they reached the top floor. Abruptly, the cawing stopped.

Sera put her hand on Archer's arm. "He's in there. That bird hates him."

"Now you know why."

They stepped into the room.

Corvus stood at the window, a black rag dangling from his hand. Beyond him, the city spread out in a winter spectacle, with the strange inversion of light and dark where the snowy night sky reflecting city lights was brighter than the buildings. Pinwheels of etheric energy burst up from the streets—horde-tenebrae, and worse, closing on their location.

Corvus did not turn. "So lovely."

Archer realized the djinn-man wasn't watching the advance of his world-ending army, but the spirit birds just outside the glass. He took in the dozens of sculptures on the window ledge and identified the motionless black tangle of feathers in Corvus's hand, in the same glance.

"Where is Bookie's soul?" He had to ask, though he doubted severed souls could be reunited with flesh. And with the rift widening, they didn't have time to find all the souls of the people below, to satiate their hunger before they destroyed the Veil.

"A Worm's spirit will never fly, so I let it go." Finally, Corvus turned. His eyes glistened with leaching birnenston. "I see he betrayed me too, given the chance."

"After you stripped his soul, he probably figured your deal was off." Archer stepped to one side, distancing himself from Sera, making room for the attack.

Corvus lifted his head. "Ah well, his work survives him. When the Veil parts, there will be demons enough for everyone."

"Not if I stop them," Sera said through gritted teeth.

In mocking reply, the vortex found them. It whirled through the room, leaving papers untouched but rattling the glass birds on the windowsill like chimes.

"You started it," Corvus reminded her. "But like your Bookworm, your task is done. You are free to go." He raised his hand. The ring on his finger winked slyly.

"Sera," Archer warned. "The ring."

Mostly dull with a hint of iridescent shine, like sunlight on gray doves' wings. The tint of a soul.

From the corner of his eye, he saw her touch the pendant around her neck. That was what Bookie had been muttering.

"*Desolator numinis*," he repeated. "The soul cleaver." No wonder the djinn-man had been so bold. With her soul sundered, she'd be as passive as Bookie, subject to Corvus's whim.

Corvus froze when Sera pulled out the matching pendant from under her shirt. "The Bookworm kept more secrets than I guessed. I doubt even he realized what his work called through from the other side. Do you know what you are?"

Her eyes gleamed violet as she framed the stone between her palms. "I might not have all the answers. But the demon told me this stone could enslave it. And Zane told us you stole his demon. So I have a damn good idea what I can try."

Corvus circled. His clawed hand flexed, startling a glimmer from his ring. "You? You would face off against me alone?"

"Yeah me. I'm the reflection of what you and Bookie invoked." Her voice rose along with the vortex wind. "You made the emptiness that drew my demon. You wanted the hole in the Veil. You got exactly what you asked for. And I am not alone."

The floor heaved. Something had shifted in the basement.

Corvus glared at Sera. "What is this sucking wound you've made? Can't you feel the void calling the darkness back? We too are demon-ridden. Let them loose."

"I won't." The vortex whirled through the room with an otherworldly shriek, like a spirit bird gone mad. It lashed her hair into a golden corona.

"If demon-kind walk the world, unfleshed, then we

will be free of them, slaves no longer." Corvus turned his poison stare on Archer. "You are old, though not as old as I. Tell her to set us free."

For a suspended heartbeat, Archer felt the gladiator's centuries of pain. Let demons and angels war on. Man needn't be the battlefield anymore.

"Nothing would change." Sera faced Corvus. "The true battle between good and evil is fought as it always has been, as it always will be, within the human heart." She stood straight, still. "I *will* seal the Veil."

"You are no healer," Corvus said. "You have always ushered in the end. Live your fate."

She shook her head. Archer dreaded the dire beauty of her in her steadfastness, and the anguish of what she denied them for the sake of an oblivious world.

"Then you will suffer eternally." Corvus raised his fist. "Only a distillation of our souls will seal the Veil. We will be trapped for eternity between the realms."

"So be it," she said.

"I will not be bound again," Corvus cried. His demon leapt into ascension, a jaundiced shadow that didn't quite keep pace with its caster. When he charged Sera, the sulfurous pall shot ahead of him.

Archer hurtled forward with an answering roar, summoning demon-fueled strength and speed. But for the first time, he knew he would fall short. All the teshuva's repentance was not enough to satiate the djinni's hunger for extinction. Once, he would have gone with fierce joy to his doom, knowing death itself had nothing more to take from him.

But now there was Sera. From deep inside, deeper than the place the demon dwelled, he dredged up a power purely human, impelled by a force that to his desperate regret he had shut away in words not said—and met the djinn-man halfway.

The *desolator numinis* swept down. An ion comet trail glittered in the vortex-charged atmosphere. Archer felt its wake pass through him, felt a part of himself fall away, a weight that had grown too heavy, and another part, a lightness that made his heart ache.

The momentum of his leap carried them both toward the window and the row of glass birds.

Sera shouted a warning, but he'd already charted the trajectory. He'd been on this path a long time. And if, at the very end, he'd come to hope for something else. . . .

Corvus's back hit the window as the vortex exploded outward. He screamed.

The glass birds blew apart, the shards a dazzling rainbow that followed Archer out into the night.

Surrounded by glittering glass and snow and a free flight of otherworldly birds, they fell.

CHAPTER 26

Sera cried out, the sound lost in the vortex howl.

Not again. She'd watched him jump from the hotel rooftop, just as she'd watched her mother leave her, not once but twice. She couldn't survive another twofold abandonment. The demons couldn't win again.

She didn't remember racing down to the riverfront. Bookie and Nanette stood on the sidewalk where a dozen frantic-looking talyan converged. Corvus was an obscene snow angel, crooked and still. But her eyes were only on the black-leather-clad shape beyond, crumpled like broken wings.

The silence was devastating. White snow melted in the pool of crimson.

She fell to her bare knees beside Archer. Her demon couldn't stop the icy pain.

Nanette reached for her. "Oh, Sera."

Niall leaned over Corvus, prodding at the slush near the djinn-man's head. "Still breathing. But this is gray matter. Damn it."

Damned . . . Sera scuttled across the snow and kicked at Corvus's body.

Niall grabbed at her. "Jesus, Sera."

She shoved the body over to uncover the hand and yanked the ring free. The stone was cracked in two. One side flashed with ragged violet lightning; the other glimmered a burnished bronze that speared her heart.

She gripped her pendant, summoning a knowledge not her own. Then she leaned forward and let the pendant swing free over Corvus, where the barest mist of breath steamed from his gaping mouth. Violence, hatred, and terror swirled in her. But at the still center was a fragile hope.

"Sera," Nanette said, "let it go."

"It's gone, all right," Sera said. "I have it now." She returned to Archer's side.

"He's gone too," Niall said softly.

"Not gone, just dead. There's a difference. Corvus took him. Now I have him." She tightened her grip on the ring.

"The djinni—"

"Never mind one djinn. We'll have all hell on us in another minute." She turned to face the cavern.

The riverside door had shivered apart in splintered timbers and bolts melted to slag. Inside, other-realm winds had scoured away the moss, etching unreadable hieroglyphics in the brick. The soulless corpses had collapsed into a tumbled Stonehenge of flesh. The building swayed with the long inhalation of the vortex like a terminal patient on his last legs.

When it finally exhaled, what would escape on its world-scorching breath?

Sera gestured the talyan back. Niall shook his head, so she ignored them. Clutching the pendant, she flattened her palm over Archer's chest. On her thumb, the ring glinted. She stared past the stone's occluding layers to the shimmering bronze heart. Just as the teshuva ascended in her, she would descend into its realm, soul and demon bound.

"C'mon, demon," she murmured. "Time to bring on the repenting."

It surged up in her like a wildfire crowning. Every nerve blazed, and the *reven* over her bare thighs sparked violet. She cast herself onto the pyre, one with the spiraling hellfire.

Now she knew why fallen angels didn't need wings.

Bearing her burden of souls, she crossed over the Veil.

The vortex breathed at her back. Threads of living color leaked into the demon realm—the hint of blue in an icy river, the blush of blood diluted in snow, the slumbering brown of dormant trees with the faintest hint of spring's green buds—achingly vibrant and utterly wrong in this place.

The threads marked her path back, just as the gray tendrils on the other side would lead demons out into the world. To close the rift, she knew she had to untangle the places where the realms had intertwined. Corvus had said souls would seal the wound where the soulless had sucked apart the Veil.

Something shifted in the mist. She whispered Archer's name.

The mist whispered back. "Sera."

A ghastly apparition coalesced from the gray. Sera recoiled when its cloudy weeping eye fixed on her. When she'd drifted into the demon realm before her possession, she'd thought it was a reflection of her wounded self.

It wasn't.

With a shock that slammed across her heart, she knew the other time she'd stared deep into that hopeless gaze—into her mother's eyes, as the car filled with river.

"Sera." The sigh swirled the gray, like an idle finger

wiping fog from a mirror to reveal a woman's face with Sera's own hazel eyes.

"Oh, Mom." Sera took a step forward, away from the bright threads. "Not you, not here."

No wonder it had all led here. Darkness engulfed her before she could take another step.

"You mustn't follow."

"Archer," she gasped.

He held her tight, the black leather of his coat like wings around her. "Demons are all around us, and the devil will lead you astray."

"*We're* demon-ridden too."

Except he wasn't anymore. The tarnish in his burned-bronze eyes had been rubbed away to a simple earthy brown, with no hint of violet, and nothing of recognition.

He frowned at her. "Have you lost your way? This is a dark place." His grip softened, and he raised one hand to touch her hair. "Only you shine."

Archer had neither demon nor soul within him. He was a cipher. No wonder hell held only confusion, no horror, for him. Was this a pale reflection of the man the demon had seduced away from life, ingenuous and gentle?

Her heart felt ripped from its mooring. How could she close the Veil now, with her mother's soul trapped on this side? And how could she so desperately want a return of the potent, dangerous man she'd come to know?

She strained against his hold. "Let me go. I have to get my mother before I seal the Veil."

Threads unraveled with a discordant note like a broken string on the harp she'd never mastered. All the hues of the living world sprayed from the severed ends, a rainbow blossom of droplets that painted the demon realm for a single heartbeat. Then they fell, faded and hard, to shatter under her feet.

Her mother's specter knelt where one of the dulled droplets had fallen. She cupped the chipped marble.

Her hazel eyes welled, and one tear dropped into her palm. The pebble bloomed into a tiny, perfect tea rose, more beautiful than anything Sera remembered growing on that Chicago windowsill. Then the petals withered, melting from the specter's hand into the mist.

Sera's heart ached. "You can't leave. Not again. Why did you go?" She raised her voice to reach the guttering silhouette. "Why?"

The specter hovered on the edge of nothingness where the flower had gone.

"No," Sera whispered. "Not again."

Archer tightened his hold. His memory might have faltered, but not his strength. "With every step you take, the way behind you unravels."

She twisted to glare at him. "I can't leave her in hell. She killed herself. Like you tried to do. Don't you remember? You failed, but I couldn't stop her."

She had hoped to shock him into releasing her, but she underestimated the man he'd been. His expression turned grim, more like the Archer she'd come to know, and he did not flinch. "If I tried to kill myself, then I too am damned."

"No. You atoned." Endlessly, but she couldn't tell him that without bringing the shadows back to his eyes.

"Then give her that."

"What?" Her head spun with memories wound tight around her heart.

"Forgiveness. Forgive and let her go."

"But I can't just . . . I have to know—"

"You'll never know."

"But she's right there." Frustrated tears smeared Sera's vision with the straying colors. How could she turn her back when she finally had a chance to quiet the doubts that had haunted her? Could she have saved her mother from the sinking car, the drowning depression, from the hell that life itself had been? Could anyone be saved?

Archer shook his head. "There are no answers." He paused. "And there was nothing you could have done."

She thumped her fist into his chest. "You don't even remember who you are, the terrible things you've done, that have been done to you. You can't preach forgiveness of anyone."

He clasped her hand against his heart. The ring she'd hooked over her thumb peeked between his fingers. Even broken in two, the *desolator numinis* shone with opal fire, as if the worldly realm had masked its true soulful glory.

"You're right. How can I convince you to let go when I've lost everything, even the memory of what I've lost." He closed his eyes and grasped her hand. "My life, my death, my fate, are in this stone. I feel it calling. Perhaps it's time I remembered."

Suddenly realizing what he intended, she strained away from him. "Without your soul, this place can't touch you."

His heart pounded under her palm, matching her racing pulse. "Maybe I needed to be touched."

"I shouldn't have said—"

Too late. He shuddered under her hand. The ring scalded her skin with icy fire. She struggled to yank back, but he wouldn't let her go. He would never let her go.

When he opened his eyes, the copper brightness glimmered and sunk behind the returning shadows, like a penny falling into a well.

"Sera," he murmured. He lifted their joined hands. His skin was unmarked, the *reven* gone. But a creased line appeared between his brows as he frowned. "I thought this quiet aloneness without even memory would be heaven."

"Ferris?" Tears jammed in her throat. "It's my fault. I brought your soul with me. You're here because of me."

"Yes, it's your fault heaven isn't enough for me now." He released her hands. "Sera, you have to go."

She swallowed hard. "I won't leave her like she left me."

"That wound is yours. You hold her here."

"No." The vortex echoed her wail.

"Yes. A hell of your making."

A chill swept through her. "Corvus was right. I've always brought on the end."

"You've always been seeking." He turned away from the faded reflection of her mother, away from the hole in the world. "But not all answers are yours to find."

"If I can't be sure—" She choked back the rest of her hopeless questions.

"You fight on. And now, as always, you fight on faith."

"Faith? You of all people would spring that on me, here of all places?"

"Where else? And who better than someone who lost everything else but found hope?"

The widening vortex, a luminous beacon to every denizen of hell, cast the edge of his jaw and his deep-set eyes into stark relief that emphasized the resolve on his face. From the beginning, his strength had borne her when she would have faltered in confusion.

She took one last step toward the lingering shade of a woman she'd never had the chance to know. "I love you. I'm sorry."

Even as the Veil between the realms unraveled, so did the knot in her heart. With a rushing clap like ethereal wings, the silhouette of her mother's specter collapsed, sending out a fleeting cat's-eye gleam of dawn light.

Mists roiled upward, as if gigantic, unseen forces stirred in the depths to fill the empty space.

Sera felt herself shaken, not in this realm, but in another. The cavern was crumbling, bricks crashing down.

The rift was massing toward critical, about to obliterate everything in reach.

She took a steadying breath. "What just happened?"

"Looked like that little piece of hell inverted, and something didn't like it. We have to get you out."

"Me? What about you?"

His hand fisted, tendons tight beneath the unmarred skin. "That army of walking corpses shredded the souls bound into the Veil. Someone—some soul—has to stay to heal the wound."

"No, I won't leave you too. This is not how it ends."

"Sera—"

Corvus burst from the churning mist, eyes white ringed. Streamers of gray clung to him like torn flesh.

At the horizon behind him, a dark band formed. The thrum of a half-heard sound sent a tremor down Sera's spine.

Archer spun her away when Corvus lunged.

"Thief," Corvus shrieked. "Soul thief. Give it back. I need to go back."

Archer circled, barring his way. "You have to leave, Sera, and seal the Veil behind you."

She sheltered in his wake. "Not without you."

"You left me before." His tone never changed, but his words folded the mist upon itself in wrinkles of deepening gray.

She flattened her hand against his taut spine. "And you tried to keep me away from what only I could do. We both did the wrong thing for the right reasons."

"We know all about good intentions."

"The road to hell," Corvus snarled. "But there's a road out." He leapt straight at them.

Archer pushed Sera out of the way and grabbed Corvus.

The dark band on the horizon resolved into individual shapes. A dozen men with spears. An elephant and a lion. A woman with a whip. They stretched as far as the eye could see. A gladiator's victims. Had Corvus conjured them out of the mist as Archer had swathed himself in isolation, as she had faced her mother?

"Let me go," Corvus chanted.

"Archer," she called, "let him go."

Archer glanced over his shoulder at her, his gaze clashing with hers. Then he sprang away.

She snapped the pendant from around her neck. She had no means to judge Corvus, no right to keep his essence. She swung the stone toward him, holding tight to the cord like a censer.

Out of the stone, a sooty bird, small as a sparrow, soared for a heartbeat toward Corvus, then plummeted, its wings fluttering, broken.

Corvus flinched away. "Not more black," he hissed. "And flawed. It mocks me still."

Seething from the horizon, the vicious crowd fell upon him. It tore him apart. With a crescendoing scream, he unraveled in a spray of blood black feathers and inky crimson splatters that stained the mist.

Sera recoiled, aghast. Archer drew her gently under his arm. He eased the pendant from her numb fingers and tied the cord behind her neck. "I always said dying was the easy part."

She tightened her grip on the ring still around her thumb. What she had to offer him wasn't easy at all.

She slipped off the cracked stone and held it up. "Your soul was in one half. Without it, your body can't truly die. Your demon, which could heal you, is in the other half."

He looked past her where black feathers clogged the mists, forcing back the light. The remnants of Corvus's soul might mend the Veil, but she had to retreat now, winding the frayed threads back with her.

"You accused me once of storming the bastion of last

vigils to force answers. So I won't ask now." She took a breath. "But releasing your soul alone, you stay dead. If I release the demon too, you live. Possessed."

"I should choose damnation a second time? Knowing what awaits me back there?"

What could she say? Pain, violence, heartache. That was on the days he wasn't battling the darkness that left his body in tatters, his soul in shadow. But he knew all that.

The ring trembled in her fingers. She hunched her shoulders, desolation a cold wash through her body that swept away any possible words.

Except . . . "This time, I will be there."

His tarnished gaze pierced her.

"I told you once not to risk your soul dying on my behalf." She held out her hand. "But whether this bond between us is fate or something we brought on ourselves, you *are* the other half of my soul. Will you live for me?"

He lifted his unmarked hand.

She slipped the ring over his finger, held him for a moment, and let go.

The vortex closed with an inverted oscillation that exploded against her eardrums and sternum, and threw her backward. The worldly realm bloomed around her, icy cold and agonizingly bright.

Archer convulsed beside her, one hand clawing for the sky. She pulled herself to her knees, reaching for him.

Just beyond, Corvus's body twitched, smearing gray matter.

"The building is coming down," Niall shouted. "Get them."

Through the rain of bricks and glass, the talyan rushed forward.

Warm, strong fingers tangled in Sera's as Archer took her hand. Hers was covered in blood, his in the bold black lines of the *reven*.

She'd remember to care about the fate of the world in just a minute. She laid her palm against his jaw, brushing her thumb under his violet-shot dark eye, and kissed him.

This time, she'd hold on, no questions asked. No why, how, or how long. Just here. Now. Him.

Then the talyan were dragging them up, though they wouldn't let go of each other, fingers entwined.

"Wait." Archer grabbed something from Corvus's stiffening hand.

The open cavern of the basement groaned as the building crumbled. She closed her eyes and held on to Archer as they fled ahead of a sulfurous wind.

Together, they ran with the retreating talyan. They ducked against the river wall away from the fountaining column of brick dust, splashing water, and horrible things she didn't want to contemplate.

Archer pulled her onto his lap, unfurling the edge of his coat around her bare legs. "I thought we were dead."

"We were." She nestled in his arms. "And damned. Who knew there're worse ways to spend an evening?"

Ecco swore. "I couldn't grab the djinn-man's body." He held out his hand, flesh blistering under yellow slime. "Something was trying to get away."

"I think the building took care of that." Nanette touched his wrist. "Hold still. I'll see if my angel will take care of you."

Ecco narrowed his eyes. "Is this one of those 'start of a beautiful friendship' moments I've seen on late-night TV?" With his good hand, he pulled Nanette closer.

Nanette frowned at him. "I'm married."

Ecco smiled. "That's cool. I'm evil."

"Come on, people," Niall said. "We have to clear out. When they find the remnants of Corvus's army, this'll go down as a fatal gas explosion in a drug den, but only if we let them see what they want to see."

The talyan made their unwitnessed retreat, apocalypse mostly averted, with no one the wiser.

Archer stood in the greenhouse doorway. A fresh scouring wind blew past.

His wounds had almost healed. Apparently, it took longer to come back from the dead than from a simple maiming. He couldn't even remember all that had happened in the demon realm. But he looked at the ring on his finger and shuddered. It had held his soul and his demon. What new dimension of power it gave him now, he wasn't quite ready to test.

In the cage dangling from his hand, the crow flapped its wings eagerly. It had recovered too. Merely stunned, he'd hoped, when he grabbed it from Corvus's dead grasp. After all, what self-respecting bird died in a fall? It had deserved a chance, considering that Corvus's rejection of its broken-winged avatar had doomed his soul to the Veil.

Archer opened the cage, and the crow burst free. It caught the Chicago wind under its wings and wheeled up, widespread feathers a fan of emphatic black exclamation points against the white-gray sky.

When he lowered his dazzled gaze, Sera waited on the sidewalk, hands thrust into the pockets of her cherry red trench coat.

"I wondered whether I'd have to break in," she said.

"I didn't change the code." Instead of watching her mull that over, he turned and made his way to the garden's heart.

She followed. "That was a crazy stunt."

He lay down on the daybed, one arm a pillow behind his head. "I knew it could fly again."

"You couldn't."

He shrugged. "Said the woman who ripped open the Veil to the demon realm."

"And sealed it again." She echoed his shrug. "Will

it hold? Can one man's soul contain all the demons of hell?"

"Corvus had a lot of atoning to do."

"And then?"

Archer ticked off on his fingers. "The horde-tenebrae of the city are wild on the streets, along with the remnants of Corvus's soulless army and at least a few untraced djinn who slipped out while the Veil was breached. For the first time in centuries, we have no historian, so Ecco might have to learn to read. You really pissed off something in hell with all your damn questions, and I don't want to guess what we'll find when the snow melts." But the snow would melt. He finally believed that. "Until then, you come here."

She edged toward the bed and sat at the far end.

"Turns out, we've got something special between us, you and me." With his free hand, he threaded his fingers through hers.

"But we don't know what it is. I went looking for the old record about female talyan and the mated-talyan bond, thinking maybe there are more like me. I couldn't find anything except a blank in the cross-references. I think Bookie destroyed the citation."

Archer considered. "Maybe he didn't want us to know we could single-handedly"—he lifted their joined hands—"triumph over unholy evil."

"Sounds almost too good to be true."

"Happens when you deal with a devil." He tugged her down against him. "Corvus and Bookie crafted a resonating evil that should have reflected only more shadows. They never dreamed that gathering darkness would sprout the seeds of its own destruction. But against the dark, hope and love grow brighter."

She curved against him, honeysuckle scent a sweet allure. "My simple Southern farmer."

He kissed her then, slow and gentle, until she whispered his name and held him as if she'd never let go.

After an eternity, she eased back, lips flushed rosy pink. "So you don't hate me?"

"For saving me?"

"For damning you again."

He tapped the back of his broken ring against her pendant. "*Desolator numinis.* 'That which makes the gods lonely.' If gods and demons get lonely when riven from our souls, how do you suppose an almost-two-hundred-year-old demon-ridden man feels when torn from his other half? And I'm not talking about my soul or my demon." He kissed her again. "It's only because of you, my love, that I feel at all."

She fitted herself to him more closely, her soft curves hiding a strength of body and will he knew would challenge him if he should ever falter. His other half? More like his better half.

"This feels right," she agreed at last. "Love?"

"Always with the esoteric questions," he murmured. "I shall have to lure you back to this earthly realm. Luckily, the demon-ridden give temptation new meaning. And for us, forever lasts."

He wondered how she'd feel about "till death do us part." Maybe on one of his good days, the Littlejohn patriarch would have some suggestions on wooing his daughter. It probably wouldn't be as simple as battling other-realm monsters.

She laid her hand over his heartbeat. "Most of the world only has today."

"I'll fight for more. But if that's all we have, then I will be . . ." He thought a moment. "Thankful."

She lifted her palm to his cheek and kissed him softly.

The war waged on, his body battered, his soul the battleground, forfeit until the bitter end. But the bright hazel of her eyes, and the warmth of her sigh, promised spring, and his heart, at last, knew peace.

Liam Niall has led the Chicago league of immortal warriors and their repentant demons for longer than he cares to remember. Four months ago, everything he thought he understood about the war against the Darkness was blown apart. Now, with the shocking appearance of a fiery new female talya, the world he's supposed to save is about to change again. . . .
Liam, meet your newest recruit.

Turn the page for a sneak preview of Jessa Slade's next compelling paranormal romance,

FORGED OF SHADOWS

Available from Signet Eclipse in May 2010

"So, what are we doing to chase these monsters—what did you call them, these horde-tenebrae?—off the streets?"

" 'We'?" Liam templed his fingers and leaned back in his chair. He waited for the hot flare of triumph at bringing another ardent, young demon fighter aboard. God knew, he needed all the bodies he could get these days.

Instead, Jilly Chan's fierce zeal made him feel older than the dirt that crept into every nook of the league's salvaged stronghold.

As for her body . . . His fingers curled, and he held his relaxed stance by force of will alone.

She paced in front of his desk, all impetuous curves and spiky nerves. "You made it perfectly clear I may not survive the demon's ascension. If I have only another hour, or another day at most, then I want to find out who—what—came after my kids in the alley. And I want to make sure it never bothers any of them again."

He tightened his jaw against the short, hard clomp of her impatient boots. She wasn't much more disciplined than the kids—the streetwise teen hooligans, more like—she worked with at the halfway house and claimed as her own. Still, he'd bent wilder spirits to their unending task. "I can't promise that."

"I don't believe in promises anyway. Give me something real I can sink my teeth into." She swung to face him, her hand cocked aggressively on the hip of her low-riding jeans. "Or I guess these demon-monster tenebrae aren't exactly real, and I don't want my teeth sunk in rotten eggs anyway. Just give me something bigger than that stupid box cutter, and I'm your warrior woman. For tonight anyway."

She was just bragging, he knew, worse than one of those kids of hers, but her words thrummed through him. Like that call-and-response echo that had lured him out to the streets until he'd found her.

He felt the tightening in his muscles, the prickle of his skin, as the demon in him stirred at even the muted battle cry in her voice. Suddenly, though he'd managed to forget for a very long time, he hated its ready and willing violence, so in tune with the young woman before him. The demon might take its steps toward repentance, but he knew every swing of his war hammer thrust him away from peace.

And the angry glitter in Jilly's eyes only pushed him farther.

But he didn't have a choice. And he'd never had a chance. "Come on then." He thrust himself to his feet and strode past her.

"Where are we going?"

"I'm giving you what you want." He led her through the empty corridors, downstairs to the storage rooms. He threw open a pair of doors and flicked on the light.

Axes, double-edged swords, daggers, razor-tipped gauntlets, and more lined the walls. Even under the buzzing fluorescent fixture, the blades shone with brutal beauty.

Jilly cleared her throat. "Box cutters on steroids. At least I know where to arm myself if World War Three breaks out."

"It already has." Liam strode into the room, then turned to survey her. He tried to keep his gaze critical as he swept her once from blue-streaked locks to heavy black shit-kicker boots. "Good weight on the bottom, at least."

She stiffened at his perusal. "You saying my ass is big?"

It took all his unholy strength to move his gaze on-ward. "I'm saying, no sense throwing off your balance with an oversized weapon."

"I've handled bigger weapons than yours."

Her bold words echoed more than the sheer reflec-tive blades accounted for. The first hint of uncertainty he'd seen in her—even when she faced the ferales in the alley with nothing more than a dull razor blade—flushed her cheeks with color, and she bit her lip.

The hunger that stirred in him at the slight vulner-ability had nothing to do with the demon. And was even more dangerous. He swallowed hard against it, and lev-eled his tone coolly. "No doubt your bravado has served you well. Did the demon come to you with the promise that now you'd finally be able to carry through with all that bluster?"

She froze at the question, but her cinnamon eyes snapped, like the tint of flames in straw.

"The demon always makes an offer we haven't the strength to refuse," he explained. "It knows us better than we know ourselves. I suppose that is the nature of temptation." How fortunate for him that he'd been around long enough to amass scars of resistance.

"I'm tempted," she said stiffly, "to grab that spiked mace and take a swing."

He forced himself to focus on work. Pairing a new talya with the right weapon was vital. "If you want to try it out—"

"Just on you."

"Ah." He rose onto the balls of his feet as the demon shifted eagerly within him. "Always happy to help."

Her hands clenched as if longing for that mace handle—or maybe just his neck. "You can't ask how people were lured to the dark side."

"Technically, we're the repenting side, which is at least a half dozen steps from the dark side." Thinking of her hands on his skin wasn't helping his focus. To a leader of demon-slaying warriors, curiosity was only slightly less useless than desire. But how had the demon cozened her, if not through her boldness?

He took a long step back—physically and mentally—and swept out one hand in a grand gesture. "Choose."

In his many years commanding the league, he'd found that a new talya's choice of weapon indicated something about the man and the demon inside him. He was getting ahead of himself, putting Jilly through his tests so soon, but the urgency that had ridden him since the appearance of her unbound demon seemed even worse when she was near.

And with her hell-bent attitude, he suspected she might soon need all the weapons she could get.

He held himself silent and still, though every muscle twitched to follow as she stalked past him to circle the room. She paused near the mace, slanted a glance at him, and kept moving.

She passed the white-men-can't-jump wall of massive, double-handed swords representing a wide swath of European history. The aesthetically organized Asian collection of kitanas and throwing stars earned not even a second look. Instead, she came around again to the blunt-force trauma corner.

But she didn't reach for the mace, which was a smaller version of his mallet of doom. "No guns? No rocket launchers?"

"Rocket launchers tend to get noticed. We try not to be. More importantly, we have to get up close and personal with the bad guys to destroy them."

"I tracked down my sister's pimp about a year ago,

trying to find out where she'd gone. He stabbed me." She put her hand against her left side, just under her breast. "Punctured a lung. Nicked my heart. But you already knew that, didn't you, from this dossier your people put together on me. Did it tell you that, even huffing along on one lung and coughing blood, I still managed to knock out a few of his teeth?"

Liam pursed his lips. "So you're saying you don't need a mace."

The protective cup of her hand slid around to settle brashly on her hip again. "I'm saying I don't need a mace."

He wanted to argue. Maybe he should argue in favor of the mace, full Kevlar—never mind that body armor interfered with the draining of the demonic emanations that were the sole reason for their immortal existence—hell, throw in a popemobile too. After all, the ferales had sniffed her out for some nefarious reason. And despite her rebellious independence, she'd come back to him because she knew she needed protection, needed his help.

He'd make her see. Finally, he shrugged. "If you change your mind. . . ."

"I'll be sure to let you know."

He withheld a snort. She'd voluntarily admit to anything that smacked of weakness only after a snowball survived August in Chicago, which was even less promising than its chances in hell.

She marched out of the weapons room but paused as he closed the door. "Sera said I'd meet the rest of the crew."

He hesitated, picturing the predatory interest of his wayward, womanless fighters. "They're recovering from last night's battles. Leave them to their rest." When she opened her mouth to protest, he added sharply, "You'll be one of them soon enough."

From the defiant flicker of violet in her eyes, he

thought soon might come even sooner. But she inclined her head and followed him back upstairs.

Instead of stopping at the main floor, he continued leading her up, their steps clanging on the steel treads, until they reached the roof. He shoved open the access door to a swirl of frigid air.

A scrim of high, thin clouds had blanked the sun into a matte white disk that leached the dimensions from the surrounding industrial district. The gray-walled buildings looked flat as cardboard cutouts, and even the graffiti had dulled.

The wind rattled Jilly's blue-spiked hair but couldn't bend it. "Why'd you bring me up here?"

"To show you."

"King of all you survey, hmm?"

"Not even a knight," he demurred. "I just want you to see what we're fighting for."

She studied the bleak landscape. "We'll be hailed as conquering heroes, no doubt."

He shook his head. This part of the test was always hard for the new recruits to grasp. "Demons stalk the Magnificent Mile as often as the South Side, but the battleground doesn't matter. This is as close as you'll get to heaven."

She pivoted to face him. The wind bit through his cambric shirt; he knew she must be equally chilled, but she stood without shivering. Though the top of her head didn't even reach his shoulder, she sized herself against him with a long, slow look even more deliberate than the one he'd given her. Was it his imagination, or did she linger over places a good, repentant demon should forget?

She made a soft noise that left him no indication of which way she had judged him. "This close, huh? And I haven't even been properly damned yet."

She took a step forward, tilting her head as if to get another perspective.

He tightened his hands into fists at his side, not against the cold but against a rising heat that seemed to spark off those cinnamon eyes. "You will be. Soon." Obviously some demon was at work that she would tease him so.

"We have hours before nightfall," she said. "Hours before I can meet your fighters. Or my demon. So let's go. Show me something to make me believe I'm better off joining you."

And that latent demon in her apparently still had power to call to him, because he—of all the talyan who should know better than to give in to temptation—followed her.

Drawn into Darkness

Annette McCleave

Between angels and demons...
Between the living and the dead...
There is the Soul Gatherer.

Serving a five-hundred-year sentence as a
Soul Gatherer—one who battles demons for the souls
of the dead—Lachlan MacGregor keeps his distance
from humans. That is, until the lovely Rachel Lewis
knocks on his door, begging for help.

As they struggle to rescue her daughter from the
clutches of a powerful demon, Lachlan finds himself
increasingly drawn to the artistic single mother. But
when Death assigns him an unbearable task, he's left
wondering who will provide for his own soul.

**Available wherever books are sold or at
penguin.com**

JESSICA ANDERSEN

NIGHTKEEPERS

A Novel of
the Final Prophecy

*First in the brand-new series that
combines Mayan astronomy and lore with
modern, sexy characters for a
gripping read.*

In the first century A.D., Mayan astronomers predicted
the world would end on December 21, 2012. In these
final years before the End Times, demon creatures of
the Mayan underworld—the makols—have come to
earth to trigger the apocalypse. But the descendants of
the Mayan warrior-priests have decided to fight back.

**"Raw passion, dark romance, and seat-of-
your-pants suspense, all set in an
astounding paranormal world."**
—#1 *New York Times* bestselling author J. R. Ward

Also Available
Dawnkeepers
Skykeepers

**Available wherever books are sold or at
penguin.com**

Penguin Group (USA) Online

What will you be reading tomorrow?

Tom Clancy, Patricia Cornwell, W.E.B. Griffin,
Nora Roberts, William Gibson, Robin Cook,
Brian Jacques, Catherine Coulter, Stephen King,
Dean Koontz, Ken Follett, Clive Cussler,
Eric Jerome Dickey, John Sandford,
Terry McMillan, Sue Monk Kidd, Amy Tan,
J. R. Ward, Laurell K. Hamilton,
Charlaine Harris, Christine Feehan...

You'll find them all at
penguin.com

*Read excerpts and newsletters,
find tour schedules and reading group guides,
and enter contests.*

Subscribe to Penguin Group (USA) newsletters
and get an exclusive inside look
at exciting new titles and the authors you love
long before everyone else does.

PENGUIN GROUP (USA)
us.penguingroup.com